DOWN IN THE FLOOD

KENNETH ABEL

DOWN IN THE FLOOD

MINOTAUR BOOKS

NEW YORK

This is a work of fiction. All of the characters, organizations, and events portrayed in this novel are either products of the author's imagination or are used fictitiously.

A THOMAS DUNNE BOOK FOR MINOTAUR BOOKS.
An imprint of St. Martin's Publishing Group.

DOWN IN THE FLOOD. Copyright © 2009 by Kenneth Abel. All rights reserved. Printed in the United States of America. For information, address St. Martin's Press, 175 Fifth Avenue, New York, N.Y. 10010.

www.thomasdunnebooks.com
www.minotaurbooks.com

Library of Congress Cataloging-in-Publication Data

Abel, Kenneth.
    Down in the flood / Kenneth Abel.—1st ed.
        p. cm.—(Danny Chaisson series 3)
    "A Thomas Dunne book for Minotaur Books"—
T.p. verso.
    ISBN-13: 978-0-312-37719-9
    ISBN-10: 0-312-37719-3
    1. Chaisson, Danny (Fictitious character)—
Fiction.   2. Hurricane Katrina, 2005—Fiction.
3. New Orleans (La.)—Fiction.   I. Title.
    PS3551.B336D69 2009
    813'.54—dc22

2008045666

First Edition: August 2009

10 9 8 7 6 5 4 3 2 1

DOWN IN THE FLOOD

For two days the water rose. Everything floated—cars, couches, broken tables from the po'boy joint at the corner, a child's abandoned doll. Black water poured into the houses through broken doors and shattered windows, swept out into the street, now a slow churning river clogged with chunks of wood, plastic lawn chairs, and the bloated corpses of dogs.

But the houses hid their dead, floating lazily in flooded rooms. Eyes open, hands outflung, the dead gazed down from the ceiling, as if surprised to find their world suddenly turned on its head, each chair, table, or TV suddenly made strange by this reversed perspective, like tiny castles placed at the bottom of fish tanks. The book left on the bedside table floats beside them; the magazine from the toilet tank floats. A newspaper floats, and a pack of cigarettes. The dish towel, the wallet, the laundry from its hamper, all float beside them, shirts and slacks with their arms and legs outflung. The coffeepot floats, but not the mug. The empty pop bottle, the sandwich bag full of disappointing grass that you planned to smoke as the storm passed over, then left lying on the coffee table when the water suddenly rushed in. The blankets off the bed, the towel left lying on the bathroom floor, the bar of soap, the plastic garbage can, the deck of playing cards, from which each card floats alone, as if the hand has now been played and lost. But mostly people—floating where they'd never expected to find water, a world gone suddenly silent and gray.

When night fell, the only light came from the flames of burning buildings. Fires burned on the dark water: those not busy burning were busy drowning. Then the gunshots began. In the morning, the first bodies were seen in the streets, floating facedown in the oily black water with their arms flung out wide, like they'd embraced it all: wind, flood, darkness, despair.

The air stank of sewage and death. The whole city had become an unflushed toilet. Men waded through it, holding children in their arms, then waded slowly back to save whatever they could carry in plastic garbage bags. And they were the lucky ones. Some drowned in their attics, gasping for a last breath of air as the water rose over the roof beams. On higher ground, they locked their doors, sat with loaded guns as one storm passed and another—more deadly— broke out where the streets were still dry. Soon the streets glittered with broken glass, which caught the flames of burning houses so that the shadows moving along the streets seemed to walk on fire.

Danny Chaisson stood watching a whole block of warehouses burning on Decatur Street, a column of thick smoke drifting across the night sky. Men moved through the darkness, lit up briefly as they passed the flames. Danny kept one hand resting on the gun stuck in his belt. Not that it would do him much good there if some- body came up on him in the darkness. He smiled, imagining what his wife would say about it. Shaking her head in disgust.

You carry a gun, you'd better be ready to use it. Round in the cham- ber, safety off, gun held low in both hands until a threat is identified. Danny'd gone through the ATF combat training course this way, keeping close to the walls of the concrete building, feeling strangely like an actor in a movie, playing at hostage rescue while the cameras rolled, until suddenly a target would pop up, and he'd bring the gun up without thinking, fire off three rounds, the way Mickie had shown him, body shots, nothing fancy, just get your shots off quick.

Danny looked off into the darkness. There were no phones, no way to find anyone in this ruined city. But it was her city too now. After five years, Mickie Vega had grown to love New Orleans as much as he did. And so, in the days before the storm hit, she'd packed up her mother and their two-year-old daughter, sent them up to stay with friends in Baton Rouge, and then strapped on her gun, gone out to do what she could to help her city survive. "It's so *wet* here," she used to say in wonder, when Danny had first met her. She'd just arrived in New Orleans, an ATF agent recently transferred from Phoenix, assigned to investigate the murder of a small-time gun dealer who'd agreed to turn informant in a series of illegal gun sales. Danny had known the guy, had met with him at the request of his boss, Jimmy Boudrieux, who ran an elaborate system of political payoffs that extended across the state from his office as speaker of the state legislature in Baton Rouge. Danny had just walked out of the restaurant when two killers walked in, shot everybody in the place. Mickie had kept after him, even after she'd started to find herself thinking about him as something other than a witness, and when the case finally exploded, she'd saved his life. When they'd married, a few months after the case came to its violent conclusion, her ATF colleagues had joked that she'd found a way to take *witness protection* to a whole new level. So she bought him a gun, took him out to the range, taught him to follow his gun through dark alleys and narrow corridors, taking out the targets that popped up with a *shoop!* in front of him, like a kid playing at war.

But this wasn't a game. And those weren't targets moving through the dark. They were other men, out searching for water, or food, or a way out of all the burning and drowning. Except not everyone in New Orleans was thinking about survival. Cities never die quietly, but they all die betrayed. By nature, sometimes, or by their own tragic beauty. Mostly by men. For two days, no help came. And now the dogs were off the chains, hunting in packs. So everybody was scared, slipping through the dark streets with guns in their hands, or kitchen knives, or just an old Louisville Slugger and the hope of one good swing before the bullet or blade finds your heart, leaves you to float away through the black water like a crumpled beer can that somebody's drained and tossed away. When you empty the heart of hope, it's fear that floods in; we drown in it, and suddenly everyone looks to us like shadows, moving through darkness. And then the shooting starts, so men go looking for guns.

She'll be okay, Danny told himself. He'd never met anyone who could take care of herself better than Mickie Vega. And the truth was, she probably had more reason to worry about him. She'd be on patrol with a heavily armed ATF Special Response Team, wearing a flak jacket and carrying a compact Heckler & Koch assault rifle, while he was out here alone in the darkness, nobody to watch his back.

Up ahead, a couple firemen stood by their truck, watching in silence as the row of warehouses burned. There was no water in the hydrants, so there was nothing they could do to fight the fires. But they stood there as if it was their job to supervise the destruction, even if they couldn't prevent it. Beyond, there was only darkness, but in the lingering glow from the fires, Danny saw that the iron grates over the warehouse doors had been ripped away and their contents thrown into the street. Somebody had backed a truck up, slung a chain around the security grates, and then punched the gas. Then they'd dug through the storage areas for anything they could haul away.

Danny walked on. He was looking for a place that didn't exist. An old warehouse, empty for almost fifty years, except for a small storage room with a padlock on the door, no windows, and a chair nailed to the bloodstained floor. Somebody had stapled old cardboard egg cartons to all the walls so nobody outside the room would hear the screams. A place where you take the hard boys who won't talk, when getting a conviction in court doesn't matter. Some cops Danny had met gazing wearily at the looted stores on Canal Street had hinted that they'd heard about the place, but when he asked them where it was, they just shook their heads. They'd never been there, just heard the rumors like everybody else: some guys on the force had used it back in the bad old days when somebody shot a cop or threatened to call the Feds. A few hours in there, and any-one would see the light. In some cases, they hinted, it was the last thing those men ever saw.

But that was back when you could get away with that stuff, be-fore they started sending cops to death row. Cops didn't use the place anymore, but it was still there, and when some politician started making noise about police corruption, some of the old-time cops still liked to hint that they knew where to get the key.

"It's a private operation now," one of the cops had said. "Word is that some of the guys who got kicked off the force a couple years back still use the place sometimes. We don't ask too many ques-tions, and they stay out of our way. That way nobody gets hurt."

Except the guy in the chair, Danny thought. *And maybe the guy trying to save him.*

Everything was history now. The whole city was like a freshly dug grave. But people still remembered it like it was, going back forty, fifty years now, a place where one day ran into the next, un-changing, like a sweet old lady sitting up on her porch and waving at the neighbors, a flask of whiskey in her pocket that she takes sips from as the day passes, until she's dazed and bleary, shouting at the children to get off her damn lawn. But get up the next morning, and she's right back out there, making sure it all goes just the way it always has, as long as anyone can remember, slow and easy as a river flowing.

But it's all a lie, Danny thought. *That's what nobody realizes, until she starts to wheeze, and then it's a cough, and when the end comes, it comes hard and fast, the ambulance with its light flaring by the curb, oxygen tanks and a stretcher with its metal legs folding up as they lift it into the back, and it's all gone, just like that. A whisper in the night.*

On Tchoupitoulas Street, a Wal-Mart was being looted. Up at St. Charles, it was a Walgreens, its front doors smashed open by a pickup truck into which some men were loading an ATM machine. On Fe-licity Street, a funeral parlor was burning. People stood in the street watching. Danny hurried past, trying not to think about that smell in the air, like a barbecue that somebody had left unattended.

Then he saw the moon shining on the street ahead; he'd reached the edge of the water. It was still rising, all across the city. *Toxic gumbo*, everybody was calling it. Full of oil and sewage, and if it had come this far, then it had flooded the old St. Louis cemeteries off Basin Street and Claiborne, so there could be coffins floating in that witches' brew, or bones, like some vodoo curse that would come back to haunt you as dysentery, cholera, or some nasty infection that bloomed in bright roses on your skin.

And unless he could stop it, there'd be another body floating in it by morning. That thought made him angry. New Orleans was dying, and there were men out there in the darkness who were ready to finish it off—clean out the cash drawer, put a bullet through its heart, and walk away. When the waters rise, you see what men value: some reach out, pull the drowning man to safety, while others just shake their heads as they turn to more important things, saying, *He should have gotten out when he had the chance.* And then there are men who'll push you under, stand on your shoulders as you drown, just to get a better grip on the rescue boat, the TV camera, or the contract to rebuild.

Out there in the darkness, a man was dying. Danny looked at that foul water. He bent down, touched it with one finger. It was spreading, slowly, filling the city. Anyone with any sense was heading south toward the river, where the ground was higher.

Danny straightened up, wiped his hand on his pants, and then waded in.

1

"Shoot me, please."

Danny leaned back in his chair, looked at the stack of deposition summaries scattered across the desk in front of him. August in New Orleans, and the ancient window air conditioner in his small office was straining to keep up with the thick blanket of moist heat that lay across the city. He'd been struggling to keep his eyes open for the last hour, as he made his way through six different accounts of a car accident up on Carrollton Avenue between a van full of Guatemalan restaurant workers and a soccer mom in a Range Rover with half the junior high school midfielders in Metairie crammed in the backseat. But when his wife called with that tone in her voice, he knew there was nothing he could do but shove it all aside and listen.

"What's she done now?"

"She just asked me if we're trying to starve our daughter."

Danny smiled. "Damn. She finally caught us."

"It's making me crazy, Danny. All she does is tell me what I'm doing wrong."

"I told you not to take the day off."

Mickie Vega sighed. "She's only here for a couple more days. She's been sitting in the house all day. I just wanted to take her out to lunch. But all she does is complain. Nothing I do seems to help."

"You show her your gun? That always works on me."

"Danny, my mother was married to a cop for twenty-eight years. You think she hasn't seen a gun before?"

"It's a pretty impressive gun." A 9mm SIG Sauer P228, which she wore in a leather holster on her hip, putting it on every morning before she went to work as an ATF agent. She'd stand in front of the mirror mounted on the back of the bedroom door, checking to make sure it didn't show beneath the jacket of her suit. Taking a moment, also, to look at her waistline, sucking in her stomach a little. Two years, now, since she'd had the baby, and she was still frowning at her waistline, waiting for the miles of running and the hours of crunches to take it back to where it was when she'd run the obstacle course at the ATF training center in Glynco, Georgia, a tough little Hispanic girl with fierce eyes and a determination to beat the good old boys in her training class, the way she'd kicked their cracker asses on the firing line. But having a baby changed everything. The muscles in her belly, which had once rippled like furrows in a hard-packed field, had stretched until she felt like a dam getting ready to burst. After the baby was born, she'd lost the weight, then lost some more when that didn't seem to be enough. She'd go to the gym every day, lift weights until the muscles in her belly rippled and her forearms were tight as a drill sergeant's. Then she'd go home, and when she opened the front door of the house on Calhoun Street that they'd moved into a few months after their daughter was born, she'd hear her daughter's tiny baby voice, and every muscle in her body would soften like hard-packed earth turning to mud beneath a gentle rain. She was a mother now, and when she heard that voice, it called out to every part of her.

And twice a year her mother came to visit, and all those muscles tightened right up again, bracing against the endless questions, every one of them implying that a *real* mother wouldn't still be going to work every day, a gun strapped to her hip. So how did you go, Danny wondered, from a young mother melting at the sound of your child's voice to telling your grown daughter everything she does is wrong?

Wrong career, wrong husband, wrong way to raise a grandchild, wrong *place* to raise any child, this city where it rains *every day* so the whole house smells like the inside of the kitchen drain. It was hard-core Chicana mama, served up on a bed of *Ay, my bones are so tired.* She'd never do that to Anna, Mickie swore to Danny, go to visit and spend the whole time complaining. But maybe you get to that age and you just can't help yourself. Her mother had been alone now for three years, since her dad died, and that was probably how she spent her day, wandering around her house in Phoenix, talking to herself, making a list of everything that wasn't right with her world. And she noticed *everything.* The upstairs toilet runs. There's dust under the couch. And what's that *smell* by the kitchen door?

"It's the garbage cans, Mom. It's August, so it smells bad."

"They don't pick up your garbage?"

"They pick it up on Tuesday. But it's New Orleans. It gets hot out there, and after a couple days it starts to smell."

But at this, Matia Vega only wrinkled her nose. In her city, her expression seemed to say, you didn't find such smells. There, the air was dry and the boys your daughter married had names like Javier, or Ernesto, or even Joaquin. Not *Danny*, like someone you'd see drinking green beer or doing that *zote* heel-clicking dancing where they leap in the air, shirt open to their waist, like an Irish boy's got anything to show you!

"He's not Irish, Mama. He's French. Around here, everybody's French."

Except the blacks, Danny could tell Matia was thinking. Not that she'd ever *say* it, but you could see her looking as they drove around New Orleans. In Phoenix, there are Mexicans and whites, and if you're Mexican, you just take the whites for granted, like the heat. There's nothing much you can do about it, so what's the point in even talking about it? But *here*, you could see Matia thinking, there were people, you couldn't even *say* what color they were. Whites, blacks, Cajuns, Creoles. And when you're done with all that, they start doing *math*: quadroons, octaroons, doubloons . . . She couldn't keep it all straight, but Danny could see it made her nervous. The first time his friend Jabril Saunders came over to the house, she looked at him like he might make a grab for her purse any moment. He was a tall black man, with a fierce light in his eye, who worked as a "community organizer" with the city's youth gangs. He'd saved Danny's life on more than one occasion, but that didn't stop him from flirting with Mickie, and before the baby had been born, the three of them had spent many nights at a blues club he owned, although his name wasn't on the lease, where they kept a table empty for him with a bottle of dark rum, a bowl of limes, and a sharp knife stuck into the top of the table like a warning, *Don't sit here, you don't belong.* Danny'd just begun to feel that the sign might not apply to him when the baby was born, and now he didn't spend his nights going to blues clubs. So a couple nights a week Jabril came to them, spent a few hours sitting on their couch playing with the baby before heading over to his club.

"Your mama don't like me," Jabril told Danny, after Matia went upstairs. And then he winked at Mickie. "Don't like seeing me around her baby girl. She afraid you might start thinking 'bout what you missin'."

Danny smiled. "If it makes you feel any better, she doesn't like me either."

"Then she got some taste, I guess."

But Danny had to admit, it was Mickie who bore the worst of it. Matia was always questioning her, her eyebrows going up before she spoke, so you could see it coming. Danny'd started joking that her eyebrows were like those question marks they use in Spanish to warn you a question's on its way:

"*¿Mercedes? ¿Porqué esta usted muerta de hambre el bebé?*"

Putting that little squeak in his voice, like Matia got when something annoyed her. Arms folded across his belly, sighing, as if he couldn't decide what was hurting him more, his back or his feet. *Ay, mama!*

Mickie would just look at him, shake her head. "We've got to work on your Spanish."

But she seemed to appreciate the gesture. Anything to lighten the mood. Not that it helped much. Mickie still got that tightness around her jaw, her eyes like the twin barrels of a shotgun as she thought about all the things she couldn't say to her mother.

"Why don't you go out for a couple hours?" Danny asked. "Go out to the range, maybe, put the hurt on some targets. That would give her a chance to fatten up our child."

"She wants to show me how to make *mole poblano*."

"I thought you made that for me a couple times."

"Apparently I'm not doing it right."

Danny winced at the thought of the anger slowly simmering in their kitchen all afternoon, building up until he got home to find Matia sitting in fierce silence on their living room sofa, her eyes fixed on the stain in the carpet they hadn't gotten around to replacing when they moved in two years ago. Mickie would be upstairs in the bedroom, cleaning out their closet with a ferocity that made him want to turn around and head back to the office, where he'd be safe with the car accidents and loan collections.

"You want me to come home?" he asked, feeling like the guy in the old war movies who takes one in the chest for the beloved sergeant or throws himself on the grenade to save his buddies. Is there a medal for husbandry?

Only at the state fair, and you gotta raise a sheep to earn it.

"No," she said with a weary tone. "You've got work to do. I just needed to blow off some steam before we start peeling the chiles. I don't trust myself with a knife in my hand."

"We'll take her to lunch tomorrow. I'll pick you up, and we'll go to Uglesich's. Show her the real New Orleans."

"I'm not sure she wants to see the real New Orleans. Can we show her Pensacola and tell her it's New Orleans?"

Danny hung up, saw that his secretary, Demitra, was watching him out of the corner of her eye. For four years they'd shared a single small office, their two desks only a few feet apart, and there wasn't much they didn't know about each other.

"Mickie callin' for help, huh?"

"Yeah, it ain't pretty."

"Her mama gettin' all up on her ass about how she's raisin' that baby?"

Danny smiled. "It's something, the two of 'em get going."

"Talkin' that Spanish at each other?"

"Too fast for me to keep up. I got those CDs in my car, *Se Habla Español*, but Matia gets going, I feel like I'm trying to catch a bus that's doing seventy down the highway, and it ain't stoppin' for *nothing*."

"You really want to catch that bus?"

Danny laughed. "Do I get a choice?"

"Depends. You don't mind not knowing what they sayin' about you, just let it go."

Demitra's cell phone rang, and she bent, dug it out of her purse. Danny looked wearily at the deposition summaries scattered across his desk. Sometimes it seemed like half the city was suing the other half, as if you could reduce the life of a place to these random moments of collision when a priest, a video-store clerk, and a Bourbon Street stripper all sat in their respective cars, watching as a Range Rover ran a light, bounced off a van full of surprised Guatemalans, scattering glass across the intersection as both vehicles spun with surprising slowness.

"She was on her cell phone," the stripper observed about the SUV's driver. "Went right past me, just talking away." The priest regretted that he was looking the other way at the crucial moment, but he heard it, saw the surprised faces of the Guatemalans as the van spun past him, and the resulting impact with a light pole that put four of them in the hospital for weeks. The video clerk confessed that he missed the whole thing; he was too busy looking at the stripper in her red Corvette. Then the cops showed up, and the ambulances, and before long the lawyers and insurance companies, ready to fight it out in court. *All of it's here*, Danny thought, picking up one of the depositions, *the whole city meeting at this intersection, like we're all just an accident waiting to happen.*

"You want to talk to him?" Demitra looked over at Danny. "He's right here, sittin' a couple feet away from me. Don't look too busy either."

Danny looked up at her, raised his eyebrows. She put one hand over the cell phone's mouthpiece, said, "Ray's brother, Louis. He's got a legal question he wants to ask you."

"Have him call me on my line. No point wasting your minutes."

Demitra shook her head. "He don't want to talk on our line. Says it ain't private enough."

Danny stared at her. "He thinks a *cell* phone is more private than my office line? Anybody can pick up calls on those things."

"He don't want to talk on no cell phone neither. He's askin' can he meet you someplace."

"Now?"

"Soon as you can make some time."

Danny glanced at his watch, then looked down at the pile of depositions on his desk. He'd known people who didn't want to talk on phones before, only met in crowded restaurants or empty parks. They'd look down at the ground as they talked, glancing over their shoulders every few minutes, watching for squad cars or unmarked panel vans, where an FBI surveillance team could be hunching over their recording gear, straining to hear the faint words coming through their headphones. But Louis Sams was the last person he'd expect to be meeting that way. He was Demitra's brother-in-law, an engineer who worked for a concrete manufacturer at a plant over on Industry Street. They'd met last summer at the wedding reception for Demitra's little brother, Shawan, a six-foot-seven-inch tight end who'd just been drafted by the Houston Oilers out of Grambling, who'd spent his college days chasing a succession of girls who were built for speed, only to marry a tiny, church-going Baptist girl he'd met at a "Do You Live in Jesus?" rally at Tad Gormley Stadium just before heading off to training camp. Even there, standing in front of the liquor-free bar with a glass of iced tea in his hand, among a crowd that clearly *lived in Jesus* every day of their lives, Louis Sams stood out—heavy-rimmed glasses, country-club jacket and tie, a big guy who looked like he'd played ball in his day, but now he looked like everyone's idea of an engineer. Jabril, who was standing beside Danny, followed his gaze.

"That somebody you know?"

"He's Ray's brother. You know Ray, Demitra's husband?"

"Yeah?" Jabril looked over at him. "Man, I know Ray's livin' that whole Cosby life, goes home to his wife, puts the seat down on the toilet. But *that* guy?" He shook his head. "That's the straightest black man I've ever seen."

Danny could only agree. Any minute, Danny expected him to pull out a calculator and start figuring up the weight tolerance of the dance floor, everybody from Demitra's side of the family out there doing the Camp Street shimmy while the Baptists looked on in stern disapproval.

Still, anything that you couldn't talk about on the phone had to be more interesting than a pile of insurance claims and deposition summaries. And Demitra was waiting, the phone tucked against her shoulder, giving him that dead-eyed stare she used when she felt he was wasting time.

"Any clue what he's got himself into?"

But Demitra shook her head. "Won't tell me. You want to know, you better go meet the man."

Danny gave his watch one last glance, then sighed. "Okay, I've

got to run some papers up to Robert E. Lee Boulevard this afternoon. Ask him if he can meet me at Deanie's after work."

She raised an eyebrow. "Black folks don't eat up in Bucktown
much."

"So give him my cell number. We can meet in the parking lot, go
for a walk by the lake. It's a good place, if he wants privacy."

She raised the phone, said, "Louis? You know where Deanie's at,
up in Bucktown? He wants to know can you swing by there, you get
off work. Take a walk by the lake."

Danny shuffled his papers. The case was a slam dunk. The woman
driving the SUV was talking on the phone and ran the light. Everybody agreed about that, except her insurance company. They'd already spent six weeks collecting the depositions, and now they'd
spend a couple months going over them, looking for something
they could use to shift liability onto somebody else. In the end,
they'd agree to a settlement just before the case went to trial, so the
only question was whether they could find something in the evidence to make the plaintiffs nervous, reduce the price they'd have
to pay for a soccer mom talking on her cell phone.

It's not exciting, Danny liked to say, *but it's a living.* Moving the
paper, like a janitor with a broom, shuffling along the corridors of
the courthouse on Poydras Street, pushing the piles of paper from
one room to the next. You go to law school, you think it'll be like you
see in the movies: a guy fighting for justice, getting up in a courtroom and convincing a jury to do what's right. That's what Danny
had thought, anyway, and for a few years he'd lived that life, putting
in eighteen months as an assistant district attorney, prosecuting
drug dealers, hookers, and petty thieves. It was the kind of job that
wore out men's souls, but Danny had loved it. Until a past he'd
thought was safely buried came back to haunt him, like a ghost that
calls to you in the night, leads you away into the darkness.

Danny sighed, pushed the papers away. There were lots of
ghosts, if you let yourself start listening to their voices. He'd spent

his whole life mixed up with corrupt cops and crooked politicians. Men had died, others had gone to prison, and Danny had a reputation now. Friends in some of the big law firms tossed work his way, small-time insurance litigation mostly, but he could tell, by the way people looked at him out of the corners of their eyes when he walked into a restaurant, that he'd never shake the scent of death that hung around long after the bodies went in the ground. So if Louis Sams was calling him, wanted to meet where nobody could listen to their conversation, Danny would bet it wasn't because he needed a lawyer to help him draw up a will. From the moment Demitra had said he didn't want to talk on the office line, Danny had heard the ghosts start whispering again. It left a strange taste in his mouth, like drinking from a well the cows won't go near.

Let it go, he told himself. *The guy just wants to talk to you in private. Makes sense, right? His sister-in-law works for you.* All that stuff about ghosts was just the memory of a bad stretch of luck. And anyway, lots of people get that feeling, living in New Orleans. It's a city with too much past, like a tide that can drown you. So what's the point of thinking about the future? It's just the promise a gambler whispers to himself as he blows on the dice.

"I'm going to take off," Danny told Demitra, getting up from his desk. "You gave Louis my cell number?"

"Uh-huh." She looked at him. "He's a good man, you know that, right? His boy's got some problems, but Louis, he ain't one of these men goes messing around in something just to be doin' it. You hear what I'm saying?"

Danny nodded. "I'm on it."

|||| When people told Danny they grew up in New Orleans, the first question he always asked them was, "Yeah? Which one?" He'd grown up in the Garden District, where you could walk past the broad windows of the mansions on St. Charles, see elegant women laugh-

ing as they sipped pale, chilled wine from crystal glasses. His mother had been one of those women, at least until his father died, his body found in a car out on River Road with a briefcase full of money on the seat beside him, a gun beside his hand, and a bullet in his brain. That was the New Orleans of his childhood, and it was gone forever, at least for him. But he'd had friends who grew up in Mid-City, or up in Metairie, who'd lived in a whole different city. Saints game on TV, beer on ice in the kitchen, your older brother and his friends out in the driveway working on his Camaro. And Demitra, she grew up over in the Ninth Ward, where families had lived on the same streets since their great-grandparents had wandered down off the plantations after Lincoln set them free.

You live in the old neighborhoods of New Orleans, you can forget the lakefront is there—a long strip of grass that looks out across the smooth water, where teenagers drink beer and throw footballs on summer evenings while sailboats carve their way across the distant horizon. It's another world, like something you'd see down along the Gulf Coast, before they built the casinos all along the beach and made you pay to look at the sunset by dropping coins in the slots. Danny stood with his hands in his pockets, gazing out across the water. Off in the distance, cars were heading back across the causeway, commuters going home to Mandeville or Covington. The sunlight spread across the water, and it felt peaceful to stand there, gazing out across all that smooth water.

He heard footsteps coming across the gravel parking lot behind him, turned to see Louis Sams making his way over from his car. He drove a white Saturn, which looked like he spent every Sunday afternoon over at the soft-wash, making it all nice. As Sams came up the grass slope onto the seawall, Danny said:

"I'll bet you don't let anybody smoke in your car, huh?"

Sams looked surprised. "No, I don't. Why?"

Danny smiled. "Just looks like you put in some time keeping it nice." He held out his hand. "Good to see you again."

Sams shook his hand, but his face didn't look like he was taking much pleasure in it. "Thanks for seeing me," he said wearily.

"No problem. What's up?"

Sams looked back at the cars parked in the restaurant lot. "You mind if we walk a little?"

Danny followed his gaze. He couldn't see anybody hanging around the parking lot, but that didn't mean they weren't there. He'd spent over a year being trailed by FBI surveillance teams, so he knew that if people wanted to listen in on your conversation, they could find a way. "Sure," he said. "Let's walk on out to the end of the breakwater."

They walked along in silence, like two old friends. When they reached the end of the seawall, they stood looking out across the water. Danny'd had conversations here before, back when he worked for Jimmy Boudrieux. Nobody thinks twice if you stand there by the water, but if somebody wants to listen in, he'd have a tough time picking up your voice over the sound of the waves. You stand there like you're admiring the view, and the guy with the sound gear has to be somewhere off behind you, while your words vanish out across the lake.

Danny waited in silence. He'd learned that when somebody is working up how to tell you about his problem, it's better to let him take his time. Whatever it was, it had Louis Sams looking like he hadn't slept in days. Danny could taste that bad water again, like he'd dropped his bucket in the wrong well.

Sams bent, picked up a rock off the breakwater, threw it way out into the lake. "Demitra tell you about my boy?"

Danny shook his head.

"He ain't a bad boy," Sams said. "He's had his problems, last couple years. Hanging out with the wrong kind, mostly."

Drugs, Danny thought. *Gangs. You grow up black in New Orleans, it's what they serve up on your plate.*

"Police picked him up two nights ago. They say they got him

dealing, and they found a gun in some bushes right by there, so they say it's his too. Lawyer I talked to says he's facing serious time."

Danny looked over at him. "Sounds like it. This lawyer, he think there's any chance you can plead him, get the charges down to simple possession?"

"Not with the gun charge mixed in there. DA says that makes him a *violent offender*, so he'll have to do time."

"They get his prints on the gun?"

Sams shrugged. "Haven't told us yet. But one of the cops says he saw my boy throw it in the bushes when he spotted their car."

"He got any prior convictions?"

"Nothing serious. Some traffic stuff."

Danny was silent, looking out at the water. The case didn't sound so serious that a DA would refuse a plea deal. Without prints, the gun charge was weak. Any decent defense lawyer could get it tossed out at trial.

"Okay," he said. "You've talked to a lawyer already. Sounds like he's working the case. So you want to tell me why you had to come way out here to talk to me?"

Sams glanced back at the parking lot behind them. "It's not like I'm sayin' what my boy did isn't wrong. He was out there on the street dealing drugs, messing 'round with guns and such, I guess he's got his share of trouble coming."

"But he's still your boy."

Sams looked at him, his expression suddenly fierce. "Damn right. And I don't like nobody using him to get to me."

Danny raised his eyebrows. "Maybe you'd better explain."

Sams's jaw tightened. But he nodded. "I go up to the courthouse for the arraignment yesterday, they bring my boy in on a chain, like they're gettin' ready to send him out to break rocks on a road gang. So I'm sitting there, waiting for his case to come up, and this man sits down next to me. Whole row of empty seats, he comes right over, sits down right beside me. I figure I'll just ignore him, but then he leans over, whispers to me, 'Shame about your boy.' And then he slips me a card." Sams dug in the pocket of his jacket, brought out a card, handed it to Danny.

Martin Seagraves, Danny read. *Special Agent, Federal Bureau of Investigation.* He handed the card back to Sams. "Go on."

"That's it. He just slips me the card, and then he gets up, walks out."

"You met this guy before?"

Sams shook his head. "It's always been another guy."

Danny looked over at him. "Another FBI agent?"

"Yeah. An agent named Franks. Tall guy. Likes to catch me when I'm eating lunch."

Danny smiled. "Just comes over and sits down at your table?"

"Yeah. I'm out on jobs a lot, all over the city. I'll grab lunch somewhere, mostly with clients. But every now and then I'll just get a sandwich someplace on my own. A couple times now, he's just shown up, like he happened to be in the place, thought he'd come over and say hello."

"It's an old cop trick," Danny told him. "The FBI guys like it 'cause it shows they can get to you anytime. They use it when they're working an informant."

Sams looked over at him. "I'm not an informant."

"Not yet, but you're going to be." Danny met his gaze. "That's why we're here, right? They've got you picked out as the inside man on a case they're investigating. First guess, I'd say there's something going on at the place where you work. It makes you uncomfortable, but not enough to take the risk of being a federal informant. This guy Franks, he comes around every couple weeks to keep the pressure on, let you know they're watching. Drops a few hints that if you don't cooperate, you might find yourself on the business end of a conspiracy indictment. But you know you're clean, so you told him to get lost. Only now they're starting to play rough, trying to get at you through your boy. So you come talk to me, because somebody told you I know the drill. That about right?"

Sams looked away. "You do know the drill."

"I've seen it, up close. How bad is it, this thing at your work?"

Sams hesitated. "Political kickbacks, mostly. Some bid-rigging. I work over at IndusCrete. We make industrial concrete for big construction projects, so we get a lot of state and local contracts."

Danny smiled. "And sometimes you've got to grease the wheels. That's just doing business in New Orleans. Things must be pretty slow over at the FBI, they're putting pressure on you over something like that."

"There's some other stuff too. Safety issues."

For a moment, neither of them said anything. Out on the lake, a sharp wind had come up, and a few heavy clouds were building up to the west. Some of the sailboats had started heading back to the marina.

"What kind of safety issues?"

Sams let the question hang there for a minute, like he'd come to a bridge he'd known was up ahead, and now he was taking his time deciding if it was safe to cross over. Danny waited. He figured Sams had come out here to tell his story, and it was just taking him a little while getting comfortable with the idea.

"Man, when I was a kid, all I ever wanted was to build stuff," Sams said at last. "Be an engineer, put up bridges and roads. Wasn't something kids in my neighborhood talked about, 'cause nobody told us we *could*, you know?" He looked over at Danny. "I've got a good job. It's not perfect, but it's what I always wanted to do, and they pay me well."

Danny nodded, but said nothing.

Sams sighed, looked out at the sailboats headed their way. "You know anything about concrete, Mr. Chaisson?"

"Just how it feels under my feet."

"It's a composite material. You got a filler and a binder. The filler's mostly crushed limestone and clay or shale, mixed with sand. The binder sticks it together, and that's pretty much just cement and water." He smiled. "Simple process, really. But that's the thing about being an engineer: you look at a building or a bridge, or this break-water we're standing on, and some engineer has worked on every part of it. There's not a thing you use in your life that hasn't been engineered. I had a professor up at LSU who used to say that engineering's what makes us human. We don't live in the world we find, the way animals do. We make the world we want to live in. And it's engineers who figure out how to do that."

"I had a professor who said it's law that makes us human." Danny smiled. "Your guy sounds more convincing."

"Anyway, water's the most important ingredient in concrete. It's what causes all the other ingredients to bind together. Too much water, and the concrete won't be strong enough. Too little, you can't work the stuff. And the water has to be pure, or you get all kinds of secondary reactions that can weaken the concrete."

"Well, there's one difference between engineering and law. Nothing we deal with is pure."

Sams nodded. "So maybe your professor was right too. Because it turns out there's not much about life that *is* pure."

Danny looked at him. "You're saying there's something wrong with the concrete?"

"Everybody thinks concrete has to dry to get hard. Actually, you need moisture for it to cure. When it gets dry, it stops hardening. Concrete with too much water loses strength, but if it gets too little water, it'll get dry without fully reacting. Concrete that's too dry can actually be weaker than wet concrete. You're pouring a sidewalk in front of your house, that's not a big deal, but you start looking at big projects, where the stress-to-weight ratio on the concrete is high, and it gets important real fast."

"What kind of projects?"

Sams shrugged. "Bridges, buildings, parking structures. You name it. The owner of the company is a guy named Gerald Vickers. He's been spreading money around up in Baton Rouge for a while, so the company's just kept growing. And that's the problem. We're working so many projects, there's no way to meet all the deadlines without cutting corners."

"So you're worried that one of these days a bridge is going to fall down."

He shook his head. "Wouldn't be a bridge. At least, not that kind of catastrophic failure. You'd start to get cracks after a while, but it probably wouldn't just fall down one day." He nodded at the seawall along the edge of the breakwater. "You want the worst-case scenario, it's water. You get soft concrete in a seawall, that's where you get catastrophic failure. We worked on some projects down along the Industrial Canal, part of the Corps of Engineers flood control system? That's the one that keeps me awake at night. You've got subgrade concrete anchored in permeable soil. One really good storm, and you watch what happens. It ain't gonna be pretty. I got family in the Ninth Ward, and I told 'em, you hear there's a hurricane heading this way, you get out. Get on the road, and don't stop until you get to Shreveport, 'cause we worked on projects all over south Louisiana."

Danny stared at him. "Can you document any of this?"

"You mean beyond my testimony?" Sams shrugged. "It's not like they leave incriminating papers lying around, but I could probably get some stuff off the computers at my office that would show you what's been going on."

"Might help. Federal prosecutors usually like to see something solid they can bring into a courtroom if they're cutting a deal. That way they don't have to worry about their witness coming apart on them, or getting scared and recanting his testimony when he gets in front of the grand jury."

"Take a little doing," Sams said, his eyes going off across the lake. "But if I can spend a little time on one of the computers, I could probably get them what they need."

"There's one thing I don't get," Danny said. "Why's the FBI coming after you? You're an engineer. They want to get your boss on bid-rigging or political kickbacks, they'd go after the money guy. That way you don't just get the businessman who's paying bribes; you get all the politicians who're taking the bribes also."

And there it was, that old tightening in his chest as he spoke the words. *They'd go after the money guy.* All the ghosts awake now, whispering. He'd been the money guy, once. Carried envelopes stuffed with cash for Jimmy Boudrieux, meeting men like Gerald Vickers in restaurants and parking lots, while the FBI got it all on tape. He'd betrayed them all, drunk the poison and then spat it out, and when the end came, Jimmy Boudrieux had sat in a car and shot himself in the head, just like Danny's father, while Danny walked away. Afterward, the head of the FBI task force investigating political corruption in Louisiana had told Danny he was a hero, but the way he said it, it sounded like he had something caught in his throat. There were people in New Orleans who still spat on the ground when they saw him on the street. Nobody likes an informant, not even the cops who employ them.

"I never had anything to do with that," Sams told him angrily. "I'm an engineer, that's it."

"So why are they after your son?"

Sams was silent for a moment. Then, as if the words were painful to him, he said, "I wrote a letter."

"What kind of letter?"

"About impurities in the water. I thought somebody should know."

"Who'd you send it to?"

"The U.S. attorney."

Danny nodded. "You sign the letter?"

"No. I didn't even say what company I worked for. Just that there were dangerous levels of impurities in the concrete on some state projects over the last several years."

"You didn't specify the projects?"

He hesitated. "I might have mentioned that some of the projects involved flood barriers and that there were also some highway bridges. But that could be dozens of projects."

"Maybe. But it couldn't have been that many, because they didn't have much trouble tracking you down. When did the FBI agent first contact you?"

"Last year. I was out on a job in Chalmette, and I stopped to eat at a burger joint on my way back to the office. That's where he first approached me."

"But it's safe to assume they'd been following you for a while."

"I guess so. But I never saw them."

"You weren't looking. Actually, I'm more concerned that somebody else might have spotted them. Anybody at work know about this?"

"God, I hope not. A guy like Gerald Vickers, he didn't get where he's at by being scared to get his hands dirty. And he's not the kind of guy who'd let something like that slide. They find out, I could end up in a ditch somewhere. Or holding up a bridge."

Danny looked over, saw real fear on Sams's face. "You tell that to the FBI agent?"

"Yeah. They say, 'We'll protect you.' Like that's all I'm worried about. Maybe they can keep me alive, but can they get me a job? I mean, who's gonna hire a guy, he's sold his last boss out to the FBI?"

Danny smiled. "Yeah, that's a problem. So what do you want to do? Sounds like they're offering to cut your boy a deal, but only if you testify. Is it worth it to you?"

"What, to keep my boy out of jail? Damn right. They got enough black children up at Angola; they don't need my boy." Sams looked at Danny with pleading eyes. "He's a good boy. He wants to go to college, be an engineer like his daddy. But there ain't nothing out there on the streets for these children except the gangs. That's all they got. I spent all these years working, keepin' my head down, I'll be damned I'm gonna watch them take my boy."

Danny raised both hands. "Hey, I hear you. It was my kid, there'd be no question. I wouldn't hesitate to testify."

"And you've done this, right? Demitra told me you helped the FBI bring down some powerful people."

"Yeah, but I won't lie to you. It ain't easy. You pay for it the rest of your life."

"They tell you they could protect you?"

"They told me, but I didn't believe 'em. You do this, it's because you believe in it. That's the only way to get through it."

Sams sighed. "Maybe it'll make 'em fix some of that concrete, keep those bridges from falling down."

Danny shook his head. "That's not what this is about. The FBI doesn't fix bridges. Maybe the state will send someone out to look at them, but if they aren't getting ready to collapse, nobody's going to want to spend the money to fix the problem. This is about sending somebody to jail. That's what these guys do. You can't fix the past. The best you can do is change the future, keep your kid out of jail, maybe stop this kind of thing from happening again."

"And I pay with *my* future."

"That's the price. You got to decide."

Sams looked away. For a long moment neither of them spoke. There were waves out on the lake now, and what looked like a sheet of rain coming in from the west.

"You think they'll cut my boy loose?"

"He'll have to plead. If you push, they'll reduce the charges to something that doesn't require jail time. But you'll need to have a long talk with your son, because if they bust him again, you won't be able to save him."

Sams nodded. "And they'll keep me safe?"

Danny hesitated. "They'll do their best to keep your testimony secret until trial, and if you feel threatened, they'll offer to put you in the Witness Protection Program. Usually it doesn't come to that. But you're talking about local police in your son's case. They see the

FBI getting involved in some kid's drug bust, somebody's going to smell a deal." He looked over at Sams. "You sure you're up for this?"

"I don't guess I have a choice."

A wind came up, blowing spray into their faces. They both turned, walked quickly back along the seawall to the parking lot, which was filling up now with the early dinner crowd. They stopped beside Danny's car, and Sams said:

"So what do we do now?"

"We go talk to the FBI." Danny unlocked his car. "After that, you do your best to keep your head above water."

2

"How much you owe me now?"

Gerald Vickers shifted in his seat, trying to find a position that didn't set his hemorrhoids on fire. "About ninety, I guess."

Jimmy Mancuso looked up at him from under his thick eyebrows, giving his eyes that dead look he used when he wanted to scare somebody. "*About* ninety?"

"Ninety-seven. And change."

"And change." Mancuso sat back slowly. "As of today, you owe me ninety-seven thousand four-fifty. That's some change. You're walkin' down the street, some bum asks if you got some spare change, that what you give him?"

"C'mon, Jimmy. You know I'm good for it. I'm just having some bad luck. You know how it is, right?"

Mancuso raised a finger. "I know how it *was*. You *were* good for it, back when you owed me twenty on them LSU games last month. Now I'm watchin' the numbers add up and I'm startin' to wonder. What I hear, you're losing all over town. You maxed out your credit over at the casinos in Gulfport, and a guy I know over at Harrah's says they got a sheet on you down there too. I hear that, I'm thinkin', this guy owes money all over the place. How's he gonna pay me?"

Little Jimmy they called him, even though he weighed almost three hundred pounds. His father had been Big Jim back in the seventies, running gambling and strip clubs all over Jefferson Parish for Carlos Marcellus. But everything was bigger now, and the way

28

Little Jimmy ate, it looked like he was just getting started. They were sitting in a po'boy place he liked on Bienville in Mid-City, a couple blocks from the cemetery. Formica tables, plastic chairs, a couple booths in the back where you could bring the kids, let them throw french fries at each other without hitting anybody else. Jimmy had a newspaper spread out on the table in front of him, a picture of people down in south Florida nailing plywood across their windows, another hurricane headed their way. A plate shoved to one side held the remains of a meatball po'boy with red gravy, and he had a basket of onion rings and some fried calamari just to pick at, dip it in some spicy mayo while they talked. *Goes on like that,* Vickers thought, *a couple years, they can just carry him up the street, put him in the ground.*

If anybody can lift him.

"Jimmy, you seen the contracts we got lined up," he said, shifting his weight on the plastic chair. "Hell, just the highway contracts alone will bring in enough to pay off everything I owe you. I got three shifts working out at the plant just trying to keep up."

"Uh-huh, but you're losing it before you make it. That's a real bad sign." Jimmy sighed, reached over to snag another piece of calamari, swishing it around in the mayo before he stuck it in his mouth. "Two years ago, you brought me in as your partner on the concrete plant, we agreed the gambling thing had to stop. That was part of the deal. I clear all your gambling debts, you agree to concentrate on the business, stop losing money making stupid bets with every Benji in town hangs out a line on a game."

Silent partner, Vickers wanted to say. *A forty percent stake, with no name on the paperwork. And you keep your mouth shut.*

Especially while you're eating.

But he'd been around cement too long not to know that you don't talk to a guy like Little Jimmy that way. Work in cement for a while, you learn that everything cracks under pressure. And guys like Jimmy Mancuso, they specialize in pressure. Staring at you with those dead eyes, like he'd just gotten a deal on your coffin, was ready to see you try it on for size. Anyway, how could he pay his debts, he wanted to ask, with somebody peeling off forty cents on every dollar he made? Wasn't he making money for Jimmy? They'd won six state contracts just last month, which would bring in over three million. Jimmy's take would be over $120,000, right there. But did that count toward his debt? Not a chance. Jimmy insisted that was a separate deal, money owed to him on an investment, never mind that he hadn't put a dollar into the company. Sure, he'd paid off the gambling debts a couple years ago, but he'd collected five times that much in profits since then. And, yeah, it didn't hurt to have a guy like Jimmy Mancuso on your side when it came time to bid on contracts up in Baton Rouge. He made a couple phone calls, and all the paperwork got moved around so only one bid met the revised specifications. They'd spread some money around, and the guys Jimmy sent to carry it were a pair of tough ex-cops who had the look of muscle, so nobody thought about taking the money without doing what they'd promised. The two guys sitting up at the bar now, eating gumbo and drinking beer, watching a ball game on the TV mounted up high on the wall. When they leaned forward to eat their gumbo, you could see the outline of the guns they wore on their belts, that bulge under their sports jackets making them still look like undercover cops. But they'd both been thrown off the force a couple years back in a corruption scandal, and they worked for Little Jimmy now. In New Orleans, you could buy ex-cops the way you buy suits off the rack; they cost a little more than regular muscle, but most of them still had friends on the force, which could be useful to a guy like Jimmy Mancuso. Not that it took much for these boys to convince people to do what he wanted: they'd show up in a guy's office, and that was usually enough to make the point. Vickers had been making large political donations for years, but all it ever bought you was a foot in the door: the politicians smiled and shook your hand as they took your money, but all they promised was that they wouldn't lose your bid or call you in front of an oversight committee when the project went over budget. Everybody paid off, so you had to do it just to keep up. But when Jimmy Mancuso was in on the deal, you saw results.

That's the thing, he wanted to tell Jimmy. He wasn't complaining about the forty percent. IndusCrete was now the largest concrete manufacturer in the state, and the plant was running over capacity. Even with the payout, he was making more money than he had before Jimmy bought up his old gambling debts and used them to muscle in on the business. But why mess with a good thing? What'd he want, *another* forty percent? He'd kill the company if he tried to bite off another chunk like that. *Just sit back*, he wanted to say, *and count your money. And so what if I lay a few bets around town?* With all that money rolling in, he could afford to wait a couple more weeks to collect.

That's what he wanted to say, but Jimmy was reaching for the calamari again, grabbing a handful with his thick fingers, like he was afraid they might swim away. "Ninety-seven and change." He shook his head. "That's some serious money. It's embarrassing. People hear I'm carrying you that deep, they start losing respect for me."

"You'll get your money," Vickers said. "I just need a couple more days."

Jimmy swirled the calamari around in the mayo, dropped them on his plate. Then he wiped his fingers on a napkin delicately. "You got until Monday. Don't make me come lookin' for it."

"Thanks, Jimmy."

"So what's this I been hearing about a grand jury?"

Vickers felt something hard rise in his throat. He reached for the glass of iced tea the waitress had set in front of him, drank some of it down, then wiped his mouth with a paper napkin. "It's nothing, Jimmy. Just some woman over at the U.S. attorney's office, trying to make some noise. I got the lawyers looking at it, and they tell me we got nothing to worry about."

"Well, they're right about that. *We* got nothing to worry about." Jimmy looked up at him. "*You* got ninety thousand reasons to worry." He stuck another a piece of calamari in his mouth, chewed it slowly. "And change."

"Anyway," Vickers said quickly, "your name's not on anything, so it's got nothing to do with you."

"Humor me. I'm protecting my investment."

"It's bullshit. They run this kind of investigation every couple years, like they figure that if they throw the net out, drag it around for a while, they might catch something."

"They got anything on us?"

Vickers shook his head. "Nothing they can use. I heard they got a letter saying we sold some bad concrete, but they get that stuff all the time. This industry, you get a guy doesn't show up to work a couple times, you have to fire him. So he writes a letter to the governor, tells him your work isn't up to code. It's just a revenge thing. Nobody pays any attention to it."

"And you let that slide?"

"What? Some guy writes a letter?" Vickers shrugged. "Sure. That's just part of the business. There's nothing you can do about stuff like that."

Jimmy sighed, shook his head. "See, that's the difference between you and me. Somebody does that in my business, he's a rat. We catch the guy, we'd show him a new way to make concrete." He looked over at the two ex-cops sitting at the bar. "How about I send Lenny and Vince out to the plant? They can ask some questions, find out who's been writing the letters."

Vickers swallowed hard, glanced over at the two men. "Thanks, Jimmy. But I don't want to put your boys to the trouble."

"It's no trouble. That's what they do." Jimmy grinned. "Hell, it'll give 'em a thrill. They can pretend like they're cops again."

Vickers said nothing. His stomach felt like he'd just swallowed a handful of carpet tacks. The last thing he needed with a grand jury looking into his business was Jimmy Mancuso's muscle boys hanging around the plant. But even without the legal problems, the idea would have left him feeling like he was sitting on three feet of metal rebar, which someone had taken the trouble to heat up before he'd taken his seat. For two years he'd paid Jimmy Mancuso his percentage of the profits, and Jimmy had been content to take the money and stay out of the way. But somewhere—deep inside him, where it burned the worst—he'd always known this moment would come: for two years he'd been waiting for the day when a carload of Jimmy's muscle boys pulled into the gravel parking lot, with something in the trunk they wanted to add to the next batch of concrete foundation blocks for the bridge on Bayou Lafourche. He'd seen all the movies: Jimmy'd show up at the bridge dedication, lay a wreath at the base of one of the support pillars. But how did they get the body in the concrete without the guys who work at the factory seeing them? Wouldn't it be easier just to dump it in the woods?

But for two years, nothing. No midnight call asking him to drive out to the plant and fire up the equipment, no wreaths floating on the muddy bayou. Just a second set of books that Vickers kept in the safe at his office, and a briefcase full of cash passed under the table at the po'boy joint at the end of every month. After a while he'd even started laying bets again. Just small ones at first, then bigger ones as he tried to cover his losses. And as his debts mounted, the fire burning in his stomach grew. Now it felt like you could make steel in there, roll it out nice and thin, make it into airplane wings or the hoods of Chevys. But what could he do? You don't say no to a guy like Little Jimmy.

"Sure, Jimmy," he said with a weak smile. "That'd be great."

llll Assistant U.S. Attorney Helen Whelan had long ago learned the value of staying cool in any situation. It was a talent that she'd mastered in law school at Tulane, rising to the challenge of even the most adversarial questioning by her contracts professor without ever seeming to break a sweat, and it had served her well through a decade of private practice with Morgan, Field and Stratton, a prestigious downtown firm specializing in commercial litigation. Twice she'd watched important clients go down in flames when Danny Chaisson turned up in her office; each time she'd rebuilt her life, slowly getting her practice back on its feet after the story had dropped off the front pages. So even now, having left private practice in a moment of midlife disillusionment to accept an appointment to the U.S. attorney's office, she might have expected to feel a chill settle over her when she got his call, asking if he could meet with her about a client who was negotiating the terms of his testimony in a political corruption investigation being conducted by her office. And yet, even with the feeling of dread that rose within her at the thought of the disasters that always seemed to follow their meetings, the moment that had tested her cool most deeply came as she ushered Danny and his client into her office, along with an FBI agent Danny knew named Marty Seagraves, got through the introductions, and then turned to Danny to ask politely:

"So how's your daughter?"

He dug out his wallet, passed her a photograph. A little girl with hair black as a raven's wing and big dark eyes, laughing, reaching out to the camera. Helen smiled, passed it back to him. "She's lovely."

Not the daughter they would have had, if their marriage had survived. She looked like her mother, Mickie Vega, the ATF agent who'd saved Danny's life, then married him, got him to settle down and stop looking for the grave that had his name on it. That's what he'd been doing for as long as Helen had known him. They'd grown up together, lived on the same block in the Garden District when they were kids. In high school he was one of those boys with haunted eyes that make you want to take him in your arms and save him from his demons. Helen had known lots of girls who'd tried, but she'd managed to resist, until their final year of law school at Tulane, when the friendship they'd both agreed upon suddenly collapsed into a passionate affair, a nightly wrestling match that left them both breathless. After graduation, she'd gone off to Atlanta to clerk for a federal judge and Danny had stayed behind, taking a job in the district attorney's office that had him working sixteen-hour days, prosecuting drug crimes and carjackings, like a man working an assembly line that just kept moving, one ruined life following the last. But Danny had loved it, enjoyed getting up in court in front of juries of auto mechanics and secretaries to argue for justice. They talked on the phone almost every night, and on weekends he'd drive up to Atlanta, or she'd come down, spending the weekend with their work spread out on his bed in the apartment he'd rented in an old house on Calhoun Street, eating Chinese takeout and then making love among the stacks of files with an urgency that left them sorting out criminal complaints from corporate litigation for an hour afterward.

And you've been getting them mixed up ever since, she couldn't help thinking with a bitter smile.

Their marriage had lasted less than two years. They'd separated a few months after he'd abruptly resigned from the DA's office, gone to work for Jimmy Boudrieux. She never forgave him for the secrets he'd kept from her—including his cooperation with the FBI investigation that brought Jimmy Boudrieux down—and when it was all over, she'd withdrawn into her tastefully decorated office on the twenty-first floor of One Shell Square, from which she could gaze down upon the city like an enchanted princess in her tower of glass. In the years since, she'd had a number of affairs, and several men had proposed marriage. But she'd turned them all down, preferring to remain at her office window, watching the traffic pass silently in the street below. Men let you down. Too full of silence and secrets to be trusted. So why not love a city instead? She loved New Orleans the way you'd love a faithless man, who drinks and gambles, but then breaks your heart with his sad smile. In fact, she loved it too much to stay up there in her glass tower, so when the offer came to leave private practice and spend a few years in the U.S. attorney's office, working on a special commission to investigate corruption in the city's construction trades, she jumped at the chance. Wouldn't the smile be a little less sad, after all, if you could grab the dice off the table, get the city to stop gambling with its future?

It was hard to keep your hands clean in New Orleans; Danny'd taught her that, coming back to give her a refresher course every few years. Working in the U.S. attorney's office brought the lesson home. She'd known on some level that an investigation of this kind would inevitably become political, but she'd never realized how quickly the flood of political donations that poured into legislative offices from Baton Rouge all the way to Washington could shape the direction of their work. Witnesses were coerced, politicians cut deals, and powerful men got off after making a single phone call to an unlisted number in McLean, Virginia. New Orleans went on, doing business under the table, rolling the dice on its future. It was disillusioning, like loving a man and watching him walk away. But she'd learned that she was stronger than she once thought: she'd learned to swallow her disappointment and focus on the battles she could win. She could smile at things that once would have broken her heart. She could keep her eye on the ball. She could even look at a picture of the child she'd never have and say, "She's lovely," without choking on the feeling of broken glass caught in her throat. That was a lesson worth learning, and she took pride in it. Nobody could accuse her of losing her cool.

Now, safely behind her desk, she felt that she'd gotten firm ground under her feet again, as they went over the written agreement Danny had prepared for his client's testimony. She read it over, asked Danny a few basic questions, then turned to Louis Sams and said:

"You can provide us with documentation of these claims?"

"Yes, ma'am."

"But you understand you'll still have to testify in open court if this comes to trial?"

Sams nodded. "But that's still a ways off, right? My grand jury testimony will be secret."

Helen glanced over at Danny, and he thought he saw her eyebrows rise slightly. "We can keep your testimony confidential until the case comes to trial, but you should be aware that grand jury testimony is difficult to control. I'm sure Danny has told you that it would be wise to take any personal precautions you feel necessary to protect yourself. We can offer you a place in the Witness Protection Program if you feel that's necessary, but that would obviously cause some disruption to your life and expose your cooperation with this grand jury."

Sams looked at her. "So basically you're saying I'm on my own."

"Grand juries leak like a rusty bucket," Danny said. "You have to be prepared to deal with the consequences of testifying before you go in."

"What happens if I'm threatened?"

Danny looked over at the FBI agent, Marty Seagraves. "What kind of security can we promise him?"

We, Helen thought. She couldn't help smiling. Danny always took things so personally. It wasn't enough just to let the FBI investigate a corrupt politician; he had to get involved, ruin his own life to bring the guy down. Or you ask him to look into a civil rights complaint filed by some local residents over a real estate development, look for ways to resolve it without getting the developer dragged into court, and the next thing you know, he's taking on the Klan, while your client, the real estate developer you were considering marrying, is looking at ten years on a wrongful death charge he'd thought was dead and buried. That was one thing about Danny: he never did anything halfway. Somebody threatened

Louis Sams, he'd probably get out there and guard the man's house himself. Bring some of Jabril Saunders's street kids to patrol the neighborhood, make sure nobody got too close.

Seagraves shifted in his chair, like they'd caught him thinking about something else and the sudden attention was making him uncomfortable. He'd aged since Helen had last seen him, lost some hair and put on a few pounds around the middle, taking it a little easier now than he used to, probably. She'd gotten a little shock when Danny introduced him—"You remember Marty Seagraves from the FBI?"—surprised to see he'd gotten so middle-aged. But then, hadn't they all started to look that way? She still caught young men looking at her on the street, but just a few days ago some kid working the valet parking at Galatoire's had called her *ma'am* in the polite tone she recognized as the way you'd talk to somebody's *mother*. It probably didn't help that she was getting out of a Volvo at the time. If she traded it in, got herself a little two-seat BMW roadster, would the valet parking guys go back to flirting with her, taking a second to check out her legs as she got out of the car?

To make it worse, she felt her lips tighten up as she looked at Seagraves, the way the nuns used to look at you in high school if you wore your skirt too short. Even now, after all these years had passed, she found it hard not to resent him for his role in the collapse of their marriage. Marty Seagraves, it turned out, had been the secret Danny'd kept from her, slipping out of the house to call the FBI agent, never even hinting that his work for Jimmy Boudrieux had been anything other than the self-destructive impulse that it had seemed to her. Had Seagraves urged him not to tell her? Was there a reason Danny had felt he couldn't trust her with his secret? Later, she'd wondered if he'd been trying to protect her. But that thought—like Danny's confession—had come too late to save their marriage.

Maybe that's the price we have to pay for justice, she thought. *Betraying those we've vowed to protect.*

"I guess that depends on the degree of the threat," Seagraves was telling Sams now. "We get witnesses to gang killings, we take them out of the city, put them up in a hotel in Baton Rouge or Mobile until trial. Twenty-four-hour guards in the room with them. I doubt we'd need to do anything that dramatic in this case. Corruption cases, we can usually work it out so it doesn't disrupt your life too much."

Sams looked at him. "Except I'd lose my job."

"That's not really my area. I'm just here to talk about security." Seagraves spread his hands. "But you testify against your boss, you can't really expect to stay on the payroll."

Sams seemed to consider this for a moment, like he'd never really thought about it that way. Then he nodded. "You're right. Maybe I should just quit my job right now, then I could testify out in the open."

Helen leaned forward, raised her hands as if to slow him down. "Actually, I'd urge you not to do that at this point. If you leave your job before you testify, it makes it easier for the defense to discredit your testimony when we go to trial. They can paint you as a disgruntled former employee who's pursuing a private grievance against the company, rather than someone who's come forward out of a sense of conscience."

"So you want me to keep working there?"

"For the moment, yes."

Sams frowned. "But there won't be anyone out there to protect me if this thing gets out, right?"

"That's true," Seagraves conceded. "It's probably not possible for us to protect you on the job if your testimony leaks. But if you get any sign that your situation isn't safe, we'll pull you out within the hour."

"I work at a concrete plant. A lot could happen in an hour."

"Your best bet if you get the feeling that something's not right is to stay in public places. Call us right away, and then go sit in the cafeteria until we get there. Or if your office has a lobby. Stay where people can see you, and you should be fine."

Sams looked over at Danny. "That what you did?"

"Not exactly. But there were other people involved."

"Usually are." Sams looked at Helen. "What happens to my boy?"

"The charges against him are local," she said, "so we can't just drop them. But should you agree to cooperate with this investigation, I'll speak to the district attorney and request that he be allowed to plead to a charge of misdemeanor possession."

"That means no jail?"

"Probation, I'd guess."

Sams nodded. "Okay. You work that out, I'll testify. But you better get on it, because I'm not saying a word until I see my boy walk out the door of that courthouse."

Helen made a note on the legal pad in front of her. "I'll make the call as soon as we're done here. We'll ask for a bail hearing first thing in the morning. The charges won't be dropped until after you testify, but that'll be just a formality. We can get him out of custody immediately." She looked up. "So all that remains is to schedule your testimony before the grand jury. Do you have any objection to doing it next week?"

"Nah. Let's just get it over with."

She reached over, pulled a calendar out of a basket on her desk. "How about next Monday? That's August twenty-ninth."

"So I'll need to put in for a personal day."

Helen nodded. "We'll schedule your testimony first thing in the morning, so it's possible that you could get back to work after lunch. But that really depends on how things go with the grand jury. It might not be a bad idea to put in for a couple vacation days. Can you find a reason to get out of town for a few days?"

"My wife's got family in Atlanta. I'll figure something out."

Helen looked over at Seagraves. "Can you put him up in a hotel over the weekend?"

"Sure. No problem."

She made a note in her file. "When you've finished your testimony, we'll put you on a plane, and you can join your family in Atlanta. Otherwise, we suggest that you go about your business as usual. Try to think of this the way you would a doctor's appointment. That's the best way to avoid arousing suspicion."

Sams smiled bitterly. "Like nothing's happened."

"That's right." Helen dropped the calendar into its basket, sat back. "Just like any other day."

3

"Someone's waving at you," Matia Vega told Danny, pointing across the restaurant to where a woman with short-cropped black hair was getting up from a crowded table, coming toward them. They were standing by the oyster bar at Uglesich's, waiting for a table to open up. "Couple minutes," the woman behind the register had told Danny when they'd come in, but that's what she always said, even at noon on Friday, when the line was out the door.

"You order up front," Danny was trying to tell Matia, handing her a menu. "When a table opens up, they'll bring out our food." He had a yellow Post-it note the cashier had handed him with a number on it they'd call out when a table came open, which he showed her as if that proved they'd get to sit down soon, but she was looking around at the cramped dining room, the crowds of late-season tourists who'd read about the place in *Bon Appétit* or *Cigar Aficionado*, and he could tell by the way she pressed her lips together that she'd made up her mind already, getting ready to start complaining about the wait, the service, the food's not right. But instead she just pointed across the room at the woman coming toward him, her hair razored short like she'd just come out of boot camp, and he suddenly knew it was going to be much worse than that. *That's how it happens*, he thought. *Somebody calling out your name in a restaurant. And your whole past comes rushing back at you, no chance to slip away.*

It was Maura Boudrieux. Once, in some lost distant life, she'd lived in a big house on Audubon Place, the daughter of one of the state's most powerful politicians, and he'd been the hollow-eyed guy who sat in the kitchen, a briefcase full of cash on the floor beside his feet. They'd known each other since they were children, but it was only in those last years that they'd recognized the same empty look in each other's eyes. She'd done all the things girls like her did: crashed the expensive sports car her daddy had bought her for her high school graduation, married badly and quickly divorced, spent time in a rehab facility out in Southern California for a collection of addictions that impressed even the former Hollywood child star with whom she shared a room. What was left but sleeping with the help?

Thinking about it now, Danny couldn't help wincing. She'd shocked him with her hunger, the sharp bones hidden just beneath her skin. Looking at him with those hollow eyes, like a famine child. And in the end, it was that hunger that had saved her. She ran, with a bag full of cash stolen from her father's safe, before the shooting started. And to Danny's knowledge, until today, she hadn't been back since, living out West somewhere, he liked to imagine, where the air was clear and dry.

"Danny Chaisson," she said now, as if the words were a twelve-year-old whiskey to be savored slowly. Her eyes took in Mickie, Anna perched on her hip, and then Matia, who was looking at her suspiciously, like she'd seen this moment coming all along.

"How've you been, Maura?"

She laughed. "Look at you. Family man."

Danny turned to Mickie, saw that the look in her eyes wasn't much different from her mother's. Seeing that put something hard in his throat, like a cherry pit he'd gotten stuck there once as a kid, but up or down, you had to move it, so he swallowed, gave a bright smile, and said, "Mickie, this is Maura Boudrieux."

Mickie raised her eyebrows. "Of course." She shifted Anna to her other hip, held out a hand. "I'm Mickie Vega, Danny's wife."

"You're the ATF agent." Maura took her hand, but her eyes took a long tour down the length of Mickie's body and back up. Then she smiled. "Nice work, Danny."

Danny saw Mickie stiffen. *Uh-oh.* He stole a quick glance at Matia. She was watching the scene with a look of quiet satisfaction, like a prophet who'd wandered in from the desert just in time to see flames descend from the sky.

"And you're the one who got away with the money," Mickie said, in a tight voice that suggested she might just reach back, pull her badge off her belt, put Maura up against the oyster bar with her feet spread, search her for weapons.

Maura laughed. "Is that what he told you? It wasn't that much money, I'm afraid. And the IRS got the rest." She looked at Anna. "Who's this lovely young lady?"

And to Danny's surprise, all the tension suddenly melted away. All three women looked at Anna and smiled.

Mickie bounced Anna on her hip slightly. "This is Anna."

"She's beautiful."

Anna looked at Maura, then buried her face in her mother's neck. Danny knew exactly how she felt.

"So," he said. "You're back in New Orleans."

All three women looked at him as if he'd just dropped a stack of dishes. Even Anna raised her head off her mother's shoulder to look at him.

Maura spread her hands. "It's been almost five years. Seemed like a good time to come home. Anyway, the food out in California never tasted right. It's like they never heard of spices out there." She glanced back at her table. "Look, I'm with some people, but we should get together, talk about old times."

Danny shot Mickie a glance. She wasn't looking at him, but Matia was watching him closely.

"Sure," he said without enthusiasm. "That'd be great."

"You in the book?"

"Yellow pages. I've got a law practice over on St. Charles."

"Yeah? I may have to come see you one of these days. My father left a real mess when he died. I could use some help getting it straightened out."

"I'm not sure I'm the right guy to help you with that."

Maura smiled. "Why not? After all, you helped make the mess." She looked at Mickie. "Nice to meet you after all this time. Looks to me like you're just what the doctor ordered." Then her eyes came back to Danny and she said, "Funny how things turn out, huh?"

For a moment he caught a glimpse of the Maura Boudrieux he'd known, all burnt matches and broken glass, then she walked back to her table, a large group of young bohemians up from the Warehouse District. She said something to them as she sat down, and the whole group looked over.

They stood in silence for a moment, until Mickie said quietly, "Looks like it's pretty busy in here today. Might take a while to get a table."

"You want to go someplace else?"

"Might be quicker."

Danny nodded, went out to get the car. Up Magazine Street, maybe, to Joey K's. Probably be a crowd there too, but at least they wouldn't have to feel like the past was hanging over them the whole time they ate. Mickie was used to it: for two years after Jimmy Boudrieux's death, if Danny walked into a restaurant, there were people who would get up in the middle of a meal, throw some money on the table, and leave. Even now there were places he knew better than to go: they'd leave him standing by the door for an hour as tables emptied and customers who'd come in behind him were seated. If he complained, the hostess would say, "Sorry, they have reservations." They'd learned to make their own reservations under Mickie's name: usually the pretty Tulane or Loyola student working the hostess desk would seat them before anybody recognized

Danny. Nobody had gone so far as to throw him out, but he'd once ordered a bowl of gumbo at a place in Mid-City only to have it arrive with a big glob of spit floating in the center of the bowl.

There were also places where the owners welcomed him, came out of the kitchen to shake his hand. That was especially true at the soul food joints up in the Ninth Ward where Jabril liked to take him. But those weren't the kinds of places where they could take Matia, showing her *the real New Orleans*. That would be a little too real for her, Danny figured.

He took his time getting the car. He knew that the moment he walked out the door, Matia would have started interrogating her daughter in whispered Spanish. *Who's that woman? How does she know your husband? You couldn't marry a nice Chicano boy?* When he pulled up, they were waiting outside the restaurant, Matia talking away, and Mickie had that look in her eye like she'd just been swept out to sea by a powerful tide and now the sharks were circling. If she'd been angry about Maura, now she shot Danny a look that said, *Save me!*

He got out, came around the car, and took Anna from her arms, saying, "How 'bout we ride up Magazine, get some catfish at Joey K's?"

"Sounds good," she said with a little too much enthusiasm, and got behind the wheel as he opened the back and slid Anna into her car seat. They had an unspoken agreement that when Matia went on the offensive, Danny would let Mickie take over the driving. *Defensive driving*, she called it. Anything to get away from the interrogation. Mickie drove like a cop, and once she pulled away from the curb, her mother couldn't think about anything but muttering prayers to keep the other cars away from them.

"I don't get it," Danny'd said after she'd come to visit them the first time. "She was married to a cop all those years, she doesn't know how they drive?"

"My father never drove like that when he was off duty," Mickie told him. "He got in the car with my mother, he turned into one of those little old men you see in the barrio, hunched over the wheel, going twenty-five with a whole line of traffic behind them."

Danny could picture it, the poor guy putting on twenty years when he came home every night, just from the weight of all the talk. He gets up in the morning, puts on his uniform, he can't wait to get out there and mix it up with all the *cholos* and *vagos* just to prove he's still alive. Hearing them call out, *Five-oh rollin'*, as he drives by, and knowing by the way they say it that's all the respect any man can get in this world.

Mickie, she could take down a hard-core felon, bust the door down on an illegal weapons dealer and put him against the wall, but she couldn't take her mother's insistent questions. *Why do you have to live where it rains so much? Why haven't you painted the kitchen yet? Why doesn't Danny have more clients? Can't he go on television like all those other lawyers? Why do you drive so fast?* Now she drove up Magazine with a fixed expression, as if lunch with her family had suddenly become the obstacle course at the Federal Law Enforcement Training Center at Glynco, Georgia, where she'd injured her knee, almost washing out of her class. She'd bought a knee brace, learned to run the obstacles without showing the pain it caused her. Couldn't she at least get through lunch?

But when Danny's cell phone rang, she shot him a look in the rearview mirror that said, *Don't you dare!*

"Sorry," he said, digging the phone out of his pocket. "I won't be a minute."

Was that relief she saw on his face? For a second she saw that flicker of hope in his eyes, like a prisoner spotting an unlocked door. But then he had the phone to his ear, gazing out the window at the passing buildings with that look people get when their mind is elsewhere. "Danny Chaisson."

"Hey, Danny," Marty Seagraves said. "Sorry to interrupt your lunch, but we got a problem."

IIII "Kinda late to be putting in for vacation days." Gerald Vickers sat back, put his feet up on his desk, and looked at Louis Sams standing there in his office door, like he was hoping he wouldn't have to come all the way into the office. "I already got three people out next week, and they put in for those days back in April."

"I'm sorry," Sams told him. "It's my wife's mother. She's going in for surgery. Kara already flew out to Atlanta last night, and she's gonna need help taking care of her dad while her mother's laid up. He doesn't get around too well since his stroke, and if they're both laid up, they'll need help until we can arrange some in-home care. He's a big guy, and Kara's not strong enough to lift him, so—"

"Okay, okay." Vickers held up a hand to stop him. "You need, what, a couple days?"

"I'll fly out on Saturday, be back here at my desk Thursday morning. And I'll have my cell and laptop with me, so you can reach me in case something comes up on one of the projects."

"All right. We'll call it personal days. But I'm still gonna expect those specs on the Madisonville project by the first."

"No problem. You got it."

Sams closed the door carefully, stood there for a moment feeling like he'd just walked out of a convenience store with a bottle of Thunderbird stuffed into his jacket. He'd done that once as a dare when he was fifteen, felt the cashier's eyes on him as he left the store. It was a place on Rampart, almost two miles from his house, but even now, almost thirty years later, he still went out of his way to avoid driving past that store, still feeling those eyes burning into the back of his neck.

"Louis can't lie to me," Kara liked to tell her girlfriends. "His face gets all red, and his shoulders tighten up like he's carrying something heavy."

It wasn't like everything he'd told Vickers was a lie. He'd put Kara and the girls on a plane to Atlanta so they could stay with her folks. But his boy, Claude, was sitting in a juvenile facility over at Orleans Parish Prison, waiting on arraignment on drug and weapons charges. And he wouldn't be joining the family in Atlanta on Saturday. Instead, he'd check into a hotel out by the airport, spend the weekend eating room service and getting ready for his grand jury testimony on Monday morning. The FBI agent, Marty Seagraves, had promised him that they could keep him out of sight for three days, until his testimony was finished. The grand jury sessions would be closed and his identity kept secret. They expected it to take two days. When he was done, nobody would know he hadn't been in Atlanta the whole time, helping out with his sick in-laws.

He went back to his office, where he had a stack of builders' specifications spread out. It was the kind of work he usually enjoyed, detail work, satisfying in its complexity. Sometimes he felt the way he used to when he was a kid, building models in his room on a Saturday afternoon while the other neighborhood kids fought and shouted in the street outside. It made him feel safe, as if there were an order to the world that made all those tiny pieces fit together perfectly to form a suspension bridge. The boys in the street could shout at the top of their voices, throw rocks at his window, but piece by piece, the bridge would rise.

He'd felt that when he first began working at IndusCrete. He'd be given a set of construction specs, and while his work on concrete moldings was only one tiny piece of the engineering that would go into the building of a highway overpass or an oil pumping station down along the Gulf, he knew that there were other engineers sitting in their offices all across the state working on their own pieces of the same project, and that when their work was done, all their work would fit neatly together as the builders poured concrete and raised steel beams, like the plastic pieces he'd laid out carefully on his desk whenever he'd started a new model, each mysterious in its shape until it was joined with the others to form something perfect and complete. He liked to drive through the city, looking at the buildings and imagining all the people it took to build each one. Every streetlight, every bus shelter, had been the work of many hands. Why couldn't other people *see* that? The teenagers who scrawled their gang tags on every wall in the neighborhood took the world that surrounded them for granted. They felt the need to mark every surface, as if that gave them some ownership. But if they could see it the way he saw it, recognizing all the care that had gone into even the simplest things, they might start to see how any city is like a bridge, in which every piece fits.

That's how he'd felt when he started his job, and the feeling had stayed with him for those first few years, until he started getting spec sheets in which the numbers didn't add up. He'd gone to his supervisor, who told him not to worry about it, that the numbers were within an acceptable range of tolerance. So he went back to his desk, figuring he had to adjust his own range of tolerance. Okay, so it isn't perfect. Let's face it, the world gets built on *good enough*. It's not pretty, but it gets the job done.

But a few weeks later, as he sat at his desk with another stack of construction specifications on a highway overpass spread out in front of him, he began to feel something hard take shape in his stomach. Maybe you couldn't expect perfection, especially in a town like New Orleans, where everything got done half fast, but you could only stretch numbers so far before you ended up with a bridge that didn't reach either side of the river, so can't *nobody* get across.

His supervisor raised his eyebrows when Sams showed him the spec sheets. He looked them over, then sighed, looked up at Sams the way you'd look at a child who comes to you crying because he's scared of the dark. "Mark it," he said wearily. "Leave it with me, and I'll run the numbers again later."

And that was the last Louis Sams had heard of it. The concrete moldings got poured, and the project went ahead as scheduled. Four years later, a state building inspector discovered cracks in the foundations. The story hit the newspapers, and a legislative committee up in Baton Rouge spent two months looking into the matter. In the end, they concluded that the damage was due to heavy rains that caused unexpected soil subsidence. The legislature voted funds to repair the problem, and when the bids were opened, InPdusCrete got the job.

So why didn't his face get red? Why didn't he get that feeling like a cashier's eyes were burning into the back of his neck? He'd gotten used to it. Just pieces of paper, after all. He marked the problems when he saw them, then sent the papers on to his supervisor. After that, it had nothing to do with him. That's what it means to have a job, right? You do what you're paid to do and keep your mouth shut. End of the week, you pick up your check, take it home to your wife so she can pay for the groceries. It ain't always pretty, but it's life: the pieces don't have to all fit together.

Except that somewhere in the back of his mind, he kept a record of every one of those papers. He knew exactly where he could find them in the thick files that had been shoved into the metal drawers that lined the office's hallway. Seagraves had walked him through the filing system twice, taking careful notes. After he completed his testimony, they'd seek a search warrant that would allow the FBI agents to seize the project files, establishing a paper trail that would support his accusations. Once they had that, they could put pressure on other engineers to testify in exchange for immunity.

"That's usually when the flood wall breaks," Seagraves had told him. "They see you've got the evidence, everybody starts cutting deals to save their own skin. Even the rats start jumping ship."

Sams wasn't sure who the rats were. Most of the engineers he worked with were good guys who did their jobs the best way they knew how. If Vickers was cutting crooked deals, they'd have to get him with the spec sheets. He also kept a file full of private notes in his office, but Sams couldn't tell them anything about what they'd find in there. They'd have to base their search warrant on the stuff in the general files, then see what they came up with once they got into the office.

But Seagraves said they needed to make the warrant as exact as possible, to convince the judge they weren't on a fishing expedition. "We'll need a list of files," he'd said, shoving a legal pad across the table. "Try to be as detailed as you can, especially about where we'll find them."

Sams had made up the list, working from memory. When he was done, it filled three pages.

Seagraves raised an eyebrow when he handed it over. "You've got quite a memory."

"Some of it I'll need to check. I'll stay late one night this week, spend some time digging around in the files."

"You feel okay about that?"

Sams shrugged. "It's nothing unusual. Half of my job is remembering what we did last time."

"What about the computers?"

"Most of it's on a general network, which anyone with a password can access. Vickers keeps the really important files on his local drive."

"You ever see any of those files?"

"Once or twice. He sent me one by mistake once, when he meant to send a different attachment."

Seagraves raised his eyebrows. "Anything we'd be interested in?"

"It was a list of state building inspectors, with a number by some of the names."

Seagraves sat back in his chair slowly. "You still have that?"

Sams shook his head. "I deleted it when I realized what it was. This was a couple years ago."

"That's too bad. Would have been useful to have before we go to the grand jury. Any chance you could get your hands on it again?"

Sams hesitated. "I'd have to get a few minutes at his computer. That may not be easy. He's got it password-protected, so the only time I can get at it may be while he's at lunch."

"Too risky?"

"Not if I'm careful."

But that was before Vickers had brought in two guys in cheap suits that made them look like cops to start sniffing around the office.

"Lenny and Vince," Vickers had said when he introduced them that morning, although no one could say which one was Lenny and which one was Vince. Vickers just waved a hand in their direction, with a look on his face like he wanted to get back to his office as quickly as possible, forget about the whole thing. "Give 'em your cooperation, okay? They're gonna look around for me, see if they can help us do things more efficiently."

Like those two guys had any idea how to make concrete. Looking at them, Sams could see that efficiency wasn't their thing, unless it was finding a more efficient way to separate a guy from his money in a dark alley.

What they looked like was cops, not the tough guys in uniform who spend an hour lifting weights after their shift ends, but the middle-aged guys who show up twenty minutes after some kid gets shot on Rampart Street, climb out of their unmarked cars like it took all their energy just to drive over from the station house, all the muscle they'd had back when they played ball for Jesuit gone now, buried under twenty years of fried chicken and beer.

For a couple hours they wandered around, watching what everybody did. In the afternoon they took to sitting in the break room, coffee cups on the table in front of them, waiting for somebody to come in for a candy bar. Then they'd start asking questions: "Hey, still raining out there? You work in the front office? What they got you doing up there?"

And the poor guy would stand there with his Snickers, wishing he'd stuck to his diet, trying to look like he was answering their questions because he wanted to, not because they scared the shit out of him. By the afternoon, a theory had sprung up that the one with red hair was Lenny, but there were others who argued—a small group of engineers crowded into the copy room, whispering—that the one with red hair was Vince. (He put powdered creamer in his coffee, and one of the engineers claimed to have heard him say, "Hey, Lenny. Grab that creamer for me, will you?") Not that it really mattered much, Sams figured. He'd watched a TV show once about how the mining companies out West had broken up the unions back in the twenties, and these two guys reminded him of the men they'd hired to stand around at the mines' front gates with ax handles, ready to rough up any union organizers who tried to slip in when the shifts changed. He brought his lunch from home, left-over chicken gumbo in a thermos, and ate it at his desk, so there was no reason for him to go to the break room.

But now everybody was packing up to leave for the day, and the two guys showed no sign of leaving. They were walking around, look-ing into people's offices, making everybody nervous. Did they think people were stealing supplies? Sams saw a couple of the engineers pack up their briefcases, then hesitate, as if nobody wanted to be seen leaving first. One secretary carefully took all the family photographs off her desk, locked them in her desk. Finally, one guy came out of his office, looked up at the clock on the wall of the receptionist's area, and said, "Is it really that late? I've got a construction meeting downtown." After that, everybody left in a crowd, hurrying to their cars like it was the last day of school and they were scared some teacher might come chasing after them with one last homework assignment.

Sams sat in his office, working away on a construction estimate that the sales guys needed on Monday. At six-thirty, Vickers came out of his office, looked around. He came over to Sams's office. "Everybody gone?" His voice sounded hopeful.

"I think I saw Lenny and Vince walking around a couple minutes ago. Looked like they were headed out to the factory."

Vickers's face fell. "Oh, Christ. I better get out there, make sure they don't fall into a mixer." He looked at the papers spread out on Sams's desk. "You working late?"

"Yeah. I want to get those estimates done on the McComb job, since I'll be out on Monday."

"Right. I forgot about that. Send me an e-mail, okay? I'll put it on my calendar in the morning." He rubbed at his forehead, looked back toward the entrance to the factory. "You'll be in tomorrow, right?"

"Yeah. I'm leaving on Saturday."

He nodded. "Then I'll see you in the morning."

Sams watched him walk away down the hall, all the office walls made of glass so you could see straight through to where the receptionist sat by the door, under the photographs of all the construction projects they'd worked on in the last five years, a new girl Vickers had hired right out of UNO, who still smiled when she answered the phone, like she wanted every caller to feel welcome. It made Louis Sams feel like he worked in a fishbowl sometimes, but there was also something reassuring about looking to your right, seeing a whole row of engineers sitting at their desks, each behind his own piece of glass, all working on some small piece of the same project.

The factory ran all night, three shifts cycling through every day, trying to keep up with all the orders. Vickers usually went out there when he was finished in the office, stood around talking to the foremen for an hour before he went home. He'd started out as a teenager pouring slabs for new houses up in Metairie, and he still loved the smell of wet concrete. Underneath the rich man, there was still a kid who liked to build things. But you can get used to having it all too easy. You start to make some money, pretty soon you forget how lucky you are, start to feel like being rich is normal. *I worked hard*, you tell yourself. *I deserve some fun.* So you get yourself a fancy car, an expensive wife, and an even more expensive bookie, and for a while every day's a party. You're doing well, but pretty soon you start to notice that there are other people who are doing better. Buying yachts, fancy houses out on Grand Isle they only use twice a year, planes to fly them to Vegas whenever they get too rich, feel like they want to slim down a little by dropping some serious money at the crap tables. Like all rich men, Gerald Vickers didn't feel rich enough. But you own a company like IndusCrete, it's like you've got a well out behind the house; you just drop in a bucket and draw up some money anytime you want. Sell some stock, borrow against the assets. When that's spent, you look around for ways to drain even more money out of the company, and you notice that the boys making the really big cash all have friends up in Baton Rouge where they sign the state contracts. So you ride up to the state capital and spread some money around. Pretty soon you got three shifts working and the money's flowing in. But now you got to pay off the loans, and all the people who own your stock expect to share in the profits. So you bid low and squeeze money from the production process. And if a bridge starts to crack a couple years after it's built, then you get on the phone to your friends upstate and make sure the whole thing gets buried under a pile of paper. You start out wanting to build things because you love the smell of fresh concrete, but by the time you're done, you can't even smell it anymore because there are less pleasant odors that have to be hidden away.

He made the choice, Sams thought, as he watched the office empty out for the night. He took a deep breath, went back to his paperwork.

Most people, they don't get one.

IIII "How did this happen?"

Seagraves spread his hands. "No way to know. A leak somewhere up in the federal courthouse, probably. You know how it works.

Somebody's got a sister who's a secretary up there, she's been there fifteen years, nobody even thinks about it. It's a small town, Danny. And as far as we know, all they got is a rumor about a grand jury. Nothing about a specific source. Our guy isn't mentioned. I wouldn't even have heard about it, except a guy down the hall on the Organized Crime Task Force knew I had an interest in IndusCrete."

Danny said nothing. He looked at the papers on Seagraves's desk, a surveillance transcript from a bug the FBI had planted in a light fixture in Little Jimmy Mancuso's favorite lunch hangout, a po'boy place on Bienville, a couple blocks from the cemetery. Danny knew the place, and he could picture Mancuso sitting at his usual table, people lined up along the bar waiting to talk to him. His favorite waiter was a little old Italian guy who'd been working in that place for thirty years, and he knew what Jimmy liked, kept the plates full of fried oysters and spicy french fries coming out every fifteen minutes, until Jimmy waved a hand lazily, got the two ex-cops who worked as his bodyguards to help him up out of his chair. If you were one of the people still waiting at the bar, you knew that you'd have to come back tomorrow, get there when the place opened at ten to make sure you made it to the table before Jimmy finished eating.

But if you owed Jimmy money, like Gerald Vickers, it didn't matter how many people were waiting at the bar, he'd wave you over, push a chair out with his foot, and say, "So? What you got for me?"

Once, Danny'd heard, a guy who ran girls out of a club up in Metairie was into Jimmy for almost two hundred thousand. He kept Jimmy supplied with girls, especially the little Chinese and Vietnamese girls Jimmy liked, taking them to bed two at a time, so the guy figured Jimmy'd cut him some slack. Every month he had a different excuse. But one day Jimmy got tired of waiting for his money. So when the guy came in, sat down at the table, Jimmy looked at him with his sleepy eyes, said, "You got something for me?"

"Listen, Jimmy, I'm gonna need some more time. I had some big expenses the last couple months. Had to bring in some new girls, keep the product fresh." Then the guy grinned. "You like the ones I sent over, right?"

Maybe the guy just misread the situation, or maybe Jimmy was in a bad mood that day. Maybe his stomach was upset, or he was sick of Chinese girls. Whatever the reason was, Jimmy surprised everybody with the speed with which he could move. His hand shot out, seized the guy's hand, then he snatched a fork up off the table, drove it through the guy's hand into the tabletop. For a moment the pimp was too surprised to react; he just sat there, eyes wide, looking down at the fork sticking out of his hand. Then he opened his mouth wide, let out a high-pitched wail of shock and pain.

"Shut the fuck up," Jimmy shouted. "I don't want to hear another sound out of you until I got my money!"

And the guy shut up. Tears were streaming down his face, but he closed his mouth, gritted his teeth, and didn't make a sound while the waiter came over, calmly pulled the fork out of his hand, then handed him a napkin to wrap up his bleeding hand. Two days later, Jimmy had his money. Nobody knew exactly how the guy got it, but for the next six months there were some very tired-looking Chinese girls working the massage parlors along Airline Highway.

"You know these two guys he's sending over to the concrete plant?" Danny reached over, tapped a finger on the surveillance transcript.

"They're muscle. Used to be NOPD, working Sixth District. Got thrown off the force during all the corruption investigations, and now they work for Jimmy Mancuso. We figure they're mostly for show. Nobody's going to mess with Little Jimmy. Not in this town, anyway. He just likes the idea of having ex-cops as his bodyguards."

"And these guys are gonna be hanging out at IndusCrete, looking for an informant?"

"That's what it says. They don't have anything on our guy. Just a rumor about a grand jury."

"It's enough. Those guys start looking, it's just a matter of time before they figure out you've got somebody inside." Danny sat back. "You have to call Louis, tell him to get out of there."

"You don't think I thought about that?" Seagraves shook his head. "He wanted to get into the files, make sure his testimony was accurate before we cut a search warrant. Anyway, he can't just stop going to work. They'll get suspicious."

"What about next week, during his testimony?"

"He's putting in for vacation time. Has to go to Atlanta to help out with a sick relative."

"So they need help sooner than he planned." Danny leaned forward. "Marty, I've been on the inside. It starts to go wrong, it can get ugly real fast."

"I'm the one who tried to pull you out. You wanted to finish the job."

"And look how that ended up." Danny took out his cell phone. "Call him. Tell him to get out of there. If you don't, I will."

"It means putting him into the Witness Protection Program. Jimmy Mancuso's involved, this isn't just a corruption investigation anymore." Seagraves looked at Danny. "Chances are he'll never be able to go back to his regular life again. Not in New Orleans, anyway. Somebody's gonna have to break that to him."

"And if he decides the price is too high? Wants to back out of testifying?"

Seagraves shrugged. "Then I guess we're back to square one. His kid goes to court, and we start looking for another witness."

"Except his name's already in the files. You got a leak over at the courthouse, he'll never be safe, whether he testifies or not."

"So I guess he might as well testify. You think you could make that clear to him?"

Danny was silent for a moment, looking at the pile of papers on Seagraves's desk. "Lousy deal for him all around."

Seagraves nodded. "It's true. I feel for the guy. And the worst thing is, he testifies, his kid could turn around and get himself arrested next year. It's not a free pass. This guy's gonna ruin his life to keep the kid out of prison this time, but I gotta tell you, I've seen the kid's file, and he keeps hanging out with the same people, it's just a matter of time before he's up at Angola."

"So maybe Witness Protection isn't such a bad idea. Get the kid out of New Orleans."

"Maybe. But there's bad stuff all over. He wants to get himself into trouble, he'll find it as easily in Salt Lake City as he will here."

Danny raised his eyebrows. "Yeah?"

"Okay, maybe not in Salt Lake. But you get what I'm saying, right?" Seagraves reached over, picked up the phone. "He needs to understand his life will never be the same."

IIII Sams put in another hour on the construction estimates, just to make sure, then took a pad from his desk, went out to the files. It took him forty minutes, but by the time he was done, he had a complete record of where the FBI agents could find the files that would be specified on their search warrant. He was just putting the last files away when he heard voices and the door that led out to the plant opened. Lenny and Vince came in, brushing concrete dust off their clothes.

"You believe this shit?" The red-haired one slid off his coat, shook it a couple times, then slapped at the shoulders. "And those guys workin' out there breathe that fucking dust eight hours straight. You want to imagine what their lungs look like?"

Sams closed the file drawer unhurriedly, carried his pad back to his office. He saw the two men look over at him, surprised, like they hadn't expected anybody to be hanging around the office this late, even though all the lights were still on. A light was flashing on his phone when he got back to his desk, but he tossed the pad casually on his desk, sat down behind his computer, and pulled up his project management system, as if he were just putting in some long hours on a job. He saw them come down the hall past the row of windows, looking like they'd just spotted a deer that had been cut from the herd.

"Working late?" The red-haired man leaned against his office door, grinning at him. "Looks like you got the whole place to yourself."

Sams looked up at him, then sat back, stretching his shoulders as if he'd spent too much time at his desk. "Yeah. Got some projects that have to get finished. How 'bout you guys?"

"Us?" The red-haired guy looked at his partner and grinned. "I guess we got a project to finish up too. Ain't that right, Lenny?"

His partner was playing with something on the secretary's desk, a little metal skier who balanced on the edge of a pencil cup. He touched it, watched as the skier began rocking back and forth as if using his poles to stay balanced. "Yeah, I guess that's right."

Vince looked at Sams. "You like working here?"

Sams shrugged. "Sure. It's a good job. Gets a little repetitive sometimes, since we're always working with concrete, but every project's got its own challenges."

"I don't know how you guys do it, sitting there working with numbers all day. I'd go out of my mind."

"Yeah, I guess you got to like math. We do most of it on the computer now. And when you're done, there's a bridge or a building you can go look at. So it's not just like sitting here doing math problems all day."

Vince grinned. "Makes it more concrete, huh?"

Sams forced a smile. "I guess that's about right. What about you guys? You finding all kinds of ways to make us more efficient?"

"Yeah, we got it all figured out." Vince shot a grin at his partner. "Stronger coffee, for one thing. Get you some Café du Monde in here, you'll get through all those math problems in no time."

"Sounds good to me. See if you can get us some real milk while you're at it." Sams glanced at his watch. "I better get these estimates done, or I'll be here all night."

Vince raised both hands. "Okay, you got work to do. I get the message. We were getting ready to call it a night anyway."

Sams turned back to his computer, trying to look busy as they walked away. When he heard the door at the end of the hall close, he sat back, feeling the tension drain from his body. The light was still flashing on his phone. He picked it up, dialed into his voice mail, and heard the FBI agent Marty Seagraves say, "Hi, Louis. It's Marty. I've been trying to reach you all afternoon, but I didn't want to leave a message if I didn't have to. Listen, something's come up that Danny and I feel you should know about. I'll try you at home, but if you get this message, can you give me a call?"

Sams erased the message and sat there for a long moment, looking at the phone. Then he shut down his computer, packed up his briefcase, and walked out to his car. The parking lot was deserted. Off to the right, the lights of the plant spilled out across the gravel, and he could smell the moist concrete being poured into precast molds. The night shift guys had parked their cars and pickup trucks along the front wall of the plant. Sams stood there for a moment in the doorway, looking at his car parked way off by itself in the dark lot. He kept his car in perfect condition, and he liked to park near the entrance of the gravel parking lot so it wouldn't get so much dust on it when the morning shift pulled out, some of the plant workers throwing gravel in their hurry to get away. But suddenly the walk across that dark lot seemed endless. *Okay, so you have to wash your car a little more often. Is that really so bad?*

He took a deep breath, set off toward his car, making himself walk slowly. It felt like when he was a kid and he'd be coming home after dark, feeling like something was sneaking up behind him the whole time, so he had to fight the impulse to break into a run. And once he'd made it to his car, pulled out onto the highway, he felt ridiculous. Nobody was after him. Everything would be fine.

At a red light, he dug out his cell phone, dialed the number Marty Seagraves had given him in case he needed to reach him after hours. The phone rang twice, and the FBI agent picked up, his voice professional even this late in the evening. "Marty Seagraves."

"It's Louis Sams. You said I should call."

"Thank God. I was starting to get worried. Are you someplace where you can talk?"

"I'm in my car. What's up?"

"We think there's been a leak at the courthouse. Nothing about you, just the fact that the grand jury will be taking evidence from a witness next week. But we'd like to pull you in, just to be safe."

Sams felt something hard form in his throat. "Did you talk to Danny?"

"Yeah. He's the one who insisted we bring you in."

"Won't that just make it obvious that I'm the witness?"

"If there's a leak, we can't be sure they won't know that once you start testifying." Seagraves's voice sounded weary. "Look, I'm sorry about this. But it's time to start thinking about your safety. Just come on in, and we'll arrange security until your testimony is over and we can get you out of town."

"This wasn't part of our deal. You said nobody would find out."

"I said we'd *try* to keep your testimony secret. But New Orleans is a small town. You get a couple people talking down at the courthouse, it's all over. There's not a whole lot we can do about that, except make sure that you're protected."

Sams was silent for a moment. "How long do I have before they get my name?"

"No way to know. They might never get it. But we need to be ready in case they do."

"Am I okay until tomorrow?"

"Hard to say. As long as you're out there, you're at some risk. Why?"

"There's some stuff I need to do before I come in." Sams looked off to his left at the lights of the downtown skyline against the night sky. "Just some personal business I need to clear up before I can close the door on all this."

⫿⫿⫿ "So? What you got for me?"

Jimmy Mancuso looked annoyed. He had a line of people waiting on him at the bar, and none of them looked like they were ready to pull a wad of cash out of their pocket, toss it on the table. Besides that, his stomach was giving him trouble. He'd had to get up and go to the bathroom three times during dinner, and his pasta alla campidanese had gotten cold. He'd had to send it back to the kitchen, get them to put it in the microwave, which ruins the texture of the tagliatelle. And now he had Lenny and Vince come in, they got cement dust all over their clothes, so when they sit down, this little cloud rises, it's all he can smell. It's a *restaurant*, for Christ's sake. He wanted to smell cement, he'd go get a muffaletta, eat it at a building site.

"That's some operation out there," Vince told him. "Those guys in the plant, they're putting in three shifts a day pouring concrete."

Jimmy raised his eyebrows. "You spent a whole day out there, that's what you got to tell me?"

"It's a bunch of engineers sitting in little glass offices, working on computers. There ain't much to tell."

"And you got no idea if somebody over there is getting ready to go to the grand jury."

Vince glanced over at his partner, grinned. "Like, are they all standing around the water cooler discussing their testimony? No, Jimmy. We didn't pick up on none a that. They're *workin'* over there. Bunch a guys doin' their jobs."

"So you got nothing." Jimmy sat back, stared at them. "What are you doin' back here, then? You got something for me, you come tell me. Otherwise you're just wasting my time."

"Okay, Jimmy. But I got to tell you, this kind of thing takes a while." Vince leaned forward, spread his hands. "You pull phone records, do surveillance on people . . ."

"Yeah? You do that yet?"

Vince looked confused. "What?"

"Look at their phone records."

"Nah, see, that's what I'm tellin' you. All that takes time. Vickers, he's got records of all the calls people make from their office phones, but nobody's gonna make that kind of call from their office. You want to find out who's talking to the U.S. attorney, you'd need to look at all their home phone records, their cell phones, pagers, all that stuff. It's a big job. We're just two guys, here."

Jimmy could feel his stomach starting to seize up again. Why was it, he wondered, you hire these guys, they're happy to sit around all day, drinking coffee at the bar, but you send 'em to take care of something, it's too big a job? He thought about saying that, but the idea of it just made the pain in his gut get worse. Instead, he said, "Tell me something. Do I pay you? What's that gettin' me?"

"Hey, I get what you're saying. You want results. And I got no problem with that. It's a reasonable expectation. All I'm saying is that we're goin' about this the wrong way."

"You got a better way?"

Vince smiled. "Yeah, Jimmy, I think we do."

4

"Thought I might find you here."

Danny Chaisson slid into the row of benches, took a seat beside Louis Sams. It was a few minutes after nine A.M., and already there was a crowd of anxious parents taking up most of the seats in the second-floor courtroom, waiting to catch a glimpse of their kids as they were led in on a wrist chain for arraignment. Sams stared straight ahead, looking like a man who'd spent much of his life hoping he wouldn't end up here, and now he couldn't do anything but keep his shoulders straight and carry the weight.

"Where else was I gonna be?"

Danny nodded. "Not much is going to happen, I'm afraid. Helen spoke to the DA last night, and they had a phone conference with the judge this morning. They'll go forward with the arraignment, then he'll make bail this afternoon. Presuming everything goes as expected with your testimony, they'll sign off on a plea bargain and a suspended sentence. If he stays clean until he's eighteen, it'll be expunged from his record."

Sams said nothing, kept his eyes on the door where they brought out the suspects waiting for arraignment.

"It's a good deal," Danny said.

"You think it'll change anything?" Sams looked over at him. "They want to put me in the Witness Protection Program. I'm gonna lose my home. My kids are gonna grow up in some other city, where they don't have family around them. And for what? People in this town, they'll still do business the way they always have."

Danny shrugged. "Might change your boy's life. Maybe a new city will be what he needs. He'll get a chance to start clean."

Sams looked away. "I'm scared for the boy. He gets used to this . . ." He jerked his head toward the front of the courtroom. "You know what I'm saying? Black kid starts down that road, he don't come back. They got him."

"So show him there's a different way."

"That's easy to say." Sams shook his head. "Boy that age doesn't look to his father. It's all about the street. They learn it from each other. You can't convince 'em there's anything else. They're so scared, all they know is how to act like killers, 'cause that's what they think it takes to keep from getting eaten alive out there."

Danny couldn't think of anything to say to that, so they sat in silence for a while. He could hear people whispering around them, everybody acting scared, like they were in church and the preacher's getting ready to raise the rod of judgment, bring it down on all the sinners.

At last he said, "You sleep at home last night?"

"I went by the house, got some stuff Kara wouldn't want to leave behind. Then I went to a hotel." Sams rubbed at his eyes wearily. "Guy in the next room spent the whole night watching porn movies. Kept the volume up loud."

"So he could hear the dialogue?"

"I guess. Didn't do much for me. I just lay there wondering what went wrong in my life."

Danny smiled. "Sounds like we need to get you into a better hotel."

"Maybe. But I've got a feeling I'm going to be spending a lot of time in hotels. Your boy over at the FBI, Seagraves? He keeps talking about putting me under protection. All I can think about is that guy in the *Godfather* movie, they got him living on an Army base.

He wants to go for a walk, they got this fenced-in area out back like a playground. Looks like they'd give a dog more room out at the pound."

"I don't think you have to worry about that. It's not like you're testifying against the Corleones here. You work for a concrete manufacturer."

Sams looked at him. "I guess it must look like I'm getting myself all worked up over nothing to people like you. Those FBI guys must think this is small stuff compared to the cases they work on. But I can't see that. From where I'm sitting, it looks like I'm losing everything."

"I know. And I'm sorry about that. But it might not turn out that way. It could be, when this is all over, you can come back. We just have to be sure right now that we can keep you safe."

Sams was silent for a moment. At the front of the room, a group of boys in orange jumpsuits were led in on a wrist chain. They were doing their best to shuffle and look tough, but Danny could see that they were scared.

"That's my boy," Sams said quietly. "Third one."

Danny could have guessed it. He looked like his father, with the same broad face and wide-set eyes, the same look like he'd enjoy nothing more than figuring out the weight tolerance of a bridge span. *Must make it tough out on the street*, Danny thought. *Maybe that's why he wants to hang with a gang. Prove that he's not scared to be out there.*

"He's not wearing his glasses," Sams said. "I hope he didn't lose them in jail."

Danny had to smile. "I'll lay money they're lying on his dresser at home. You picture him going out to hang with the homeboys wearing glasses?"

"Yeah, you probably right." Sams gave a sigh. "I guess I should be glad. At least I don't have to worry about him shooting somebody, he's leaving his glasses at home."

"Not on purpose, anyway."

They waited for forty minutes while the judge sorted out the first two cases, then the bailiff called out, "Claude Sams," and the boy stood up, trying to look like he didn't care about nothing that was going on, was just taking the opportunity to stretch his legs. The lawyer Sams had hired to represent his son got up, went forward to the defense table. The other boys watched as the public defender who'd been handling their cases sat down, started looking through some papers, and Danny could see they were wondering what was going on, why this new guy was going up there to talk to the judge about Claude, when their guy just stood up, read from some papers, and then sat down again. Didn't even look at them, hardly. Like none of this was about *them*, just business that had to get done before everybody could go get their lunch.

Danny didn't recognize the lawyer. He was a young black guy, probably only a couple years out of law school over at Loyola, trying to get his own practice going, working criminal cases, doing some real estate transactions, anything he could scrape up. Danny watched him talk quietly to the judge, then the judge nodded, consulted a paper he picked up off the bench, and passed it to his clerk. The clerk read off the charges in a bored voice, and the lawyer entered a plea of not guilty. Then the judge ordered Claude Sams held over for trial, made a note on some papers, and the next case was called.

It all took less than five minutes.

"That's it?" Sams looked over at Danny as his son sat down, and the lawyer packed up his papers, slipped out the back of the courtroom.

"It's pretty straightforward. They're just moving the papers. All the real action happened this morning on the phone." Danny glanced at his watch. "I should get back to my office. Can I drop you with Marty? He'll get you set up in a hotel."

"I have to go to work."

Danny looked at him, surprised. "At IndusCrete?"

"That's where I work." Sams stood up, looked over at where his son sat gazing at the floor with a bored expression. "There's some information on a computer there. And there's some personal stuff I don't want to leave behind."

Danny stared at him as he slid out of the row of seats, then quickly got up, followed him out into the hallway. "You think that's safe, going back to work?"

Sams shrugged. "Don't really have a choice. I didn't hear about the leak until after I left the office last night. I can't just walk away."

"That's the point. You get the call, you're supposed to walk away."

"Did you?"

Danny hesitated. "It was a different situation."

"You keep saying that, but all I can see here is *my* situation. I got a family to protect, but that doesn't mean I can just walk away from all my other responsibilities. When I'm gone, somebody else at my office is going to have to finish up my projects. I can't just leave it all in a mess on my desk."

"Why not? You walk out of here and get hit by a bus, they'd have to go through your files, figure out where things stood. How's this different?"

Sams looked at him. "You serious?"

"I'm worried about your safety. That serious enough for you?"

"Look, shit happens. You can't grow up in the Ninth Ward, not know that's true. But I get hit by a bus, it's somebody else's problem to clean up the mess. I'm done. My life insurance is paid up, I got a little money put away for my kids, they want to go to college. I've lived up to my responsibilities, so I got no more worries. They put me in the ground, everything after that is not my concern. But if I'm still around, I got to live with myself. I'm an engineer. I don't do my job right, stuff falls down. So if I'm not gonna be there to finish up a job, it's my responsibility to put a note in the file so the next guy knows what to watch out for." He waved a hand at all the buildings around them, the steady stream of traffic going past on the street. "That's the only way any of this works. We all in this together. You see what I'm saying?"

Danny said nothing for a moment. Maybe what Sams was saying was true, but *we all in this together* only works if everybody plays by the same rules. Every city, every civilization, was balanced on a narrow point between civility and self-interest. But then there's always a guy like Jimmy Mancuso, who looks at the world and thinks it's every man for himself. Why should he pay taxes so somebody else's kid can go to school or some old lady in the projects has a heart attack, she knows there'll be an ambulance she can call to take her to the hospital? Jimmy *hated* school, and he don't much care for doctors either, but when he needs one, he's gonna pay for a helicopter to fly him to Houston, get that guy who cuts on the Arab oil sheikhs. You got the money, the world's your oyster. And if you got to cut some throats to get it, hey, that's the way the world works. A guy like that doesn't care about anybody else. The only reason he obeys a law is if he thinks it's in his interest. He stops at a red light, it's not because he's a patient guy, willing to let some other guy have his turn to go; it's because he knows that if he runs the light, some guy in an SUV is gonna plow into his Caddie, leave him splattered all over the intersection. But even then, it's all about power. If you're the guy in the SUV, you see him cut through that intersection in front of you, you better punch it, make sure you hit him hard enough to kill him, because Jimmy ain't gonna call a cop or a lawyer. He climbs out of that Caddie, he'll have a gun in his hand, and he ain't gonna stop to worry about who was at fault.

But how do you say that to a guy like Louis Sams, who pays his taxes early, plays by the rules, does his best to keep his kid off the street? He's the guy you never hear about, who makes the whole system work. Most people, Danny'd found, were just doing their best to stay afloat. Like the city, they spend their lives trying to keep their balance between their hopes and their fears, doing whatever it takes to feed their kids, pay the rent, keep getting up every morning and going to work. They look around, and it looks like everybody else is doing the same, but then they notice the guy who's getting away with murder, and it makes them angry. They watch their TV in the evening, and the world's full of snakes and rats. All the commercials—and most of the shows—tell them that they should be living better than they do, that if they don't drive a fancy car, wear expensive clothes, or sleep with beautiful women, they're losers. And that only makes them angrier: *Why should I hold up my end, when everybody else is grabbing what they can?* And before long, the politicians start to catch the smell of that anger, like meat sizzling on a flame. So they spread on the hot sauce and serve it up, an old-time southern political barbecue, full of angry speeches about people who don't live like you, don't look like you, don't share your values. Why should you pay your taxes to help people like that? Hell, it's every man for himself in this world, sink or swim, eat or be eaten, and we *like* it that way! Work hard, get rich, send your boy off to war: it'll make him a man. And while you're at it, send me some money and I'll send you a genuine prayer cloth, blessed by my own perfumed hand, that'll take away all your ills. 'Cause we got the *blessings* in this land!

Just don't call us when your kid gets sick or the water's rising, 'cause you're on your own, son.

Danny sighed, shook his head. "I'm not going to try to talk you out of it."

"Wouldn't do no good if you tried."

"Can I at least get you to check in with me every couple hours, so I don't worry?"

Sams laughed. "Is this what federal protection is like? They treat you like a child?"

"That's probably not far off."

"Great. Something else to look forward to when I'm finished ruining my life."

"They're just doing their job." Danny smiled. "Like you."

"Okay. I hear you." Sams looked at his watch. "How 'bout I give you a call around eleven-thirty? You be in your office then?"

"If I know you're going to call." Danny hesitated. "Look, follow your instincts. You'll know when it's time to get out. Something don't feel right, you get a chill up the back of your neck you don't like, you go. Agreed?"

"All right." Sams extended his hand. "Listen, thanks. I know I'm complaining a lot about all this, but I appreciate your lookin' out for me."

"We all got to look out for each other." Danny smiled. "Only way any of this works."

|||| "I know a guy likes to say smokers are the last free men." Vince leaned against a wall, looked down at the cigarette butts scattered across the sidewalk outside the Federal Building.

"That so?" Lenny flicked his ash into the gutter. "He spend much time standing around outside buildings?"

"That's exactly what he's talking about. Everybody else is back in their cubicles working away, the smokers keep sneaking out to get some poison in their lungs. Raises everybody's health insurance, but they don't fucking care. Smokers, they screw up the whole system."

Lenny raised his eyebrows, took a drag from his cigarette. "You buy that?"

"Sure, why not? Makes as much sense as anything, right?"

Lenny said nothing, just looked out at the traffic passing in the street, his eyes expressionless.

Yeah, Vince thought, *it makes sense. As much sense as standing around all day talking to a guy who never says a fucking **word**.* He didn't mind that they went out on a job, he had to do all the talking. Hey, no problem. He could talk all day, that's what the job required.

But they'd been partners for almost four years now, spent the whole day hanging out in restaurants waiting for Jimmy to finish his business, driving him all over town, sitting in the car while he got all up in some guy's face, standing real close so the guy could smell the meatballs on his breath, too scared to back away even when he thought he was going to gag. It was funny if you thought about it, but the job wasn't really what you'd call *exciting*. So you really going to blame him, trying to make the time pass, maybe have a laugh or two?

But Lenny, man, it was like talking to a stump. The guy just looked at you, no expression, like you dropped a rock down a dry well.

Almost two hours they'd been standing there, watching the people who worked in the offices come out one by one for a smoke. It was kind of gross, actually, watching them all puff away like they were trying to get as much smoke in their lungs as they could before somebody noticed they were gone. Every time a woman came out, Lenny would look over, raise his eyebrows. Asian woman, black woman, Hispanic—it didn't matter. Vince would shake his head wearily. The woman they were waiting for was named Maribell Cadieux. *You ever seen an Asian woman named Maribell Cadieux?* He was getting ready to ask Lenny that after the third time it happened, but then he realized, what's the point? Lenny would just look at him blankly, then light up another cigarette.

Anyway, the last time Vince had seen her, she'd had red hair and was throwing beads off a Mardi Gras float. Her husband, Marcus Cadieux, was a cop working out of Eighth District Vice. Vince had worked with him for a couple months back when he was still on the force, went to a barbecue at his house in Metairie one Saturday for the LSU-Tulane game. Their front door had a carved wooden heart on it, with the words MARCUS 'N MARIBELL burned into it. In their living room, they had a glass case full of Maribell's collection of tiny porcelain cats. Each cat was posed in a different position—

some rolling on their backs, some chasing balls of yarn, one looking like he was trying to catch a fly. Before he left, Vince snuck in there, used a credit card to slip the lock on the display case, and positioned two of them so it looked like they were fucking. On Monday, Marcus sat sullenly at his desk, glaring at the cops who'd been at his house that weekend.

"What's wrong with Cadieux?" one of the other cops asked when he went sullenly out for coffee.

Vince shrugged. "You got me."

"His wife find out he's been banging hookers again?" The cop grinned. "You heard he gave her a case a couple years back? Picked it up from some hooker on Magazine Street, brought it home to the little woman."

"And they're still married?" Vince shook his head. "That's devotion, man."

"He told her he got it working undercover."

"Can't argue with that."

The cop grinned. "Duty calls, right?"

But that was getting to be a while ago, now. Back before Vince had gotten caught up in a corruption investigation, lost his job when he refused to testify against other members of his unit, including Marcus Cadieux. What he knew could have put them all away for long stretches playing drop the soap up in Angola, but he'd kept his mouth shut, taken the ride alone. No jail time, but a quick ticket to nowhere—out the door, on the street, an ex-cop with no job, no friends, and no hope, all your stuff in boxes in a crappy apartment up on Airline Highway after your wife threw you out of the house. So you sit there, gun in your mouth, just waiting for the bang to make that nasty taste go away. Six months he'd lived like that, unable to work up the courage to pull the trigger, until one night he was sitting in a bar up on Veterans, watching all the stereo salesmen hitting on secretaries and medical transcriptionists, when who walks into the place but Jimmy Mancuso. Little

Jimmy was a silent partner in half the bars in Metairie, made his rounds every Thursday night to count the crowd and collect what he figured he was owed. That was his system: he could estimate a bar's weekly take just by counting up the women tapping their paste-on fingernails on the bar on a Thursday night. You walk in a place, see a bunch of women all dressed up like they'd get down on their knees for a piña colada, and you knew that was where all the guys who worked at the Toyota dealership and the appliance outlets and Waterbed Warehouse were going to stop after work. He had a formula, count the fingernails, multiply by the number of mojitos it takes the average guy to start looking like Brad Pitt, pay me. Anyway, Vince watched Jimmy walk in there that night, looking like somebody'd taught a hippo how to get up out of the mud and walk into town, and he realized this was his chance: one shot, everything on the table, play the cards you been dealt. So he got down off his stool, walked over to where Little Jimmy was standing next to the bar, said in his toughest cop voice, like he was getting ready to roust a dealer on a street corner:

"Hey, Jimmy. Remember me?"

And what did Little Jimmy do? He got that tired look on his face like he'd played this game before, said, "What's the problem, Detective? I can't come in here, get a drink no more?"

Vince laughed. Then he leaned in real close, said quietly, "You're behind the times, Jimmy. I ain't on the force no more. I'm just some guy in a bar with a gun in my pocket and nothing to lose. Which means I got only one question for you. How much you paying for protection?"

Jimmy looked at him closely. "Too much, I guess."

"You used to have those two guys looked like they spend all their time in the gym pumping iron."

"They're out in the car."

Vince sighed, shook his head. "Too stiff to get up and walk in here, huh? I always figured they were mostly for show."

"You got a better suggestion?"

"Depends." Vince grinned. "How you feel about cops?"

"I got no problem with cops. Long as they keep their mouths shut and do what I tell 'em."

"That's why I'm here. 'Cause I know how to keep my mouth shut."

Jimmy was silent for a moment, then he belched slightly. "Then I guess you better go outside and tell those two guys you just stole their job."

So, in a way, Vince felt like he owed it all to Marcus Cadieux. If it wasn't for guys like that, still working the force while he was out on the street, looking away real quick whenever they saw him, then he wouldn't be working for Jimmy now. Pretty good work, really. Decent money, no paperwork, and if you felt like doing a tap dance on some guy's face, you didn't have to worry about some news crew filming the whole thing. And, hell, if they did, you just ride out to the TV station, mention Jimmy's name to the news director, and the whole thing's history, you walk out with a nice home movie to show the kids.

As for Maribell, she worked as a secretary in the U.S. attorney's office, and Vince was guessing she had no idea how deep her husband was swimming in shit every day when he put on his coat and tie, got in his car, drove down to Eighth District Vice to put in another day keeping New Orleans safe for all the whores and pimps just trying to make a living selling their product to frat boys down from Texas Tech looking for a party. Vince thought about that glass case full of porcelain cats she kept in her living room and couldn't keep from smiling. You work vice down in the French Quarter, you get to see cats in all their poses.

"That her?"

Vince looked up, surprised. Lenny was looking at a woman coming out the door, pausing to light up as soon as she hit the open air. She'd put on some weight, but her hair was still that weird red, like she got up every morning and washed it in Kool-Aid. Vince nodded, tossed his cigarette into the gutter, where it gave off a slow curl of smoke in the hot still air. He leaned against the wall, gazing out at the traffic passing on Magazine Street. She came over, stood a few feet away, gazing off into the distance like she was waiting for the sky to open and the trumpet to sound, but until then she'd pass some time with a Marlboro Light.

"So, I told the guy," Vince said loudly, "the stuff I know, I could put all those guys down at Eighth District away. You know what he said?"

Lenny looked at him. "What'd he say?"

"He don't care. It's a federal case. U.S. attorney has an informant, but nobody can find out who it is. Some guy who works over at the concrete plant." Vince spread his hands. "So what can I do? We don't get that informant's name, I'll have no choice. They'll put me in front of the grand jury, and I'll have to give up those guys from the Eighth District." He shook his head sadly. "Some of those guys, it won't just be jail time. They'll lose everything. IRS will go after them on back taxes, take their house, their cars, everything."

Out of the corner of his eye he could see Maribell looking over at him like she'd just swallowed a handful of ashes, but he took his time, lit up another cigarette. Then he blew the smoke up at the sky, lazily, like none of this made any difference to him. It was somebody else's problem. Nothing to do with his life. Then he glanced over at her, real casual, like he'd just realized she was staring at him.

"Hey," he said, letting his eyes get wide with surprise. "Don't I know you?" Then he grinned. "Man, this is a small world, huh?"

|||| Sams hated getting into the office late. Everybody sitting in their glass cubicles looked up at you as you came in, so you felt like they were all wondering what made you think you were special, strolling in two hours late like you owned the place. But it wasn't

even that, really. Engineers take pride in how hard they work, and so coming in late made every guy sitting at his computer look smug, as if you'd failed some kind of test, proved that you were the weakest dog in the pack. Some guys tried to sneak in the back way, their jackets slung over their shoulders and their shirtsleeves rolled up, like they'd been out in the plant all morning pouring concrete. Others stopped at the coffee machine, made a point of announcing wearily that they'd been in meetings with clients all morning, or out at a job site getting mud on their shoes. Once, Sams caught a guy carefully stepping into a deep puddle in the gravel parking lot, trying to get his Florsheims to look like he'd spent the last two hours in a swamp.

All Sams wanted was to clear the last few papers off his desk, pack up some personal stuff when nobody was looking, and then get away. He felt the way he always did the day before leaving for vacation: slightly distracted, overwhelmed by all the stuff on his desk, like he should really spend a few minutes organizing his paper clips and putting the correct caps on all his pens so he could leave feeling like everything was in order. Instead, he wrote up some quick notes summarizing the outstanding issues on the jobs he'd be leaving behind, slipped them into the files for somebody to find when they cleaned out his desk in a couple weeks. The FBI guys would have thrown up their hands. *You're leaving notes? Why not just send everyone an e-mail, let them know you're not planning to come back?* But they didn't get it. He was an engineer. Telling him just to walk away from unfinished jobs was like draining all the water out of a pool and then handing him a towel. Anyway, he did the same thing before taking four days off to take the kids to Disney World last year; he cleaned off his desk, stuck notes in all his files, even emptied out his personal e-mail folder, just in case the plane crashed. You want somebody knowing you saved a bunch of Cialis ads and e-mails promising baldness remedies? His luck, he'd survive the crash, then die of shame.

He put in a couple hours, staying at his desk when all the other engineers left for lunch. Most of them brought their lunch, ate it in the break room, but at least it gave him a few minutes to clear the personal photographs off his desk, take down his framed degrees from the wall beside his window, and roll up the drawing his youngest daughter, Shondra, had made, showing him like a superhero, holding up a bridge to keep it from falling into a river. At least he thought it was him. He had muscular arms that bulged like Carl Weathers's when he was punching it out with Rocky, but he was wearing a tie, there was a pocket protector in his shirt pocket that held an impressive collection of pens, and his hairline looked like it was going faster than the crumbling bridge. When she gave it to him, he'd thanked her, given her a kiss, then waited until she went up to get ready for bed to show it to his wife. "You think that's really how she sees me?"

"You're her hero. She asked me a couple days ago what you did, and I told her you kept all the buildings from falling down."

"Yeah? That's what you told her?" He laid the picture on the kitchen table, came up behind her where she stood at the sink, put his arms around her waist. "How 'bout you? Am I your hero too?"

"You do these dishes, you'll be my hero. I'll even sew you a cape, you think it would make you happy. We can call you *Husband Man*."

He laughed. "Damn, woman. You do know how to bring a man down to earth."

"Only place a man should be." She peeled off her gloves, handed them to him. "But I'll meet you upstairs in a little while, you want to show me your superpowers."

He couldn't help smiling at the memory as he rolled up the drawing, tucked it into his briefcase. Maybe that's enough, just to be a decent husband and a father to your kids. You watch TV, it makes you feel like your life's a failure if you don't spend your time either saving the world or bending it to your will. But life is merciless to men in their forties. All your neon-lit dreams fade to simple daylight, and it's all you can manage to get up every day, go to work, pay your bills, and do your best to keep a minimum safe distance from mirrors and young women. If your daughter draws you a picture to hang on your office wall, and your wife still smiles at you some evenings, then you're ahead of the game. But that don't make you no hero.

At twelve-thirty, he saw Vickers come out of his office, walk down the hall, pausing to tell the receptionist that he was headed out to grab some lunch. Sams glanced along the row of glass cubicles. For the moment they were all empty. He reached over, slid a CD from the pile beside his computer, then stood up, walked down the hall to Vickers's office, and slipped inside.

Gerald Vickers was the kind of guy who wanted you to know his tribe. He'd hung LSU football memorabilia around his office, including photographs of himself on the sideline with the team at the Fiesta Bowl, standing next to a state senator who'd had a boy playing on the squad. There were photographs of Vickers on vacation in Cancún, deep-sea fishing, tossing beads from a float during Mardi Gras. But Louis Sams had seen it all, spent time admiring the photographs when he'd first interviewed for the job, and every year since, when Vickers called him in for his annual performance review. Now all Sams could focus on was the computer on Vickers's desk. Like all the other engineers, he had unrestricted access to the office network, where they kept the active project files on a shared drive. But every now and then something would come up where Vickers had to forward you one of the files he kept on the local drive of his office computer. Just once, he'd sent the wrong file by mistake, and when Sams opened it, he'd been shocked at what he saw. He knew some of the guys on that list of names, state building inspectors who had to approve a bid before contracts were awarded. Was Vickers paying them all off? Then he'd panicked. What would Vickers do if he realized his mistake? Sams thought about it, then quickly wrote an e-mail to Vickers saying, *I can't seem to open your attachment. Could you try sending it again?* At least that way he could claim he'd never seen the document. A few minutes later he received an e-mail with the right attachment, and neither he nor Vickers ever mentioned the incident. He figured Vickers hadn't caught his mistake.

Now he sat behind the desk, saw that Vickers had been in a hurry to get to lunch, and so he hadn't bothered to log off his computer. It only took a few moments to slip the disk into the computer, open the list of files on Vickers's hard drive, and copy them over onto the disk. Then he closed the list, popped the disk out of the drive, slipped it into his pocket. He paused for a moment at the door listening, then opened it a crack. The row of glass cubicles was still deserted; the engineers had seen Vickers leave, and now they were lingering over their lunches. Sams returned to his desk, and when they emerged from the lunchroom he was hard at work, looking harried with all that he had to do before his vacation.

By two, Vickers was back from lunch, and Sams had finished making notes for all his project files. All that remained was to send a few e-mails to clients to update them on the status of their projects, then compose a project summary for Vickers to let him know where everything stood before he left for vacation. He'd just started that when he looked up, saw the two ex-cops, Vince and Lenny, go past, headed for Vickers's office. They both looked in at him as they went past his office, and he saw Vince flash him a grin. For some reason, it unnerved him. They talk to him for five minutes, suddenly they're his best friends now? All down the row of glass cubicles he saw men look up, follow them with wary eyes as they continued down the hall, vanished into Vickers's office, and pulled the door shut behind them.

They didn't look at anybody else.

You'll know when it's time to get out. He sat there, staring at the door to Vickers's office. *Anything don't feel right, you go.*

Sams stood up, closed his briefcase, and snapped the latches shut. Just a short stroll along the hall, looking at his watch like he had an urgent appointment, wave to the girl working the phones at the receptionist's desk, and he'd be out the door before anybody knew he was leaving. *Don't think about it*, he told himself. *Just go.*

He almost made it. He was only a few steps from the door that led to the reception area when he heard a door open behind him, and Gerald Vickers called out, "Louis? Could I have a word with you before you leave?"

He should have kept going. He knew it even as he turned to look back at Vickers standing there in the door of his office, with the two ex-cops walking toward him, watching with curious eyes to see if he'd run for it.

Vickers gave him a friendly smile, waved him back toward his office. "Just a couple quick questions," he called out. "Won't take a second, then we'll send you on your way."

Sams hesitated. He was standing beside the door to the men's room, and now his hand slowly rose, and as if by its own volition, came to rest on the door. "Be right there," he said. "Just got to make a quick stop."

And he pushed the door open without waiting for a reply, ducked into one of the stalls. He stood there for a moment, not moving, feeling a wave of panic sweep over him. They knew. He felt sure of that. Was it the leak, or had he made a mistake, left some clue when he copied the files off Vickers's computer? His hand went to his jacket pocket. If they searched him, they'd find the disk. He drew it out, looked around frantically. Behind him he heard the door to the men's room open, and somebody came in, whistling softly. There was something slightly off-key about the whistling, and Sams knew instantly that it was Vince, coming in there to keep an eye on him so he didn't try to climb out the window beside the sinks. Directly in front of him, a dispenser holding toilet seat covers was attached to the wall. Sams leaned forward, saw that there was a slight gap between the back of the dispenser and the tile wall. Quietly, he opened his briefcase, drew out a sheet of paper. He took a pen from his pocket, wrote on it—*Danny Chaisson! REWARD!!* and the lawyer's phone number—then folded the paper around the disk to protect it. He slid the disk carefully into the gap, stood there for a moment thinking, then took his pen and scrawled *VICKERS SUCKS!* on the front of the dispenser in crude block letters. He felt strange doing it, embarrassed by the feeling of satisfaction it gave him. He'd never written on walls, even as a child sitting in the school bathroom. But he figured it would only be a matter of days before Vickers saw it and called the company that serviced the bathrooms to get the dispenser removed. All he could do now was keep quiet about the disk and hope that the man the company sent out to do the job would be tempted enough by the promise of a reward to call Danny.

"Hey, you okay in there?" Vince's voice sounded like the whole thing was a big joke, this guy trying to hide in the bathroom, like he thought that could save him. "You want me to call an ambulance?"

Sams reached down, flushed the toilet. "I'm done."

5

"You see this?"

Mickie reached for the coffeepot, rubbing at her eyes sleepily. She glanced over to where Danny was sitting at their kitchen table, watching the small TV set on the counter. "What?"

He nodded to the television, where a local weatherman was standing in front of a map of the Gulf of Mexico, sweeping his hand in a broad arc up from the Florida Keys to the Louisiana coast. "They're talking about the hurricane. Looks like we might get a direct hit."

She looked at him. "Didn't it just hit Miami yesterday?"

"It's turning north. The weatherman's saying the most likely track brings it right through New Orleans."

"How strong is it?"

"Category Three at five this morning, but it looks like it'll get stronger as it comes up through the Gulf. The governor declared a state of emergency for all the coastal parishes last night, and they're talking about evacuation plans."

For a moment neither of them said anything. The television switched to shots of storm damage in Florida, trees down, pieces of aluminum siding blowing along the rain-swept streets.

"It could swing east toward Pensacola," Danny said, "like the last couple they got all excited over."

"You really want to take that chance?"

Danny hesitated, looked up at Mickie standing there in her

bathrobe, Anna still asleep in her crib upstairs. "I was just talking to a guy who worked on the levees."

"Yeah? What did he say?"

"Start driving, and don't stop until you get to Shreveport."

Mickie raised her eyebrows. She took a sip of her coffee. "You know I'd have to stay if there's an evacuation. We've got an emergency plan to assist local law enforcement."

"Even if the city floods?"

"That's when they'd need us."

They could hear someone moving around upstairs. Matia slept on a pull-out couch in the baby's room when she came to visit. Every morning she complained about the mattress, but when Danny and Mickie offered her their bed, she refused. She got up several times during the night, and she liked to lie there in the darkness, listening to the baby breathing.

"Maybe I should put your mother and Anna in the car and drive them to Phoenix," Danny said. "We could stay with her until it's clear what's happening."

"Can you do that?"

He shrugged. "If they announce an evacuation, we gotta go somewhere. My guess is that every hotel between here and Dallas will fill up by tonight. If the levees hold, we'll turn around and come back. If not, then at least we've got somewhere to go."

"What about your cases?"

He smiled. "We get hit by this storm, I don't think the first thing on people's minds is going to be calling their lawyer. Not for a while, anyway."

They heard Matia clear her throat at the top of the steps and then start down the stairs. She did that every morning, like she was taking a moment to count the steps, suspicious that they might have added a couple during the night. When she came down, she kept one hand tight on the railing, taking it one step at a time.

Every morning Danny silently counted her steps, like a prisoner scratching the days on the wall of his cell.

She shuffled in, looked at them both, then over at the television. "What's wrong?"

"They're saying on the news that we might get a hurricane," Mickie said quietly.

Matia rolled her eyes. *"Madre de Dios,"* she whispered. As if the rain and the smells weren't bad enough, now there was a hurricane coming. She looked at her daughter with something like triumph in her eyes. *You see? What did I tell you?* But then, just as suddenly, all that vanished and her eyes widened. "What about the baby? We can't stay here!"

"Danny's going to drive you back to Phoenix," Mickie told her. "You'll take Anna with you, until we see what things look like here."

"And what about you?"

"I have to stay. ATF has a disaster plan, and they'll need every available agent."

Matia looked at Danny. "You agree with this?"

"I'm not happy about it, but it's not my decision."

She shook her head in disgust. "The baby will need her mother." She pulled her robe more tightly about her. Then she looked at the television. A reporter was standing on the levee next to Lake Pontchartrain, making great sweeping motions with his hand, as if to show the waves crashing over into the neighborhoods beyond. "When do we leave?"

Danny looked at the television. They were showing the storm's projected track again, a shaded cone that spread out from the storm's current position just north of the Keys and ended up covering most of the Gulf Coast from Houston to the Florida panhandle. The darkest part of the cone ran along the Louisiana coast over to Bay St. Louis. "It could still turn. Might make sense to wait and see what they say as it gets closer."

Mickie watched as the television switched to a map of the city, showing the portions most below sea level. It was followed by an animation showing how flooding could fill the city like a bowl. "There's only four roads out of this city," she said. "You wait, you're going to get stuck." She drew her robe tighter. "If the storm turns, you can always come back."

"Okay. We'll pack up this morning, get on the road." Danny drained his coffee cup, put it in the sink. He glanced out the window. The sky was a perfect blue, and the late August heat seemed draped across the ancient oak trees that lined their street. It seemed impossible, somehow, to imagine that hundreds of miles out in the Gulf a storm was churning its way toward them. He'd grown up hearing people talk about what would happen to the city when the big storm finally came, and every year there was a storm that looked for a couple hours like it might be the one. But the storms always turned, headed for Pensacola or Pascagoula, like a curveball spinning out of the strike zone just as the batter starts to swing. Over the years, people in New Orleans had grown used to lying back, watching for the moment when the storm's track broke, making it swing east toward the beach condos along the Florida coast. Do it enough times, you could drop your bat in the dust, take the base on balls.

But everybody knew it was a dangerous game. All it took was once, a single hard pitch that didn't break, went straight down the middle of the plate, so all you could do was stand there and watch it go past, and you were out, man, no second chance. All over town, he thought, people were watching their televisions and having the same conversation. *Do we go? Where do we go? When do we leave?* The city went on with its business, just another hot Saturday morning, but there was a quiet buzz of anxiety. It was out there; it was coming. The bars up in the Irish Channel and down on Bourbon Street would fill up today with people hoping to party the storm away. They'd be drinking Hurricanes, like a tribe making offerings to the storm's blank-eyed god. But on Sunday they'd wake up, feeling sick to the bone, and turn on their TVs, then quietly start packing the car. By that time, I-10 would be a parking lot, and it wouldn't take long until some guy with a hangover and a gun under his seat started waving it out his window in frustration. Better to be sitting in a hotel room in Houston or Dallas, watching it on television. And then, with a slight feeling of panic, Danny wondered how many people across the city were having the same thought. Mickie was right. Get on the road as soon as possible. It was going to be a long trip, no matter when they left.

Danny's cell phone rang. It was in the pocket of his jacket, hanging over a chair in the living room. He saw Mickie look at him skeptically.

"People won't call their lawyers, huh?"

"It's probably Demitra, letting me know she won't be in the office on Monday."

Matia raised her eyebrows. "If there *is* an office on Monday."

Danny went into the living room, dug the phone out of his coat pocket. He could hear Matia in the kitchen, talking in Spanish now. Probably telling Mickie it was all his fault, making her live in a city where it never stops raining.

"Hey, Danny," Marty Seagraves said when he answered the phone. "I'm glad I caught you. I was afraid you might have left town."

"We're packing up, heading out later this morning. How about you?"

"I gotta stay. FBI's part of the federal emergency response, so our whole office is going on emergency duty. My wife's heading up to Memphis with the kids to stay with her sister."

"Yeah, it's the same story here. ATF is on a call-up, so Mickie's staying, but I'm heading out to Phoenix with her mother and Anna."

"Lucky you. At least you'll be dry." Seagraves hesitated, then said, "Listen, I don't want to hold you up any, but I just wondered if you'd heard anything from Louis Sams."

"What do you mean? He's not with you?"

"No, he never showed up last night. I've tried his cell phone a couple times, but he must have it shut off, because all my calls just go through to voice mail. I figured he might have heard about the storm and headed out to stay with his family in Atlanta. It doesn't look like there's going to be any grand jury testimony on Monday."

Danny felt his throat go dry. "Marty, that's not the kind of guy Louis is. He wouldn't just leave town without calling you."

"You say that, but we see it all the time. People get second thoughts when it comes time to get up in front of the grand jury and testify. We have to get the U.S. attorney to request a continuance, send the marshals after them. It was up to me, we'd put 'em all in protective custody for a couple days before they testify, just so we know where to find them."

"You really think he skipped?"

"Danny, that's the best-case scenario. You got another number where I can try him?"

"Let me make a few calls."

Danny hung up, stood there thinking for a moment. Then he dialed Demitra.

"This better be important," she said when she picked up.

"Demitra, it's Danny."

"I *know* it's you, honey. I got caller ID. What I *don't* know is why you calling me at home on a Saturday morning. Can't be because you need me to come in and work today, 'cause that'd be just craziness."

"Demitra, you heard from Louis?"

"Louis Sams? No. Why?"

"He was supposed to meet someone last night, and he never showed up. I wondered if you knew where I might find him."

There was a long pause. Danny could picture the expression on her face, like a car suddenly turning onto the highway, coming straight at you with both headlights up high. All you could do was brace yourself for the crash.

"Danny, I asked you to help Louis out. You didn't get that poor man into some kind of evil, now, did you?"

It was the kind of question she always found a way to ask him, which left him feeling like a sheep as it staggers away from the shears, bare skin twitching awkwardly in the cold morning air. She had a gift for it, the way some people can shuck an oyster with one quick flick of the knife blade. It was one of the reasons she got along so well with Mickie. The first time they'd met, in Danny's tiny office on St. Charles, they'd taken one look at each other and recognized the common ground they shared, like two women raising the same unruly child.

He didn't know what to say. Had he put Sams in danger? He'd tried to talk him out of going to work. Was that enough? But even as he'd urged him against it, he'd known that Sams wouldn't listen. Danny wouldn't have, if it had been his choice. But that was the problem: it *had* been his choice, once, and he'd nearly gotten himself killed.

"I'm sure it's nothing," he said to Demitra, hearing the words fall flat even as he said them. And then, as if to shore them up, he added before he could stop himself, "I'll find him."

He regretted the words as soon as he'd spoken them. He was leaving town in a couple hours. What could he do?

He stood there for a moment, thinking. Then he shoved the phone into the pocket of his jacket, went back into the kitchen.

"Something's come up," he told Mickie. "I think I have to stay in town."

She looked at him, and he could see a storm starting to gather in her eyes. "What do you mean?"

"Louis Sams has gone missing. He was supposed to meet Marty Seagraves last night so they could put some protection on him. He never showed up."

"And how is this your problem?"

"He's my client. I set up the deal for his testimony."

She raised her eyebrows. "So it's your fault if he doesn't show up?"

"I saw him yesterday morning, and he told me he was going back to work. I should have stopped him."

"Danny, there's a hurricane coming. The whole city may have to evacuate. I don't see what you can do."

Matia was standing with her arms folded, looking at Danny as if she'd seen this coming. He could see satisfaction in her eyes, as if it was worth being swept away in a storm just to see everything she'd warned her daughter about him proved true.

"We could run Anna and your mother up to St. Tammany to stay with Etta," he said. "She's been wanting to spend some time with Anna, and they'd be a good ten miles back off the lake, away from the storm surge."

Etta Jackson was an old woman who'd lost her husband to some teenage boys trying to prove their manhood by tearing up an old slave burial ground a few years back. Danny'd helped her out, and in return she'd brewed up some midwife's tea to help Mickie get her strength back after a car accident gave her a scare about the baby. Since then, they'd driven across the Lake Pontchartrain causeway several times a year to have dinner at her house, and she'd sit with the baby on her lap, singing quietly until Anna fell asleep, like she was casting a spell.

"Danny, any storm that hits New Orleans is going to blow through St. Tammany twenty minutes later. There might not be a storm surge, but the wind alone could pull Etta's house down."

He rubbed at his eyes. "You're right. I should call up there, make sure she's got someplace to go."

And that was it, the moment that always came for Mickie, when she remembered why she loved him. When they'd first met, she'd thought he was a screwup, one of those guys who'd learned to make it on their boyish charm, even as the years passed and the world spun away from them. He'd walked around New Orleans in a leather jacket and jeans, like he was always looking for the next party. But then, the whole city struck her that way. She couldn't get used to the air, the way you could feel it against your skin like a lover who's slipped into your bed, pressed himself against you. And the heat was full of smells, both fragrant and foul, that came to you like distant music you could hear even from underwater. A lazy, self-indulgent city, she'd thought at first, that could never make up its mind between living and dying. But then, as she got to know it, she realized that she'd had it wrong: at a party, she met a woman in her late sixties who sat with great dignity on a sofa, greeting friends, making no effort to cover up her bald head, the result of eight months of intensive chemotherapy for the cancer that would kill her within a year. She was sipping a glass of champagne, in which she'd floated a single leaf of mint. After that night, Mickie saw that woman as an image of the city, living deeply until she died, drinking it in even more deeply because she knew that death was close. But even that seemed too simple, an easy metaphor that still missed something about the place. It wasn't until she met Danny that she realized what it was. In New Orleans, she realized, everyone carries the knowledge that it can't last, that maybe it *shouldn't* last. But grace is wearing your shroud with style, drinking champagne at your own funeral, with one perfect mint leaf floating in the glass. In a way, it's the most human thing we do: we strike the match with a flourish even when we know the fuse is short. What else is there to do? Danny had gotten used to living that way, and as she got to know him, she realized that he was carrying a weight no one could see, a past hidden in shadows and lies, like a bayou winding its way through the stench of garbage, pollution, and rot. You live in Louisiana for a while, that's a smell you get to know. Danny had grown up surrounded by it, had come close to drowning in that filthy water before he'd made up his mind to do what he could to drain it away. The leather jacket, the easy grin, it was all there to hide his anger, and the deep sense of responsibility that made him put his life on the line when he smelled that stench rising around him.

How do you tell a man who's spent his life building dams that nothing he does will keep the water from rising? It drove her crazy sometimes, but secretly she loved this weight he carried, like ballast for his soul. He believed that every man was his brother's keeper, believed it not as something you repeat on Sundays while your mind drifts to other things, but as the shared burden we each have to lift every day.

"I'll call Etta," she said. "You go see what you can find out about Louis."

He looked at her. "You sure?"

"Yeah, no problem. ATF won't go onto emergency orders until tomorrow. I'll call some of our friends up in Baton Rouge, see if Anna and my mother can stay with them until the storm passes. I can drive them up there this afternoon. It makes more sense than sending you out to Phoenix with them." She looked at her mother. "You won't mind looking after Anna for a couple days, right? We'll pack up everything you need."

Matia frowned. "Will Anna be safe there?"

"It's in the middle of the state. You might get some wind damage, but you'll be well out of the storm's path."

She sighed, spread her hands. "If you think this is the best thing, then that's what we will do."

"I do, Mama." Mickie looked at Danny. "Why don't you pack up a suitcase? We'll take it up to Baton Rouge with us, so it'll be there if you need it."

She said it quietly, Danny noticed, that voice she used when things needed to get done quickly and without question. It seemed to come naturally to her, but he knew it was the result of hard training, like field-stripping a semiautomatic pistol or moving calmly to suppress gunfire when the natural thing was to dive for cover. The first time he'd heard her use that voice, she was saving his life, and the violence that followed seemed a grim necessity, something accomplished at a cost to both of them. But they'd come out alive, and he'd learned not to argue with that voice. But what struck him now was the way Matia looked at her daughter, surprised at the suddenness with which her daughter had vanished, replaced by a woman who quickly took charge of a situation. This voice was new to her, Danny saw, and he guessed that there was something in it that reminded her of her husband. *What a strange thing, he thought, to see coming out in your daughter.* Would he see his own habits of mind coming out in Anna? It was a troubling thought. There was so much he'd like to spare her.

But Mickie had set her coffee cup down in the sink, and it was clear that the discussion was over. She reached for the phone, started calling their friends up in Baton Rouge. He almost felt sorry for them. Confronted with that voice, how could they say no?

He went upstairs, took all their suitcases out of the hall closet, laid them out on the bed. He packed the smallest one with his clothes, threw in some important papers and a box of old family photographs he'd carried around ever since his mother died. He gathered up all the photos of Anna, their wedding photo, and his favorite shot of Mickie in full combat gear, running the obstacle course at the Federal Law Enforcement Training Center in Georgia. Then he pulled out a gym bag he kept under the bed, packed it with a couple days' worth of clothes and his toiletries, just in case he got stuck. He was almost finished when he heard Mickie come upstairs, pause to peer into Anna's room, then come down the hall to their bedroom.

"Janice and Barry can let my mother and Anna use their guest room," she told him, "and they've got a futon in their family room, if we need it."

"That's great."

She looked at his suitcase, which was open on the bed. "You're taking everything, huh?"

"Only the things that can't be replaced." He looked around the room. "You see anything I'm forgetting?"

"It's just stuff, Danny." She came over, laid a hand on his arm. "I know why you feel you have to stay, but promise me you'll be careful, okay? I want to know you'll get out before the storm comes."

"Hey, you know me."

"That's what worries me."

He put his arms around her, leaned in to press his lips gently against the spot at the base of her neck that always made her sigh. "You can count on it, okay? There are some things even I know better than to try fighting."

For a moment neither of them moved. They stood there in their bedroom, and Danny found himself wondering why they hadn't spent more time doing this when they'd had the chance. Their small house, which often felt chaotic in the mornings as they both rushed to get ready for work and get Anna off to her babysitter, suddenly seemed quiet and peaceful, their bedroom full of soft morning light.

The quiet before the storm, Danny thought. And now he felt a great sadness fill him, knowing that this moment would vanish before he could catch hold of it, find a safe place inside himself to tuck it away.

Mickie raised her head, listening.

"Anna's awake," she said. "I should go get her up."

Danny nodded. He opened his arms, and a moment later she was gone.

|||| "What are you talkin' about?"

"Jesus, Jimmy. Don't you watch the news? There's a hurricane coming. Looks like a big one. People are packing up, leaving town."

Jimmy laughed. "That's all? You scared of a storm? I been living in this city all my life, and every summer there's some hurricane gonna wipe the place off the map. You know how many times I left town all those years? None. And I'm still here. Those weather guys just give them warnings to cover their ass, so one day, we get a big storm, they can say, 'Hey, don't look at me. I did *my* job.'" He waved his hand dismissively, like he was shooing away flies. "Day comes that a storm hits this city, you know where I'm gonna be? Right here, eatin' ribs and gumbo. I say fix me a drink and *fuck* the storm. I look like I'm gonna blow away?"

Gerald Vickers said nothing, but he had to admit Jimmy had a point. It would take a serious wind to move him off that chair, and the way he was putting away the pecan pancakes and bacon strips, it looked like he meant to stay awhile. The man had some serious ballast; his ass alone was probably rated up to Category Five.

But it wasn't the wind that had Gerald Vickers worried. All night, since he first saw the storm track they were predicting on the eleven o'clock news, coming right up the Mississippi River into New Orleans like it planned to get a room at the Royal Orleans, spend the weekend partying on Bourbon Street, his stomach had been getting tighter and tighter, as if somebody had wound a rubber band around it, started to twist it just to make sure he got the message.

"See, here's the thing, Jimmy. It ain't the wind you got to worry about, this kind of storm." He leaned forward, spread his hands. "I mean, the wind's bad, but see, what you really got to worry about is water."

"You know, I think I heard that somewhere." Jimmy stabbed a piece of bacon, shoved it into his mouth. He looked at Vickers with a bored expression as he chewed. "Where did I hear that?" He let his fork hang in the air, made a face like he was pondering a problem. "Oh, yeah, I know. On like every weather report for the last *thirty years*." He dropped his fork in his plate, disgusted. "You know what I call people like you? Weather pussies. You hear there's a storm coming, and you get your panties all up in your crack worrying about something *might* happen if it don't turn off toward Mobile, like it *always does.*" He crumpled up his paper napkin, threw it on the table. "There, you fuckin' ruined my breakfast. You satisfied? Saturday morning, I look forward to my breakfast. It's something I enjoy. No rush, nobody all up in my grill about business. I can sit back and enjoy my food. But you got to come in here, get me all worked up 'cause you saw the news last night and the weatherman said we're gonna get some rain. It's New Orleans. We get rain every day. That's why it smells like somethin' died all the time. You hear what I'm saying?"

Vickers swallowed carefully, nodded. "Yeah, sure. It's just, I got some concerns about the levees, you know?"

"What, you mean all the concrete you been pouring in there, you don't think they'll hold? That much concrete, you coulda built the Great Wall of China." Jimmy picked up a piece of bacon with his fingers, syrup trailing off it. He considered Vickers while he ate it. "So what you're saying is you don't have complete confidence in your product."

"It's not just the concrete, Jimmy. They ran some tests about twenty years ago, and the soil isn't up to grade either. Enough water pressure, it just turns to mud and melts away. So even if our concrete holds, the whole seawall could wash out if we get the kind of flooding they're talking about coming up the canals from Lake Pontchartrain." He sat forward, lowering his voice. "But you watch, if something happens, nobody's going to be talking about bad soil. With this investigation the U.S. attorney's been running, the first seawall that washes out, I'm the guy who eats it."

Jimmy grinned. "Listen to you. You been watching *The Sopranos*?" He wiped his fingers on the paper napkin, but they were still sticky from the syrup. He caught the waitress's eye, held up his napkin. She nodded, took a handful from the serving station, brought them over. Jimmy ate here regularly, and they knew his needs. "Look, you just told me that there's about six different reasons the levees could go. Concrete, soil, water pressure. So what are you worried about? Something happens, we spread some money around, they blame the other guy." He waited as the waitress handed him the stack of napkins, took one and tossed the rest on the table. "Anyway," he said, wiping his fingers, "I thought we took care of that investigation for you."

"That's the problem," Vickers said, his voice urgent. "Your guys identified the witness, one of my engineers. Real straight-arrow guy, but his kid's got problems, and the Feds put pressure on him."

"I don't give a fuck about his kid. A rat's a rat, period. You know what we used to do with rats, my neighborhood? They had rats all up in those empty lots, big black rats. We'd go out there hunting 'em with baseball bats. Hit 'em on the head, toss 'em in a bag, then throw the bag in the river." Jimmy grinned. "Sometimes they weren't all dead, and you'd see the bag wriggling as it floated away."

Vickers tried not to think about the rats squirming around in the bag. "See, that's the thing, Jimmy. Your guys, they found the rat. And that's great, really. A load off my mind. But see, I thought when they found him we'd, kind of, *talk* to him."

"Talk to him." Jimmy looked at him, his face blank, like they'd suddenly started talking in Portuguese and he was trying to figure out what he'd missed. "You wanted us to have a *chat* with him."

"Yeah. Convince him to back off. Show him how it's in his interest not to testify."

"I'm pretty sure my boys will make that clear to him." Jimmy belched, and a sudden smell of bacon and maple syrup drifted across the table toward Vickers. "Especially Lenny. He don't say much, but he can be real convincing."

Vickers swallowed hard. "I'm sure that's true. But see, there are like ten witnesses who saw me call this guy into my office yesterday. It was two in the afternoon, and everybody was at their desks. You know, we got these glass cubicles, so all my engineers can see what's going on in the office."

"Yeah, so?" Jimmy grinned. "You worried somebody is gonna testify against you? I think they'll get the message that ain't a good idea."

"Jimmy, if something happens to this guy . . ."

"What's gonna happen?" Jimmy leaned forward. "Look, did he walk out of there on his own two feet?"

Vickers looked at him miserably, then nodded.

"Anybody drag him out? Somebody put a gun to his head?"

Vickers saw where this was going. He shook his head, resigned to playing out his part until Jimmy reached his inevitable conclusion.

"So what are you worried about? You had a talk with the guy, expressed your concerns about his testimony, and he walked out." Jimmy spread his hands, eyes wide. "What can you do? He could have stayed and talked it over, but he's a big boy, makes his own choices."

"Everybody saw your guys follow him out of there, Jimmy."

"So? They're busy guys. They can't hang around your office all day. I mean, you're a charming guy and all, but no offense. They finished their job, so they left. End of story."

Vickers leaned forward, rubbed at his face with both hands. He was tired. Try getting a good night's sleep, you feel your whole world crumbling around you. "Look, I'm just saying . . ."

"You're just sayin' nothing." Jimmy's voice was suddenly angry. "You ask me to fix this mess, so okay, I fixed it. Now you're scared that it might cost you something, so you come in here, ruin my breakfast, telling me the whole city's about to get blown away, and what's it *really* about? You're scared somebody's gonna say you weren't *nice* to this rat who was trying to send your ass to jail." He picked up another napkin, rubbed at the syrup on his fingers viciously. But the napkin only got stuck, leaving bits of white paper stuck to his fingers. Annoyed, Jimmy rubbed his hands together, scattering the shreds of paper across the table like falling snow.

"You want the truth, I'm sorry I ever got involved. Wasn't my ass in the sling."

"I'm grateful, Jimmy. I really am. But I just don't want anything . . ."—Vickers hesitated—"anything *irrevocable* to happen to this guy. He turns up dead, and they got a whole row of witnesses can connect me to it."

Jimmy's eyes clouded. "Who said anything about killing this guy? You ever hear me say that?"

"No, but I just assumed—"

"You assumed *what*? That my boys wouldn't hesitate to cancel some guy's ticket just to save your sorry ass? That how you think I run my business?" Jimmy picked up a fork, and Vickers watched nervously as he used it to flick the bits of paper off the remains of his pancakes. Like everyone else, he'd heard stories. "You had a talk with the guy, now they're having a talk with him. Might take a couple days, but they get results."

"What about the storm?"

"What about it? They just have to talk a little louder, make sure he can hear them over the wind."

Vickers sat back, pressing his palms against his thighs, hoping that could keep his hands from shaking. He looked around at the empty restaurant. Nobody was thinking about breakfast today except Jimmy. A couple waitresses were standing around a TV set mounted on the wall behind the bar. They had it tuned to a twenty-four-hour news channel, which had preempted all its war coverage and politics to give the weather its day in the sun. As he watched, the screen filled with footage from Miami, trees down, traffic lights sideways blowing in the wind, roof tiles peeling off and blowing away. Then they switched to a map of the Gulf, and there it was, that red line that seemed to lead the storm right up through all that wide open water into New Orleans. Vickers felt his stomach tighten up again, forced himself to look away.

"I just can't catch a break," he said. "Everything's coming at me all at once."

"When it rains, it pours, huh?" Jimmy pushed his chair back, stood up. "Now get out of here. I gotta go take a leak."

⫼ It was a small room, with a stained cement floor and egg cartons fixed to all the walls and the door. The only piece of furniture was a wooden chair mounted on four metal brackets in the center of the floor.

"Sorry 'bout the mess," Vince had said, grinning, when they took the hood off, let him look around. "Somebody should get in here with some bleach, clean up that floor. But I guess we'd only mess it up again. Lenny, he kinda likes it the way it is. Ain't that right, Lenny?" He looked over at his partner, grinned. "Says it's got feng shui. And he's got a point there. It's spare, but functional. Why mess with a winning formula? If it ain't broke, I say don't fix it." He nodded to the chair. "We call it the throne room. See if you can guess why."

The stains on the floor were worst, Sams couldn't help noticing, around the chair. They looked like rust, or dried mud. He couldn't bring himself to think about it any more deeply than that.

"You want to see the coolest thing?" Vince turned, shut the door behind him. "Check it out. You can't even see the door. It disappears when you close it. Unless you look real close, you can't even see that little lock. Just looks like a piece of one of the egg cartons broke off." He gestured around at the walls. "You imagine how long it took to save up all those egg cartons? I first saw this place, I thought, *Damn, that's some serious cholesterol!* I pictured some old beat cop, eats eggs and bacon every morning, saving up all the cartons in his basement. I mean, I was *impressed*. Then I find out they just rode over to Farm Fresh Eggs, walked out with stacks of egg cartons. You could get one of these off the wall, that's what it would say on the other side. Farm Fresh. But they're glued on there pretty good. And people who spend any serious time in here, they usually got other stuff on their mind."

"Minds," Lenny said, his voice surprisingly soft.

Vince looked at him. "What?"

"Minds. They have other stuff on their minds. You use the plural."

Vince grinned. "Jesus, he speaks. Okay, so I stand corrected." He turned back to Sams, shook his head in amazement. "Almost five years I've been riding around with this guy, he never says a word. Turns out he's correcting my grammar the whole time. Just too polite to say anything." He gave a laugh. "I guess it finally got to him. Either that or hell's freezing over. But where's my manners?" He went over, stood beside the chair, patted it gently. "Sit down. Take a load off."

He was right, Sams thought now. When they closed the door, you couldn't even see it. They'd left the light on when they went home for the night, sometime after midnight, and somewhere in the fog of his pain he'd heard the scrape of the key as they locked the door behind them. He lay curled up in the corner, just the way he'd seen his dog do once when he was a kid, after mixing it up with another dog. He'd found a blood trail, followed it out into the backyard to his father's toolshed. The dog had squeezed into a space under a set of low shelves, had lain there panting softly, one paw tucked carefully under it. That's how he'd found it, and nothing he did—whistling, setting out bowls of food and water just inside the entrance to the shed—could coax him out.

He understood now. It was the pain, which made you want to curl into a tiny ball, small enough for your mother to come over and pick you up, hold you on her lap, make it go away. His mother had died six years ago, and nothing she could do would have helped, but he curled into a ball anyway. And then there was the shame. They'd beat him like a dog. It was a thorough, professional job. Unhurried, unemotional, invisible to all but the most experienced emergency room doctor. It almost didn't seem like violence, more like two surgeons working on a patient. Lenny was the real master; he found ways to hurt Sams that Sams could never have imagined. Lenny had a talent for finding tender spots on the body that would show no bruise. If it hadn't been for the pain, and the vomiting that followed, Sams might almost have admired his gift. He was serious and silent while he worked, like a musician picking out a complex melody in a minor key.

By the time they left, the only visible injury he'd sustained was a nasty cut on his forehead from when he'd slipped out of the chair, hit his head on Lenny's knee. He lay there on the cool concrete floor, feeling the blood run down one side of his face. His eyes were closed, but he could picture it blending into the stains that had been left there by other men. Had they all cried out for mercy as he had? Did they all feel this shame when it was done, or were they simply grateful that the pain had ceased, glad to lie there, curled on their sides on the cool floor for a few minutes while the men who'd beaten them went off to get a cold beer? He had no doubt it was thirsty work.

From time to time the pain would recede, like a tide drawing out to expose the rocks hidden beneath. He'd take a deep breath, open his eyes. The room spun, but if he made a great effort, he could make its whirling slow. He wondered, if he lay here long enough, could he count the eggs all these cartons might have held? It struck him as sad, so many eggs left unprotected, their fragile shells cracked, the yoke draining away. *The yoke's on you*, he thought. His father had enjoyed saying that whenever they ate eggs. It became a family tradition, and when he grew up, had his own children, he'd said it to them. That's how families get made. You have to break a few eggs, crack a few jokes. Until the day when your children stop wanting to hear them. And then the yoke's on you after all.

The pain came back, rushing in on him again with a force that made him groan, close his eyes, panting like a dog. For a moment he thought he might vomit again. He'd skipped lunch, so he'd had nothing since breakfast. How could there be anything more in there? After a while, the tide of pain went out again. In books he'd read, they talked about pain coming in waves. But that wasn't right. It swelled up within you, filling every empty space in your body. Something hot and wet, like lava or burning gas. It would have been easier if they'd just killed him. Why *didn't* they just kill him?

He'd told them about the disk. He'd denied everything at first, but they just laughed. Then they went back to work on him, and soon enough he told them everything they wanted to know.

Except where to find it. The thought might almost have made him smile, but the muscles in his jaw hung slack as a sail when the wind dies away. But he clung to that idea: he'd deceived them, a last shattered fragment of his pride. *It's in my desk,* he'd told them, then leaned forward like he might throw up again to hide the flash of defiance in his eyes. They'd go out to the plant, but they could search all day and they'd never find it.

So then they'll come back. And they'll hurt you some more until you tell them where it is. He knew this was true. There was nothing he could do about it. But as long as they didn't have the disk, as long as he still had the strength to deceive them, they'd have to keep him alive.

He opened his eyes again. The ceiling was missing a few panels, leaving holes where he could faintly see metal beams up in the darkness. Somebody had climbed up on the chair, he realized, knocked down those panels trying to escape. But it was a false ceiling, just some acoustic tiles hung on thin metal bands from the beams way up there in the darkness. The building was a warehouse; he could tell by the smell, that familiar mix of dust and damp concrete he'd gotten to know when he worked in a furniture warehouse for two summers during college. Work all day in heat way up over a hundred, metal roof above you, so you lose two pounds just from sweat, then go out in the evening, make it back in ice-cold beer. This room was cool, even in August. *Must be on the ground floor*, he thought. The concrete he was lying on was probably the building's slab. Maybe IndusCrete had poured it. Depended on how old the building was. And whether the owners cared how long it stood. It smelled like it had been around awhile, and the bloodstains on the floor told a history of pain. Maybe one of the old cotton warehouses down along the docks, over a century of dust and black men's pain drifting through its empty rooms.

In a few hours they'd come back. They'd sleep late, have a nice breakfast, then ride out to the plant to get the disk. When it didn't turn up, they'd come back here, ready to go to work. There was no hurry. They had all weekend. By Monday he'd know with absolute clarity what any testimony before the grand jury would cost him.

But for the moment there was only the pain, and that was enough. He lay there, curled around it, understanding at that moment how the world would end—each of us with our pain, alone.

|||| Danny turned into the parking lot at IndusCrete, hearing the oyster shells crackle under the tires of his car. For some reason, it made him think of when he was a boy and his parents would take him down to Pensacola on summer weekends. They'd stay in a beachfront motel, nothing fancy, the kind of place where the rooms were attached cabins with fishing nets draped over the sliding glass doors that led out to the beach, and his parents pulled the car right up to the door of your room so the kids climbed out of the backseat barefoot, hopping like gawky frogs over the sun-baked shells in their bathing suits and towels, smelling like cocoa butter and salt water. It was the endlessness of childhood he'd felt in those days, watching his mother walk down to the water's edge to dip a wary toe in the surf. Later, she'd wade out, turning her back to the incoming waves with a grimace as they rose and crashed around her, and when she reached the calmer water beyond the breakers, she'd

ease into a languorous sidestroke, chin raised with a strange, queenly dignity to keep her hair from getting wet as she swam. Just a few strokes, then she'd emerge like Venus from the waves, come walking up the beach, dripping, to lie on the beach towel his father had spread out for her under a tilted beach umbrella that had to be adjusted each hour as the sun moved slowly across the sky.

What a strange thing to remember, Danny thought as he got out of the car. *What will Anna remember like that?* What lost world would haunt her the way this one haunted him? He tried to imagine how she'd see her parents as she grew older. Would it be this sunlit memory, or the darkness that had followed? We cling to our myths of Eden, the way children carry a scrap of old blanket to rub between their fingers when they go to sleep. What vanishes isn't a perfect world, just the childlike eyes that allowed us to see it.

He was surprised to see that the plant was still running, even while a couple of guys were up on ladders hanging sheets of plywood over the office windows. Danny walked over to them.

"Looks like they're keeping you busy."

One of the guys, who was holding the plywood in place while his partner used a power drill to screw it into place, looked down at him, his face expressionless. "Help you?"

"The boss around?"

"Shift boss or big boss?"

"I'm looking for Gerald Vickers."

The man looked at his partner. "Hey, you seen the man today?"

The other guy finished driving a screw through the plywood, lowered the drill. "Probably up at his house, getting it ready for the storm. I heard he pulled a couple other guys out of the plant, made 'em ride over there and board the place up."

Danny nodded. "He's over by the country club, right?"

"I look like the kind of guy he invites over for beers?" He took another screw from his tool belt, lined it up. "There was anybody in the office, they could tell you. But they all took off last night."

"Hey, you know Louis Sams? Black guy, works in the office?"

Danny saw the two men exchange glances.

"Not since yesterday," the first man said. "I heard he left early." Then he grinned. "Maybe he wasn't feeling too good."

Danny looked at him. "That what you heard?"

"Sure. He took off after lunch. Maybe it was something he ate."

Danny stood there for a moment, watching the man with the drill drive another screw through the plywood into the window frame. The drill gave a high whirring sound, which dropped a pitch as the screw bit into the metal frame. Then he walked back to his car. He sat there for a moment, thinking. The morning was clear and bright; the shimmer of heat rising off the hood of his car looked like the last thing you'd see as the life drains out of your body.

He took out his cell phone, dialed Marty Seagraves. When he picked up, Danny said, "I need a home address for Gerald Vickers."

"You think that's a good idea? You're not a cop. He's got no reason to talk to you."

"So I shouldn't even try?"

"How about I go with you?"

"You got time for that?"

Seagraves hesitated. "All right, I'll give you the address. But listen, don't go pushing the guy's buttons just to see if you can ring up the cherries, okay? He does business with some unpleasant people, and there's no point letting on how much you know."

"I don't have time to play games."

"I'm just saying it doesn't hurt to be smart."

"That's interesting. I'll have to try that sometime."

He waited while Seagraves got the address from the surveillance reports on his computer, then he scribbled it down on a pad he kept in his glove box. Vickers lived on Nassau Drive over in Metairie Club Gardens. Just writing down the address made the anger boil up within him. It was one of the wealthiest neighborhoods in New

Orleans, beautiful homes spread out along streets lined with cypress and oak trees, swimming pools gleaming in the sunlight. You feel like playing some golf, you just walk on down to the end of the street and you're at the country club. Gracious living, like squeezing the juice out of every day. You've had enough, you toss the crushed rind away, watch while the poor folks scramble to snatch it up, just in case you got lazy, left something for somebody else just this once.

Vickers had his workers out at the house, boarding up his picture windows in case a branch blew off one of those picturesque oak trees that shaded his street. But who, Danny wondered, was going to board up *their* windows, if that hurricane decided to pay New Orleans a visit? The man pays you, so you work for the man, and it's up to you to watch out for your own ass on your own time. Would he let them go home early if the city had to evacuate? Somehow Danny doubted it.

Danny drove over to Metairie Road, got off at Friedrich, and followed it back up into Metairie Club Gardens. The only people he'd ever known who lived up here were corporate lawyers and doctors, along with a state legislator so openly corrupt that he didn't even try to hide his sudden wealth. Danny had been waiting for years to see his name among the news reports of federal corruption indictments, but this guy had been either lucky or smart: he got out of politics, went to work for an oil services company that had recently made huge profits from a few favorable decisions by the state legislature. Lately Danny had seen him standing among the city's leading philanthropists in photos taken at a charity gala. Who says there are no second acts? In New Orleans, redemption was as easy as hanging your laundry out in the next hard rain. All it took to become respectable was cash, and it didn't matter if the money had a funny smell. In this climate, everything stinks. Just means you need to add more spice.

Gerald Vickers's house was a sprawling imitation of a West Indies plantation house, with wide, shady porches that extended all the way around the house and broad picture windows on which two men were now hanging sheets of plywood. Vickers paced on his front porch, glancing up at the sky nervously from time to time, as if he expected the hurricane to arrive at any moment, like a guest who comes too early to the party, finds his hosts in their bathrobes, bickering. Watching him, Danny felt strangely disappointed. He seemed too nervous and worried to be the villain Danny had imagined. Just a guy who'd gotten in over his head, wanting to get rich, like anybody else, but without understanding that a deal with the devil has to be signed in blood.

Danny got out of the car, walked over. He paused with one foot on the porch steps, called up, "Mr. Vickers?"

Vickers turned, surprised. He'd been caught up in his contemplation of the empty sky, not recognizing that danger always approaches from the unwatched quarter—the cloud of dust rising in the east while the sunset is streaked with crimson, the white flecks on the distant wave tops as the women crowd along the pier, waving their handkerchiefs at the sailors by the rail. He looked at Danny without recognition. He seemed annoyed at having his thoughts interrupted, but his expression suggested that he was too polite to show it.

"Yes? Can I help you?"

"My name's Danny Chaisson. I'm an attorney here in town." Danny glanced at the two men hanging the sheets of plywood. "Is there somewhere we could speak in private?"

Vickers's face took on a wary expression. "What's this about?"

"One of your employees. Louis Sams."

Vickers visibly stiffened. "What about him? Is something wrong?"

"You sure you want to have this conversation here?"

Vickers looked at the two men, saw that they were listening, even though they kept their attention on their work and their faces carefully expressionless.

"Come inside," he told Danny in a toneless voice.

The air outside felt like a baker's oven, but as Danny followed Vickers through the door, the sudden burst of air-conditioning was like being whipped with silk. Ceiling fans spun lazily nine feet above their heads, not because the rooms were warm, but as if to suggest there could be no better life than this one, effortless and languid. The house smelled like cleaning solvents, as if a troupe of maids had just spent the morning polishing every surface to a shine, but in the background Danny could smell that somebody had been making gumbo. He never got used to the smell of rich men's houses, like a life you could pour into a jar and screw the lid tightly on.

Vickers led him down a long corridor of polished oak floors, past a kitchen done in dark marble and Spanish floor tiles, where an elegant woman in her late forties stood with a glass of iced tea in her hand, watching a weather forecast on a small television on the counter.

"That you, Gerry?" The woman glanced over at them, and Vickers paused in the kitchen doorway. "Still no change. They're saying landfall before dawn on Monday." She caught a glance of Danny, looked surprised. "Oh, I didn't realize we had company."

"Mr. Chaisson's a lawyer," Vickers said quietly, and for a moment Danny thought he caught a tone in his voice he recognized. Like a husband who's been caught at a party talking to a pretty woman, quickly finding a way to explain it. "He wants to ask me some questions about one of my employees."

"Nothing wrong, I hope."

"He's disappeared," Danny said. "I'm concerned for his safety."

The woman's eyebrows went up. "Oh, dear. I'm sorry to hear it." She looked at her husband. "Is there anything we can do?"

Vickers looked as if he'd swallowed a handful of glass and now he was trying not to bring it back up. "I'm just learning about this myself," he said. "Obviously, we'll help in any way we can."

His wife nodded, looking suitably somber for a moment. Then she turned to Danny, said, "May I offer you some iced tea, Mr. Chaisson?"

And suddenly Danny found himself feeling sorry for Vickers. By any measure, he was an unattractive man, short and heavyset, with a florid face and dull red hair that had begun to retreat like an army whose defenses have given way after a long siege. How had he won this elegant woman's heart, except by providing her a life of comfort, with a lovely home in the city's most expensive neighborhood and maids to clean it? No doubt the gumbo he could smell was made by a cook who rode the bus in from the Ninth Ward to cook up down-home favorites on the cast-iron Aga. And while her husband went out to shake the fruit from the trees, his wife sat in her kitchen drinking iced tea and watching the maids until it was an hour when one might reasonably switch to mojitos or Tom Collinses, or else she went out to play tennis at the country club with other elegant women whose faces grew more lean and stretched with each comfortable year.

"No, thank you." Danny gave her his most reassuring smile. "I'll try not to trouble you any longer than necessary."

Vickers led Danny to the end of the hall, where a door opened on a wide den with a picture window that looked out across a gleaming swimming pool to the wooded golf course beyond. He seemed at a loss for a moment, then sat down behind a large mahogany desk, pulled his chair in close, so he seemed to be hugging the desk to his belly, trying to disappear behind it like a man crouched in a trench.

"I'm deeply concerned about what you've told me," he said to Danny. "But I want you to know that I don't make a habit of involving my wife in my business dealings."

Danny gave him a hard stare. "I guess that makes sense, considering your business partners. How you think she'd feel about Jimmy Mancuso?"

Vickers stiffened. "I don't know what you're talking about."

"The FBI has tapes, Gerald. You think they let a guy like Jimmy Mancuso walk around, they don't listen in on everything he does?" Danny sat down in one of the leather chairs Vickers had set up facing his desk. Guys like Jimmy Mancuso know how hard it is to make a federal criminal case; they count on the fact that the FBI might know what the bad guys are doing, but what they know and what they can sell to a jury are two different things. You keep a good defense lawyer on retainer, and even a hard-shell federal prosecutor will hesitate to bring an indictment unless he's sure he's got the case wrapped up tight. And even then, with a tough lawyer and a little pressure on witnesses, you can still walk away at the end of the day. Buy the jurors dinner at Galatoire's, send 'em each a nice present so everybody in town knows you had their home addresses the whole time. That's how a guy like Little Jimmy handles the FBI.

But Gerald Vickers heard "The FBI has tapes," and his whole face went tight. He looked like one of those Stone Age hunters they find frozen in a glacier, still clutching his spear. Or what was that other weapon they carried? *Atlatl.* Danny couldn't help smiling. He'd always loved that word as a boy.

"Louis Sams," Danny said. "Where is he?"

"I don't know. I'm his employer, not his keeper." Vickers shot him a nervous look. "He left work early yesterday. Said he had a family emergency."

"Did he say where?"

Vickers shrugged. "Atlanta, I guess. That's where he was headed this weekend. Someone in his mother's family had a surgery."

Danny studied Vickers's face. Sweat had broken out along his hairline, and Danny saw a drop run slowly down his neck, vanishing inside his collar. He was lying; his eyes looked like caves where an animal goes to hide.

But the story was just close enough to the truth to make Danny hesitate. Was it possible that Sams had left town in a hurry? Had something come up in Atlanta?

"Now that I think about it," Vickers said in a sudden rush, "he definitely said Atlanta. We were in my office. He came in to tell me while I was on the phone, so I guess it slipped my mind." He paused, as if his mouth had suddenly gone dry and the words were like bricks that wouldn't take shape in his mouth without something to hold the dust together.

Danny looked at him silently for a moment. Then he glanced out through the picture windows at the gleaming pool beyond. "This is a great house," he said. "Be a shame to lose it."

Vickers stood up, his face angry. "I'm going to have to ask you to leave."

"Sit down," Danny told him. "I'm giving you a chance. This is the moment when you get to decide how your life's going to go. You're lucky you get a choice. So think hard. This how you want things to go for you? You want your wife to see you sitting in a courtroom next to Jimmy Mancuso?"

Vickers looked down at his desk, and his whole body seemed to lose shape, like a balloon slowly deflating. "I didn't want anything to do with this," he said with a pained expression. "It wasn't my idea."

"People always tell me that when it's too late." Danny leaned forward so Vickers had to meet his eyes. "But the thing is, you *are* in it now. Whatever's happening, you're part of it. The only question is where you'll be when it's over. You do the right thing right now, you might not end up sitting at that defense table with Jimmy. It won't be easy, but you can still make things right."

"You don't know what you're asking." Vickers looked away. "You know what Jimmy does to people who betray him?"

"Yeah. And I know what they do to guys like you in prison too. A guy like Jimmy Mancuso isn't going to wait around to see if you betray him. He's got one business, and it's protecting his own ass.

The moment you got involved with him, you became a potential liability. Every time he looks at you, he's thinking, *Do I need to unload this guy?* You keep making money for him, you're fine. But the moment he has to start worrying about you, that balance starts to tip. Looks to me like you're past that point already."

He watched Vickers's eyes move across the room, as if taking stock of a lifetime's worth of things he'd once desired, which now, Danny imagined, looked as strange to him as the relics dug from an ancient tomb. Was it this stuff—the bronze golf trophy, the autographed baseball in its Plexiglas case, the photo of Vickers shaking hands with the governor at a highway dedication, the family photographs, his wife smiling in the sunshine on a boat in Cancún—that he'd traded for his soul?

"You're going to lose it all anyway," Danny told him. "You know that, right?"

Vickers looked at him. "So I'm just supposed to sit here and take it?"

"I'm offering you a way to land on your feet. That's what you should be thinking about now."

"Yeah? So you're trying to *help* me? I should thank you for coming in here, telling me I'm gonna lose my house and spend the rest of my life playing drop the soap in the shower in some federal prison?" Vickers shook his head angrily. "I've worked hard for what I've got, and I'm not giving it up just because you walk in here and start jerking my chain. Life's tough. But I've got no choice. You don't fuck with a guy like Jimmy Mancuso. And I don't see him doing any time, so you'll excuse me if I don't get too scared of going to prison." Vickers stood up, walked over to the door. "Now, if you'll excuse me, I've got to finish getting my house ready for the storm."

He walked Danny out of the house, shut the door behind him without another word. The two guys hanging plywood glanced over at him, then silently went on with their work. Danny walked back to his car, which was parked in the dappled shade of a mature oak at the edge of the street. He'd hit a dead end. But what had he expected? All you can do is take your best shot. Vickers had built his elegant wife a house from glass and pale wood, and all he could think about was hanging on, boarding up the windows against the wind. Did he really think those boards would hold if the storm blew through? It didn't matter, finally. He did it because it was all he could do. Cross your fingers and watch the weather on TV, trying to turn the storm with your will, sending it off to Tampa or Texas. Hang on, figure up the luck that's still left to you, the way a poor man might count out the coins in his pocket, slowly, trying to make it enough to buy himself one last drink. And if it worked this time, the storm turning aside at the last moment as it always has in the past, then why worry about something as small as a federal grand jury? You've still got coins in your pocket, and anyone who wanted to take them away would have to peel them out of your hand, one broken finger at a time.

Danny got on Airline Highway, picked up the expressway headed back toward the city. He wasn't sure what to do next. He'd driven past Sams's house over on North Prieur Street. There were no lights on in the house, no car in the driveway. He'd knocked on the door, but nobody answered. So what now? There was an odd smell in the air, like after a lightning strike, although the sky was empty of clouds. And the city had a strange, still feeling, even though the traffic was almost as heavy as usual. It felt like everybody was waiting for something that didn't seem real, could barely be imagined. *Like the whole city has gambler's eyes,* Danny thought. That look you see around a roulette table when the wheel is spinning and there's nothing more you can do, just stand there and watch the little silver ball begin to fade off the rail, skidding toward a number you didn't pick.

Danny's cell phone rang. He reached over, dug in the pocket of his jacket on the seat beside him, managed to pick it up before it rang through to his voice mail.

"I hope your news is better than mine," Marty Seagraves said.

"Nothing yet. What do you have?"

"Local police found his car parked behind a rib joint over on Claiborne. It was behind a dumpster, so nobody saw it until they started hauling out trash this morning."

"Any reason he might have left it there?"

"Not that I can see. Nobody who works there knows him, and it doesn't look like he ate there last night."

"So somebody dumped it?"

"Too soon to say." Seagraves's voice sounded weary. "Listen, Danny. There's too much going on for us to get any help with this. The local police have their hands full getting ready for the storm, and we're going on to emergency orders this afternoon. I'm under a lot of pressure to set this aside until after the storm. There's no solid evidence to suggest we're looking at anything but a guy who got nervous and took off. And it looks like we're going to have much more pressing business shortly."

"You know something I don't?"

"The mayor and the governor are going on television this afternoon to announce an evacuation. We're looking at a major storm. They're predicting it'll reach Category Five by tomorrow morning."

For a moment Danny said nothing. He was coming up on the Central Business District; its glass towers suddenly looked terribly fragile to him. "You're serious? Category *Five?*"

"That's what the National Weather Service is predicting."

"And the levees are only rated to Category Three?"

"That's right. We're telling everyone to get out of town as soon as possible. It's time to go, Danny."

Danny looked out across the city. "You really think the whole city can evacuate? What about all the people who don't own cars?"

"They're going to open up the Superdome as a shelter."

Danny looked over at the Dome rising up between the two arms of the expressway. "They really think it'll hold up in a Category Five?"

"The engineers say it'll stand up to winds as high as two hundred miles per hour, but nobody's ever tested that. So you can imagine, we've got a lot on our plate just getting our own office ready. I wish there was more I could do for your guy, but it looks like we're going to be up to our necks the next few days, so I'm afraid he's gonna have to wait. This thing hits, I don't think the grand jury is going to be hearing testimony anytime soon."

Up to our necks, Danny thought as he hung up. If the storm got to Category Five, that might not be an exaggeration. He looked out at the city spread out below the expressway. Was it really possible? Could the whole thing be underwater in less than two days? Like everybody else, he'd spent his life hearing the warnings: the city was built below sea level, one good storm surge could turn it all back into swamp. He'd read somewhere that a Category Five hurricane brought a wall of water over eighteen feet high. The only storm that strong he could remember was Hurricane Camille. His parents had driven him along the Gulf Coast a month after the storm had destroyed everything in its path. His father had pointed out the car's window at the empty lots, where not a tree or a wall remained, and said, "There was a hotel here. Over there, they found a thirty-eight-foot boat up in a tree, a half mile from the harbor. The storm surge was twenty-five feet high when it hit the beach. That's like four men my height standing on each other's shoulders."

Danny had sat in the car's backseat, trying to imagine a wave that tall sweeping in across the coastal road they were driving along, carrying away houses and hotels—every brick, every pipe, everything but the concrete foundation slabs, which now lay exposed, like the bones of some long-dead animal. Was that what would hit New Orleans? That wasn't what the experts talked about; the Mississippi's alluvial delta south of the city would absorb any wave coming in off the Gulf. No, what had them worried wasn't the violence of a wave crashing over the city, but a tidal surge pouring into Lake Pontchartrain from Lake Borgne, which was really more like a bay than a lake, open to the Gulf along its eastern end, swamping the coastal marshes that usually kept the two bodies of water separate, so that the lake rose over its banks, rushed up along the city's drainage canals, and then burst through the fragile levees to spill into the city, filling it right up until it reached sea level—as much as ten feet in some parts of town   like water pouring into a bathtub. It wouldn't be the apocalyptic violence that Camille had wrought on Pass Christian and Bay St. Louis, one vast crashing wave that swept all away, but a slowly rising tide in which every-thing floated, the whole city sloshing around like the junk you see floating in a canal—people, houses, uprooted trees, snakes from the bayou, the dead rising from their crumbling tombs, sewage, chemicals from the plants out on Old Gentilly Road and the Belle Chasse Highway. Buildings wouldn't be destroyed by wind, but their roofs would be ripped away, becoming flying debris that crashed through windows and walls, and then the rest would sim-ply float off the foundations with the rising water. Nothing would be left in some parts of the city, and what did remain would be so fouled by that black tide of sewage and chemicals that when the water receded, there would be nothing left to save. What the storm didn't destroy, the bulldozers would have to plow under. In the end, nothing would be left except a few miles of the old city strung out along the high ground next to the Mississippi like the last beads on a piece of frayed string.

For a century, everyone had known it was coming. Just a matter of time and luck. People went on with their lives, did their best not to think about it. And was that really different from people any-where? Everyone lives on the edge of a cliff, doing his best not to think about the fault line that runs under the house, or the few years of drought that will turn the whole state to dust, or the pollu-tion pouring out of the factory, or the ghetto simmering with rage, or the forest fires that sweep down from the hills, or the tsunami that must descend one day on the island paradise, or the social contract that's torn apart by greed, as easily as one might crumple a sheet of paper, toss it away. The end is always coming, but we can't bear to look. New Orleans just makes it all clear, a city where the roots force their way up through the sidewalks and you can smell the rotting garbage in the air, where nothing can be hidden for long.

All it took was time. That's what Danny had learned from living in New Orleans: the roots were there, just under the concrete, straining to break through. Gerald Vickers was on the edge. He couldn't hold it together much longer. A little pressure, and he'd crack open, spill everything he knew. But time, it seemed, was the one thing none of them had. In thirty-six hours, none of this would matter anymore. The greed, the corruption, the beautiful homes with their swimming pools and lush gardens, all the things men fought over, even thought worth killing for, would be carried away by the wind or drowned under eight feet of water.

But Louis Sams was out there too. Danny felt sure of it. He'd been snatched off the street, his car left in a place where nobody might see it for days. If Jimmy Mancuso felt secure, he'd be dead by now. But killing a witness was risky, especially if the prosecutors could connect you to his disappearance. Jimmy's boys might have hesitated, looking for a way to make him disappear without it coming back to haunt them.

And suddenly Danny realized that they had nothing to worry about. In a few days, the city would be full of dead.

He felt his throat tighten. A whole city of victims. Who'd care about one man? Natural disaster shatters the illusion that we matter. There are no individuals when the floodwaters rise. Victims, Danny knew, are faceless. We might remember the cute child who vanished, or the pretty young woman whose life was cut short by the predator's soul-destroying madness, but even their tragic smiles fade from our memories, replaced by all the other faces who fill the newspapers in the months that follow, feeding the world's hunger. But there are no smiling photos when people die together. Instead, the newspapers show bodies scattered along a road like so much trash, or a vague shape floating facedown in the flood, arms flung out, like he's looking for the cross on which he'd once hung, now vanished beneath the waves.

It's time to go, Danny. Seagraves was letting him know there was nothing more anyone could do for Louis Sams. He hadn't wanted to say it straight out, so he just apologized that he couldn't be more help, figuring Danny would get the message. Time to head north, away from the wind and water. Save yourself. We'll come back and bury the dead when it's all over. But looking at the city, Danny couldn't help feeling that there was still something here worth saving. You grow up in a city, it's more than just a place in your mind. It's the way people wave at each other every morning on their way to work, the way people line up on the median strip on St. Charles, waiting for the streetcar, the music drifting out of an apartment window, where some Tulane students are still going at it, reluctant to let the party end. Can you just let all that stuff go, take off for someplace dry to watch on CNN while it all gets swept away? Cities matter not because they're pretty or historic or interesting to visit, but because they force people to care about each other, every day. Every city is a disaster waiting to happen. But that's not the whole story. The only way a city can survive, even for a day, is by an endless series of unspoken agreements. Every man matters, if only for a moment. That's what people who've never lived in a city don't understand, Danny thought. They think of cities as anonymous places, but nothing could be further from the truth. You can't care about everybody, but you have to care about somebody every moment of the day. You wait your turn at the stoplight, at the grocery store, at the bus stop. Even the cemeteries are full of silent crowds. Respect is what keeps the knife from your throat. A city can be the worst of places, full of anger and violence and fear. But it's also the best, a place built on endless small acts of cooperation and agreement. You work together or nothing works.

That's why it's important that nobody gets left behind, Danny thought. The girl crying on the bus, the homeless drunk on his filthy bed of cardboard, the clerk in the DMV, every one of them catches somebody's eye. Everybody matters. If we stop caring, even for a moment, then you might as well walk away and let the levees crumble before the flood.

Danny got off the expressway, took St. Bernard up to Paris Avenue. He wasn't leaving Louis Sams behind. But time was short, and what he needed now was help.

llll "So what's the story? This guy talk?" Jimmy Mancuso held up his coffee cup for the waitress, and she picked up the coffeepot, started to bring it over to give him a refill. But Jimmy waved her away. "Make some fresh, okay? I hate drinking from the bottom of the pot."

The girl went away, rinsed out the pot, and then Jimmy watched her dump the old grounds, tear open a plastic packet, and toss the prepacked filter into the pot.

"Damn right he talked," Vince told him. "You ever see Lenny work? He's an artist, man. They'd ever let him do this when he was on the force, we'd have cleaned up the whole city."

"You believe this shit?" Jimmy nodded toward the waitress. "*This* is how they make coffee now? It just comes in a filter like that?"

Vince looked over. "Yeah, Jimmy. They been doin' that for years."

Jimmy shook his head. "Jesus, no wonder it tastes the way it does."

"You should go over to the French Market, get you some at the Morning Call. They got great coffee."

"I don't *want* to go over to the French Market, okay? There's no place to park over there, you don't have to walk six blocks. I'm gonna do that for a cup of coffee? Fuck that. What I want is to sit here, eat my lunch, then have a decent cup of coffee. Is that too much to ask?"

Vince sighed. "You want to hear the rest of it or what?"

Jimmy looked over at him, scowled. "What rest of it? You just told me the guy talked. Lenny's a fucking artist. What else is there to know?"

"There's a disk."

"A what?"

"A computer disk. He copied some files off the computer in Vickers's office, hid the disk out there before we brought him in."

"So the Feds don't have it."

"No. It's hidden out at IndusCrete."

"They know about it?"

Vince shrugged. "Hard to say."

"You mean you didn't ask him."

"Not exactly, no. He told us where he hid the disk. It's in his desk."

The waitress came over with a fresh cup of coffee, set it down in front of Jimmy, took the old one away. He reached over, grabbed a handful of sugar packets out of the bowl in the middle of the table, tore them open, and dumped the sugar into his coffee. "Go get this disk and bring it to me."

Vince smiled. "So you don't want us to tell Vickers about it?"

"Nah. This thing's all over, I'm gonna have a little talk with him, let him know we got to change the terms of our arrangement."

"Okay, soon as Lenny gets back, we'll head on out there."

Jimmy looked around. "Where'd he go, anyway?"

"He went over to the French Market. He wanted some coffee."

|||| Among his other interests, Jabril Saunders owned a muffler shop on Paris Avenue called Muffel-Auto. "Drives the Italian guys up the street crazy," he'd told Danny once. "They keep tellin' me

I'm pronouncing it wrong. Way they say it, it's like, *Moofeletta*." He grinned. "Got all that Italian flavor in your mouth, but you don't get the joke. So I told 'em, where I live, up in the Ninth Ward, we don't eat that shit anyway. I'll leave that for my Italian brothers, like to go on down to the Quarter, get them a muff at Luigi's. Way I see it, you eat all that olive paste, you *think* you been eatin' a muff."

In New Orleans, Danny had learned, that's how it was with all kinds of things. What made sense in one part of town was all wrong at the other end of the streetcar line. Jabril kept talking about *putting something back into the community*, and the muffler shop was one way he put that into action. He used it to train boys from the neighborhood in job skills.

"Man, they need it too." Jabril shook his head. "And we're not just talking about how to service a transmission. I mean, like, showin' up for work on Monday. Schools don't teach 'em that. You look around where these boys live, all the hardworkin' people are invisible. Their mamas, they get up early, take the bus downtown, work in some office all day, so they ain't ever around. You look around the neighborhood, the only people you *see* puttin' in long hours on the job are the dealers. They out there every night, 'cause if they ain't, some other guy come steal their corner. Those boys got them some serious work ethic. Them and the hookers, 'cause they know it's *primal* out there. Capitalism in its purest form. You got to guard your territory or you dead."

"And a muffler shop isn't?"

"Not like that." Jabril laughed. "Look, it ain't like I'm makin' much money off it. But we got to have more daylight businesses up in the neighborhood, so these boys can see what it means to go to work in the morning, come home at night. And why should my people have to drive up Claiborne, hand their money to some white guy, they need a new muffler? Hell, we been muffled all our damn lives. Ain't nothing we don't know about that, except how to ring it up in the cash register."

Now, if you pulled in there, you'd hear the clatter of tools, the high-pitched whine of the lug driver, boys shouting to each other as they swarmed over your car like angry bees. Jabril had set up an office in the back, put in an expensive stereo with speakers out in the main garage, and he liked to sit back there, playing blues and classic soul. *Teaching 'em their heritage,* he called it. When he wasn't around, one of the boys would crawl through an air duct, unlock the office door, and they'd pump up the bass, put on Juvenile, Ghostface Killah, and Danja Mowf. Danny'd driven past with Jabril a couple of times when they could feel the music shaking their car all the way down the block.

Jabril just shook his head sadly. "Don't know why anybody need a muffler. You can't hear your car, way they play that music."

But there was pride in his voice as he said it. Some of those boys had been working short for the drug gangs, carrying the product the older boys sold so they wouldn't face felony time if they got busted, before he'd pulled them off the street and taught them there was another way to live. He'd sent two boys from his afternoon crew off to Dillard and Grambling by demanding that they get their teachers to sign off on their high school attendance every day before he'd let them in the door. One of them was talking about law school, and Danny felt sure that it was only a matter of time before Jabril started dropping hints to Mickie about how he's working too hard, needs to get him some help.

That's where Danny found Jabril now, in the back office of the muffler shop, feet propped up on his desk, watching the hurricane reports on a silent television mounted on the wall while the hip-hop boomed from the stereo. There was a line of cars waiting outside the shop's roll-up doors, and his boys were working hard, doing oil changes, topping off fluids, installing new batteries.

"You're doing good business," Danny shouted over the music as he came in.

Jabril leaned back, lowered the volume on the stereo, and Danny saw a couple of the boys out in the shop look up angrily. "Got all these people need their cars serviced before getting out of town. Half the places in town are closing up. Somebody's got to take care of 'em. Lot of them say they're gonna wait until tomorrow, see what the storm's doing before heading out."

"Roads are gonna be packed."

Jabril nodded. "Stop-and-go all the way to Baton Rouge, and in this heat you'll have cars breaking down, people running out of gas, all kinds of problems. I'm telling 'em, go tonight. If the storm turns, you can come home. But where they gonna go? These people, lots of 'em don't have the money to go spend the night in a hotel. Nobody give 'em a credit card, 'cause they've never had one. They *might* have a checking account, but mostly they deal in cash. You know how hard it is to get a hotel room, you don't have a credit card? They're living paycheck to paycheck anyway. Most of 'em probably just drive north until they run out of gas, pull it over and sleep in the car."

"With a hurricane blowing through?"

He shrugged. "It's either that or stay here. What about you? You getting the family out of town?"

"Mickie's taking Anna and her mother up to stay with some friends in Baton Rouge, but she's coming back tonight. ATF is part of the emergency plan."

Jabril raised his eyebrows. "And what about you? You goin' down with the ship?"

"Not if I can help it. But something's come up I have to deal with. You know Louis Sams?"

"Demitra's brother-in-law? The guy walks around with a calculator?"

"Yeah. He got himself into a tough spot, and now he's gone missing."

"And you think you can find him with a hurricane blowing into town?" Jabril sighed, shook his head. "Man, I've seen you ride into

Dodge on some lame horses in the past, but this one won't even make the stable."

Danny smiled. "That some of your folksy wisdom?"

"You know it, son. Time you started listening to it."

"Look, it's probably nothing, but I feel responsible for the guy. I went by his house, and I was just out at his office. It's closed up for the weekend, but they had some guys who work in the plant out hanging plywood on the windows. One of them said they'd heard he got called out of town suddenly. Family emergency."

"Yeah? So?"

"He wasn't supposed to leave town. We agreed he'd call me if anything came up."

Jabril shrugged. "Maybe he took off because of the storm. Lots of people leaving town."

"You don't understand. He's scheduled to appear before a federal grand jury on Monday. You have something like that coming up, you don't just take off without telling anyone."

"Shit, I would."

"They're not investigating him. He's a witness."

"Don't matter. You start talkin' about a grand jury, I'm doing the two-foot shuffle. Nothing good *ever* comes out of a federal grand jury. Might as well throw a rope over a branch. Somebody's gonna end up swingin', and you'll have to forgive me if I'm jumping to conclusions here, but I don't see a whole lotta white boys hanging from no trees."

"I don't think that's really the fear this time."

"So what is?"

"The people he's testifying against."

Jabril winced. "You see what I mean? Anytime you walk into that courthouse, that's it. You better watch your ass."

"We tried to set up some protection for him, but he didn't really trust it."

"Would you?"

Danny shook his head. "It's hard to give up your life. I always think it must be what my grandmother felt when she had to go into a nursing home. You spend your whole childhood waiting to become independent, and now they expect you to give it up."

"You really think you can find him now?" Jabril spread his hands. "These people he was gonna testify against have him, there's not much you can do."

"No way to know unless I try."

"And you think that makes more sense than getting ready for the hurricane?"

"Life doesn't stop just because a storm's coming."

"See, that's where you wrong. Life stops, everybody leaves or waits it out, and if we're lucky, life starts again after it's gone." Jabril sat back, looked at Danny for a moment. "So what do you need me to do?"

IIII By five, when the mayor and the governor went on TV to urge the city's residents to evacuate, Jabril had over forty boys on the street. In two hours they'd knocked on doors all along Louis Sams's street, talked to the women who worked behind the counters in the local corner stores, even questioned the pair of hookers who worked the next block. Nobody had seen Sams in a couple days, but they hadn't seen anything unusual going down on the block either. Two of the older boys slipped the lock on the back door of Sams's house, called Jabril on a cell phone from his bathroom.

"He didn't leave town," they told him. "There's a suitcase on the bed, but it's only got a couple things in it, and his toothbrush is right here next to the sink."

"Look around," Jabril told them. "What else you see?"

The boy with the phone turned slowly, his eyes moving across the room. "Laundry basket's full, and there's stuff piled on one side of the bed. Looks like his wife ain't been home for a couple days."

"Keep looking," Jabril told him. "What else you see?"

A pad next to the bed had some phone numbers scribbled on it. The boy read them off, and Jabril repeated them. One was Danny's office. Another was the private cell phone number Marty Seagraves gave out to people if they needed to reach him after hours. Danny didn't recognize the other two, but one of them had an Atlanta area code. He wrote the numbers down.

One of the boys, who kept all Jabril's accounting and business records on a laptop he carried around in an old backpack, protected by the most advanced data encryption programs available on the open market, fired up Sams's computer and scrolled through his files.

"Brother's security is a joke," he told Jabril. "But it don't look like he got nothin' to hide. Buncha work files, couple porn downloads. He likes Asian girls. Nothing too nasty. They all smiling and shit. Happy little Japanese girls. I guess they like people looking at 'em naked."

"We ain't interested in none a that," Jabril told him. "Just look 'round, see if there's anything tells us where he might be."

The boy laughed. "How 'bout Japan? Wouldn't mind goin' there myself, meet some a these girls."

Jabril rolled his eyes. "Tell you what. You find something, I'll buy you some sushi. How'd that be?"

"Man, I don't eat that shit. You buy me some fried catfish, I'll let the girl sit on my lap while I eat it."

Over the speakerphone, they heard his fingers flying across the computer's keys. "Booked a plane ticket for his wife to Atlanta, couple days ago."

Danny sat forward, closer to the phone. "You see any reservations for him?"

"Just that one. Don't mean he didn't book a ticket, but it wasn't on this computer. You say he's got a computer at work?"

"That's right."

"Could have done it there. I'd have to get into that computer to know for sure." More keys clicking, and then the boy sighed, said, "Ah, man, look at this. Don't know why I didn't think to look before now. Man's got himself a remote access program."

Danny looked at Jabril, who shrugged. "What's that?"

"Lets him get into his office computer from home. That way, you get home from work, you say, *Damn, I left something at the office*, you don't have to get back in your car, drive over there to get it. You just fire up your computer, type in your password, and you can get on your office network, even access your local drives." They heard more keys clicking. "This guy got kids?"

"Yeah, three."

"You know their names?"

Danny frowned. "His boy's name is Claude, but I don't know about the two girls."

The boy on the phone hit some keys. "Any way you could find out?"

Danny thought about it for a moment, then dug out his cell phone, called Demitra.

"Tell me you ain't calling me 'cause you *need* something," she said when she picked up.

"Just a quick question. You remember the names of Louis's daughters?"

"Yeah. Shondra and Tenille. Why?"

"No reason," Danny said quickly. "Just couldn't remember. That's Shondra?"

"Uh-huh. And Tenille, like she knows the Captain." Demitra sighed. "Poor little girl don't even know what you talkin' about, you say that, but she gonna have to spend her whole life listening to people make that joke."

"Thanks," Danny said. "You taking off soon?"

"We was just heading out the door when you called. Heading up to Natchitoches. I got a cousin up there we can stay with. You?"

"I got a couple things to take care of still. But you drive safely, okay? I'll see you real soon."

"God willing, and the river don't rise."

Danny hung up. "He's got a daughter named Shondra," he said into the speakerphone, "and another one named Tenille."

"How about his wife's name?"

"Kara."

There was a silence, with the only sound the clicking of the keys as the boy typed quickly. "Okay, we're in. Lotta files here. You interested in somethin' particular, or we just messin' around?"

Danny hesitated. "I'd have to look at it to know."

"You want me to burn you a copy?"

"Can you do that?"

"Sure. He's got some CDs here on his desk. You want, I could make you a whole set." They heard the boy typing. "Man, somebody needs to talk with these people 'bout their network security. Their firewalls are a joke. You can just open a door, walk right in."

"Hang on," Danny said, leaning forward. "Are you saying you can get into the whole company network?"

"I'm in there now. Everything but the local drives. Have to get access to the office to get at that stuff. You want copies of what I got?"

Danny thought about it. "How long would that take?"

"Most of the night, probably. Have to go get me a couple zip drives."

Danny looked over at Jabril. "This is unreal. You know he could do that?"

Jabril shrugged. "We just dinosaurs, man. These kids, they're gonna eat us alive."

"I don't know what to tell you," Danny said to the kid on the phone. "Ninety percent of that stuff is probably meaningless. Without an engineer to help me, I wouldn't even know what I was looking at. Could be there's something important there, but I won't know until I get a chance to go through it. And the truth is, we don't have much time."

"You mean 'cause of the storm? Won't take me that long, and hell, I'm not going anywhere."

"You're not evacuating?"

"I got my whole family here. My grandma, she can't walk. How we gonna get her out of town?"

Danny shot a look at Jabril, who looked at him with expressionless eyes. "You understand what they're saying could happen here? The whole city could flood."

"Yeah, I heard that. But where we gonna go? Can't afford no motel, even if we could fit everybody in the car. Anyway, we up on the third floor. Won't be no thing."

Danny raised his eyebrows, but Jabril just spread his hands.

"Been sayin' this for years," he told Danny quietly. "You want to evacuate this city, you need a plan. Lots of poor people in this city. They got to have someplace to go, some way to get there. You want to do this right, you got to open up every National Guard armory and high school gym from Baton Rouge to Shreveport, get school buses runnin' every hour. Shoulda started last night."

"What about you?"

Jabril shrugged. "I'm like you. I sent the girls up to Shreveport this morning with their mama. But I can't just leave. I got too many people count on me. Somebody got to watch out for 'em. So I'm here until the sun rise."

Danny stared at him. It had never occurred to him that Jabril might be planning to stay and ride out the storm in New Orleans. He'd figured they'd stick it out until tomorrow, then get on the road with everybody else. Traffic would be a nightmare, but at least they'd be out of the flood zone before the storm hit. But now he had to wonder. How many people were planning to stay? New Orleans was a city of gamblers: casino, quarter slots, backroom poker, or floating crap games, it made no difference. They loved to gamble, and if they bet on the Saints, they expected to lose. But were they really ready to gamble with their lives?

"What's the story?" the boy on the phone said. "You want this stuff or not?"

"Do it," Danny said quickly. "Keep track of your time, and I'll pay you for it."

"Sounds good to me. You pay for the zip drives too?"

"Whatever you need."

"Okay, I'm on it."

They hung up, and Danny sat back, feeling strangely exhausted. "You're really planning to stay?"

Jabril shrugged. "Thirty years they been tellin' us it's every man for himself. That ain't the way it works in my world. Somebody's got to watch out for the people get left behind."

"You really think you can help them if the city floods?"

"Don't look like they gonna get much help from nobody else." He sighed. "Fact is, people I talk to, they just don't believe it. They figure somebody's in charge, gonna take care of it. I say, 'Yeah? You seen *anything* lately make you believe that?' But they watch TV, all these people come on, tellin' 'em they got nothin' to worry about, except maybe two girls up in Boston might want to get married. Lot of 'em got boys in the Army. They want to believe we at war for a reason, same way they want to believe somebody gonna be there watchin' out for them if this storm comes through. Our whole country's a faith-based initiative, man. Take somethin' awful big to wake people up."

"Be a hard way to wake up, you find water rising over your roof."

"You right about that. But these people so used to feelin' like they drowning, you can't blame 'em for wondering how this can be worse. Fact is, nobody cares about them. White folks get out, that's all that matters. We got to do for ourselves, same as always. So I'm gonna stay right here, make sure that happens."

Danny looked at his watch, then stood up, looked out at the evening starting to settle over the city. "I better get going. I want to catch Jimmy Mancuso before he leaves town."

Jabril looked at him with surprise. "You going to see Little Jimmy?"

"He's the guy with the muscle in this thing. If they grabbed Louis to keep him from testifying, Jimmy's the man I got to see."

"You want company?" Jabril started to get up. "Jimmy ain't known for his sweet disposition."

But Danny waved him off. "I know Jimmy. Your being there wouldn't help."

"Yeah? He got a thing about people like me?"

"You know any mob guys who don't?"

"All right." Jabril raised both hands, sat back in his chair. "But you tell the man right up front that I know where you are. You don't show up here in a couple hours, I'm gonna go out there, pay him a visit. And then he know what it's *really* like to be one of the Sopranos."

⁣|||| "Will you turn that shit off already?" Jimmy Mancuso shook his head in disgust. He was sitting with his back to the television mounted over the bar, which also meant having his back to the door, a position that made him feel distinctly uncomfortable ever since somebody showed him some photographs of a guy back in the twenties got shot in the back of the head and fell face-first into his plate of tagliatelle. But the waitresses in this joint couldn't stop watching the weather reports. Two days now, they'd been standing around at the end of the bar, staring up at that guy standing in front of a map of the Gulf Coast, waving both hands slowly up toward the mouth of the Mississippi like he was a traffic cop showing that fucking storm the way. For two days Jimmy had gone about his business, doing his best to ignore the lousy service and the undercooked food, even sitting with his back to the door, where any clown could walk in and put a bullet in his head, just so he wouldn't have to look at the damn thing. A couple more days of this, and he'd probably pay somebody to do it himself. Bang, splat, end of story. Then they could all take off, get on the expressway with all the other idiots heading for Baton Rouge and Houston, just leave him lying there. What the fuck would he care?

"The thing is," he told Danny, "it's just fucking *boring*. They stand there, all day, staring up at that weather map, and nothing ever changes! It's like watching a train coming toward you, no brakes, and your car's stuck on the tracks. But it's way out on the fucking prairie, the whole place as flat as a Chinese crack whore, and the train's only doing, like, three miles an hour, so you sit there for, what? Three *days*? Just watching it come. And the . . . What's he called? The guy drives the train?"

"The engineer," Danny said, expressionless.

"That's right, the engineer. He keeps blowing the whistle—*Woo! Woooo!*—every two seconds, like maybe you just went to sleep there, and if he blows it enough, you're gonna get the message and move your fuckin' car." He reached for one of the fried cheese sticks on the plate in the middle of the table, looked at it for a moment with something like disgust, and then dropped it back onto the plate. "Whole thing's got my stomach upset. Can't enjoy nothing. It's almost worth leaving town just to get away from it, but I'd just be sitting in traffic for two days, end up in some motel in Monroe or Alexandria full of people from New Orleans, all of 'em sitting around watching the Weather Channel. Might as well stay here." He looked at Danny. "How you been, anyway? I heard you're, what? Like a *lawyer* now?" He grinned. "Man, I remember you used to walk around town with a big old briefcase full of cash. Every guy in town thought about takin' you down sometime. Only thing kept you alive was I told my guys, 'Don't fuckin' do it! They'll just send some other guy out, I'll end up having to pay twice.'"

"Sounds like I should be grateful."

"Damn right. You should. Not that I didn't have second thoughts when I heard that you ratted out Jimmy Boudrieux. But we was all sick of him anyway. Time for a change." He leaned forward, shoved the plate toward Danny. "Cheese stick? Grab one. I hear they're good for the heart."

"Thanks. I just ate a little while ago."

Jimmy shrugged. "Never stopped me." He took one, dipped it in some marinara sauce, shoved it into his mouth. "So what's on your mind, anyway?"

"Concrete."

Jimmy's eyes narrowed. "Yeah? What about it?"

"I hear you've been making it."

"Not me." Jimmy grinned. "I had some business associates got into concrete a few years back. I ain't seen them around lately, so I guess it was a solid investment."

"I've got a client who works for a concrete company," Danny said. "Louis Sams. He's an engineer over at IndusCrete."

Jimmy took a moment to lick the marinara sauce off his fingertips. "Sounds like you need to get you some better clients. I gotta say, so far I ain't too impressed."

"I like to think of it as a boutique practice. Small, but lots of personal attention. But see, the thing is, when you got a practice the size of mine, you can't afford to *lose* any clients."

"Yeah, I guess I can see how that could be a problem." Jimmy gave a slight smile. "There some reason you're telling me this?"

"I went to see Gerald Vickers this morning. He's a very nervous man."

Jimmy sighed. "This storm, it's got everybody spooked. Guy like that, he must be pretty worried about his property."

"How about you? You worried about your property?"

Jimmy raised his eyebrows. "Me? Nah, I'm pretty liquid. I'll come out okay."

"You chose a bad partner, Jimmy." Danny smiled. "He's the kind who'll sweat under cross-examination. Little drops running down his face. You know how that looks to a jury? They get embarrassed and they want to look away. But they can't. So they just sit there, watching it. It's like a car wreck. You can't look at anything else."

"See, I got a different vision. I don't see Gerald Vickers up on a witness stand. Ever."

"That part of staying liquid?"

"Damn right. I know when to cut my losses." Jimmy glanced at his watch, then sat back, considering Danny's face. "You got some balls, comin' in here like this. Everybody always said you had more balls than brains, and now I see what they meant."

"I'm just trying to help you out, Jimmy."

"Help *me*?"

"Sure. You're not seeing the whole picture." Danny spread his hands. "I'm just a lawyer. How do I know all this?"

Jimmy looked at him. "Go on."

"You think we're the only ones talking about this?"

"What do you mean?"

Danny looked down at the table, then slowly brought his eyes up to meet Jimmy's. He raised one hand, touched his ear. "You ought to start taking walks, Jimmy. You spend too much time in restaurants. Walking's good for the heart."

Jimmy thought about this for a moment. He looked at the table, then slowly leaned down, peered under it. He had to grab the edge of the table to steady himself, and Danny heard him grunt with the effort. At last, he straightened up. His face looked flushed.

"I hate walking," he said angrily. "You know how hot it is out there this time of year?"

Danny smiled. "It's not the heat, Jimmy. It's the humidity."

Jimmy looked at him for a long moment. Then he shook his head slowly. "You know what I think? I think you're full of shit." He leaned forward, jabbed a finger toward Danny. "You come in here tryin' to put the spooks in me. But I look at you, and you know what I see? I see a guy trying to play two eights like it's a handful of aces. You got nothing. Just some bullshit story you're trying to sell me, like you're doing me a favor. Well, don't fuckin' do me any favors, okay? I know all about favors. I been doing people favors for twenty years, and when I'm all finished doing them favors, I end up owning their business. Nothing's free. I want something from you, I'll let you know. You hear what I'm saying?"

Jimmy's face was bright red, and he was breathing hard now. Danny glanced over at the waitresses, saw they were listening, the TV playing silently behind them. "Yeah, Jimmy. I hear you."

"And don't fuckin' tell me what's good for my heart! Everybody's always tellin' me something's bad for my heart. You know what I say? Fuck that! I eat what I want. I feel like some exercise, I'll go get me a whore. You don't like it, you can go climb on your hamster wheel like all those other fuckin' lawyers I see goin' to their health clubs, and you can spin it until you *die*! Me, I live in New Orleans. I'm gonna sit here and eat some good food, maybe drink me a Dixie beer on the side, and you and all the heart doctors and the TV weathermen and the fucking FBI can kiss my fat ass!"

Danny got up from his chair. "Okay, Jimmy. I get the point."

"Yeah? You get the *point*?" Jimmy reached over, picked up a fork from the table. "I'll fuckin' show you the point!"

He grabbed the table, started to get up, and the expression on his face made Danny take a step back. But then Jimmy froze, a surprised look on his face. He made a sound like a strangled cough and slumped back in his chair. He looked up at Danny with a per-plexed expression. Then he suddenly winced.

"Shit," he gasped. The fork fell from his hand.

"Jimmy?" Danny hung back, keeping his distance. "You okay?"

"I can't fuckin' breathe!" Jimmy gripped the table, threw his head back, his mouth and eyes wide. "I feel like somebody just stabbed me."

"You need a doctor?"

Jimmy glared at him. "Fuck you, okay? I'm fine!"

"You don't look fine."

In fact, Jimmy looked about as far from fine as a man could get. His face was turning bright red, and now he grunted, doubled over in pain, so his forehead was practically resting on the tabletop. Danny looked around. Jimmy's usual bodyguards, the two ex-cops who drove him around town, were nowhere to be seen. All the waitresses were crowded around the television behind the bar, their eyes glued to the storm coverage. On the screen they were showing footage from Florida after Hurricane Andrew, rows of suburban houses reduced to piles of rubble.

"Oh, Christ," Jimmy gasped. "I think I'm fuckin' dying here."

"Hey," Danny called out to the waitresses. "Somebody better call 911. I think Jimmy's having a heart attack."

They all turned to look over, and Danny couldn't help thinking of a herd of deer standing in a forest, staring with wide eyes at the car going past.

"I'm not having a heart attack!" Jimmy tried to straighten up. "Somebody fucking poisoned me!"

For a moment nobody moved. The waitresses just stared. On the television a man was standing in front of the ruins of his home, weeping. And then, suddenly, Jimmy made a sound like the brakes giving out on a semi truck, and he jerked forward against the table, clutching at his chest. The nearest leg of the table snapped under the sudden weight, and the table skidded out from under him, so that Jimmy pitched forward onto the floor like a huge fish flopping onto the deck of a boat. With that, one of the waitresses grabbed for the phone behind the bar, and Danny knelt down beside Jimmy, realizing two things with an equal sense of dread: Jimmy Mancuso wasn't breathing, and this wasn't exactly the situation Mickie had been imagining two years ago, when she made him go down to Charity Hospital, take the free CPR class they offered to the public every Thursday evening under a banner that read LEARN CPR! A LIFE IS WORTH SAVING!

Every life? Danny couldn't help wondering. But there hadn't been any time to debate such questions, and the dummy on which they'd had him practice what they called *the kiss of life* had looked like a nice young guy, who probably had a wife and young kids. So Danny'd kept his mouth shut, practiced what they taught him until he felt like he could do it in his sleep.

Now he bent over Jimmy, got a thick whiff of fried cheese and marinara sauce that almost made him gag, but he made himself put it out of his mind. Jimmy was lying on his stomach, his face turned to one side, eyes closed. Danny couldn't hear any breath coming out of his mouth or nose. He slid his hands under Jimmy's chest, tried to roll him over, but it was like trying to flip a Volkswagen onto its roof.

"I need some help here," he yelled to the waitresses. A couple of them hurried over, and together, with Danny counting off, they managed to roll Jimmy onto his back. Danny tipped Jimmy's head back, opened his mouth and made sure that his airway was clear. He felt for a pulse in the carotid artery, sliding two fingers down from the trachea into the soft flesh at the side of Jimmy's neck, then pressing gently. Nothing. He put both hands on Jimmy's chest, found the hard bone of the sternum, laced his fingers together, locked his elbows straight, and began compressing Jimmy's chest, counting off as they'd taught him, "One, and two, and three, and . . ." When he got to fifteen, he tipped Jimmy's head back, thought, *Well, shit,* then took a deep breath, bent down, and pressed his mouth over Jimmy's, blowing the breath deep into his lungs.

As he straightened up, went back to compressing the chest, he couldn't help thinking, *Jimmy ever finds out you did that, he'll probably have you killed.*

6

"You're shittin' me." Jabril threw his head back, laughing. "You really gave Jimmy Mancuso the kiss of life?"

"Seemed like the right thing to do."

"Right for Jimmy, maybe. You ask anybody else how they feel?"

"What did you want me to do? Stop and take a poll?"

"Wouldn't have been a bad idea." Jabril grinned. "Voice of the people, you know? We see how Jimmy does with the common man. Vote yes, he lives. Vote no, he's in the ground. Like *American Idol*, only with mob guys."

"That's cold-blooded, man."

"You think? We're talkin' about a guy who was getting ready to stick you with a *fork*. Hell, Jimmy, he'd probably cut off a piece and *eat* it. He has a heart attack, I say let him die. Whole city probably be better off."

Danny shrugged. "Well, it's too late now. He's up in the cardiac ICU at Charity. I spent half the night up there, talking to doctors."

"Yeah? You wanted to make sure he got the best treatment, huh? You gonna head back over there today, see how he likes the food?"

"I don't think he's going to find the food to his taste for a long time. They got him on IVs right now, tubes going everywhere. He survives that, they'll have him eating lettuce and cucumbers from here on out."

"Couldn't happen to a nicer guy." Jabril sat back for a moment, hands behind his head, clearly savoring the idea. "Hell, that might actually be better than lettin' him die. You imagine Jimmy eating salads? Low-salt diet? Be like torture for him."

"Anybody ever tell you that you've got a sick sense of humor?"

"Me?" He grinned, shook his head. "I got a healthy sense of perspective. Ask anyone."

A boy came in, glanced at Danny, said, "My mama say we got to go to the Superdome tonight."

Jabril looked over at him. "Your mama's right. That's where they tellin' people to go."

"You don't need me?"

"Nah. You do what your mama say. This ain't no time to be messin' 'round. Everybody got to hang together, right?"

"Or we hang separately," the boy said.

"Damn right. That's what I taught you. Now you get on home, help your mama get ready."

The boy nodded, but Danny could see he wasn't convinced. All over the city, people had that same look. Like they didn't quite believe it, all the warnings, the evacuation order, that look in people's eyes as they packed up everything that would fit into the backseat of their car, got out on the road, where traffic was at a dead stop, everybody waiting in an endless line to get out of the city, growing more anxious and angry with every passing hour, just the way the experts had predicted. But even as they did all this, they kept looking up at the sky, which was as bright and hot as newly blown glass. Secretly, in the backs of their minds, they couldn't help thinking it would all come to nothing, as it always had before. They were out here, suffering in the heat and traffic for nothing. The smart people, everyone couldn't help thinking, were the ones who ignored the warnings and stayed home: they'd wait out the blow in the comfort of their houses, throw a hurricane party to use up all the ice and cold beer before the power went out, then sleep it off in the sweltering heat while they waited for the PG&E trucks to roll through their neighborhoods, getting the electricity back on in time for them to catch the first LSU game, the world going on as it always had. Meanwhile, they sit in an endless line of traffic, crawling along I-10, afraid to run the air-conditioning in case they ran out of gas before they reached Baton Rouge. In the backseat, the kids whine and fight. Beside them, the wife seethes, biting her tongue to keep from saying, "I *told* you we shoulda left yesterday." She's right, of course, no question about it. But if she says it now, so help him God, he'll slap her. So she sits there, keeping her mouth shut tight, wondering why she'd ever married him, Lord knows there'd been other guys, and had she wasted her whole life, like her mother had predicted?

Slowly, the city was emptying out. Danny had felt it from the moment he woke up, a silence settling over the streets as people packed up their cars and headed for the interstate, like people shuffling toward the exits when the movie's over. It was close to ten when he got out of bed. He'd slept later than he'd planned. But then, he'd spent much of the night at the hospital, waiting to see if Jimmy Mancuso made it through those first couple hours after the EMTs had pressed the defibrillator paddles to his chest and shocked his dying heart back into life.

He still couldn't say why he'd followed the ambulance over to Charity Hospital, stuck around as they wheeled Jimmy into the emergency room, and then later up to the cardiac intensive care unit. Maybe it was because nobody else had. Jimmy's father had been killed in a mob hit up in Jefferson Parish in 1987, and his mother had died a couple years later. He had a brother who was doing twenty-five-to-life in a federal supermax prison in Kansas after trying to take out a contract on a federal prosecutor, only to find that the hit man with whom he was bargaining in a motel room on Airline Highway was really an undercover FBI agent, and the backup team in the next room had gotten the whole conversation on video. No wife, no kids, Jimmy ate his meals in restaurants and got himself serviced by whores a couple times a week. He had a couple of corrupt ex-cops who hung out with him most days working as his bodyguards, but they weren't around when his heart stopped. Danny had stood there, watching as they wheeled him out to the ambulance, and he'd realized that there was nobody to care if the man lived or died. The waitresses shook their heads, went back to standing around the television, and the ambulance crew went about their business as if they were moving a large but delicate piece of furniture. It was hard to feel sorry for a guy like Jimmy Mancuso. If there was anybody who deserved to die alone, it was him. He'd done everything he could to make it happen. Still, something had made Danny follow the ambulance crew out into the parking lot as they wheeled him out, watch as they'd struggled to lift him into the back of the ambulance, and then get into his car and follow in the wake of the siren and flaring light as they rushed him to the hospital.

When Mickie called, he was sitting in a waiting area outside the emergency room, three rows of plastic seats, most of them full of people coming down hard off a Saturday night in New Orleans: a young guy dripping blood from a knife wound in his upper arm, a woman pressing ice against a broken nose while her husband paced nervously nearby, a teenage girl with a deep, wracking cough and needle tracks all down one arm. Just the sight of it all made him want to bury his head in his hands. Where did all this suffering come from? Was it simply what rose off the city on a hot summer night, like smoke off the hood of a car when it's been driven too hard and the bearings start to go?

Just then his phone had rung, and when he picked it up, he heard Mickie's voice say,

"Where *are* you?"

"I'm in the emergency room up at Charity—"

"Jesus, Danny! Are you okay?"

"I'm fine. It's not me. Jimmy Mancuso had a heart attack, and I had to do CPR on him until the ambulance came."

There was a long silence. He said, "Hello?"

"You're serious? You saved Jimmy Mancuso's life?"

Danny rubbed at his eyes wearily. "You're going to give me a hard time about this for the rest of our lives, aren't you?"

She laughed. "Damn right I am. This is too delicious. I can't wait to tell the guys over at FBI. I'm sure they'll have lots of other suggestions about people you can help out. You know, you could, like, fly to Karachi, in case Osama bin Laden chokes on his falafel, you'd be right there to give him the Heimlich maneuver."

"You figure Osama eats falafel?"

"I don't really care. But it'd be a pita if he choked on it, huh?"

"Jesus, Mickie. How long you been working on that one?"

"What can I say? It just came to me. So you planning to stay there with Jimmy all night, or should I make you some dinner?"

Danny heard her moving some pans around on the stove, realized that he was very hungry. "I guess there's no reason for me to stay here. I'll come on home."

They'd had dinner, feeling the quiet of the house surrounding them. Danny realized it was the first time they'd been alone together in this house. They'd bought it after Anna was born, and Danny had spent a week getting her room ready before they'd moved in. Their first night in the house, as he and Mickie had started to open a bottle of champagne they'd saved for this occasion, Anna had begun to cry, and they realized she'd come down with a high fever. They'd spent that first night sitting up with her, trying to keep her comfortable while they waited for the antibiotic their pediatrician had prescribed to bring her temperature down. Since that night, they'd gotten used to the idea that life spun wildly around them at a pace they'd never learn to control. It took them a month to get the kitchen unpacked, and there were still boxes stashed under all the beds, which Danny had simply shoved out of the way as they tried to get the house ready for Matia's first visit. He couldn't remember what was in those boxes now, but whatever it was, they'd lived without it for almost two years, so he figured there was no hurry to get them unpacked.

But now they found that they were alone together in a quiet house. Danny opened a bottle of wine, and they drank most of it with dinner. Later, they made love, fell asleep with music playing the way they used to before Anna was born. For a moment it felt like the world was young again, but they both wondered silently when they would ever feel so young again.

When Danny woke up the next morning, Mickie was gone. She'd left a note by the coffeemaker that said:

I'm on duty until after the storm. Call me when you leave town.
DON'T EVEN THINK ABOUT STAYING!
I love you.

Mickie

He made some coffee, turned on the television. Every channel was showing weather maps. The storm had not turned. As of seven A.M., it had reached Category Five intensity. A mandatory evacuation order was in effect for New Orleans. The Superdome would open at noon as a "refuge of last resort."

Danny drank his coffee, ate some yogurt and half a banana that Mickie had left in a piece of plastic wrap on the counter after slicing the other half into her cereal. When he finished, he washed out his bowl and cup, put them next to Mickie's in the dish rack beside the sink. Everything looked so neat and orderly, just as it did every morning. He shut off the television, spent a few minutes emptying the refrigerator of everything that could spoil if the power went out. He dumped all the food into a plastic garbage bag, dragged it out to the heavy plastic garbage cans in the driveway behind the kitchen. Only then did it occur to him that if the hurricane struck, the garbage cans would probably blow away. They'd end up half a mile away, going through somebody's plate-glass window like a cannonball. He stood there looking around for a moment, then got a piece of rope from the trunk of his car, used it to tie the cans to the metal railing on the back steps. He went into the kitchen, got some strapping tape, and used it to tape the lids down. Afterward, he felt kind of silly. What were the chances something like that would hold in a Category Five hurricane? Maximum sustained winds up to 175 miles per hour, the weatherman had said, with gusts over two hundred. At that speed, the wind would strip the roof from every house in the city, blow down wood-frame buildings, pick up the storage shed in his neighbor's backyard and hurl it down the street like a bowling ball, taking down trees and light poles like they were weeds.

He went back into the house, stood there looking around. When they'd bought the house, the thought had struck him that he'd probably spend the rest of his life here. That was how people lived in New Orleans; once you settle down, buy a house, and start to raise kids, you've planted your feet in the mud, and you quickly take root there, so that when your kids are grown, they come home to the same house where they grew up, feeling how strange it is to look around and see that so little has changed. That's how Danny had felt, until his mother finally sold the big house on Octavia Street where he grew up, and from that moment on he'd felt strangely unsettled, drifting around the city with no sense of belonging, as if the first good wind to come along might carry him away.

Now that feeling seemed prophetic. But it turned out the whole city felt that way. He knew people whose roots went deep, their families going back five generations in a single neighborhood, even on a single street. But roots won't hold you when the wind blows this hard. It turned out they weren't rooted at all—not trees, just leaves that could be carried away on the wind.

He locked the door behind him, got into his car, and drove away without looking back. He wanted to get on the road to Baton

Rouge as early as possible. He felt bad about Louis Sams, but he'd done what he could, right? And Mickie was right: it would be crazy to stay, with a storm this deadly. But before he got on the highway, he had one stop to make. He headed over to Paris Avenue, found Jabril on the phone in the back of the muffler shop, while several boys worked to get everything of value off the floor of the shop and onto a stack of wooden shipping flats that they'd stacked up along one wall.

Jabril looked up at Danny as he came in, raised one finger while he listened to something the person on the other end of the line was saying. Danny took a seat in one of the plastic chairs that faced the desk, looked around. The computer was gone from Jabril's desk, and they'd taken down the photos that usually hung on the wall, group shots of the boys who'd worked there over the years climbing all over a smashed-up car with sledgehammers or messing around out in the garage, squirting each other with windshield wiper fluid. One end of the desk was piled with file boxes, and Danny saw that they'd emptied out the bottom two drawers of the metal filing cabinet beside him.

"Nobody askin' you to stay," Jabril said into the phone. "All you got to do is stop by the restaurant for a couple minutes on your way outta town. My buddy's sitting right here. We can head over there, take a quick look at the tape, get you on the road in, like, twenty minutes. You think you could do that for me?"

Danny looked at Jabril, raised his eyebrows, but Jabril waved him off.

"That's great," he said. "I'm grateful. You ever need anything, all you got to do is call me." He glanced at his watch. "How 'bout we meet you there in twenty minutes? Yeah. And hey, say hello to your sister for me, okay? You tell her she don't *even* need a reason to call me. You got that?" He grinned at Danny. "Man, I *know* she's your sister. That's why I'm *tellin'* you. You just give her the message, okay? And we see you in twenty."

He hung up the phone, sat back, grinning. "Man, I got to tell you, I'm *good*. You don't need no cops, this town. You want to find out who done something, all you got to know is who to call."

"What was that all about?"

"You still want to find out what happened to your man Sams?"

Danny stiffened. "Is there a reason we're using the past tense now?"

"Nah, man. It's nothing like that. Turns out I got a kid works out in the garage whose uncle manages that rib joint where they found your man's car. They got security cameras that cover the whole parking lot. Cops told him to pull the tapes when they impounded the car, but I guess they've been too busy with this storm coming to pick them up. They're just sitting over there in the guy's office. He's meeting us there in twenty minutes, so if you want to look at 'em, we should roll."

Danny followed Jabril out to his car, feeling like a leaf that had fallen into a storm drain, slowly circling the pipe that would eventually carry it away. He tried not to look at his watch or think about the traffic he'd have to fight to make it to Baton Rouge before the storm swept in. And secretly, he felt ashamed. He hadn't come to Jabril's to work the case. As he drove over, he'd been thinking out ways to convince him to leave town. *You can't help these people by getting yourself killed,* he'd planned to say. *It's after the storm when they'll need you most. Somebody's going to have to fight the rich guys who want to rebuild the city in their own image. To men like that, a city's just property. Real estate. Somebody's got to be here to remind them it's the people who matter.* He'd had his arguments all worked out in his mind, and if those didn't work, he'd planned to get dirty. *What about the women? How do you think they'd feel, you're not around?*

But there was no way he could make that argument now. He felt like he'd reached out to grab Jabril's hand as the current carried him past, only to find himself pulled neck-deep into the flood. No point in fighting the tide now, just let it carry you and watch for a chance to pull yourself clear.

Bones Bar-B-Que was on South Claiborne near Jackson Avenue. The place was locked up, and the only car in the parking lot was a Cadillac with three small children crowded into the backseat, along with a pile of suitcases that looked like it might topple over on them if the car took a sharp right. The trunk was stuffed full of televisions and stereo gear, so full that they couldn't get it closed, had to wire it down with an old coat hanger that they'd twisted into an elaborate knot. The car's suspension groaned as the driver got out, and for a moment Danny couldn't help thinking of the pictures he'd seen of Dust Bowl refugees waiting at the California state line, gazing out at the world through hopeless eyes.

Jabril pulled up next to the Cadillac, and Danny saw the woman sitting in the passenger seat shoot them an angry look. Like everyone else, she was anxious to get on the road, put some distance between her family and this city, the way you move away from a gambler when the dice come up wrong. From the exhausted look in her husband's eyes as he walked over to them, Danny could see that she'd been making this point the whole way over to the restaurant.

"Damn," Jabril said under his breath. "You see the look on that woman's face? She'd sour the milk."

But he got out, wearing his most charming smile, said loudly, "Man, you my *hero*! You making the game-winnin' play here today, and don't let *nobody* tell you that ain't true!"

His name was Victor Green, and he'd worked his way up from grill cook to restaurant manager by putting in long hours and never complaining. For years, he'd worked nights at the grill, getting up early every morning to take business management classes at Delgado. Now he owned a small house over on Deslonde Street and worked longer hours than ever, going in to the restaurant every morning at eight to meet the delivery trucks and staying until the place closed at midnight. He wore a thick ring of keys on a chain hooked to his belt, and some nights, when one of his cooks didn't show up for his scheduled shift, he still filled in behind the grill, breathing in the smoke and burnt grease as he slapped ribs on the fire, dished up helpings of coleslaw and fried okra. Then, while the waitresses wiped down the tables and the cooks cleaned up the kitchen, he sat down to ring up the night's sales totals, do a quick stock inventory, and check the staff's time cards to make sure nobody had gotten a friend to clock them in for an extra lunch shift. It was a hard life, but he didn't complain. That was his wife's job, and she handled it with gusto.

"You can be quick, right?" he asked Jabril as he unlocked the kitchen door.

"You bet. We just need to take a look at that tape."

Green nodded toward the Dumpster at the rear of the lot. "That's where the car was. I wouldn't have seen it, except one of my cooks forgot to take out the kitchen trash on Friday night. I got here yesterday morning, it was starting to stink, so I hauled it out there, saw the car back there."

Danny glanced up at the security camera mounted on the edge of the roof. "That camera sees back there?"

"No, but we got another one mounted on the back wall," Green told him. "So nobody tries to get up on the roof back there. We had a guy tried to break in by climbing down the vent ducts a couple years back. Got stuck in there, and we didn't hear him until we lit up the grills. Took three fire trucks to get him out of there. He'd been in there almost twelve hours. Broke my heart to tell the guy we don't keep any cash in the place after we close up." He got the door unlocked, held it open for them. "You sure this is legal, right? The cops told me I should hold the tape for them."

"You're still holding it," Jabril told him. "We just havin' a look while you hold it."

"I don't want to lose my job."

Jabril looked at him. "You really think that's your main problem right now? I'd say, you still *have* a job in a couple days, you damn lucky."

Green led them in through the restaurant's kitchen, which still had the faint smell of smoke lingering in the air. There was a small office off one side of the kitchen with a large glass window so the manager could keep an eye on the cooks. Green unlocked the door, turned on the light. "I got it right here," he said, taking a computer disk out of the top drawer of his desk.

Jabril raised his eyebrows. "I thought you said you had a tape."

"Just a habit. Tape's the old way. All our cameras are digital now. You can store more on a computer disk, so the cameras have a longer cycle before they start recording over the old images." Green switched on the computer on his desk. "Used to be a problem. We used to get kids messing with our drive-up speakers. I'd get in on Tuesday morning, find somebody drove through and tossed a paint balloon at our sign. You got a tape, all you can do is hope they slowed down enough so you can see their license plate. With the computer, I can freeze the image, blow up any part of it I want. Get you a nice clean shot of the plate, send it right off to the cops by e-mail."

They waited for the computer to finish loading, then Green slid the disk into a drive, hit a few keys, and the image from one of the security cameras filled the screen. It was the parking lot behind the restaurant, sun shining down on the empty pavement. Green slid the mouse over the on-screen video controls, used it to drag a bar that made the image fast-forward so quickly the screen blurred. "It's about halfway through," he told them. "I should have set a memory code. We could have jumped right to it."

He released the bar near the halfway point, and the image went back to normal speed, showing the same parking lot at night. He slid the mouse back over the video controls and clicked the fast-forward button, and now Danny saw cars enter the screen, passing through the camera's field of vision quickly, like the drivers had decided it might be fun to hit the gas as they swung around the back of the restaurant, laying some rubber down in the parking lot. And then suddenly one of the cars stopped, backed into the small space behind the large garbage Dumpster.

"Here we go." Green slid the mouse over the rewind key, backed the image up, and then let it play at normal speed.

Danny recognized Louis Sams's white Saturn as soon as it entered the frame. All he could see of the driver was his hands at first, resting on the steering wheel as the car entered the frame, stopped, then backed into the space behind the Dumpster at the top right corner of the screen.

"White man," Jabril said. "You can see the light reflecting off his skin."

Green nodded. "He gets out of the car in a second, and you can get a good look at him."

And sure enough, a moment later the car's door opened and a white man got out, walked casually out of the frame like he was going back along the side of the restaurant toward the street. Green rewound it, and Danny leaned forward, watched closely as the man got out of the car and walked away.

"Can you freeze it on him?"

"Sure," Green said. "You want me to blow it up so you can see his face better?"

"Even better."

Green rewound it, then let it play until the man got out of the car. He froze it, advancing the image a frame at a time until he got one he liked. He hit a key and the cursor changed into a magnifying glass, which he used to draw a graphics box around the man's face, then he hit another key, and used a tiny hand to drag the edges of the image out until they filled the screen. The image pixilated for a moment, then came back into focus. The man had red hair, cut short, and he was smiling as he walked away, like he'd just thought of something really funny.

"You want me to print you a copy?"

Danny straightened up, his eyes angry. "Thanks. That would be great."

Jabril looked at his face, and he didn't like what he saw there. "You know this guy?"

"Yeah. Vince Leitch. He's an ex-cop, used to work Sixth District Vice. He works for Jimmy Mancuso now."

"That surprise you?"

"No. Just makes me wish I'd let that fat son of a bitch die."

|||| Jimmy Mancuso lay in a hospital bed on the cardiac ICU ward, tubes running into both arms like they were using him to filter water, running it in one side and out the other. Almost a dozen wires ran out of the neck of his hospital gown, going to an electrocardiograph machine beside the bed, and he had a small oxygen tube taped to his nose. His eyes were open, and he was gazing up blankly at a television mounted on the wall, where a weather map was showing the hurricane closing in on the Louisiana coast.

"You look like somebody forgot to turn out the lights," Danny said, as he pulled up a chair beside the bed. "They got you charged up yet, or you running on battery power?"

Jimmy looked over at him, as if just moving his eyes down from the television took a huge effort of will. "Fuck you," he whispered hoarsely. His voice sounded like somebody had ripped out his larynx and replaced it with scouring pads.

Danny smiled. "That's the spirit. Same old Jimmy. Don't let a heart attack stop you, right?"

Jimmy took several deep breaths, tried to speak, but nothing came out. He swallowed painfully, and on his second try he managed to whisper, "Where am I?"

"You're in the hospital, Jimmy. You had a heart attack."

"*Which* hospital?"

"Charity."

Jimmy's eyes closed for a moment, but then he rallied, gathered his breath, and whispered, "Touro."

"What?"

He closed his eyes, summoned up his strength again, whispered, "Not Charity. *Touro.*"

"Sorry, but it's Charity," Danny told him. "We didn't have a chance to ask your preference. This was the closest emergency room. You're lucky you're even alive. They had to put a tube in your artery, do an emergency angioplasty on you." He leaned forward, smoothed the sheet out next to Jimmy's hand. "You want to be someplace nicer while you recover, you can get them to move you in a couple days."

Jimmy's eyes drifted away. Danny saw that he was watching the television again. The sound was off, but they were showing a clip Danny had seen that morning, the FEMA director in Memphis or Baton Rouge assuring a reporter that all appropriate preparations were being made to help those in the storm's path.

"Listen, Jimmy. I got a question for you."

Jimmy's eyes came back to Danny's face. "I saw it," he whispered.

Danny had been about to go on, but something in Jimmy's face made him pause. "What did you see?"

Jimmy swallowed. "Light," he said hoarsely. "Bright light."

Danny stared at him. "What light?"

"Tunnel. Light." He closed his eyes. "Lots of voices, calling my name."

"You mean like you were dead?"

Jimmy nodded. "I saw my mother."

Danny had seen a photograph of Jimmy Mancuso's mother once in the *Times-Picayune*. She was an enormously fat woman in a black dress, standing beside her husband's graveside two days after the mob hit that claimed his life. She looked angry, like she was impatient with the slow pace of the funeral service, was thinking about picking up the coffin and tossing it in there herself. Not exactly the kind of mother you'd want to find waiting for you on the other side of death's dark river, but maybe Jimmy had more pleasant memories of her. Danny tried to think of something appropriate to say, but Jimmy was lying there with his eyes closed as if he were trying to re-create the experience, and Danny suddenly didn't want to interrupt him.

"Beautiful," Jimmy whispered. "Like floating. In sunlight." He opened his eyes. "All my sins, washed away. Clean. Like a baby."

Danny found the image of Jimmy floating like a baby in sunlight slightly revolting. Had this whale of a man ever been a baby, cradled by his mother as she washed him in a warm bathtub? Was it possible that even a man like him, who took pleasure only in greasy fried food and his own acts of violence, could be washed clean at the moment of death? He found it strangely disturbing to think of death as nothing more than a spiritual laundry, where even a man like Jimmy Mancuso could find peace. He'd read somewhere that in a recent poll three-quarters of Americans expressed the belief that they would go to heaven when they died, but only fourteen percent believed that their neighbors would. *Wishful thinking,* Danny had thought. *Nobody thinks they're going to hell. But they wouldn't mind sending other people there.* We all think that we're innocent, even if our dreams are violent. But can you still be washed clean of your sins if an innocent man like Louis Sams is suffering at your hands?

"Jimmy, I know your boys grabbed Louis Sams," Danny said. "We've got a security camera picture of Vince dumping the car. You can still get out of this clean, but I need to know where he is. We don't have much time."

Jimmy had closed his eyes, and now Danny heard his breathing grow shallow. He glanced over at the heart monitor in alarm, but the waves rolled steadily across the screen. He'd fallen asleep.

Danny sat back, frustrated. *Now what?* He looked over at the bedside table. A small plastic tray contained the personal belongings that Jimmy'd had on his person when they brought him into the emergency room: a gold Rolex, a tiny gold cross on a chain that he'd worn around his fat neck, a thick wallet, an empty gold money clip, and a cell phone. Danny looked at the money clip, wondering how much cash Jimmy had been carrying when they brought him in. It only took a couple seconds while all the doctors were busy stablizing the patient for the contents of a money clip to disappear. But mob guys didn't use credit cards; they liked to carry a thick roll of hundred-dollar bills, so they could pull it out at restaurants, impress everybody with the size of their wad. Some hospital orderly or nurse's aide had probably hit the jackpot last night. Whoever it was had left everything but the cash—not cleaning the guy out, just taking a little tip for saving the guy's life. Still, Jimmy'd raise hell about it when he got back on his feet. Probably get his boys to find out everybody who worked in the emergency room that night, go around doing a Joe Pesci on them until he found the person who'd lifted his cash or got it all back. Doctors too. Grab that rubber stethoscope they all wear around their necks, wind it a little tighter until they coughed up the cash. Just his way of letting the world know he was back on his feet and feeling good, ready to go back to work.

Danny stood up to leave. Jabril was out in the corridor, talking up the nurses on duty, getting that little smile on his face whenever one of them said something, like he'd just been thinking the same exact thing. Danny had never seen it fail. They could be driving through the backwoods, and Jabril would stop to ask some woman directions, before you knew it he'd have her smiling, taking out a pen to scribble her phone number onto his palm. *Ten minutes*, Danny had told him on the way up in the elevator. That's all he figured he'd need either to get the information out of Jimmy or arrive at the certainty that it wouldn't be possible. It was a long shot, he knew, but he had to try. At least he could tell himself that he'd tried, and now there wasn't much more he could do except get in his car and head for Baton Rouge with the rest of the crowds pouring onto I-10. By morning it would all be ancient history.

He turned to go. Jimmy's cell phone rang. He had it set to vibrate, so for a moment Danny looked blankly around the room, trying to identify the humming sound, like a drill biting into wood. It came and went twice before he got it figured out, two short bursts, and then he saw the tiny phone skittering across the plastic tray that held Jimmy's possessions. He stood there looking at it, and the phone promptly fell silent. Whoever had called him was talking to voice mail now. Did a guy like Jimmy even use voice mail? In the movies, mob guys drive around town using pay phones so the FBI can't tap into their lines, get the whole operation on tape in a week. Wouldn't a cell phone be even easier to intercept? But everybody walked around using them now. You want people to know you're an important businessman, you have to stride along crowded sidewalks shouting buy orders at your broker. Jimmy probably couldn't resist. Danny'd seen drug dealers talking on cell phones over by the projects. They'd take the call, then hang up quickly, walk over to the pay phone on the corner to call back. What they didn't realize was that the narco cops had the pay phone wired up. It turned out that was a whole lot easier than trying to get a line on all the cell phones used by the kids who hung out on that corner. But maybe that was how Jimmy used it: just a message service, so people could reach him, then he'd call them back from a more secure line.

Danny reached over, picked up the phone. He hesitated for a second, then flipped it open. Jimmy had let the power run down. If he didn't charge it soon, he'd wake up during the night to hear it beeping at him, then it would shut down. The screen told him there was a new message, and gave the phone number. He hit a couple keys, brought up Jimmy's speed dial. The first name on the list was *Vince*. It was the same number as the message that had just come through.

Danny looked down at Jimmy, his face empty of its usual expressions of anger or guile as he slept. *He's seen the light*, Danny thought. *He's got nothing more to fear.*

He hit the enter key, and the phone started to dial the number. Danny raised it to his ear, listened as it rang twice, then connected.

|||| Vince hung up the phone just as Lenny came back from the men's room, shaking his hands the way he did to dry them, because he didn't like using the towels. "Got his voice mail."

"You leave a message?"

"Fuck, no. I just told him the disk isn't where the guy said."

"That's a message."

"It's not a message. It's an *update*. A message is, like, all the details."

Lenny shrugged. "He said don't leave messages."

"So why's he got the damn voice mail? He wants to know who called, you got to leave your name, right? That's a message."

Lenny didn't reply. He looked around at the engineer's office, trying to imagine what it would be like to spend your life working in a glass box. Just the idea of it made Lenny's throat tighten up, like a movie he'd seen on TV when he was a kid, where a guy was underwater fighting with an octopus, and every time he cut off one of its arms with his knife, another one wound itself around his throat. For years he'd had nightmares about that, until the day he joined the police force and found out how it really felt. Everybody looking over your shoulder, Internal Affairs guys hanging around all the time, trying to catch you using the wrong fork when you eat.

That was the thing about working for Jimmy Mancuso: everything was nice and clean. You had a problem, you solved it. You never came away feeling like the octopus had you by the throat.

Not that there wasn't still bullshit to deal with. Like this deal with the disk. They'd searched the guy's desk, found a whole pile of disks next to his computer, but none hidden away in the drawer. Vince grabbed all the disks just in case, but it was clear to Lenny that they were blanks the guy used to back up his work. There was a box of disks with labels for all the jobs the guy was working on, so they grabbed those too. Now it looked like they were going to have to search the place more completely, or else go back and beat on the guy some more until he told them what they wanted to know. Both, maybe. Vince could stay and search, while he went back to the warehouse. That way, when the guy tried to come up with another lie, Lenny could just get on the phone and check it out.

Lenny was just about to say this when the cell phone in Vince's hand rang. Vince looked down at the number on the screen, said, "Okay, it's Jimmy." Giving him a look as he said it, like, *See? I left a message, and now he's calling us back.*

He hit the button to answer the call, said, "Damn, Jimmy. Where the hell you been? I been trying to call you all day."

"Is this Vince?"

There was a long pause. Lenny saw Vince take the phone away from his ear, look down at the screen again, like he wasn't sure he'd read it right. Then he frowned, raised the phone back to his ear. "Yeah, this is Vince. Who the fuck is this?"

He couldn't bring himself to look at Lenny as he said it. The whole thing was like some joke they'd set up just to prove him wrong. Okay, so he'd left a message on Jimmy's phone. How was he supposed to know somebody else had it? What did Jimmy do, just leave it lying around?

"Jimmy wanted me to call you," the guy on the phone said. "He's up in Charity Hospital. He had a heart attack."

"No shit? He okay?"

"He's been better. They had to shock him. He's in the cardiac ICU now, and it looks like they've got him hooked up to every machine in the place."

"Jesus. Can he talk?"

"Not a whole lot. He wanted me to call you and say you should let the guy go."

Vince paused. "Who the fuck is this?"

|||| "Danny? Where are you?"

The anxiety in Mickie's voice made Danny wince. "I'm still in the city. Something's come up."

There was a long silence. He waited, the phone pressed to his ear, picturing the expression on her face—eyes narrowed, lips tight with anger or disapproval. He only caught a glimpse of that face on rare occasions, mostly when she got a call from her office with bad news about a case she'd been working. He thought of it as something she put on every morning along with her semiautomatic pistol and Kevlar vest. She was sitting at her desk now in the ATF field office up at the east end of Veterans Boulevard, looking out the window with that same expression on her face, like she could pick him out of that vast sprawl of city, make him look up at her with the force of her disapproving gaze, so that he'd turn his car around and head out of the city before the storm of her anger broke around him.

"You seem to think I'll be happier as a widow," she said finally. "Or is it that you think Anna will be better off growing up without a father?"

"Mickie . . ."

"At least tell me you've got someplace to take shelter during the storm."

"I'm working on it."

She sighed. "Danny, we got about twelve hours before this thing hits. It's time for you to stop messing around like it's business as usual and get serious about your own safety. There's a mandatory evacuation order in effect. They don't do that just to see who's listening. You have to leave."

Danny glanced over at Jabril. "Mickie feels we're not taking our safety seriously."

Jabril raised his eyebrows. Without a word, he reached back, pulled his seat belt around his chest, and fastened it.

They were waiting at a red light on Claiborne, getting ready to make a left onto Poydras. There was almost no traffic on the street, but around them crowds of people were streaming along the sidewalks toward the Superdome, carrying blankets, coolers, and sleeping bags. For a moment it struck Danny that it could have been a game day, the Saints getting ready to kick off their season. But the people heading toward the stadium didn't look like they could afford Saints tickets. They were poor, and black, trailing small children or wheeling elderly relatives in wheelchairs. They shuffled through the dense heat with empty faces.

The light changed, and Jabril edged through the crowd crossing the intersection onto Poydras, headed downtown. "My people," he said bitterly. "Storm's about to wipe out the city, and this is what we got to offer them."

Within a few blocks, the crowds had vanished and Poydras Street looked like it had been swept clean of all life. Danny had driven through downtown at four A.M., back when he worked for Jimmy Boudrieux, and he'd seen more traffic at that hour. He couldn't help thinking of those horror movies you see on TV where some guy wakes up in an empty city, discovers he's the last man alive, except for the army of zombies stumbling through the darkness, hungry for his flesh.

"Just a couple more hours," Danny told Mickie. "I can't just abandon this guy."

"You keep saying that, but I don't see you leaving town."

Jabril looked over at him. "She knows we're not the only ones sticking around, right? There's lots of people planning to ride it out up in my neighborhood."

Danny nodded. "Listen, Mickie. You should know that the mandatory evacuation's a joke. There's lots of people who can't leave town before the storm hits. We get it bad, they're all going to need help."

"You heard that, or you know it for a fact?"

"Jabril's sitting right here, and he says there's still people over in his neighborhood."

"Do the local cops know that?"

Danny looked over at Jabril. "Local cops know about all those people staying?"

Jabril shrugged. "They'd have to be blind not to. There's people up in all the stores, buyin' flashlights and water. I don't think they goin' camping." He shook his head. "Some of those people, they'd leave if they could. Somebody'd thought to send some buses into those neighborhoods, they could get more of those people out."

"Sounds like a mess," Danny told Mickie. "They didn't send in any buses to help people evacuate."

"Jesus. And they've been working on this evacuation plan how long?"

"Just forty years. Since Betsy flooded the city. That's how long they've had to get it right."

Mickie was silent for a moment. "FEMA did a study last year, and they figured a hundred thousand people would still be in the city after a mandatory evacuation order. Everybody without a car, basically. They estimated as many as sixty thousand dead if the city floods."

"So where *are* they?" Danny shook his head angrily. "They should have had school buses on every corner, picking up people who needed to evacuate. There must be thousands of school buses just in Orleans Parish. Now it's too late." Danny looked out at a homeless guy wandering along the street, pushing all his stuff in a shopping cart. "You know where you'll be tonight?"

"Right here. Most of our staff's evacuated to Baton Rouge. They're setting up a temporary command post up there. But the Special Response Team is staying in the office to keep it secured. Everybody's worried about the case files, so I guess we'll be here until it's over. After that, we've got orders to assist local law enforcement."

"You feel safe there?"

"We've got a safe area in an inner hallway, away from all the windows, and we're up five floors, so I'm not worried about flooding." Mickie paused. "Danny, it's you I'm worried about. You really have to get out of here. You don't leave soon, you'll be on the road when the storm hits."

"Soon as I talk to a couple of Jimmy Mancuso's muscle boys."

"You think that's safe?"

"I've got Jabril with me. When we're done, I'm out of here."

"Take Jabril with you, okay? Don't let him try to stay."

Danny looked over at Jabril. "Mickie says I should make you come with me when I take off for Baton Rouge."

"She just don't want you to know we gonna meet up, soon as you gone." Jabril glanced over at Harrah's. "You believe the casino's still open? Got to be some hard-core gamblers, they still in there playin' the slots."

"I gotta go," Danny told Mickie.

"Okay. Stay safe, all right?"

"You too. I'll try to call you again before we take off." He hung up, slipped the phone into his pocket. "The guy said Spanish Plaza, by the fountain. You can drop me off right up here at the light."

Jabril pulled over to the curb, looked over at him. "How you want to play it?"

"Straight up. I talk to the guy, see if I can get him to cut Sams lose."

"And if he won't?"

"That's why I want you to hang back. He walks away, you can follow him, see where he goes." Danny had slipped Jimmy's cell phone into his pocket before he left the hospital, and now it went off, vibrating urgently against his thigh. "He's trying Jimmy again."

"Tell him to call Charity." Jabril smiled. "He can send a get-well card."

The buzzing against Danny's thigh abruptly stopped. "Damn. I was just starting to enjoy that." He opened the door, got out. "I'll call you if he takes off. Looks like the tourist lots are closed, so he's probably parked on the street somewhere."

Jabril nodded. "He comes this way, I'll pick him up." Then he leaned over, looked up at Danny. "Stay loose, okay?"

"Not much else I can do at this point."

Danny walked back past the World Trade Center, crossed the streetcar tracks, and headed toward the fountain in Spanish Plaza. Most days the place was full of tourists taking pictures in front of the fountain, but now it was empty. A man stood looking out across the river, his hands in his pockets. He had red hair and wore a bright yellow sports shirt, like he'd just come from the golf course, where he'd spent the morning knocking balls into the long grass with a bunch of dentists.

"Where's your partner?"

Vince turned, looked at Danny. "I know you. You used to make the rounds for Jimmy Boudrieux."

"That was a long time ago."

"I heard you hung him out for the Feds. That true?"

Danny shrugged. "You hear all kinds of things, this town. I heard you got thrown off the force for shackin' up with hookers on the job. That true?"

Vince grinned. "Shit, you got me there. I always figured it came with the job. Nobody told me they changed the rules."

"Way I heard it, they cut you slack until you developed a taste for boys."

The grin vanished from his face. "Where'd you hear that?"

"Like I said, you hear all kinds of things." Danny leaned against the metal railing, looked out across the river. "Ship traffic's really cleared out. Don't you wonder where they go, there's a storm like this coming up through the Gulf? You see the satellite pictures of this thing? Fills up the whole Gulf, from here to Yucatán. You're a freighter, there's no place to hide."

Vince was looking at him warily. Then suddenly his face relaxed and he grinned. "Damn, you almost had me there for a minute. Got all up in my face, now you're talking about some stupid shit like we're best friends. Me and my partner, we used to do the good cop, bad cop routine. I just never seen one guy try to play both roles."

Danny raised both hands. "Okay, you got me. So what do you say we save us both time and just talk straight?"

Vince laughed. "I'll bet you couldn't talk straight if you tried. You're a lawyer, huh?"

"That's right. And you're holding one of my clients."

Vince's eyes widened. "That what you think? You got the wrong guy, man."

Danny took the security camera printout from his back pocket, unfolded it, and handed it to him. "Cops won't think so. Anything happens to him, they'll come looking for you."

Vince looked at the photograph. "I guess you got lots of copies of this, huh?"

"All I need."

He nodded, folded up the photograph, handed it back to Danny. "So you figured you'd just call me up and sell me some line about how Jimmy's in the hospital and he wants me to cut the guy loose."

"Jimmy is in the hospital. You can go pay him a visit. But all that means is that you have to start thinking for yourself. The way I see it, I'm giving you a chance to walk away clean."

Vince turned, looked out across the river. "You're right about the ships. Whenever I come out here, the whole river's full of ships. Now it's like they all just disappeared. Where'd they go?"

"Upriver, I guess. They probably headed for Baton Rouge, or Natchez. Someplace where the wind won't be so strong." Danny looked at him. "You turn my guy loose, you could go find out. That's where everybody else is going. Better than trying to babysit a hostage during a hurricane."

Vince shrugged. "I do what I'm paid to do until Jimmy tells me to do something else."

"Jimmy's in the hospital. He's not in any shape to tell you much of anything at the moment. Anyway, you really want to be stuck here during the storm? Looks to me like it's time to cut your losses and get out while you can."

"Storms pass," Vince said. "But guys like Jimmy, they never forget. And that's trouble I don't need."

Danny looked down at the photograph in his hand. "I'll have to go to the cops."

"That's not much of a threat. If you thought they could do something, you'd have gone to them first." He looked up at the sky, heavy clouds starting to roll in from the south. "I got a feeling the cops are going to be busy with other things for a while."

And just then, before he could summon up a reply, Danny heard a sound like whispering behind him, and then a gust of wind snatched the photograph from his hand, sent it flying out across the water.

Vince laughed. "Looks like it's not your day."

|||| "No luck, huh?"

Danny shook his head. "You see him come out this way?"

"*This* way?" Jabril leaned forward, looked out along the street. "Ain't nobody come out this way except you."

"Damn it!"

Jabril looked at him, surprised. "What happened, man?"

"I let him walk away. He headed up along the Riverwalk, like he was going toward Jackson Square. I hung back so he wouldn't see that I was following him, and I was just getting ready to call you when he cut back around the aquarium, like he was coming back this way. I lost sight of him for maybe a minute, but by the time I got there, he was gone."

"Sounds like he made you following him." Jabril reached down, started up the car. "There ain't many people around, and he had to leave his car somewhere." He pulled out, headed up past the ferry landing, made a left on Canal, then circled back to cruise along past the casino, both of them watching for a guy with red hair. Dust whirled through the streets, trash blowing along the sidewalk.

Neither of them spoke. On their third loop, Jabril kept going down past the Convention Center, where they saw another large crowd of people lining up to get in, some of them carrying mattresses piled high with personal possessions.

"My head feels like it's caught in a vise," Danny said.

"Pressure's dropping." Jabril leaned forward, looked up at the darkening sky. "Looks like we might be in for it."

"I blew it. I had a shot, and I blew it."

Jabril shook his head. "You never had a shot. Not with these guys. That ain't how they work. Only reason they do anything is because Jimmy Mancuso tells them to do it. And it sounds like he's got other things on his mind."

"So they're going to hold on to Sams during a *hurricane*? That doesn't make any sense."

Jabril looked over at him. "You want the truth? They'll probably just shoot him and dump his body. This storm goes down the way it looks, they'll be bodies all over town. By the time the cops find him, you won't even be able to tell he was shot." He glanced over at the crowds lining up at the Convention Center. "Just another dead nigger."

"You're saying there's nothing we can do about it?"

"Storm's blowing in, Danny. We've run out of time. I'm gonna drop you back at your car, and you're gonna take off for Baton Rouge. Go play with your daughter, watch it all happen on CNN."

Danny said nothing for a long moment. Then he shook his head. "I can't do that."

"You don't get a choice. Anyway, you won't do nobody no good staying here. You'll just be another victim they got to rescue."

They drove back to Paris Avenue in silence. The sky darkened, and the first rain started to come down in sudden, wind-blown bursts, splattering the windshield of Jabril's car as if somebody had tossed buckets of water at them as they went past. By the time they turned onto Paris Avenue, the streets were empty and the traffic lights were blowing around.

"I should have made you leave a couple hours ago," Jabril said. "You're gonna have a nasty drive."

Danny said nothing. He was trying to think of what he'd say to Demitra to explain why he'd left Sams to his fate when the storm hit. Jabril looked over at him and, as if reading his thoughts, said, "You did everything you could, man. Don't go blaming yourself for this."

"It's not like I get a choice. If Louis dies, I'm the one who's gonna have to live with that."

"Look around, man. Lots a people are gonna die tonight. Only question now is, are you gonna be one of them?" Jabril looked out at the rain hitting the streets. "Time to stop messing around, Danny. This is gonna be bad for real, and you got a kid to think about. You can worry about the guilt later."

"You got a bunch of kids. How come you're staying?"

"I told you, these are my people. Nobody else is watching out for them."

"And you think you can?"

"Don't matter what I think." Jabril turned into the parking lot of the muffler shop. "Only thing that matters is what I *do*."

He brought the car to a stop, looked around. "Wasn't your car parked right over there?"

Danny leaned forward, looked out at the parking lot. "Yeah, it was. I left it right in front of the door."

"Well, *shit*." Jabril's face was angry. "Some people got no respect."

Danny sat back. "People are scared. I guess someone was looking for a way out of town."

"So they stole a car off *my* lot? They better be scared, that's all I can say." Jabril pointed to a security camera mounted on the roof of the garage. "I got video cameras too. And I won't be giving the film to no cops. I'll see about this one *myself*. And it better not be one of *my* boys, I'll tell you that."

He sat back, looked at Danny. "So I guess you stayin' now."

"I guess so."

Jabril looked out at the rain, falling in sheets now on the empty streets. "Then we better get where we goin', 'cause it's on its way."

"You think we should go to the Dome?"

Jabril gave him a weary look. "I guess that depends. How much you trust your government? You think they got this shit figured out, or you think it's gonna be bush league, like everything else these guys touch?"

"Okay, I see your point."

"I got a rule: stay away from any place where the guy who runs it doesn't have to spend the night there. You think we ride over to the Dome, we'll see any of the people who made these emergency plans?"

Danny smiled. "Might be hard to go on TV and tell everybody

what a great job you're doing if you actually have to sleep there. So you got someplace else in mind?"

"People count on you, you got to be ready." Jabril put the car in gear, swung around, and made a left on Paris Avenue, heading back downtown. "At least that's how it works where I come from."

7

In the darkness, women were singing. Quietly at first, so Danny could barely make it out over the sound of the wind, then louder as the howling grew stronger and they started to hear windows shattering all along one wall. They'd lost power sometime during the night, and now the faces around him were lit only by the dull glow of a battery-powered storm light that someone had hung on a hook in the middle of the room. Two floors above them, Danny could hear the roof groan and flex as the wind tore at it, but the building was old and heavy as a stone that had lain in the same place for a thousand years while the world shifted and changed around it. The metal sign on the front of the warehouse—ST. CLAUDE SHIPPING AND STORAGE—had sheared off during the first hour, and they'd heard it crash to the ground, then skid away down the street as the wind snatched at it.

"Shit," Jabril said quietly. "You know what I paid for that sign?"

But now the women were singing, hymns they'd sung every Sunday in churches where the choir swayed and clapped and cried out to Jesus as the faith poured through them. They sang them slow and quiet now, almost under their breath, as if they knew that Jesus had plenty to attend to at the present moment, but they wanted him to know they were there, hanging on, waiting for the sky to clear.

There were almost two hundred people crowded into the open piece of floor Jabril's boys had cleared on the third floor of the warehouse on St. Claude. By the time Jabril and Danny pulled up, most of the space was full and there was a small crowd waiting outside, mostly people from the neighborhood who'd heard that Jabril Saunders had opened up his warehouse to people who needed shelter from the storm. Jabril took a look at the crowd and set his boys back to work clearing more space.

"We should be okay on food and water," he told Danny, "but toilets could be a serious problem if we gotta stay here a couple days."

They'd stolen some portable toilets from a construction site by the railroad tracks up on North Galvez, used a truck to haul them back to the warehouse, where they'd emptied them into a storm drain and hosed them out with bleach. They'd set them up next to the stairs on the second floor, with a battery-powered storm lamp hanging from a beam for when the power went out.

"The city floods, those things will be floating around out there anyway," Jabril told Danny. "You imagine? You're on the roof of your house, waiting to be rescued, and you see a toilet float past? Might make you think about what's going to be in that water, those levees give way."

Before night fell, they'd moved the trucks out of the fenced-in parking area, lined them up in the shelter of an old grain warehouse next to the river, where the ground was high enough that Jabril figured they'd be safe from flooding. They parked their cars there too, and then walked back through the pelting rain to the warehouse, climbed the three flights of stairs, and waited for the storm to arrive.

"You see those bricked-up windows?" Jabril pointed to a row of squares where someone had closed up some openings along the lowest floor of the warehouse's façade. "That's where the flooding came up to during Betsy. Just under seven feet. Everything above that should be okay, but we're putting everybody up on the third floor, just to be safe."

"What about all the stuff in the storage units on the first floor?"

"That's why I'm paying flood insurance. People come back, find their stuff is ruined, they fill out a form and the insurance company cuts them a check."

At the time it had sounded reasonable enough. But now, with the wind howling around them, windows shattering, and the roof beams groaning like the unsanctified dead, Danny could only hope those women knew what they were singing about. "It's Gonna Rain," they sang, and "Wade in the Water." Their faces shone in the strange light of the storm lamps, swaying slowly, eyes closed. A couple of the boys had earphones in, lost in their own private music, but after a while the batteries started dying and they slipped the tiny plugs out of their ears, sat there listening to the women singing away the storm.

To his surprise, Danny realized he wasn't the only white person in the room. A small group of British tourists had wandered the wrong way out of the French Quarter after their hotel had turned them out, looking for shelter at the Convention Center. They'd stopped to ask directions, and Jabril took one look at them dragging their luggage, soaked from the pelting rain, and waved them inside. They sat against one wall, looking self-conscious and scared, until a couple of the women brought them over some water bottles and boxes of dry cereal. After that they seemed to relax, and Danny saw one of the local women listening as they all talked at once, gesturing back toward the French Quarter, like they'd all just been waiting for a chance to tell the story of how they'd ended up here, an adventure none of them had envisioned when they booked their vacations with travel agents back in Bristol and Guildford.

Welcome to New Orleans, Danny thought. When you check in, the tourist hotels hand you a map of the French Quarter, and the desk clerk takes out a red pen, draws a circle from Jackson Square out to Burgundy, saying, "I wouldn't go beyond here. It's not safe." And every year some tourist gets mugged on Rampart Street near Louis Armstrong Park, ends up in the hospital. *Be sure to carry a map of the area to avoid wandering off of the beaten path,* the guide-books say, *and use extra care at night to stay where people are. If a block seems a little too quiet, turn back onto one of the main streets of Bourbon, Royal, Chartres or Decatur.* But tourists don't pay much attention to the local news, so one Sunday morning they wake up late, nursing a hangover, wander out to find the streets deserted and all the bars locked up, with storm shutters pulled down over the windows and heavy iron grates drawn across the doors. Most of the big hotels remained open, and their guests would drag mat-tresses into the hallways and ride out the storm there. But the small hotels were old buildings built around open courtyards, and their staff had evacuated or were crowding into the Superdome with the rest of the city's working poor. What could those places do but shut their doors and point their guests toward the public shelters, where they would spend the night getting to know the *other* New Orleans, the one beyond the crude circle drawn on their maps?

At least they'll have a story when they get home, Danny thought. Looking around the room, he wondered how many of these people would still have a home when the storm had passed. He'd been through hurricanes before, but he'd never heard a wind this vio-lent. It had the sound of endings, roofs sheared off, trees splintered, water rising. One boy sitting near Danny had a radio, and during the first few hours he kept calling out news reports: "Power's out in Grand Isle." "It's down to Category Four. And it's turning east a little, heading for Mississippi." (Cheers.) "Lotsa flooding in Plaquemines and St. Bernard." (Silence.) "Jackson Barracks is underwater, and the pumping stations are losing power." (Groans.)

And then, abruptly, the power went out. The radio station he'd been listening to went off the air. He spun slowly through the dial, but all he got was static. It sounded like the wind howling outside. He shut the radio off.

That's when the women began to sing. Danny looked at his watch. Just after midnight. The eye of the storm wasn't even supposed to pass over until around eight A.M. How could something so violent last so long? The hours crept past. The wind grew louder. For a while Danny slept, until a loud crash awoke him, a piece of flying debris smashing into the building somewhere below them. Around him people sat with their eyes open, gazing at nothing. There was nothing to say, and their eyes looked empty of thought or feeling. For some reason, Danny remembered the old movies they used to show on television Saturday afternoons—a submarine full of men waiting silently, listening as a destroyer searches for them with its sonar, the faint ping, growing louder, then fading, the hours passing slowly, and then, suddenly, panic, the crash of the depth charges around them, water bursting from pipes, men fighting for their lives. But it was that look in their eyes as they sat there, waiting for the destroyer to find them, that Danny felt he suddenly understood. Fear makes men hollow; it empties all the feeling out of you, leaves you staring blankly at nothing as the hours pass, until at last what you fear becomes real, rushing in at you with all the sudden terror of the sea bursting through the walls and crushing the life out of everyone.

After a while Danny couldn't take it anymore. He got up, picked his way among the groups of people sitting on the concrete floor, and went out into the outer corridor. The windows on this floor were still holding so far, and there was a strange glow in the darkness that Danny couldn't make out, until he realized that one of Jabril's boys had strung up a bunch of glow sticks, like you get at Mardi Gras, so people could find their way to the toilets downstairs.

The wind rattled the glass in its frame. Beyond, the night was so dark that Danny felt as if he'd fallen into a well, but he could sense the wind's presence just beyond the glass, like a tangle of snakes, hissing and spitting in their rage. Then it struck him that this was a stupid thing to be doing, standing near a window in the middle of a hurricane. Wind that strong could tear a splinter off a roof tile and turn it into a bullet. The window was no protection. It was only a matter of time before it shattered, burying glass shards in the wall behind him.

He went back into the storeroom, closed the door behind him. Nearby a woman was working her fingers over a set of rosary beads. Her lips moved silently, her eyes staring off into the darkness. Mickie had a necklace of polished wood beads that Anna found fascinating. She'd climb up on her mother's lap and carefully touch each bead with her forefinger, as if counting them. It made Mickie nervous; she was always afraid that Anna would be unable to resist the urge to grab the necklace and pull, scattering beads everywhere.

"Maybe I shouldn't wear it," she fretted to Danny every time she put the necklace on. "You know how easy it would be for a child to choke on one of these beads?"

"So don't wear it."

Danny didn't much care for the necklace anyway. It was a gift from an old boyfriend back in Phoenix, and she had several necklaces Danny had given her that she didn't wear as often.

"It goes with my outfits," she insisted, fingering the beads. "It's nice, but not too dressy."

But secretly Danny suspected she liked to play with the beads as much as Anna. He'd caught her fingering them as she worked at her computer, the way other women twirled their hair. He'd always enjoyed watching Helen while she studied for law school exams at the kitchen table. She'd twirl her long hair into elaborate braids while she read, then quickly unbraid it with an expert flick of her finger. He'd always found it oddly arousing, which was probably one reason she'd always scored a few points higher than him on every exam.

Somewhere a chunk of metal crashed against the brick wall of the building, making everyone jump. Danny shook his head, startled out of this silk web of memory. *Just as well*, he thought, finding an empty spot along one wall. *That's a train of thought you don't want to ride to the end.*

But it was hard to resist. All around him he could see people swimming in the deep water of memory. They sat staring off at nothing, their thoughts turned inward on that vast landscape that spreads out behind our eyes. Were they thinking about their homes? Children they'd raised in those small shotgun houses? The way people used to come out on summer evenings and sit on their front steps, calling to each other across the street as the light slowly faded from the sky? The streets they'd grown up on in the Ninth Ward or New Orleans East were more than just neighborhoods; they were the closest thing to villages you'll find in America. Some families had lived there for seven generations, going back to the first freed slaves to wander out of the cotton fields and find their way downriver to work along the wharves and in the cotton warehouses east of the French Quarter. The land those freed slaves built on was swamp, and their children grew up with mud between their toes. But there was enough land there for them to put down roots, and when the city finally got around to paving those streets, you could almost forget the broad stream that used to run down the middle of St. Claude whenever it rained hard, or the way a house that had been there thirty years could suddenly start sinking as the ground turned to soft mud beneath it. Try hard enough, and you could forget that for years. But now, suddenly, Danny could see those memories come pouring back into their eyes as they listened to that wind howling in off the Gulf.

Hours passed. The women sang. Sometime before dawn, Danny slept. He woke up to find the wind still howling, but now a faint band of gray light, the color of an old bruise, was visible under the door that led out to the corridor. He got up and found his way down to the portable toilets on the floor below. When he came back, Jabril was waiting for him, sitting against the wall with his head leaned back and his eyes closed. For a moment Danny thought he was asleep, but then his eyes opened, considered Danny with their thoughtful gaze.

"You got some sleep, huh?"

Danny shrugged, sat down beside him. "Not much else to do till it's over."

"My people been sayin' that for a long time." Jabril stretched his shoulders, working the stiffness out of his neck. "So I was talkin' to this guy over there, says he knew Jimmy's boys when they worked vice over in the Sixth District."

"Yeah?"

Jabril nodded. "He says they used to have a place they took people, they wanted to talk to them privately. Off the record. Some kind of warehouse out east of the Quarter. Cops don't use it anymore, but they all know about it. Anybody gets out of line, they find an egg carton taped to their locker, like a warning."

Danny looked at him. "Why an egg carton?"

"They put egg cartons on all the walls so nobody can hear you scream."

"Seriously?"

"That's what the man said."

"He know where this place is?"

"No, but the cops do. You get assigned to the division, they drive you past, show you where it's at."

"As a warning?"

Jabril shrugged. "Or else they figure on usin' it again. Times change, but people don't."

"You think that might be where they've got Louis?"

"Could be worth a look." Jabril got up, rubbed at his back with one hand. He raised his eyes up to the ceiling, listening. "Sounds like the wind's gotten stronger, last hour. Must be right over us by now."

"You think we're gonna make it?"

He shrugged. "Last report I heard, the eye was going east of us. Means the wind'll be coming south across the lake now. If we haven't lost the levees yet, that's when it'll happen. All that lake water's gonna get pushed back up into the canals, like a drain backing up." He looked down at Danny. "If it ain't the wind, it's the water. That's what my daddy used to say."

"Sounds like a philosophy."

"He spent his whole life in New Orleans. I guess he'd know."

Jabril wandered off into the darkness, picking his way among the bodies crowded onto every inch of the concrete floor. Danny sat there, trying to picture the wind lifting the lake out of its bed, hurling it against the city's levees. He'd been out at the lakefront when a wind came up, and he'd seen waves come crashing across Lakeshore Drive out by the yacht club. And that had been just a sudden, brisk wind, the kind that makes the flags snap out in front of the seafood restaurants and the girls turn their backs, laughing, as the spray off the water soaks their faces. What would a hurricane do?

He'd never thought much about the drainage canals before now. You barely noticed them as you drove around the city, until you found yourself on a dead-end street in some residential neighborhood, facing a levee. You had to backtrack, find your way back to a major street, cross the canal on a bridge that gave you a brief glimpse of water before dropping you back in among the houses. *Minimum Payment City*, Danny'd always called that part of town. He'd worked collection agency cases all through those neighborhoods, as the credit agencies went after the boat, the bike, the rented bedroom suite when the monthly checks stopped arriving in the mail. He knew the guys who lived in those houses. They'd gone to high school together, played ball on the same dusty fields across the city. After graduation, they got jobs installing car stereos or working oil rigs out in the Gulf. He'd run into some of them around town while he was at Tulane, riding around with high school girls in their Camaros, shaking their heads when they learned Danny was still in school. *Man, you know how much I'm making on the rigs?* By the time he finished law school, most of them were married, had a couple kids already, and the bills were piling up. You could see them hanging on, doing their best to live the life they felt promised, but if you looked in their eyes, you could see them quietly drowning.

Now Danny thought about those rows of tiny houses up along the canals and wondered if they'd listened to the storm warnings, gotten out in time. *Leave it*, they'd been told. *Leave it all behind.* Leave the house, where the dog paces behind a chain-link fence from the motorcycle under its weathered tarp to the boat on its trailer next to the driveway. Leave the rented bedroom suite, leave the big-screen TV and stereo gear; leave the credit card bills and collection notices, the kids' report cards and the wedding album, the home videos and the Disney Channel and the porn bought in the back room of the Waterbed Warehouse up on Veterans Boulevard. Leave the Saints jersey and the fishing gear, the collection of seashells the kids picked up on the beach at Sanibel Island, the prom dress and the water pipe (but not the stash); leave the stack of frozen microwave dinners in the freezer, but pour out the milk, so it won't go bad. Leave the bags of chips and three cases of beer you'd bought for the start of football season, when you'd invite the couple down the street and their kids to come over on Sunday afternoon to watch the game on TV. Leave the electric guitar you never learned how to play, and the stack of cassette tapes and concert T-shirts in your closet from the days when your only dreams were rock 'n' roll. Take the kids' birth certificates and the marriage license and your union card, but leave the title to your car and your home insurance papers by mistake, something else to worry about during the long drive north into Mississippi. Leave it all, your whole life. Looking back, you'd thought it would add up to more.

Mickie's office was right in among those neighborhoods, on Veterans close to the Seventeenth Street canal. Danny closed his eyes. What was she thinking at this moment, listening to the wind howling around the glass bank tower where ATF had its offices? They were on the fifth floor, above any possible flooding, but he couldn't help worrying. The wind would be battering the building, smashing windows, making it sway slightly like the mast on a ship. The agents would be crowded into inner hallways or the file room in the center of the building, away from the windows, waiting out the storm with empty eyes, just like everybody else. When it was over, they'd emerge to find that the wind had whipped through the broken windows to toss paper around the offices so deep that they had to wade through it like snow. And then what? When they looked out the broken windows, what would they see? Streets strewn with debris and fallen trees, or a lake spreading out from their building in all directions, the whole city drowning? He'd called Mickie one last time just before the storm came ashore, and he could still feel the heat of her anger on his face.

"You're *where*?"

"In Jabril's trucking warehouse on St. Claude. He's got it set up as a storm shelter. There's a couple hundred people here. They needed a safe place to ride out the storm."

"So you decided to stay? Even after you promised me I wouldn't have to worry about you?"

He winced. "I couldn't help it, Mickie. My car got stolen."

"Your car got *stolen*?" She gave an exasperated sigh. "There's hardly anybody left in the city. How the hell did your car get stolen?"

"I parked it at Jabril's muffler shop while we were up at the hospital. Somebody must have needed a way out of town."

"Well, at least the car thieves have some sense." She was silent for a moment. "You're safe, though?"

"It's a solid building, and we're up three floors, so I'm not too worried about flooding. We've got plenty of food and water, so we should be fine for a couple days."

"If it's a couple days, then we're all in deep trouble."

Just at that moment he lost the connection. He tried calling her back a few times, but he couldn't get a signal. Either the cell phone towers had blown down or his service provider had lost power. He closed the phone, shoved it into his pocket. Days later, he'd find it there, the battery dead, like a souvenir from a more innocent time. Mickie's office had a battery-powered satellite phone that they'd used when they were staking out some backwoods compound in the red-clay woods up in north Louisiana, where some minister of the Church of Aryan Identity preached God and guns beneath a cross made from the barrels of two .50-caliber machine guns. Sometimes they'd have to stay up there for a week, watching the pickup trucks come and go from the compound through their telescopic sights, waiting until their surveillance turned up enough evidence of illegal gun dealing to justify a search warrant. Danny would get phone calls with a strange hollow sound, Mickie's voice sounding like she was talking through a metal tube, but it was better than nothing. Silence made him crazy. He'd hated it ever since he was a kid, sitting on the stairs of the big house on Octavia Street where he'd grown up, watching his father's wake break up shortly after his mother ran upstairs in tears, the last mourners filing out in awkward silence. The house, which had always echoed with laughter and politics, suddenly seemed like a letter that'd been torn and let fall slowly to the ground. He'd sat there listening. Somewhere upstairs, his mother was crying. Water ran in the kitchen where a maid was washing dishes. And way off in the distance, a car idled on the side of a country road, a man sitting behind the wheel smelling the scent of the Mississippi in the warm night air, before a single gunshot draped the whole world in silence.

Stop it, Danny thought angrily. *What's happening outside is bad enough. You won't help anything by torturing yourself.*

That's what Mickie would have told him, if his phone had worked. Or the women who'd spent the night singing while the storm swirled around them. He'd been through hurricanes before; they had to blow over, and there was nothing anyone could do but sit there listening to its roar, angry and dark as the thoughts that haunted him, until the rain finally died and the sun came out, showing you a city that looked as if it had been beaten flat with a hammer. You pick up a broom, start sweeping up the broken glass. For a few days you live as they did a hundred years ago, without electric lights or air-conditioning or television news, but it all slowly comes back, and within a few weeks you find that life has returned to normal. People sit on their porches drinking beer and talking into the night, the way they have for generations. Music plays from somebody's window, and tourists line up outside the bar at the corner where they serve the best fried oysters in town.

But in all those years spent sitting in darkness while the storm howled outside, Danny had never heard a wind wail this loud or last this long. What would they find when they finally emerged into the surprising quiet of a hot summer day? Would there be anyone left to sweep up the glass and sit on their porches, drinking beer while they waited for the power to come back on?

A boy sitting a few feet from Danny got up, went out to the stairs. A moment later he was back.

"There's water comin' in down there," he yelled out from the doorway, his voice cutting through the shriek of the wind.

Danny saw people all around him raise their heads, look up at the boy wearily. He expected to see fear in their eyes, but they didn't seem surprised. Jabril got up, came over. "Show me."

Danny got to his feet, followed them out to the stairs and then down to the second floor. From there, in the dull glow of the emergency lamp hanging next to the toilets, they could look down the loading ramp into the darkness of the first floor, where something was moving not far below. Jabril reached up and lifted the storm lamp off its hook, held it over the ramp. Water caught the light.

"Damn," said the boy. "You see how high it is? Couple more feet, it'll be at the toilets."

"It must have come up pretty fast," Danny said. "I was just down here a little while ago, and I didn't see anything."

"Levee must have gone." Jabril raised the lamp, looked around on the floor near them, but it seemed to be dry. "Must be flooding all through the Ninth Ward."

A crowd of people had followed them, and now they stood along the stairs leading up to the third floor, looking down in silence at the black water rising on the floor below. Jabril looked up at them, said, "Everybody stay where you at, and we be fine. Just some water, that's all."

Danny saw something floating in the water. A sneaker, upside down, its laces trailing behind it like something it was trying hard to forget.

"If water's come up this high," one man said, "then all our houses is flooded."

"That's why you here, right?" Jabril hung the lamp back on its hook, looked up at them. "This about what we figured would happen. We got no choice now but to live it. Gonna need each other more than ever now, 'cause ain't nobody else gonna be there lookin' out for you."

"That's a fact," a woman said bitterly. "Won't even see us, unless we go floatin' by on a big pile of money."

Danny saw them all look at him. He suddenly felt uncomfortable. Without thinking, he leaned down, fished the sneaker out of the water, tossed it onto an empty patch of floor. It left a trail of water behind it, lay there on its side with a puddle spreading out around it. They all looked at it for a moment, and then slowly the people gathered on the stairs turned, went back upstairs.

"You really think that's true?" Danny looked at Jabril. "They'll just let people drown?"

"Wouldn't be surprised. They ain't shown no sign they care up till now." He shook his head. "Local people, they'll be there. Probably out there already, riskin' their lives to save folks trapped in their houses. But I wouldn't put much hope on nobody else. Camera's rollin', they might come get you. Got to have somebody for the president to hug, he comes down here."

They went back upstairs. Two of the windows had shattered, and the wind-whipped rain was soaking the floor along the outer hallway. There was enough light outside now for them to see that the street below was flooded up to the eaves of the smaller buildings at the end of the block.

"I hope nobody tried to ride it out in their houses," Danny yelled over the wind. "They'd have no place to go now."

"You know some folks did," Jabril shouted back. "Sit there with a shotgun, afraid somebody might break in and steal their stuff."

They stood there for a moment, looking down at the whitecaps rolling along St. Claude Avenue. But the rain stung when it hit your skin, quickly soaking through your shirt, and Danny didn't like the way one of the remaining windows was rattling in its frame, like it was getting ready to explode, throwing shards of glass across the hall. They slipped back into the large central storeroom full of silent people contemplating the end of the only world they'd ever known, and then had to shove the door hard against the wind to get it closed.

|||| Louis Sams could hear the egg cartons crackling. It was a strange sound, like somebody walking over pebbles. It woke him out of a deep sleep, and only then did he realize that the cement

floor around him was wet. He thought for a moment that he'd pissed himself, and a feeling of profound humiliation settled in his chest. Was this what they'd reduced him to? He opened his eyes, but the room was pitch-dark. He couldn't see a thing. He reached out with one hand, felt that the floor all around was covered in a thin puddle of water.

They've got a new trick, he thought wearily. *Something new to show you.*

He closed his eyes again, let his head rest against his arms. They'd shoved a hose under the door, probably, and now they'd keep it running all night so he couldn't sleep, had to lie there and get soaked, shivering on the cold cement floor. But then he noticed that the water had a funny smell, like the sewage ditch that ran behind the plant out at IndusCrete. And why wasn't it running across the floor and draining out through the grate under the chair? They'd installed that drain so they could hose the room out when they were finished using it, keep the smell of blood and fear and stale piss to a manageable level the next time they had to spend some time in here. But the water wasn't draining. Instead, it was rising, almost half an inch already.

Slowly, he got up onto his hands and knees. His muscles felt like they'd been boiled away, leaving only the stringing tendons hanging on the bone. The water was up to his wrists already, and rising quickly. He crept along the floor, wincing as his knees pressed against the concrete. Every few seconds he swung one hand about blindly in the darkness, until one of his fingers collided painfully with the chair. He cursed, shaking the pain out of his hand. But now he knew which way he was facing, and he turned toward the chair, got his hands on it, and felt around underneath it until his fingers found the drain. He pressed his hand against it, palm down, but there was no suction. In fact, he felt water pushing against his hand. He realized it was flowing up through the drain into the room.

What the hell was going on? He felt a sudden panic seize him.

The water was up to his elbows already. He grasped the chair, used it to pull himself up to his feet.

"Hello?"

His voice sounded weak. He cleared his throat, took a deep breath, and tried again.

"Hello? Anybody there?"

The effort made him dizzy. He had to lean over the chair, resting his head on his hands for a moment. There was no answer. Had he really expected one? When they weren't working him over, they ignored him. Why would that change now?

But were they really flooding his cell? His mind flashed on a movie he'd watched on TV late one night, a serial killer who took pleasure in drowning his victims in a glass box, filming it to watch later. At the time, it had struck him as a ridiculous way to kill someone. How much water would it take? Like filling a swimming pool. And the pressure of that much water filling up a box would shatter the glass. *They should have talked to an engineer,* he'd thought as he shut the TV off, got up to go upstairs to bed. He wasn't thinking straight. The water was up over his knees already. Nobody could pump that much water into a room unless you had high-velocity pumps rigged up, the kind they used over at the aquarium that looked like a pair of jet engines, and made almost as much noise. The water had a bad smell, and it was coming up through the drains. In New Orleans, that could mean only one thing.

Back when he was a kid, it rained so much one August that the emergency pumps broke down and all the drains in his parents' house started to back up. But even then it was only enough to make the toilets overflow and cover the bottom of the bathtub with a foul black sludge, so that even after they got the storm drains cleared out and the water went down, his mama had to scrub at it with bleach before she'd let anyone use the shower. Another time a barge had broken loose and crashed through a levee on the Intracoastal Waterway, and they'd had water in the streets up to his waist for two days. But even then it came up slowly. Nothing like this, with the water rising almost an inch a minute, soaking his pants pockets now, and still rising.

How much water would it take to flood the city this deep so fast? Something would have had to punch huge holes in the levees, so that the whole lake was draining off into the low-lying neighborhoods. Somewhere inside him, he felt something begin to work its way to the surface. He didn't recognize it at first, and then he tried to fight it down, but it rose within him with a force that couldn't be resisted, almost choking him when it reached his throat.

"I told you so," he whispered, his throat raw. "Don't say I never warned you."

But there was no pleasure in it. And soon he felt the water reach his chest, and he let go of the chair, feeling it lift him gently in that endless darkness, up toward the ceiling where he knew that he'd drift for a moment in a last pocket of air before the water filled the room completely, left his body bumping against the egg cartons they'd glued to the ceiling until the waters slowly receded and he became just one more piece of debris left behind by the flood.

‖‖ "This is bullshit."

"Shut up, okay? I'm listening."

Lenny stood at the head of the metal stairs that climbed up through the warehouse, his head turned slightly to one side, looking down into the dark water below. For a while they'd heard the guy calling out for help, but it was quiet now. Vince sat on an overturned plastic bucket, clicking his flashlight on and off impatiently. "You really think he's still alive down there? The whole place is full of water."

Lenny said nothing. For almost twelve hours he'd barely said a word while the storm came barreling in, shaking the ancient building, shattering windows and blowing shit around on the top floors, where the windows had been smashed long ago. Vince had spent the whole time running his mouth, worrying about his car, his house, even—no lie—the fucking *banana* tree that he had growing in his backyard. He'd come back from meeting the guy on the phone with a worried look in his eyes, spent most of the night—as the winds started to rise around them—telling Lenny all the ways they were screwed.

"The guy's a *lawyer*. He's got me on film, getting out of the car."

"So you borrowed it." Lenny nodded toward the storage room. "Give me another hour with this guy, he'll say you were doing him a favor, taking it out to get it washed."

"He'll say that now, but what will he say when he gets out of there?" Vince shook his head. "Jimmy's off the board, man I called over to Charity, and the lawyer wasn't lying. They got him up in the cardiac ICU. Sounds pretty bad. So what if he dies? Where's that leave us?"

"You saying we should just cut the guy loose?"

"I'm saying we got to start lookin' out for ourselves in this thing."

Lenny rubbed at his forehead, feeling the muscles there start to tighten up like they used to whenever he caught a whiff of Internal Affairs guys starting to nose around. "So we don't get the disk?"

"I don't know, man. That disk could be all we got to cut a deal, the Feds come after us."

Lenny looked at him sharply. "Cut a deal on who? *Jimmy?* You remember what happens to people who try to cut a deal on him? Last guy got his balls spiked to a chair with an ice pick."

"It was his hand, and he got it spiked to a table. Anyway, Jimmy's on life support. You really think he's our biggest worry at this point?"

"You want to take that chance?"

Vince shook his head. "See, you can afford to think that way. They don't have your picture getting out of the guy's car. I'm the one who's gonna take the fall if something happens to this guy. But we get hold of that disk, we don't have to say a word about Jimmy. It's the construction guy, Vickers, who's been paying everybody off. They want us to cut a deal, that's who we give 'em."

"Okay, so we'll get the disk."

But just as Lenny said this, they heard a sound like metal siding shearing off a building and crashing to the ground.

"Jesus!" Vince went over to the door, looked out at the storm howling outside, rain blowing sideways. "This shit's gonna be murder on my banana tree."

Then the lights went out. Lenny ran out to his car, dug some flashlights out of the trunk, came back soaked to the skin. They stood just inside the warehouse's loading dock, watching the storm, as if hypnotized by its violence. All kinds of stuff blew by in the street—stop signs, pieces of billboards, a phone book that tumbled along the pavement like an octopus making its way along the sea floor.

"Some fucking storm," Vince said.

Lenny shrugged. "I seen worse."

Then the water started to rise, the street filling up so fast it surprised them. When it reached the loading dock and started pouring into the warehouse, they retreated up to the second floor.

"What about the guy?" Vince pointed his flashlight down at the water rising steadily in the darkness below "We can't just let him drown."

"Fine," Lenny told him, just to shut him up. "Go get him."

But when Vince started down the stairs to the first floor, he found water already halfway up the stairs, swirling around down there. Then he heard a strange, high-pitched squealing sound that sent a chill through him. He shone his flashlight around, saw rats swimming in the black water, and quickly retreated back up the stairs.

"Fuck that," he said. "There's a whole rat *navy* down there."

A pair of eyes glittered on the steps below them, looking up at them. Lenny drew his gun, pointed it at the shining eyes, and fired. The shot echoed through the empty warehouse, and the eyes disappeared. But the water kept rising, and soon they could hear the rats scurrying around on the stairs only a few feet below them. Lenny fired again, and something let out a shriek of pain.

"They want to get up here," he said. "I can't keep shooting them."

Another rat appeared at the top of the stairs. Lenny kicked at it, but it evaded him, ran off to hide somewhere.

Vince looked around. There were some old broken shipping pallets on the floor. He went over, kicked at one of them. A rat leapt out from under it. "Son of a bitch!" Vince jumped back, watched the rat scurry away into the darkness. "They're fuckin' everywhere." He gave the pallet a nudge with his foot, watching apprehensively a moment to see if something else appeared, then reached down, pulled at one of the planks. The wood was rotten, and he was able to break it off by stomping on the frame where the rusted nails held it together.

"Here, use this." He tossed the plank toward Lenny. "They try to climb up here, you hit 'em with that." He bent, started pulling at another plank.

Lenny looked at the board, then pointed his flashlight down at the steps. Dozens of eyes glittered up at him now. "I don't know, man. There's a lot of rats down there."

Vince broke off another plank, hefted it like a baseball bat. "C'mon, man. Didn't you ever play that Whac-A-Mole game? They stick their heads up, you whack 'em." He came over, stood on the opposite side of the steps. "Got to pass the time somehow."

Over the next hour the water rose to within a few feet of the top of the steps. Every few minutes the rats would make a rush at the opening in the floor, squealing as they poured out of the darkness into the small patch of light cast by Lenny's flashlight. They'd both curse and start swinging wildly, while the rats would dart this way and that, trying to escape into the darkness beyond. They'd get a few, but more would escape. And soon Vince began to catch himself glancing behind, as if the rats might be forming up back there in the darkness to attack, pissed off at losing so many of their friends. *They're just rats,* he kept telling himself. *They'll go hide in the darkness, find someplace to wait out the storm.*

"You know what the difference is between us and rats?" he said to Lenny during one of the pauses in the action.

Lenny looked up at him wearily. The floor at his feet was smeared with blood, and the water below was full of the bodies of dead rats, where he and Vince had swept them off the floor when they'd driven back the latest assault. He took a pack of cigarettes out of his pocket, shook one loose, stuck it in his mouth.

"You mean besides the fact that we're the ones smashing them with boards?" He flicked his lighter, his face going pale in the re-flected flame.

"We're organized. Rats, they don't work together. They all come running up here, trying to get out of the water, and when we start smashing them, it's every rat for himself. You don't think they could take us, they got their act together?"

Lenny took a second getting his cigarette lit, then snapped the lighter closed, slipped it into his pocket. "What, like jump us and take our guns?"

"They start biting you on the ankle, tell me you wouldn't drop that board and run." Vince grinned, then started hopping around, eyes wide with terror. "You'd learn to tap-dance right quick."

"Yeah? Well, I seen you do some dancing already." Lenny blew smoke into the air between them, and it hung there. "Looked like one of 'em was trying to crawl up inside your pants."

Vince gave a shudder. "Man, don't even say that shit."

"I ain't the one brought it up."

"Yeah, well, we better hope they never get organized, that's all I'm saying." Vince looked down at the water between them. "Man, that's some nasty-looking water. Looks like it's got chemicals floating in it."

Lenny looked down. "The rats are gone."

"What the fuck are you talkin' about?"

"You see any rats down there?"

Vince crouched down, pointed his flashlight into the darkness. The stairs were empty. The only rats he could see were the dead ones floating in the water. "Where the fuck did they go?"

"Maybe they got a better offer."

"Fine with me." Vince straightened up, tossed his plank aside, and wiped his hands on his pants. "You think it's like a ship? They take off when it's getting ready to sink?"

"You blame 'em?"

"Hell, no. This shit's over, I'm gone."

"What about your guy?" Lenny nodded toward the stairs. "You were ready to go get him a few minutes ago. Now you're just gonna leave him there?"

"You kidding? He's fucking dead. Look how high the water is down there! The rats are probably eating him right now. They got sick of us beating on 'em and smelled some fresh meat."

They both stood there for a moment, listening. But the only thing they could hear was the roar of the wind and the soft lapping of the water against the steps below them.

"He's dead," Vince repeated. "What we should do, this thing's over, is drag him out of there and leave him someplace. Storm like this, the cops aren't gonna be looking at any fucking videotape. They're gonna be finding bodies all over the place. What's one more?"

"Rats are back," Lenny said, pointing down at the water.

Vince looked down, saw dozens of eyes glittering at him. "Shit."

He bent over, picked up his board. "But you watch, they still ain't organized."

|||| In the afternoon, the wind finally began to die down. Jabril and Danny went up on the roof, stood there in the pelting rain silently looking out across the flooded city toward downtown. The glass office towers in the Central Business District looked like somebody had given them a good shaking; most of the windows were gone, so Danny couldn't help thinking about a kid he'd known in high school who got so drunk at a party that he tripped over a planter, knocked out two of his front teeth on the sidewalk, then stood up grinning, like he'd just pulled off a terrific stunt.

"Damn. You see the Superdome?" Jabril pointed, and Danny saw that large sheets of the building's roof had been peeled away, leaving the metal frame exposed. "Lot of people in there last night."

"You think the roof fell on them?"

Jabril shook his head. "Can't tell from here. Looks like the skin just peeled away."

Off to the east, they could see people standing on their rooftops, surrounded by a vast lake of black water. A Coast Guard helicopter flew over, and a man came along St. Claude in a boat. He waved at them, called something up to them, but they couldn't make out his words. A few blocks to the west, the water seemed to be shallower, and they could see people wading through it up to their chests.

Danny looked over at Jabril. "You got a plan to get all these people out of here?"

"We've got a couple inflatable rafts on the second floor. Trick'll be getting them out of the building." He leaned over the edge of the roof, looked down at the water below. "We'll have to use a second-floor window, I guess. But there'll still be a drop. Have to rig up a ladder, probably." He straightened up, looked out across the city. "Not clear where we'd take 'em, even if we can get out. We've got food and water. Might be better just to stay here, see if the water goes down."

"You've got more people down there than you figured on. You think there's enough for everybody?"

Jabril hesitated. "For a couple days, if we go easy on it. We're not out of here by then, I guess I'll have to send some of my boys out to look for more."

Off in the distance, they heard a sound like gunshots. Danny looked over at Jabril. "That what I think it was?"

Jabril nodded, his face somber. "That's what'll kill us. People start looting and shooting, we're fucked. They'll just back off, say it's a city full of no-good niggers, and leave us here to die."

"Doesn't look like they've done much so far."

Jabril nodded. "Yeah, so far it's about what they didn't do. Didn't build up the levees, like they promised. Cut the funding for it, what? Two years ago? Didn't have an evacuation plan that got the people out. Didn't do much, except go on the TV and tell everybody how bad it was gonna be." He waved a hand at the flooded streets below them. "It ain't easy to be ready for something like this. Especially with a city like New Orleans, where everybody's been rollin' the dice for thirty years. I'll give 'em that. But now we find out what they about. We know they good at makin' enemies. Let's see how they treat the people countin' on them."

Danny was silent for a moment, looking out across the city. "I don't think you should wait to start getting people out of here," he said at last. "Something like this, it's not like we can go home and start cleaning up. They're going to have to evacuate the city until they get it drained and then start over." He felt something hard take shape in his throat. "None of us are going to see our homes for a long time."

"I guess you right." Jabril shook his head sadly. "It's gonna be a long road for these people. Some of them have never left New Orleans their whole lives."

"Well, their lives have changed."

"No lie." He turned back toward the stairs. "I guess we better take a boat and go find out where to bring these people."

"You don't need me, right?"

Jabril turned, looked back at him. "You goin' someplace?"

"I've still got to find Louis Sams," Danny told him. "If you can get me to the Sixth District, I want to see if anybody can tell me where they might be holding him."

Jabril shrugged. "Suit yourself," he said. "But I doubt they're gonna be in much of a mood to talk. Looks to me like they got other things on their minds."

As he turned away, Danny heard a popping sound in the distance. A moment later, from much closer, came laughter, and then the sound of breaking glass.

|||| "What street is this? I think my grandma's house is up here."

The boy kneeling in the front of the boat looked back, annoyed. "How should I know what street this is? You see any street signs?"

The boy behind him rested his paddle on the side of the rubber boat. "They at the corners, man."

"I *know* they at the corners. But they also under the water. What you expect me to do, read the sign while we goin' over it?"

Jabril looked over at Danny. "I hope you ain't in no hurry."

"I'm all right."

They were drifting in a slow current among the ruins of houses and neighborhood stores. Danny and Jabril sat in the back of the boat, using their paddles to steer, while the two boys up front kept an eye open for submerged trees, streetlights, chunks of wood that the storm had ripped off people's roofs, anything that could catch on the bottom of the boat and rip it open. The rain was still falling, lightly at times, at other times in blinding sheets, and every few minutes a wind would kick up and blow them against the roof of a submerged house. They could see columns of smoke rising from burning buildings off in the distance, and the wind blew it toward them, so that when the sun finally started to break through the heavy clouds, it made the day look strange, like a fog that had settled across everything and was now lit from within by its own dense light.

"C'mon, man," the first boy said, "I thought you said you grew up around here."

"I did grow up around here. But it ain't never looked like this. I wasn't lookin' at nobody's *roof.*"

That's what they could see, just sloping roofs surrounded by a flat expanse of water, with the top branches of a tree sticking out here and there.

For the first hour they made it no farther than three blocks from the warehouse. They'd launched the boat from one of the second-story windows, climbing down a rope net slung out the window to get into it. But as soon as they set out, heading west toward the city center, they heard distant cries for help, saw that people were stuck on their roofs over in the Ninth Ward.

"Turn it around," Jabril told the boys. "We'll go get those people first."

They made six trips, but with each one, they got farther into the neighborhoods and found more people who'd climbed out onto their roofs as the water rose, some of them coming up through the attic, punching holes to get out when the water trapped them there. One man had carried an ax into his attic, started using it on the plywood sloping above him when he felt the water reach his ankles.

"Jesus," Danny said, as they helped him into the boat. "How many you think didn't get out?"

"Probably a lot," Jabril said. "They get in these houses, they'll find a whole bunch of dead people up in their attics. Fingernail marks on the wood, where they tried to claw through."

One by one, they ferried the people they rescued back to the warehouse. Pretty soon they started to see other boats doing the same thing. And then the Coast Guard helicopter showed up, lifting people off their roofs in rescue buckets while the water swirled wildly in the downdraft of the blades. Danny shielded his eyes, watched as the helicopter pulled away, a young woman dangling from a long safety line below it like a doll while the crew winched her up.

"Where you think they're taking those people?"

"Airport, maybe?" Jabril pushed off from the roof, used his paddle to fend off some branches floating in the water. "Whole city can't be underwater."

"Sure looks like it." Danny dug in with his oar, as the two boys up front got them turned around, headed back toward the warehouse. He could feel a blister coming up on his left hand, where he was pulling hard on his paddle. "They were saying on the radio last night that Jackson Barracks was flooded even before the worst of the winds hit us. That's where the National Guard outfits keep all their gear. Means they won't be much help in any rescue work."

Jabril raised his eyebrows. "Nobody figured out they might get flooded? You look around, you can see that place ain't on high ground. So how come they didn't move their equipment out before the storm hit?"

"I guess nobody thought of it."

He shook his head. "Pretty bad, you got to go rescue the National Guard."

"Yeah, I guess they're in over their heads."

Jabril shot him a look. "That woulda been funnier, it wasn't so true."

Somewhere near Andry Street, they came across a body floating facedown in the water. He wore an undershirt and striped pajama bottoms, like he'd just gotten out of bed, was on his way to the bathroom sleepily when the flood came rushing in. Now he drifted lazily in the middle of an intersection, arms outflung. They all looked at him, but nobody said anything as they went past.

Jabril looked up at the sky. "Starting to get dark out here. We better get back."

Surprised, Danny looked at his watch. It was after eight. They'd been out here paddling around for six hours, and they could still see people sitting on their roofs, waiting for somebody to come get them. In the last couple hours they'd started seeing police out working the same streets in fishing boats, searchlights mounted on the front. They might be able to keep up a rescue operation after dark, but anybody without a light would run himself up on a submerged tree or a street sign in the first five minutes.

"You think you could do me a favor," Danny asked, "while we still got some light?"

"What's that?"

"Can you get me to some dry ground? I'll get across town to the Sixth District from there."

Jabril looked at him. "Man, you can't walk around this city by yourself in the dark. People take one look at you, they see a white guy who needs somebody to go upside his head with a baseball bat."

One of the boys in the front of the boat laughed. "He's right, man. That's what I'd see, for sure."

"Anyway, you get *any* sleep last night?"

Danny shrugged. "Couple hours, maybe. But I can't just leave Sams out there without trying."

"Nobody sayin' you should," Jabril said. "But you ain't gonna be no use to him tonight. Come on back with us, get you some sleep, we'll get you where you need to go in the morning."

Danny looked up at the darkening sky and realized he was very tired. But he shook his head. "Can't do it, man. This is something I got to do."

Jabril raised his eyebrows. "You talkin' like you got a choice. Way I see it, this is my boat." He grinned. "Least I'm the guy who stole it.

So it goes where I say, and I say it's goin' where you can get something to eat and a night's sleep before you go runnin' off across the city. Tomorrow we're gonna start taking all our people out of here, and we'll take you out in the first boat. That suit you?"

Danny thought about sleep, and he couldn't help feeling grateful to Jabril. "Yeah, I guess that makes sense."

"Damn right it makes sense." Jabril nodded to the boys, and they started turning the boat around, getting it headed back toward the warehouse. "Anyway, tell me you won't miss hearing all them women singin' again."

"Might save my soul."

"Hey, somebody got to do it."

IIII "Phones must be down."

Gerald Vickers's wife looked at him with something like pity. "Well, of *course* the phones are down. It was a hurricane."

They were staying in an executive suite in the Four Seasons in Houston, the room costing him almost four hundred dollars a night, even with the AAA discount, but that was where her friends were staying, so what could he say? She had one of the cable news networks on the television, and so far it didn't look too bad. One of the reporters on the scene had said something about flooding in the Ninth Ward, but what the hell did they expect? You build on a damn swamp, you might get some flooding, right? But so far it sounded from the news reports like the rest of the city had come through okay. He had an inspector on the pad over at the Corps of Engineers, a couple more at the Orleans Levee Board, but when he tried to call them, all he got was a busy signal. So he stood there, arms folded, watching the reports on the TV, while his wife flipped through the room service menu, said, "I think I'll have the sea bass. How about you?"

Like he could think about eating. "You order for me," he told her. "You know what I like."

"They have a twelve-ounce peppered New York strip loin, with roasted potatoes and spinach. How does that sound?"

"That's fine." On the television, a reporter was inside the Superdome, pointing up at the damaged ceiling. You could see the sky through the hole, and some of the people who'd spent the night there came on camera, talking about what it was like when the wind blew the roof tiles off and the rain started pouring in on them.

"Look at that poor woman. Isn't that horrible?" Janine reached over, hit the mute button on the TV remote, and picked up the phone. "I'm going to get us some crab cakes as appetizers, and they have a white chocolate cheesecake for dessert, with pecan caramel. Doesn't that sound delicious?"

"Sounds great."

She dialed room service, tucked the phone between her shoulder and ear. "Should I order wine with dinner, or do you want a beer?"

But now Vickers was frozen, staring at the television in horror. They'd cut away to a chopper shot over the northeast section of the city, and he could clearly see water pouring through a wide gap in the levee along the northern section of the Seventeenth Street canal. "Son of a bitch," he said, and grabbed the remote from his wife's hand, trying to bring up the sound. But instead he managed to switch the channel, and he found himself watching two cowboys having a shoot-out. "What the fuck?" He stared down at the remote. "What did you do to this thing?"

"What did *I* do? You're the one who snatched it out of my hand." She leaned forward as he frantically started pressing buttons at random. "Give it *here*. You're just making it worse."

He passed her the remote, and she managed to get it back to the news, brought the sound up in time for him to hear a reporter say,

"... and we're getting reports of serious flooding throughout the eastern part of the city from levee breaks on both the Seventeenth Street and Industrial canals. We don't yet know the full extent of damage, but rescue efforts are under way in the city's Ninth Ward, where residents have been plucked off rooftops by boats and helicopters." He looked up at the camera, his face somber. "For a few hours, it seemed as if New Orleans had dodged disaster today, but now the city's worst fears appear to be coming true."

Vickers sat down, feeling all the strength go out of his legs. "Shut it off."

"He said the eastern part of the city." Janine looked over at him. "We're in Metairie. That's west of the canals, right?"

"Just shut it off."

She raised the remote and the TV went dark. "Does this mean you don't want dinner?"

||| A dull gleam of light along the black water. Louis Sams raised his head and peered into the darkness ahead of him. Where was it coming from? It seemed like a miracle after so many hours in darkness, but in the last few hours he'd begun to wonder about the difference between miracles and accidents. Was there a hand guiding him to safety, or had the water simply carried him up through the gap in the acoustic ceiling, where his hand brushed against an iron support beam in the darkness, found itself grasping at that solid form that rose above the water, so that he was able to pull himself up, lying there on the beam as the water reached its height of flood only inches below the concrete floor above? Miracle, or fluid dynamics? Water flows through an open hole, sweeps everything that floats with it. If the flood is an act of God, then so is the rescue. But for an engineer, that's a hard concept to swallow. The city wasn't drowning as an act of God's wrath, but because of engineering failures, construction shortcuts, and a failure of political will. Spend

the money to build the levees high and strong, and they'll keep the water out. Refuse to allow the contractors to corrupt safety inspectors, and they won't collapse when the flood rolls in. Lying there in the darkness, his arms wrapped around the metal beam, he knew that his salvation came not from God, but from some anonymous construction engineer, who'd thought to strengthen the floors of this warehouse with cross-bracing. He ran one hand up the length of the beam to where it met the concrete floor. A good, solid beam, smooth and cool to the touch, with the faint smell of rust. Men made such things to support their dreams. It was how the world hung together against wind and rain, how it rose above the reach of our hands, and kept rising, as if on a flood of dreams, until something else made by God or man brought it down. But for now Louis was grateful simply to rest his head on the cool metal, close his eyes, and feel the breath still stirring in his lungs.

He slept. When he finally opened his eyes, he saw the faint light shining on the surface of the water. He stared at it for a long time, wondering if he was imagining it. He'd heard that men who lived in darkness for days on end saw ghost lights as the nerves in their eyes fired from habit or despair. But when he moved his head, he saw the light shift slightly, as a reflection on water would. If he'd created it in his mind, wouldn't it follow his eyes as they moved around the darkness? He raised his hand, reached out toward it. He could see the faint outline of his fingers blocking the light.

Was it daylight? He lowered his hand until it touched the surface of the water six inches below him. It hadn't risen any more while he slept. He closed his eyes and pictured the room in which he'd been held. The ceiling had been about nine feet above him, but they'd gone down a couple steps when they shoved him into the room. So there must be close to ten feet of water. He tried to imagine that much water filling the streets of New Orleans. Cars down there, like bottom-feeding fish. You could stand on the roof of a car and barely have your head above the surface. Some houses would be completely underwater. He thought about his own house, a one-story shotgun that he and Kara had bought on North Prieur six months after they got married, where they'd raised their kids and figured they'd live until they retired. But the thought of what the house must look like now was too painful, so he pushed it away.

He opened his eyes, looked at that faint glow on the water. Light meant a way out. He could stay here, clinging to this beam, until the water went down, or he could swim for it. How long would it take them to drain ten feet of water out of the city? Weeks. He'd die if he stayed there. Dehydration, probably. *Water, water, everywhere* . . . Life was just full of little ironies. Almost nobody starves to death; it's dehydration that gets you. He could just reach down, scoop up a handful of water, raise it to his mouth. But the water would be full of bacteria, sewage, toxic chemicals from the plants out on Almonaster and Chef Menteur Highway. He'd get dysentery, lie here groaning and fouling his pants until he was too weak to cling to this beam, then just slip into the water and drown. Might happen if he swam too, but at least he'd stand a chance then.

And it was the water that had saved him. Raised him up out of that cell where they'd beaten him like a dog. They'd put that water in the street, he felt sure. But it had set him free. Little ironies.

So it was swim for it. He'd stay close to the walls where he could, in case he got into trouble. If the guys who'd built this place had put in cross-bracing on one wall, then they'd probably put it all through the place. He could go from beam to beam, resting when he got tired. He'd gone days without food, and his muscles felt like rubber. But he felt sure now that he could make it. Iron and irony. Just stay close to the walls and let the water carry you. Men like this, they don't understand that the world only grants them a short time to run out the line before the hook seizes tight in the flesh of their mouths. There have always been men like them, whose talent isn't to build, but to destroy. There have always been lazy men, greedy men, violent men who will beat you like a dog. And for a while, the world seems to pour its treasures into their pockets. Stealing is easy, they learn. And you can kill a man without a thought, the way you'd toss away a cigarette when you'd smoked it down to the filter. But it all comes back at you one day. Iron and irony. Men keep building, despite them, and eventually the debt always comes due.

He was going to be there to see that they paid. If it took swimming through this black water, then that's what he'd do. And when it was done, he'd go back to his family and leave all this behind him. The city was gone, he knew. But he could make a new home anywhere, if he had his family with him.

He let go of the beam, slid into the black water. Something brushed against him as he swam, but he ignored it, kept his eyes on the faint glow that grew brighter as he approached it. He started to reach for a beam, caught sight of a row of glittering eyes gazing at him, drew his hand back quickly. *Rats*, he realized, *lined up like cars on an overpass.* He swam on, trying not to think about what might be floating in the water.

Gradually the light seemed to become more solid, not just a faint glow on the water, but filling a space above it. It moved slightly, so that the darkness seemed to change shape; for some reason, he thought of his mother's hands shaping dough between them, the way he'd watched her do it when he was a boy sitting at the kitchen table and she was making biscuits. Then he saw a set of metal stairs rising out of the water through a gap in the ceiling above, heard the faint sound of voices.

"Man, I'm hungry," he heard Vince say. "We should have caught some a those rats. Cook 'em up for breakfast."

"There's one layin' over there," Lenny said. "Nice fat one. You can use my knife to clean it."

His heart sank. But there was nowhere else to go. He couldn't stay in the water. His body ached from the beatings they'd given him, and he could feel the strength starting to drain from his arms. He swam over to the stairs, grabbed hold of them, looked up into the light. Lenny and Vince were standing beside the opening, holding splintered boards that looked shattered at one end, like they'd been smashing them against the floor. Vince raised his board over his head, then froze, staring down at him. "Jesus," he said. "Where the hell did he come from?"

Lenny gazed down at him for a moment, then carefully laid his board aside, drew his gun from the holster on his belt, pointed it at Sams. "Same as all the others," he said, and gave a thin smile. "Just another big old rat to me."

8

"Wake up, man. Water's risin'."

Danny opened his eyes, found Jabril crouched next to him among the sleeping people, shaking his shoulder. "What?"

"Water's up on the second floor. We got to move everybody up to the fourth floor, get those portable toilets up here where it's still dry."

Danny sat up, looked around, confused. It was still dark, the only light coming from Jabril's emergency lamp. "What time is it?"

"Can't wait, man. Got to happen now."

The fourth floor was crowded with industrial packing cases, and the floor near the windows was covered with broken glass from the storm. It took them almost two hours to clear enough space for everybody, then they strung up an emergency lamp on the steps, started moving the people up there in small groups. They were still in the middle of that when one of the boys called out to Jabril, "Them toilets getting' pretty wet down there."

"Keep movin' the people," Jabril told him. "We'll see 'bout the toilets."

Danny followed him down the stairs. Water was ankle-deep on the second floor, with a smell like chemicals and sewage. Jabril tipped one of the toilets slightly, feeling its weight.

"These things are pretty full."

"You got a couple hundred people up there," Danny said. "What do you expect?"

Jabril let the toilet down, shook his head. "I didn't figure on this many people. We got to get 'em out of here. Water keeps risin' like this, we'll be up on the roof pretty soon, somebody have to come rescue us."

"We'll need more boats."

Jabril nodded. "Have to go find us some in the morning." He looked at Danny. "Could use your help, man."

"Okay. No problem. Just tell me what to do."

"Well, first thing we got to do is get these things moved." Jabril nodded to the toilets. Then he grinned. "Hell, you a lawyer. You should be *good* at this."

Two hours later they had the toilets lined up beside the stairs on the third floor. They staggered upstairs, and a woman took one look at them, made a face, and said, "There's a wash bucket and some disinfectant over there. See if you can get that smell off you."

They did their best. The woman brought them over another bucket full of soapy water, told them, "Strip off them clothes and soak 'em in this. We'll lay 'em out on the roof to dry in the morning."

Danny looked at her. "I don't have any other clothes."

Jabril grinned at him. "Man, you somethin' else." He looked at the woman. "See if we can find some clothes that fit him. Otherwise, we all gonna be embarrassed."

She went away, came back a few minutes later carrying an old LSU T-shirt and the pants from a red tracksuit. "Don't match," she said, handing him the clothes, "but they should fit you."

Danny was too tired to care. He put on the clothes, tossed his dirty ones into the bucket to soak, then found an empty piece of floor so he could stretch out.

Two hours later, Jabril was shaking him awake.

"Light comin' up," Jabril told him. "We got to get out on the water, find us some boats."

Danny glanced at his watch. It was a few minutes before six. He sat up, saw that Jabril was holding a mug of instant coffee.

"Here." Jabril handed him the mug. "We got some bread and peanut butter, when you hungry."

Danny nodded. His mouth felt like something you dredge up out of a bayou in a bucket. Jesus, two days without a toothbrush. "You got any toothpaste?"

Jabril nodded. "Even got a toothbrush. Some of us thought about this before it happened."

"Your car get stolen?"

"Nah, that was you, man. People in this town, they know better than to mess with *my* ride." Jabril stood up. "C'mon. You can use my toothpaste. When you done, you just lean over the stairs, spit into the water."

Danny did the best he could using his finger, then rinsed his mouth out with bottled water. At least it took that taste out of his mouth. He drank the coffee, spread some peanut butter on a slice of bread and ate it. One of Jabril's boys had a little camp stove going, and Danny got him to boil up some water for a second cup of coffee.

"Go easy on that stuff," Jabril told him. "We got a lot of people gonna start wakin' up soon, they smell that stuff."

"Might be the last cup I get for a while," Danny said, stirring it. "You think Morning Call's open?"

"Be surprised." Jabril took a handful of water bottles out of a carton, started loading them into a backpack to take with him in the boat. "Have to see what the rest of the city looks like. It's anything like around here, they gonna have to reopen up in Baton Rouge."

The boat was tied up under the same window they'd climbed out of the day before, and they tossed their stuff into it, climbed down the netting. It was a bright morning, the sky clear, but the water had risen a couple feet overnight. They could see more people standing on roofs of apartment buildings that had upper floors that had still been dry the night before.

"Damn," one of the boys said. "Where all these people keep comin' from?"

"I guess they figured they'd be okay yesterday. Water wasn't up to their floor, they'd just wait it out." Jabril looked at Danny. "You got any idea where we can find some more boats?"

"Most of the dealers are up by the lake. But there's a couple boat-yards on North Galvez, other side of the Industrial Canal."

"Sounds like it's worth a try."

They paddled up St. Claude toward the Industrial Canal. People were making their way out of the Ninth Ward in canoes or rubber boats. There was even a guy lying on an air mattress, lazily churning the water behind him with his feet. As they went past, he grinned and raised an open can of beer at them in a drunken salute. The remains of a six-pack hung off one side of the air mattress, like he was keeping it cold in the water.

"Got the whole day off work," he called out. "Now all I need is to find me a beach!"

The boys in the front of the boat cracked up at that. "Head north," one of them yelled to him. "Looks like the Gulf Coast is up in Slidell now!"

They paddled on, and Jabril said, "You believe that guy? Whole city's drowning, and he's havin' himself a party."

"He's gonna be havin' himself a case of cholera," Danny said, "he drinks from those cans he's got floating in the water."

They reached the bridge over the Industrial Canal, found a crowd of people sleeping on it, others sitting along the top of the levee, staring back with exhausted eyes at the light coming up on the floodwaters spread out before them. One of the boys hopped out, and they dragged their boat onto the bridge span. Jabril called to one of the men standing there, "How's it look on the other side?"

The man had a shirt draped over his head to protect himself from the sun that had begun to heat up the pavement, and it made him look strangely like a biblical prophet. "Was dry last night, but I heard there's water all up through City Park, and it's rising all over." He shook his head sadly. "Whole city's gonna be underwater pretty soon."

They tossed their paddles in the boat, heaved it up between them, carried it through the crowd to the other side of the bridge. From there they could see the city spread out before them. For a couple blocks the streets were dry, and the water beyond looked shallower, but as they looked north toward Galvez Street, they could see flooding everywhere.

"Must have lost a couple levees," Jabril said. He looked at Danny. "Looks like your boy Sams was right."

Danny nodded. "Won't do him much good now."

They carried the boat through the ankle-deep water in the streets north of St. Claude. When it reached their knees, they set the boat down, climbed in, and paddled the rest of the way up to North Galvez, where they found the boatyard behind a high chain-link fence. Somebody had cut through the lock on the gate, and they paddled in. A pair of guard dogs stood on a loading dock surrounded by water and started barking as they paddled past. One of the boys laid down his paddle, drew a pistol out of his pants, looked over at Jabril.

"You want me to shoot them?"

"What for? They ain't botherin' us. Somebody gonna have to come out here and rescue them pretty soon."

At the back of the boatyard, they found a stack of wrecked boats that had been blown into a pile against a building. But just beyond was a large metal building, like an airplane hangar, with its doors standing open. Inside, they saw a row of empty trailers standing in three feet of water.

"Looks like somebody beat us to it," Danny said.

"Cops, probably. Took 'em a couple hours to get out there and start rescuing people yesterday. Had to go find some boats first."

At the back of the building they found two small fishing boats under canvas tarps. When they pulled back the tarps, they found there were no engines on them.

"Shit. You believe that?" Jabril tossed the tarp aside angrily. "All they left us was this and that pile of storm wrecks outside."

Danny thought about it for a moment, then he said, "You get a good look at those wrecked boats when we went past?"

"Not really. Just a pile of busted-up boats. Why?"

"You think any of those might have an engine that still works? We found one, we could mount it on one of these boats, and we'd be in business."

Jabril raised his eyebrows. "Worth a look."

They paddled back out to the pile of wrecked boats, and Danny climbed out, balanced carefully on one of the wrecks, and looked over the engines. "I think we could salvage some of these," he called back to Jabril. "Might take a couple hours."

"Be quicker than trying to bring all those people out of there in rubber boats."

It took all morning. They pulled two engines off the wrecks at the top of the pile, found that the propeller shaft on one was bent, while the other had a crack in its block. One of the boys climbed up on the pile with Danny, and they shoved some boats aside, found an engine that looked like it was in good shape lying in the stern of a smashed speedboat. They hauled it out, loaded it into the raft, and paddled back to the boats. They got it mounted on one boat's frame, and then Danny sat back, said, "We'll need some fuel."

"I saw a couple gas pumps back there at the front of the yard," one of the boys offered. But Jabril shook his head. "Won't work without power. We'll have to find another boat with some gas in it, siphon it out."

But the yard was empty, stripped of anything that could still float. They pulled a fuel hose off one of the wrecked boats, tied the rubber boat to the back of the skiff, and paddled it out through the gates. On Poland Avenue, they came across a car that had water halfway up its doors. The gas cap was just above the waterline, so they smashed the car's window with a paddle, and one of the boys reached in, released the latch on it. Jabril slid the hose into the gas tank, and they managed to siphon out enough gas to get the engine running.

A block north of Claiborne, they found another abandoned car and topped off the outboard's tank. Then they headed for the bridge, tossed the rubber raft on top of the boat, carried it through the crowd of people standing up there.

"Jesus," one of the boys said, looking off to the north. "You see that?"

Danny looked over, saw that the flood wall had completely collapsed, water pouring over the levee into the streets beyond. The water had rushed in with enough force to crush houses, toss cars around, and he could even see a barge that had been swept in, running aground against a house on Jourdan Avenue. They set the boat down, stood there looking at the breach, watching as debris came floating down the canal and was carried across by the current flowing through the hole in the levee.

"Let's go," Jabril said quietly, and they picked up the boat, carried it the rest of the way across the bridge.

As they got ready to launch the boat, a woman came up to them. "Can you go check on my mama? She was in her house over at Caffin and Tonti."

Jabril looked up into her eyes, hesitated, then said, "Yeah, sure. We'll go take a look."

A man called out, "My sister's up on Dorgenois. Can you get up there, look for her?"

"What block?"

"Up by Forstall, across from the high school."

A crowd quickly gathered, people calling out street names. Jabril held up both hands, said, "We'll do our best, okay? But we got to get our own people out, too."

But the crowd kept calling out addresses to them, even after they climbed into the boat, got the engine started, and sped off up Claiborne. Jabril shook his head, his face somber. "That was wrong," he said, raising his voice over the roar of the outboard. "I shouldn't have said none a that."

"Why? It's true."

"*Our* people?" He shook his head again. "That ain't right. Something like this happens, they *all* your people. You got some way to help 'em, that's what you got to do. Can't go dividing people up, sayin' some of them yours and some ain't. That kind of bullshit is what got us into this mess."

Danny was silent. Jabril's words felt like an accusation. After a moment he called out, "So why ain't we headin' to Caffin and Tonti?"

Jabril nodded. He turned the boat north, away from the warehouse, and headed up through the flooded streets into the deepest section of the flood zone.

|||| "What we need's a boat."

"You think?" Lenny shook his head in amazement. "Man, that's some sharp thinking. You come up with that all by yourself?"

"Hey, fuck you, man. I don't see you comin' up with any brilliant plans."

They were standing by the window, looking out at the water lapping against the side of the building only a few feet below them. Sams sat against a wall, his hands bound behind him with a piece of old rope they'd found lying around. All day the heat had been building, and now his shirt clung to him like they'd just pulled him from the water.

"The disk wasn't there, asshole," Vince had told him as he stood there, water dripping from him. "You thought you could just send us away, we wouldn't come back?"

For a moment Sams had stared at them blankly. What disk? And then it came back to him, like something from another lifetime. How could they still be worried about something like that, with the whole city underwater? It seemed crazy, like stealing an empty wallet. Didn't they realize there was nothing left to fight over? That life was over, swept away in a few hours like something they'd all dreamed.

He'd seen two dogs in a yard rip each other bloody over table scraps. Why shouldn't he expect men to be the same way? We've built a society based on stories in which some men win and others lose; the habit's hard to break, even when the wind comes and the waters rise. For every man who sets about building a raft large enough to carry his neighbors, there are two more who see a chance to grab what they can get, or simply keep playing out the hand they were dealt before the storm blew the cards from their grasp, tossed the table over the neighbor's roof, and scattered the chips among the distant, leafless trees. Sams wanted to raise his hand, like a fighter who'd come to the end of his strength, saying, *No más, no más.* But these men hadn't heard the bell, or simply had no interest in endings that weren't on their terms. They were still playing out the crime story when a much vaster crime—the culmination of all the town's casual corruptions, the politicians' lies, the negligence of powerful men—was unfolding all around them. And so Sams had to play along or die. They wanted the disk. Once they got it, they wouldn't need him anymore.

He had expected them to beat him when they dragged him out of the water, but they simply tied his hands, shoved him against the wall, and left him there while they went to the window to figure out how to get their hands on a boat. His head slumped against his chest. A puddle of filthy water spread out around him.

"I'll tell you what," Vince said, "Jimmy makes it, he owes me a new car."

Lenny looked at him. "How you figure that?"

Vince pointed down at the street. "You think I would have left my car parked on the street in this neighborhood, I wasn't in here doing something for him?"

"You got insurance."

"Sure. But you want to imagine how long it's gonna take to get an insurance company to pay up on something this big? And that's before they start telling you your policy don't cover flooding." He shook his head. "Ten feet of water in the streets, man. Somebody better fucking pay."

"What you gonna tell 'em? You parked your car down here during a hurricane 'cause you wanted a free wash?"

"I had business down here!"

"Yeah? So what kind of *business* you gonna tell 'em you doin' down here in the middle of a hurricane?"

"We work security." Vince gestured around at the abandoned warehouse. "Somebody had to make sure this place was secure. Nobody got in here, messed up the place."

Lenny raised his eyebrows. "You don't think they'll come look at the place?"

"Where they gonna get the time to go around, look at all these flooded buildings? You *see* what's happening out there?"

Lenny leaned out the window, gazed up the street toward the highway overpass. "Is that a boat?"

"Where?"

Lenny pointed. "Up there. By the overpass."

"Shit, you're right." Vince peeled off his shirt. "I'll get his attention. He comes over here, you wait until he's right up close to the building, then show him your gun."

"That's your plan? You're gonna wave your shirt around?"

"You got a better idea?" Vince leaned out the window, started waving his shirt, calling out, "Hey! Over here!"

They both watched as the boat kept going, following the over-pass out of sight beyond a row of industrial buildings.

"Okay," Vince conceded. "So this could take a while."

|||| "Getting late. You sure you want to try getting across town?" Danny looked over at Jabril wearily. They'd spent most of this second day moving people off roofs, working their way through the flooded streets until the skiff and the rubber boat were full, then ferrying them down to the bridge at St. Claude Avenue, where they could get their feet on dry land. They'd had to stop twice to siphon off more gas for the boat's engine, and once it died on them, wouldn't start again until Danny pulled out the spark plugs, cleaned the connection, and primed the engine with more gas. Now it was late afternoon, and they stood on the bridge, looking out at the rising water on the west side of the Industrial Canal. Two days since the storm hit, and there were still people waiting on their roofs to be rescued in the Ninth Ward. But now the water was rising across the whole city, and it was hard to know if there was anywhere that would be safe.

"I gotta try, man," Danny told Jabril. "I can't just leave the guy out there." He looked over toward the river. "I just need to get across town to the Sixth District. Looks like I could make it if I stay close to the levees, work my way along the river."

"We come this far," Jabril told him, "we'll take you up to the Quarter. Looks like it might still be dry over there."

They left the skiff with some of the people they'd rescued sitting on the bridge, carried the rubber boat three blocks to where the water started just beyond Poland Avenue, launching it along the north side of St. Claude, where the water was deeper. It stayed fairly shallow there, and at places they had to turn north a block or two to find enough water to keep paddling. But even here they came across people wading through it, carrying their belongings wrapped in garbage bags, over their heads. A handful of cops passed them in a motorboat, headed for the Bywater Hospital, ignoring the groups of young guys headed back into the flood zone carrying food, disposable diapers, beer, and, in a couple cases, brand-new electronic gear—boom boxes, car stereos, even a big-screen TV that two guys had balanced on a board they were struggling to carry over their shoulders.

Jabril called out to them, "You got power?"

"Nah," one of the guys carrying the TV shouted back. "It's out all over. All the wires is down."

"So what you plannin' to do with that TV?"

The guy grinned at him. "Power's comin' back sometime. And it was just sittin' in a store window. Somebody was gonna get it. Might as well be us."

But their group was moving on up the block, and now the two guys had to hurry to catch up to them.

"Let's go," Jabril said to the boys up front. "That shit just makes me sad."

Danny heard disgust in his voice, and none of them said anything as they dug in with their paddles. But they'd only gone a few hundred feet when they heard a loud splash behind them. They all looked back, saw that the two guys who'd been carrying the TV were now standing a few feet apart, arguing loudly.

"I said go *left*!"

"I went left!"

"You went right!"

"The hell you say!"

They still had the board, but the TV was gone. Lying at the bottom of the water, Danny realized, where it would stay until the water went down, just another piece of storm junk. One of the men tossed the board aside now, turned back the way they'd come. His partner just stood there, staring after him.

"Where you going?"

"To get another one!"

"Fuck that! That shit's heavy!"

"That's 'cause it's a big-screen TV. You wanted a big-screen, it's gonna be heavy!"

They were still arguing as the boat rounded a corner, making their way past a row of flooded cars. It all struck Danny as absurd, like something from a fevered dream. What would they see next? Sharks cruising along Causeway Boulevard? Fishing boats tossing their nets on Esplanade Avenue? He had to remind himself that below every roof they passed was a life to which someone would never return.

The water got lower as they paddled west toward the Quarter. Windows appeared above the waterline, and the tops of doors, then porches where people stood, watching them in amusement as they paddled past, the water shallow enough now to wade through without getting your belt buckle wet.

"Nice boat," one man called out. "Your yacht go down in the storm?" And the rest of his family standing on the porch burst out laughing.

They don't know, Danny thought. *They see a couple feet of water in the street, and they have no idea what's happened a few blocks east of them.*

He expected Jabril to say something to the guy, but he just kept his eyes fixed on the block ahead, where the street rose until Danny could see the broken yellow center line through the shallow water. At Louisa Street, right in front of Mandich, their boat scraped against the bottom, and they ground to a stop.

"Last stop," one of the boys up front said, and he got out, standing knee-deep in the water, held the boat so it wouldn't float away. Danny dropped his paddle in the bottom of the boat, went forward, and stepped down into the water. "You sure you don't need me?"

Jabril kept his seat in the back of the boat. "You done your part. We'll start bringing our people out in the morning, see if we can find some way out of this city."

Danny nodded, started to turn away, but Jabril called to him:

"Hey, Danny. Hang on."

Danny turned, looked back at him. "Yeah?"

Jabril looked at one of the boys in the front of the boat. "Give him your piece."

"*What?*"

"Go on, give it to him. Man's gonna be walkin', could run into trouble. I got more back at the warehouse."

The boy got a look on his face like Jabril had just told him there'd be no Christmas this year. "C'mon, man, I *like* this piece!"

But Jabril just narrowed his eyes slightly, looking at him hard, and after a moment the boy said, "Well, *shit.*" And he lifted his Miami Heat jersey, took a semiautomatic pistol from the waistband of his tracksuit pants, held it out to Danny. "I want that *back.* You hear me?"

"Sure, no problem." Danny shoved the gun into his pants, then hesitated a second, pulled out his shirt so it hung loosely over the bulge. He looked over at Jabril. "Thanks."

"You sure you be all right?"

"Yeah. You've got other things to worry about. You want me to send somebody out to check on you?"

"What, like the police?" Jabril laughed. "You find 'em, you tell 'em we're fine. They run into trouble, we'll send out a boat, pick 'em up."

And with that, the boy standing in the water pushed the boat out, jumped in as it started to turn, and they paddled away, back the way they'd just come. Jabril raised a hand as they rounded the corner. And then they were gone.

Danny turned, waded out of the water. The street was covered with broken glass and roof tiles that the storm had blown off the nearby buildings. A sheet of plywood lay against a lamppost, nails sticking out of its edges where the wind had torn it off of a window, blown it along the street for six blocks, and left it lying in the street. There was a hastily scrawled message on it in black spray paint: U LOOT U DIE!

Danny looked back at Mandich. It was an old creole restaurant where Jimmy Boudrieux used to meet with local politicians to cut deals over oysters bordelaise and fried eggplant. The water was a few inches up the door. Trees were down everywhere, and some houses looked like they'd been hit by a bomb—roof gone, walls collapsed in on themselves, just a ragged pile of wood.

He walked up to the corner of Clouet Street and was relieved to see that the Saturn Bar had survived. It was the kind of place he'd always loved, a tiny neighborhood bar, full of junk, leopard-print booths, and little round black Formica tables, with old table lamps the owner, an old guy named O'Neil Broyard, had bought at garage sales. Photographs and garish murals on the walls and ceiling, Eartha Kitt on the jukebox, a little garden out back where Broyard grew tomatoes, satsumas, squash, peaches, and Japanese plums that he put in a box on the bar for people to take home. You want a fancy drink, go uptown. But he'd give you a Dixie in the bottle or a straight-up martini, show you his collection of baseball caps.

A couple blocks ahead, Danny could see more water. He'd have to head south through the French Quarter to get around it. The city's first settlers had built on the high ground near the river, left those who came later—the freed slaves, the laborers who worked on the docks—to fill in the swamps that lay between the river and the lakefront and build their homes there. Now the streets leading south into the Quarter looked dry, but when he looked north, Danny could see only water, spreading out in all directions. The whole city seemed to be underwater. It was exactly what the storm warnings had described, but he still found it strange to look up those familiar streets and see light shimmering on water, the way it looked if you took a boat out into the bayou at first light, sat under the shelter of an ancient oak tree, waiting out the rain blowing across the surface of the water like a whispering breath. But the water filling the streets looked black and oily, like the waste ponds he'd seen lining the roads near the chemical plants up by Baton Rouge when he was a boy. He thought about the people he'd seen wading through that water, and it made him feel sick.

There's nothing you can do about it, he thought. *So focus on what you can fix.*

He headed south, through the Quarter, along streets that were dry but looked strangely stripped, as if every loose piece of the buildings had been shaken loose, tossed into the street. Glass crunched under his feet, and he had to step over power wires lying across the street like snakes. Every few blocks, he'd come across someone standing in his doorway, gazing out at the shattered street with empty eyes. One man sweeping the glass off the sidewalk in front of his building straightened up, called out, "You comin' from the Nine?"

"That's right."

"How they doin' over there?"

"It's gone. Water up to the roofs. Flooding all up St. Claude, and it looks like everything north of the Quarter is pretty wet."

The man pursed his lips slightly, as if he might say something, but then he just shook his head, went back to his sweeping.

Danny kept going, through the heart of the French Quarter, all the bars and antique stores shut up tight, their metal security grates pulled down across their doors. But many had lost windows, and you could see that the wind had scattered things around inside. On Camp Street, he saw a sports car and an SUV crushed by bricks where the façade had crumbled off a building. The fire escape dangled off the building, a twisted knot of metal. Sheet metal lay in the middle of the street, blown off the roof of a building down the block.

A huge cloud of smoke rose on Canal Street, up by the I-10 overpass. The palm trees that usually lined the median ground had been sheared off by the wind and lay scattered along the street like spent missiles. Store windows had been smashed, and several of the stores looked like they'd been looted. But now there was water in the street, and it was mostly empty, except for a guy wading along the median ground a few blocks to the north, his arms full of track-suits he'd found in a sporting goods store.

A couple uniformed cops were standing there in front of the Marriott. Danny didn't recognize any of them, but he went over, said:

"Hey, what's burning up there?"

"Tire center," one of the cops said. "Been burning since this morning. There's fires all over, but that one's putting out most of the smoke."

They stood there for a moment, watching a pickup truck turn onto Canal up at Claiborne, trying to make it down the street through the water. It went slowly, looking like a boat cruising along, finally turned off onto Basin Street.

"I need to get over to the Sixth District," Danny said. "You guys hear anything from them?" One of the cops, a patrol sergeant, looked over at him, then took off his cap, rubbed at his eyes wearily. "We got a couple of their guys down at our command post at Harrah's. I heard the rest were in a hotel over by the Convention Center during the storm, then they headed back up to their station. But that was before the water started rising. There's a couple feet over by the Superdome already. They're only a couple blocks from there, so they could be getting wet."

Another cop said, "You don't want to go over to that part of town, anyway. They got people looting, shooting at each other. They broke into Coleman's before the storm was even over. Some guy got shot over a flashlight."

Danny looked over at the empty stores on Canal Street. "Worse than here?"

"This is nothing. We got reports they're looting all over. Somebody said there's people riding around in boats over in the Ninth Ward, stealing things off all the bodies floating in the water."

"I just came from over there," Danny said. "The only boats I saw were rescuing people off roofs."

The cop shrugged. "Just telling you what I heard."

"So it's true? The Ninth Ward's underwater?" The sergeant was black, and Danny saw that his face was suddenly anxious. It's easy to forget that cops are just blue-collar guys, who live in the same neighborhoods as the people they arrest. Danny suddenly felt bad for these guys, working emergency shifts while their homes vanished in the flood.

"Yeah, it's pretty bad. Over ten feet in some places. There are people trapped in houses, up on roofs waiting to get rescued. The Coast Guard had a chopper in there last night, and they were lifting people off roofs."

The sergeant looked at the water, silent. "Thirty years, I lived up in there."

"You get everybody out?"

"Yeah. They all up in Arkansas with my in-laws. But what you saying is true, my house is underwater."

Danny looked down at the water lapping at their feet. "Looks like that's true for just about everybody."

"It's a hell of a thing to see." The sergeant shook his head. "Whole city's gone. Hard to see how it'll come back."

One of the other cops looked over at him. "You think? It's happened before."

"This bad?"

The cop shrugged. "How should I know? I wasn't around to see it. But you look at those pictures from Betsy, it looks just like this. They fixed the levees, pumped the water out, and people came back. You don't think that'll happen again? Hell, a city like this, you can't keep people away."

"Shit, I don't know. How many times you got to lose everything before you start to think about getting out of town?" The sergeant looked at Danny. "My wife, she's been saying for two years we should move up to Arkansas, be closer to her folks. I asked her, 'What you 'spect me to do up in *Arkansas*? I'm a New Orleans cop.' All I know is this city. Somebody points a gun at a tourist, steals his gold watch, I know where the guy goes to sell it. Buncha kids start messin' 'round on the Upperline, I know their mamas, can get 'em to straighten those boys out. That ain't exactly a transferable skill, you know?"

"Even if it comes back," Danny said, "it won't be the city we know."

They all stood there in silence, gazing up Canal Street. At last Danny shook his head, turned to the sergeant. "You said you saw some Sixth District guys down at Harrah's?"

"That's right. At least they were there when I left. We've got a command post set up under the portico. There were cops comin' in from all over the city."

"Thanks. You guys stay dry."

"Don't look like any of us gonna do that."

Danny walked down Canal toward the casino. A half dozen squad cars were lined up in the valet parking driveway, with some picnic tables and folding lawn chairs. Uniformed cops stood around looking dazed. One of them was wandering around, picking up the plastic bags and old newspapers scattered along the driveway by the storm, like all he could think to do without orders was straighten up the place.

"I'm looking for Sixth District," Danny told him. "You know where I could find them?"

The cop shrugged. "We got people scattered all over. Phones are down, radios don't work. Nobody knows what's going on. Broad Street's flooded, so they evacuated headquarters over here."

"But you seen any Sixth District guys?"

"Somebody said they were staying at a hotel over by the Convention Center last night. I got no idea if they're still there."

Danny left him, walked over to where some other cops were sitting at a picnic table eating packaged sandwiches like they sell to tourists out of the corner markets. "Any of you guys from the Sixth?"

One of the cops looked up. He was an African-American officer in his late twenties, broad-shouldered, with a shaved head like a ball player. "Yeah. Who's asking?"

"I'm trying to track down some guys who used to work Sixth District Vice a couple years ago. They work for Jimmy Mancuso now."

The cop shook his head. "I only transferred in a couple weeks ago. I'm lucky I can find my locker."

"You know where I could find any of the guys who've been working there for a while?"

"Shit, you got me, man. They put us all up in downtown hotels, in case the city flooded. Not that it helped any. Rain was blowing so hard it was coming through the window frames. Then all the windows started breaking, and pretty soon the rain's comin' in everywhere. Water running down the walls, everything. So the storm finally passes, and we all come out, the city looks pretty bad, but there's no flooding, so we figure we got lucky. We ride back over to Felicity Street, and the station's still standing. Half the squad cars are under telephone poles, and we got no power, but we figure we'll hook up a generator, we're back in business. We'd parked some other cars up on freeway ramps to keep them safe if there's flooding, and this morning the captain sends a bunch of us up there to bring 'em back. That's when we saw the water. We're up there on the expressway, where it splits off I-10 by the Superdome, and we can see that there's water everywhere up by the cemeteries. So we send a guy back to the station to let 'em know, and I mean we're up there maybe fifteen minutes, it's already down by Carrollton and we can see it's comin' our way. So we jump in our cars, head back over to the station, and everybody's in a panic over there. Somebody says they got a report there's ten feet of water heading downtown. They're all picturing those tsunami waves we saw on TV last year. We try to tell 'em it ain't like that. It's more like you leave the bathtub running, and it spills over, starts to flood the floor. It's rising maybe a couple inches an hour. But everybody's ready to run for the hills. It's like the *Titanic*'s sinking, and they're all scrambling for the boats." He shook his head. "Anyway, so we all pile into the squad cars we got left, and we drive back over to the hotel. I'm thinking we're a block from the river, that's the highest ground in the city. We'll be fine there. But everybody's screaming, 'We're all gonna drown. We've got to get out!' I mean, we're in a five-story building, right? You get water rising *that* high, it's time to build the ark, 'cause you're not gonna find dry land from here to Arkansas. So my lieutenant asks the captain, 'Are you ordering us to leave the city?' And the captain says, 'I'm not ordering anyone to go. It's up to you.' Next thing you know, they're all piling back in the squad cars and they're heading for the bridge. They figure it's still dry on the West Bank, or else they can spend the night in their cars up on the bridge."

"But you didn't go?"

The cop shook his head. "We were stayin' in a hotel about forty yards from the Convention Center, and there's, like, twenty thousand people in there, more showin' up all the time. You're gonna take off, leave all those people behind? So I stay, and a couple other guys stay. There's a couple guys still over at the station on Felicity Street, holding down the fort. Everybody else takes off. I heard they're all over in the parking lot of the Breaux Mart on General Meyer in Algiers." He looked down at his sandwich, then pushed it away, wiped his hands on a napkin. "Somebody told me they set up a command post over here, so I walked over to see if anybody knows what's going on. They got a bunch of people out looking for boats right now, a couple more trying to find some searchlights, so we can get out on the water and do more rescues tonight. We heard there's people stuck on roofs all up through the Ninth Ward."

"You heard right," Danny told him. "Looks like most of Lake Pontchartrain's flowing down Galvez Street right now."

"Jesus. Ain't that some shit." The cop got up, tossed the remains of his sandwich into a plastic garbage bag. "I was over in Iraq last year, and that place is pretty messed up. But it wasn't nothing compared to this."

"You said there were some other guys from Sixth District who stayed around. You know where I can find them?"

"Try over at the hotel. Hampton Inn, over by Gaiennie Street. I think a couple of them were working the area around the Convention Center. That's Eighth District territory, but I heard most of their people are up at the Superdome. They're gonna try to keep everybody there until they can get some buses in to evacuate them."

Danny glanced over in the direction of the Superdome. "Looked from where I was like they had some serious storm damage over there."

The cop shrugged. "I heard they lost some roof panels, but that's it. Nobody hurt, apparently."

"And you said there's still some Sixth District guys up at Felicity Street?"

"Was when I left. They were saying they planned to stay."

"You got any idea how deep the water is over there?"

"Couple feet, maybe. That's what everybody's saying, anyway."

"Thanks." Danny left him and wandered through the crowd of cops. Some TV crews who'd ridden out the storm in downtown hotels had parked their satellite trucks in the street nearby and were setting up their gear so they could shoot storm updates for the national networks. Danny thought about asking one of the technicians if he had a satellite phone he could use to get in touch with Mickie, but the guy was busy trying to keep his generator running while the reporter got ready to go on camera, rolling up his sleeves so he looked like he'd been fighting his way through the floods. As Danny watched, the reporter picked up his microphone, waited for the signal from his producer, then looked into the camera, and said:

"New Orleans is a city battered by high winds and rising water tonight, and some say that the City That Care Forgot has forgotten many of its citizens. . . ."

Danny turned and walked away.

IIII "Nurse?" Jimmy Mancuso tried to sit up, but they had him strapped down on the narrow bed, IV tubes running everywhere, so he could barely move his hands. He was lying in a hallway lit only by emergency lights, both walls lined with patients' beds, so close the nurses had to squeeze between them whenever they needed something from the equipment closet at the end of the hall. They'd moved everybody out here when the windows started shattering, unplugging all the machines that could be unplugged, running extension cords when they couldn't. Then the power gave out, and for a few moments they all lay there in the dark until the hospital staff got everything switched over to emergency generators. Hours later, when the wind started to die down, Jimmy could hear the generators through the broken windows. It sounded like a truck idling, and he kept expecting to hear somebody climb up behind the wheel and drive it away. Another patient lay across the hall from him, breathing through a ventilator that hissed slightly, like a balloon with a slow leak. There was no air-conditioning, and once the storm had died away, the heat began to build up in the hall until it felt like an oven where they were being slowly baked. All night Jimmy lay there sweating, trying to remember what it had looked like, that bright light that drew him forward, bathed him in joy.

But it seemed a long way off now. The storm had woken him, and at first he'd thought he was still dreaming, but then the nurses came hurrying in, disconnected all the machines, and wheeled him out into the hallway, where they pushed him against a wall, left him there. He lay there, staring up at the stained ceiling panels above him, feeling that bright light fade slowly from his mind as the heat settled around him and the foul smells of the sick filled his nose and throat.

Hours passed. He started to see faces he recognized in the ceiling tiles. Not Jesus, or anything crazy like that. Just guys he'd had to take out over the years. Their faces took shape up there, then slowly faded, and pretty soon he'd see another one. Like a slide show. When it got to the end, it started over. They didn't say anything, just looked at him silently, like this was something they'd been waiting for, they had nothing better to do now that they were dead than hang around in the hospital ceiling, counting the days until his heart gave out.

When he was in Catholic school, he'd asked some old nun what the dead did up in heaven. They kept saying if you're good, you go to heaven for all eternity. So how do they keep 'em all busy? Do they, like, show movies?

"In heaven, they sing hymns," she told him. "In hell, they burn." Then she looked at him and pursed her lips. "You're not much of a singer, are you?"

Secretly, he'd always figured the dead spent their time watching the living. What could be more fun? It's like a soap opera that goes on forever, only they don't cut away when people climb into bed. When he was a teenager, that thought had really messed up his sex life. Every time he got to messing around with a girl, he suddenly imagined all these dead people *watching* him—his grandma, all the old ladies who used to turn around and stare at him when he made noise in church, and even that old nun, who'd dropped dead a couple of months after he'd asked her that question. She'd collapsed one day in the convent dining room, and he'd heard that when the ambulance guys arrived, they opened up her robes, found that she was wearing a canvas sack against her skin, which had rubbed the flesh off her shoulders and ribs, leaving rashes that had become infected. By the time it made the rounds of the school, the story had become even more disgusting. *She was wearing burlap underwear,* one boy whispered. *It took all the skin off her tits and ass.* Anyway, this was not the person Jimmy wanted to imagine watching him when he finally got a girl's shirt off. But he couldn't help it. Once he'd gotten that idea in his head, it was like those dogs who get hungry when you ring a bell, only this wasn't doing his appetite no good at all.

So now the faces were looking down at him, and he couldn't help thinking that they didn't look like they'd been doing much singing. Or much burning either. They looked like they'd been waiting. Watching him all this time. Counting up every plate of fried oysters, every Chinese whore.

"Look, it was just business," he told them. "Nothing personal, okay?"

But this didn't seem to satisfy them. They just stared at him, as if the only thing that mattered to them was that he was lying there on this hospital bed in a fucking hallway of Charity Hospital, sweat dripping off every part of him, while some guy moaned in pain.

And then the power went out again. There was no storm this time, but the sound of the engines he'd gotten used to hearing suddenly died away, and all the lights went off. At the end of the hall, one of the nurses looked up as the battery-powered emergency lights came on above the exits. "Now what?"

"The water's getting too high," another nurse said to her. "They can't run the generators. They're afraid it'll short out the whole electrical system."

"So what are we supposed to do without power? We've got all these patients on life support."

"We'll have to bag the ones on ventilators and respirate them by hand."

"For how long?"

"As long as we have to. Run downstairs and get some other nurses off the other wards. Anyone who's not on a priority case. We'll have to do it in shifts."

The nurse hurried away, leaving Jimmy lying there in darkness and silence. What were they talking about, water? The only sound he could hear now was the soft moaning of the man a few beds away. But even in the darkness, he could feel the faces gazing down at him. *The streets are full of water, Jimmy.* Their eyes were full of weary sadness now. *It's coming right in the hospital. And you know whose fault that is, right?*

"Fuck you," Jimmy said angrily. "Go crawl back in your hole." He reached over, peeled off the tape holding the IV line to his arm, and with a grunt, yanked out the needle. Hurt like a bastard, but he'd fucking had it, lying there. Yeah, okay, so he'd had some chest pain. He felt fine now. Little tired, maybe, but nothing he couldn't handle. All he needed was a couple days in his own bed, some decent food, he'd be fine. His fingers fumbled with the straps holding him to the bed, like something you'd do to an *animal*, for Christ's sake. He got some slack in it, then worked it loose, yanking it out of the buckle that held it in place. For a moment he lay there, out of breath. Then he carefully peeled away the tape on his upper lip that held the oxygen tube in place, tossed it aside. There were still some EKG sensors taped to his chest, but the nurses had unplugged them all during the storm when they came in to move his bed out into the hall, so he just left them on there. He sat up slowly. The sheet was soaked where he'd been lying on it.

He eased his legs off the side of the bed, sat there for a minute catching his breath. Okay, so maybe he wasn't a hundred percent. At least he could get a cab, go over to Touro, get a decent room. He knew a guy who'd had a heart attack; two days later, he checks out of the hospital, checks into the Royal Sonesta, hires a nurse to come sit by his bed, feed him off the room service tray. You gotta be sick, that's the way to do it. Not lying here with these poor bastards, got nowhere else to go to die.

With a grunt, he shifted his weight to the edge of the bed, slid slowly off until his bare feet touched the floor. The floor was damp, and for a moment he thought his legs wouldn't hold him, he'd end up lying there on the dirty floor, wishing he'd stayed in his bed.

He looked up at the faces watching him from the ceiling. "You'd fucking like that, wouldn't you? See me go down on my ass?"

But he slowly felt the strength come back into his legs, and by hanging on to the edge of the bed, he was able to stand up, get his balance. He was wearing a hospital gown, open across the back. The strings weren't long enough to tie it around him, so it just hung there, letting his ass hang out. They'd cut his clothes off him in the emergency room. That's what a nurse had told him, anyway. Hundred-dollar silk shirt, custom-tailored pants he'd bought at a fancy boutique in Vegas, and they take a scissor to them, leave him lying there in something that looked like your aunt Eunice would wear, she goes down to the kitchen to get her coffee in the morning. They should give you two gowns, at least, so you can wear one in front and the other in the back, you don't have to walk around the hospital feeling like you're carrying a couple of hams, and everybody's getting ready to drop their chow, you go past.

What he should do was find his phone, call up Lenny and Vince, get them to bring him some decent clothes. But all his stuff was gone, or lying in one of the empty rooms they'd moved all the beds out of during the storm, broken glass all over the floor where the windows had shattered and the rain had come blowing in. They probably had phones in those rooms too. But no way he was going to go in there, walking on all that broken glass, nothing on his feet.

The nurses had a phone. He'd just take a stroll down the hall, use the one on their desk. Get somebody over here to pick him up, take him home, or at least to a decent hospital, where they wouldn't leave him lying around in a damn hallway all night.

"What, you don't think I can do it?"

The faces gazed down at him, expressionless. They were reserving judgment on the matter.

"Bite me," he told them. "Just watch."

He took a cautious step, still holding on to the bed. For a moment the hall whirled and spun before him. He took a deep breath, tightened his grip on the bed rail. Slowly, it settled. He saw that an old man in one of the beds across from him was watching him. He had an oxygen tube taped to his face, but his mouth was open, making him look like a fish gasping for air.

"What the fuck are you looking at?"

The man looked away. His face was the color of ashes blowing away in the wind.

"You can lie here and die if you want," Jimmy told him, "but I got stuff to do."

And with that, he let go of the bed, took a step, then another. He caught hold of a metal IV stand, used it to catch his balance, then pushed off, staggering down the middle of the hall between the rows of beds lined up along the wall. Wide eyes followed him as he went past, but nobody said a word. They all looked like it took every ounce of their energy just to keep breathing. *Suckers,* he thought. *Just lie there and suck air, until someone comes around, notices they're not breathing anymore.* He kept going, taking his time, and when he made it to the end of the hall by the nurses' station, he thought about turning around and taking a bow. But he wasn't sure he could pull that off without falling over on his knees, and anyway, fuck 'em. He wasn't doing it for their amusement. The nurses were all gone, everybody off in the darkness somewhere dealing with emergencies. He caught hold of the counter to steady himself, eased around behind it, and picked up the phone on the corner of the desk. Nothing. He punched a couple buttons, but it didn't help. The phone was dead. Everything in this fucking place was dead or dying. Except him. He was leaving, and if they didn't like it, fuck 'em.

He made it to the end of the hall, found a stairway. The only light came from emergency lights over the doors. Below, the stairs led down into darkness. There was a foul smell, like you get by the ocean when the tide goes out, leaves everything rotting in the sun. It made him gag, and he almost turned around, went back to his bed. But the thought of lying there in the darkness made him feel like cutting his own throat with a broken bottle, so he gripped the railing with one hand, started down.

Behind him, the faces followed. He could feel them back there, slipping from one shadow to the next, like they thought he wouldn't notice.

"You enjoying this, huh?" He stumbled, caught himself on the railing. "Stick with me, you'll get the whole show."

He went down two flights, then almost fell over something lying on the stairs next to the wall. He peered down at it angrily; it looked like a golf bag, but what kind of asshole would leave his golf clubs lying in a stairway? Then he realized that there were lots of them, lined up along one wall all the way down the stairs. And suddenly, without quite realizing it, he knew what they were.

Body bags. The basement must have flooded. They'd moved the dead bodies out of the morgue and into the stairway. That's what the smell was: rotting bodies. As he stood there, he heard voices, and two black orderlies came up the steps carrying another plastic body bag between them. They looked up at him, surprised.

"What you doin' down here? Nobody's supposed to be in here. You got to use the other stairs."

Jimmy opened his mouth to say something, then closed it again. He took a step back, feeling his way with his hand on the wall. He couldn't take his eyes off the limp vinyl sack they carried between them; it sagged in the middle, like a hammock slung between two trees.

"Go on," the orderly said, his voice angry now. "Get on back to where you come from!"

Jimmy retreated to the landing above them, paused there in the darkness. He watched the two men take a better grip on the body bag, then haul it up a few more steps, lay it down there next to the wall. They turned, started back down the stairs, and he heard one of them say:

"How many more they got down there?"

"Couple more. But they all wet. Floatin' around."

"Bad scene, the dead risin' like that. Like the last days."

"You think this is bad? Think about what all this water's doing to the cemeteries. Way some of those tombs over in St. Louis are crumbling, they'll have coffins floating around everywhere."

"Man, that's just gross."

And then there was only their footsteps, echoing up the stairs. He stood there for a long moment, looking down at the bodies lying along the wall.

"It ain't nothing," he whispered to the shadows behind him. "Just dead people."

But he could feel the shadows pressing in on him, like a weight on his heart. *You were looking for the way out*, they whispered. *Well, there it is.*

There was no light here. Nothing but darkness, and the stench of bodies that had been lying in the heat for hours. He took a cautious step back, but a wave of dizziness swept over him, like wind bending the trees back, and he lost his balance, felt himself grabbing helplessly for the railing. The shadows crowded in. He could feel their breath on his face, their hands slapping at his, and then he was falling back into the darkness. And as he fell, all he could think was:

Well, ain't this some shit.

|||| Outside the Convention Center, people were standing around like they expected a bus to pull up at any minute, take them out of the city, back to a world that made sense. You can learn to take

things for granted in America. Hit a switch, and the lights go on. Turn on the tap, and there's water that's clean enough to drink. Open the refrigerator, there's something to eat. You can carry your plate into the living room, sit down in front of the TV, turn on a ball game. Everybody in the stands is smiling, having fun. And at the end of every inning, while the players are grabbing their gloves and heading out into the field, you get commercials that promise you everything in your life can be bright and shiny and new.

So what can it feel like except a betrayal when you hit the switch and the lights don't come on, when you're stuck in a public storm shelter with twenty thousand people, no power or water, and everybody feels their nerves starting to fray? If you live in Desire or Tremé, you recognize the gang signs some of the young guys in the crowd are flashing at each other, and you start to wonder how many of them left their guns at home, and how many had them shoved down in their pants, under the oversized shirts they all wore, hanging loose, so even if they weren't carrying, you had to wonder.

Danny saw that most of the older men had stripped off their shirts, and the sweat was already dripping off them. They sat in what shade they could find with a slightly dazed look. Danny tried to imagine how hot it must be inside; he'd gone to Mardi Gras balls in there back when he was in college, and it was hard to picture twenty thousand people sitting on the floors of those vast window-less rooms, where the city's wealthy came once a year to drink champagne from a crystal fountain and dance the night away in their beaded costumes and masks.

"Hey, Danny!"

He looked over, surprised, saw a young black man emerge out of a small cluster of young men and come toward him. It took Danny a minute, but then he recognized him as Jules, who worked back in the kitchen at the Pearl Oyster Bar on St. Charles. Danny's office was in a building just up the street, and for years he'd been parking his car illegally in an alley that ran the length of the block. He gave the guys who worked in the kitchen at the Pearl a few bucks every month to keep an eye on his car through the screen door that opened onto the alley, and Jules had once earned himself an extra twenty by running up to Danny's office to warn him that there was a new traffic cop out there getting ready to have his car towed. Danny had hurried downstairs, caught the cop just before he called it in. It cost him seventy bucks—twenty for Jules, fifty for the cop— to keep his car out of the city impound lot, but after that the cops had left his car alone.

"Hey, Jules. How you doin'?"

Jules shook his head. "Not so good, man. They got us packed in there like cattle, no water, no food, and it's *hot* in there."

"Any storm damage?"

"Nah, we got through that okay. Sounded bad, stuff crashing around, but nothing happened. I heard the roof fell in on the Superdome, killed, like, a hundred people."

"Where'd you hear that?"

"Word's goin' around. Everybody heard it."

"Yeah?" Danny raised his eyebrows. "Cop back on Canal Street told me they just lost some roof panels. Nobody hurt."

"You believe that?"

"Sounded like he knew."

Jules shook his head. "Man, they got to keep a lid on it. They worried everybody hear about it, they have to start tellin' us the *truth*. You know what I'm sayin'?"

Danny didn't, exactly, but he shrugged, said, "Anyway, they got enough problems. Whole city's underwater."

Jules opened his eyes wide. "For *real*? How bad?"

"Ninth Ward's gone. Most everything east of the Industrial Canal looks about the same. And there's flooding up by City Park. Water's comin' all the way down Canal Street, but it's still pretty shallow. I can't really tell what the rest of the city looks like."

"Jesus," Jules said. "I *know* people who stayed in their houses last night all up through there. You tellin' me they all dead?"

Danny hesitated. "They could be fine," he said. "Lots of people got out. They're on their roofs, and there's rescue boats going all through those neighborhoods. Helicopters lifting people off houses. It's a whole big operation."

But Jules was looking back at the Convention Center now, and Danny could tell he was anxious to get back to his group and start spreading the bad news around. A hundred dead in the Superdome? That ain't nothing, man. They got *thousands* drowned over in the Ninth Ward. Whole city's underwater.

Bad news spreads to fill the low places in your spirit, Danny thought. When a city suffers, it's like the poison you drink together, which keeps you all connected to what's been lost. People start whispering, and it comes flooding in, spreads everywhere in minutes. There's nothing anyone can do.

"Look, I gotta go," he told Jules. "I heard there were some cops staying up at the Hampton Inn. You know if they're still over there?"

"I don't know, man. Only cops I've seen since yesterday took off. We got all these people over here, you'd think they'd send some cops over to keep things quiet, but I ain't seen 'em." He shook his head. "It's just us. Bunch of people got no place else to go." He left Danny standing there in the middle of the street, walked back toward the entrance to the Convention Center, vanishing into the crowd. Danny stood there for a moment, looking at the faces of the people whose eyes looked back at him emptily. Almost all of them were black, and for a moment Danny couldn't help thinking of the television news footage he'd seen of refugees in Liberia or Sierra Leone, who'd just staggered out of a war zone with nothing but what they could carry, looking as if hunger and heat had emptied them of all hope. But this wasn't some war-torn city in West Africa; this was America, the city where Danny had grown up, lived his entire life. Not an easy life, maybe, compared to some. But still, looking at these faces, he couldn't help feeling that he'd spent his years skating on a frozen pond; now the ice was breaking up under him, and he'd caught a glimpse of what lay hidden in the depths. New Orleans was two cities; he'd always known that. One had fled from the storm, and what they'd left behind was a city that was poor, black, and until this moment mostly invisible to those who spent their lives skating on that white surface. Danny had seen this other New Orleans many times before. His friendship with Jabril had shown him the city he'd ignored growing up, where families spent their whole lives just struggling to hang on, working long hours for minimum wage in the city's restaurants and tourist hotels, keeping the party going for those who thought of New Orleans the way the tourist brochures still described it, as the City That Care Forgot. But you could only see the city that way, Danny had realized, if you forgot to care about that other New Orleans, the one that worked hard, as their ancestors had worked hard to keep the great plantations running, the one that the tourists never saw, out there in the neighborhoods from which all the legendary music and spicy food had first emerged, and where the idea of a government that took care of its citizens was just a distant rumor.

Danny turned away, walked on up the street to the Hampton Inn at the corner of Gaiennie Street. A white cop in mirrored sunglasses and an NOPD T-shirt, wearing a semiautomatic pistol in a shoulder holster, his badge hanging from a lanyard around his neck, sat in a folding lawn chair in front of the glass doors, an M16 lying across his lap. He watched Danny walk toward him, his hand resting on the rifle, until Danny called out, "This where I find Sixth District?"

"What's left of it. We had most of the division staying here last night. Now there's only about six of us." The cop looked over at the crowd standing in front of the Convention Center. "We're taking turns guarding the place, so nobody gets into our stuff."

"So you're the only one here?"

"Last couple hours, yeah. Everybody else either took off across the river or they're out working rescue."

Danny followed his gaze. From here, the people standing in front of the Convention Center were just a crowd. You couldn't see the exhausted expression on people's faces.

"You got anybody over there?"

He shrugged. "Eighth District might, but I haven't seen any cops. Lot of those people over there just showed up yesterday. We heard they were sending them down from the Superdome when that got filled up, but I can't tell that anybody's in charge over there. Truth is, we aren't even supposed to be down here. Captain had it set up for us to stay at the Pontchartrain Hotel over on St. Charles, so we'd be right there in our district. But we got there a couple hours before the storm hit, the whole place was locked up and everybody had left town. So one of our guys who works security down here sometimes had a key to this place. We all just came down here, rode out the storm." He looked at Danny, his sunglasses reflecting Danny's image back at him, like he'd suddenly decided to take an interest. "So what you need with the Sixth District, anyway?"

"I'm looking for a couple of guys used to work up there. They got canned a couple years back, work for Little Jimmy Mancuso now."

"One of them has red hair?"

"That's right."

"Yeah, I know those guys. What you want with them?"

Danny hesitated. "I'm looking for a friend. I heard they might know where he is."

"You're looking for a friend." The cop looked at Danny, gave a harsh laugh. "Man, my family took off yesterday, I got no idea where they are. Half my unit's missing, they could be anywhere. We got people never showed up for duty, half of them probably got caught in their houses when the water rose, we'll find 'em in a couple weeks when they get the water drained out of the city, start looking for bodies." He waved a hand toward the Convention Center. "Hell, I heard there's twenty thousand people over there, maybe twice that up in the Dome. How you expect to find *one guy*?"

"They're supposed to be holding him in a place the police used to question people off the books. Some kind of old warehouse with an interrogation room they used, back in the bad old days."

The cop looked away, his eyes going over to the people standing on the neutral ground up the block by the Convention Center. "The bad old days, huh?" He was silent for a moment, then he shook his head. "You're asking the wrong guy. I don't know nothing about any of that stuff."

"You know anybody who would?"

He lifted the M16 off his lap, leaned it against his chair. Then he eased up on one elbow, dug an old bandanna from the back pocket of his shorts, used it to wipe his face. Then he carefully folded it, shoved it back into his pocket, adjusted his sunglasses, and picked up his rifle, laid it back across his lap. "Patrol sergeant could probably tell you," he said casually. "He's been there forever."

"You know where I could find him?"

"Last I heard, he was still up at the station." The cop had an empty tone to his voice now, and he wouldn't meet Danny's eyes. "Captain wanted somebody to stay there, keep an eye on things."

"You mean the Sixth District station up on Felicity Street?"

"Uh-huh. Can't promise he's still there, though. Depends on the flood."

Danny looked up at the sky. The light was fading. Off to the east, the last banks of clouds from the storm still lay thick on the horizon, dark and heavy as an unhealed wound.

The cop followed his gaze. He reached up, took off his sunglasses. Danny saw that his eyes were exhausted.

"Getting dark soon," the cop said. "You should find yourself someplace to spend the night. I been hearing shooting from over beyond the expressway for the last couple hours. I wouldn't want to be walking around out there tonight."

"I guess I'll take my chances."

The cop looked up at him for a moment, then shrugged. "Okay. Your funeral. But I got a feeling all the animals are gonna come out tonight. It ain't gonna be pretty."

"It wasn't ever pretty," Danny said. "We just never noticed before now."

⫼ "All right, listen up, people." ATF Assistant Special Agent in Charge Jim Fisher stood in the bed of a pickup truck on a Veterans Boulevard overpass surrounded by water, looked down at the small group of agents gathered around him. They wore combat gear and body armor, carried assault rifles and night-vision goggles, but they all looked tired. They'd spent the night listening to the wind howl around their building up at the end of Veterans near the Seventeenth Street canal, and by the time the worst of the storm passed over them at midmorning, most of the windows had blown out, leaving their offices soaked by rain and ravaged by wind. When the wind finally died down enough for them to leave the shelter of the hallway where they'd all waited out the storm, he'd looked down onto Veterans from the shattered windows of his office and found that the streets were slowly filling with water. It took them almost five hours to find enough boats to get their team and equipment to high ground, and then they'd only managed it because one of his agents, Mickie Vega, had proved surprisingly skilled at hot-wiring a Ford 4×4 with a suspension lift kit and off-road tires that they found parked in a nearby parking garage. She'd smashed the driver's window with the butt of her rifle, swept the broken glass out of the driver's seat with one gloved hand, then climbed behind the wheel and popped the hood.

"You sure you know what you're doing?"

She shot Fisher a look. "I'm Mexican. We learn this stuff in grade school."

She put the truck in neutral, set the emergency brake, then got out, went around to the front of the truck, and raised the hood. Then she leaned in, spent a moment sorting through some wires in the electrical system, and when she'd chosen one, yanked it out. "Sorry, guys," she said to the agents gathered around the truck. "I'm afraid we won't be able to run the heater."

She connected one end of the wire to the battery, ran it to the coil. Then she followed the positive battery cable down into the engine, found a small wire near where it entered the starter, and used a screwdriver to cross the two wires. The starter whirred. She shifted her position slightly, touched the two wires again, and this time the engine sparked, caught, and the truck started up. She straightened up, slammed the hood of the truck, and got back behind the wheel. She leaned in over the steering wheel, pushed the flat blade of the screwdriver down into the crack between the wheel and the steering column, then gave the wheel a quick jerk, unlocking it. She looked up at Fisher. "Okay, what's next?"

They'd used the truck to make two trips through the floodwaters, until the water got too deep and they had to leave the truck on an elevated section of highway. But by that time they'd managed to get over to a boat dealer on Airline Highway that had come through the storm with almost no damage, tow away a couple of small fishing boats, which they launched off an overpass. They'd found a couple of searchlights at a sporting goods store nearby, mounted them on the boats for night operations, and now they'd split up into two teams, ready to go.

"Listen up," he repeated now, although they were all silent, looking up at him with exhausted eyes. He glanced down at the sheet of paper in his hand, where he'd scrawled some quick notes. "Best I can tell, we've got search-and-rescue operations going on across the flood zone that extends throughout the eastern part of the city.

NOPD is also requesting help with foot patrols. They've already had major looting in some areas, and there are a couple of reports of guns being looted out of stores across the city." He looked up at the agents. "I don't need to tell you that the last thing we want is to see a lot of heavily armed looters running around, so while it may be too late to secure all gun stores across the city, we should give that priority." He looked down at his notes again. "There have been some reports of shooting at officers conducting rescue operations in the flood zone, and several hospitals across the city have requested help securing their buildings against looting. It's only a matter of time before every addict in the city starts going into withdrawal, and it won't take them long to figure out where they can go to get what they need." He folded the paper, stuck it in his pocket. "Tonight we're all working rescue. There's a lot of water out there, and we don't know how many people still need help. Keep your weapons secured unless you run into trouble. These people just need somebody to get them to dry land. In the morning we'll meet back here for a situation assessment, and if it looks like the locals have the rescue operation under control, I'll put one team on securing the gun stores and we'll do what we can to provide some security where it's needed. That means rapid response, so try to get some rest and food when you can." He looked around at the agents. "Understood?"

They all nodded. "Okay, let's do it."

They climbed into their boats, and Fisher saw Mickie Vega start to strip off her body armor. "Vega, what are you doing?"

She paused, her Kevlar vest dangling from one hand, looked over at him. "We're going out on a rescue mission. You think the threat level warrants taking the risk that we'll fall overboard wearing body armor?" She waved a hand at the boat. "I'm an okay swimmer, but this is a small boat, and I don't really see the point of raising my handicap."

Fisher saw the other agents looking over at him, waiting for his reply. "Okay, you're right. Use your discretion on the body armor. If you come under fire, I want everybody taking appropriate precautions. If not, then you can stow it in your boats."

He saw the other agents start to strip off their armor. Mickie folded up her vest, tucked it under a seat at the front of the boat. For a moment Fisher wondered if he should feel offended at her words. Was she questioning his command authority? But then he realized there was no operational precedent for *anything* they were doing: commandeering civilian vehicles, conducting marine rescue operations, assisting local law enforcement in areas beyond the bureau's mandate. Nobody had written up any plans for hurricane relief, so they were just making it up as they went along. He had well-trained agents, so it was time to give them some discretion, let them show what they could do under their own initiative. He'd been about to climb into the same boat as Vega, but now some impulse made him change his mind.

"Vega," he called out. "You're in command of your boat. See if you can get some situation reports if you run into other law enforcement, and we'll meet back here at dawn." And with that, he climbed into the other boat, nodded to the agent behind the wheel, and gripped the windshield as the agent hit the throttle, making the boat fishtail slightly as it headed out Polk Street toward the deep water out around City Park.

Mickie felt the other agents' eyes on her as she tucked her rifle under the seat, watched the boat vanish into the flood zone. "Okay," she said, straightening up. "Looks like we've got another long night ahead of us, so let's get to it. They headed east, so we'll swing up through Lakeview, see if we find anybody up there, then work our way east from there." She met each of their eyes in turn. "That work for everybody?"

They nodded, and one of the agents grinned. "Your command," he said. "Just point the way."

Damn right, she thought, as the agent behind the wheel fired up the engine. *But you wouldn't have said it if I was a man.*

IIII On Tchoupitoulas Street, Danny came across a Wal-Mart that was in the process of being looted. The front windows were smashed, and he saw people walking out with their arms full of stuff. Most of them emerged carrying the kind of stuff they'd need to survive—bottled water, packaged food, one guy even emerged carrying an inflatable beach raft, and Danny couldn't help thinking of the guy he'd seen floating on a raft like that a few hours earlier. Where was this guy headed? Was he planning to paddle out into the flood zone looking to help?

But many other people came out of the store carrying clothing, appliances, DVDs, and computer games. Some of them were pushing shopping carts full of stuff. Danny had once seen some footage of a pre-Christmas sale at one of the suburban department stores. They'd announced that they would open the doors at eight A.M. When the crowd waiting outside the store reached several hundred, a TV news crew showed up, and they managed to film the moment when the doors were thrown open and a herd of anxious shoppers trampled each other, sending twelve people to the hospital, in their rush to get at the bargains. That was how people acted under *normal* circumstances, so now that it felt like the normal rules had been swept away, no traffic on the streets, all the guardians of order vanished, having fled the city for higher ground, it felt strangely like a carnival, the day a king is swept from power by workingmen carrying baseball bats and sawed-off broom handles. For a few hours the flag is torn down and trampled into the ground, and an old man stands on the street corner, weeping with joy, while he slaps at a picture of the tyrant with his shoe.

But there was no joy in these people's faces. A boy ran past

Danny carrying a video game player. "It's all free in there," he yelled to Danny. "Everything's all fucked up!"

Civilization had been blown from the streets, and for a moment groups of young men were indulging the fantasy that gets enacted on the streets of Beirut and Berlin and Freetown, when a boy with a gun proclaims himself the city's king, struts through the streets, taking everything that has always been denied him. Danny stood there watching it, and he thought, *They'll start shooting soon.* Why not, after all? The world had been destroyed around them. Chaos had come at last, as they had always known it would. How could a system so corrupt last? Now it was as if the animals had broken out of their cages to find their keepers had fled, leaving sacks of food lying around, just there for the taking. But how long would it be, Danny had to wonder, before the jackals started to feast on the deer, and the rabbits ran through the streets in terror, feeling the wolves close behind, their breath hot against their backs, the razor teeth closing on their terrified throats?

Danny turned, walked on. It was starting to feel like an epic journey, Dante wandering through hell or Odysseus adrift on his wine-dark sea. Except what he'd seen struck him as too strange even for hell, and nobody would ever compare the floods he'd crossed to wine. They had an oily look, and a smell that could make you gag in the late August heat. It was hard to imagine that anything that water touched would ever be clean again. Just as it was hard to believe that these people who'd emerged from their homes to find that those who ran this city had fled, left it to sink into the sea around them, would ever accept the old ways again. The whole city would have to be scrubbed clean, not just of these toxic waters, but of the corruption that had caused it, and the casual way that the powerful had allowed its weight to fall upon the poorest of its citizens.

A moment later Danny saw the first car he'd seen moving along the streets since the storm, a police cruiser, which raced past him, lights flashing, and turned into the parking lot in front of the Wal-

Mart. Danny turned, stood there watching as a pair of uniformed officers climbed out of the squad car, guns drawn, and walked calmly in through the store's smashed front door. A few seconds passed, and then suddenly a torrent of people began to spill out of the store, their arms full of merchandise, the crowd quickly scattering in every direction. *There it is,* Danny thought angrily. *Half the city's drowning, but at least they've secured the Wal-Mart. At least their priorities are clear.*

A moment later one of the cops came out carrying a large box. He went over to the squad car, popped the trunk, and shoved it in there. His partner came out carrying more stuff, and they loaded up the squad car. Danny saw that some of the people they'd chased out of the store were hanging around the edges of the parking lot, waiting their chance to get back in there. It made him think of those TV wildlife shows where you see the hyenas scattering when a pair of lions show up to feast on their kill; they hang back, just beyond the lions' reach, waiting until the big cats have eaten their fill, and when the lions walk away, they move back in, stripping the last bits of meat from the bones.

Danny headed up across Magazine Street toward St. Charles. A few years back, before he'd met Mickie, he'd spent a lot of time sitting in Rue de la Course up by Magazine and Ninth Streets, killing time while he waited to go meet one of Jimmy Boudrieux's political contacts with an envelope full of cash. There was a girl who worked behind the counter that he couldn't take his eyes off. Not beautiful, exactly, but with a strong face, a pierced nose, and fierce dark eyes. For weeks she never said more than a few words to him as she got him his coffee, ran a wet rag across his table quickly, then walked away. One morning she was wearing a T-shirt with the name of a punk band on the front, with the neck and sleeves cut off. As she bent to wipe off his table, he saw that she had some words tattooed on her back between her shoulder blades. But all he could see clearly was one word—THE. She straightened up, walked back to the counter, and Danny realized that the strange feeling he had in his chest was his heart, beating hard. *Women you can read,* he thought. *What'll they think of next?*

It took him another week to work up his courage, but one morning, as she brought him his coffee, he said, "Can I ask you a personal question?"

She set his coffee down in front of him, looked at him. "Depends. What's the question?"

"You've got something written on your back."

"Yeah." She gave a slight smile. "And you want to know what it says."

He shook his head. "That would ruin the mystery."

"So what's your question?"

"What's a guy have to do to see it?"

She studied his face for a moment. "You tried prayer?" And she laid his check on the table, walked away.

Danny couldn't help smiling now, remembering it. Weird how that memory came back to him at this moment. Was that all any city was, or any person, just a web of memory on which we hang the present? Walking across the shattered city, he'd been unable to escape the sensation that he was seeing everything double, like a drunk pressing his hand over one eye as he weaves his way home so the sidewalk will stay in one place. What he saw unfolding around him was so strange that his mind couldn't make sense of it; instead, he kept seeing each place as it had once been only days, weeks, or months ago, full of life and light and people going about their daily lives. But now he had to wonder, had any of that ever been real, or was it just a pleasant dream from which they'd been violently woken?

At St. Charles, a Walgreens was being looted. The front doors had been smashed, and people were hauling out boxes of medical supplies and bottled water. One guy came out wheeling a rack of sunglasses. Danny saw two men hauling away an ATM, some others back in the pharmacy, tearing the place apart. While he watched, a young kid rode up on his bike, got off and locked it to the bike rack, then went inside, like nothing was out of the ordinary. He emerged a few minutes later carrying two cartons of soda, which he strapped to the book rack on the back of his bicycle, and rode away, weaving slightly from the extra weight.

Down the block, some people were standing in front of the Avenue Pub, bottles of beer in their hands, like they were watching a Mardi Gras parade. Danny walked over.

"How long has this been going on?" he asked a kid who looked like he might be a Tulane student.

"What? You mean the looting?" The kid shrugged. "Started about an hour ago. We were inside having a beer, and we heard this loud crash. Some guys drove a pickup truck through the front door. They were hauling out the registers, the night-deposit safe, anything they could get their hands on, and tossing it in the back of the truck. Then they drove away, but I guess the word must have spread, because everybody else showed up about ten minutes later, and they've been cleaning the place out ever since."

Danny was surprised to see that the beer in his hand was cold. "This place open?"

The kid laughed. "Man, they never shut. Couple guys rode out the storm in there, and we came over when the wind was still blowing. They got a generator running out back, so the beer's still cold. You want a burger, they're runnin' the grill."

Danny realized he was starving. He hadn't eaten anything since the women at Jabril's warehouse had fixed up some sandwiches for them out of a cooler before they set out in the boat. But he wanted to get up to Felicity Street before it got completely dark.

"Maybe I'll come back. You think they'll still be open later?"

"Bartender said they're not shutting down. It's been getting pretty scary out here, but I'd rather be sitting in there than back in my apartment. Wind blew a tree against it, busted out a whole wall. Everything's soaked." He laughed. "Hell, I may just live here."

"You could do worse."

Danny walked back up St. Charles, keeping to the opposite side of the street from the looting at the Walgreens, then headed north on Felicity. Trees and power lines were down everywhere, and one house had been split almost down the middle by a falling light pole. He saw a grocery store on St. Andrews being looted, and he passed a funeral home that was on fire. A crowd of people were standing in the street, watching it burn, but none of them said a word as Danny went past. He covered his mouth with his hand, trying not to think about what might be causing the stench that drifted in the thick smoke. At LaSalle Street, he saw that the street was shining. There was almost no light in the sky now, but he saw the glow of the fire behind him gleaming on the street. He crouched down, looked at it more closely, then slowly extended one finger, touched the damp pavement. Just a thin film on the street, but it felt like it was flowing along the surface of the street. And as he crouched there, he saw the waterline creep away behind him, moving slowly south down the block. He straightened up. He only had a couple more blocks to go. He could see the Sixth District headquarters up ahead, just another dark building on a block of dark buildings.

He stood there looking at the water. *Toxic gumbo.* Somehow, this seemed like a moment of decision. How far was he willing to go to help a client? Was he ready to risk dysentery, cholera, a bacterial infection sinking roots into his skin? People were dying out there in the darkness. *What can you do about it? You're just one guy. All you'll do is make yourself sick.*

But that's an empty thought, he realized, and a feeling of anger swept over him. Just a way people forgive themselves for doing nothing. You do what you can, even if it isn't enough. You do it, and you *keep* doing it, as long as you can, because that's what you'd want somebody to do for you when the day comes that you see the water start to rise. No excuses, no medals. You do it because all we've got is each other, no matter how much people try to convince you otherwise: no world except the one we make by our acts of mercy and courage and kindness, or by our hatred and hollowness of soul. *Choose the world you want*, he thought, *because you make it every day.*

He waded in. He could feel the water squelch under his shoes. By the end of the block, he was making small splashes with each step, and as he crossed the intersection, it felt like when you go out to the store after a hard rain and you have to run through the puddles. But you couldn't jump these puddles; the whole street was covered with water now, so that it felt more like wading up a shallow stream against a current that flowed past the other way. He could feel it get deeper as he went. By the time he reached the police building, it was over his ankles. The station was dark, but one of the doors stood open. Danny started up the steps, pausing to shake the water off his shoes.

"Hold it right there."

Danny froze. A flashlight came on, blinding him. After a moment it moved down his body, pausing at his waist.

"You want to show me what you got under your shirt?"

"It's a gun," Danny said.

"I didn't figure it was a toaster oven. Looks like you carry right-handed. That right?"

Danny nodded.

"Okay, so here's what I want you to do. Lift your shirt slowly with your right hand, then reach across with your left and slide the gun out with your thumb and forefinger. Set it down on the steps next to your feet. I got a shotgun pointed at you, so just take it *real* easy." Danny did as he was told. Then he straightened up, showed his empty hands. "That better?"

"Uh-huh. Now just shove it over against the wall with your foot." The flashlight stayed on Danny's feet until he'd pushed the gun away. "That's fine. Now why don't you tell me what you want?"

"You Sixth District?"

"That's right." The flashlight went off, and a moment later a battery-powered emergency light came on. Danny saw a black police sergeant sitting on a folding chair behind a metal table, which he'd turned on its side so that it faced the door like a barricade. He was wearing his combat rig, including his Kevlar vest, military-style helmet, and a shoulder holster. He lowered his shotgun and switched off the light. "Not taking any crime reports at the moment, if that's why you're here. Whole city's a crime scene right now. All I can tell you is stay in your house. Anybody comes 'round you don't recognize, that's why you got a gun."

"How come you're sitting here in the dark? Don't you guys have a generator?"

"Uh-huh. Puts out enough power to run the lights, anyway. But you take a close look at those doors, you'll see why I ain't in no hurry to be showing no lights. Last couple hours, people been ridin' past, taking shots at the building. Seems like everybody out there's runnin' around with guns. Half of 'em think it's a big party, they're out there shooting off their guns, and the other half are lookin' for some serious payback. I'm not gonna make it easier for 'em."

Danny's eyes were starting to adjust to the darkness now, and he could see the cop's outline behind the table. "But you're still here."

The cop shrugged. "Somebody's got to stick around. I'm duty sergeant, so I guess it's me."

"*Just* you?"

"You see anybody else?"

Behind him Danny heard the crack of gunshots from up the block. He glanced back at the street nervously. "You mind if I get out of the door?"

"Probably be a good idea."

He moved around behind the table, pressed his back to the wall, out of direct line with the doorway. "They're really shooting at the station?"

"Had a couple rounds come through the window in the next room a couple minutes ago. Got worse after it started getting dark. You got a bunch of young guys walking around out there, they figure the usual rules don't apply. Ninth Ward's all flooded, the power's out, and everybody with any sense boarded up their house and left town. Those guys out there don't know whether to party or get pissed off. Just a matter of time before they start heading over to the Garden District, burning down all those rich folks' mansions." The cop looked over at Danny, "I'm surprised you made it here in one piece. You walk up from St. Charles?"

"Yeah."

"They finish emptying out the Walgreens?"

"There's still a pretty good crowd. They were dragging out the ATM when I went past."

The cop laughed. "Good luck to 'em. You need a stick of dynamite to get those things open. How'd the streets look?"

"There's trees down everywhere, power lines . . ."

"I've seen all that. How's the flooding?"

"You got almost a foot out there on the street right now."

"Shit." The cop stood up, looked out over the table into the street beyond, but he couldn't see anything. "I went out there about an hour ago and it was still pretty dry."

"Well, it's rising now," Danny told him. "You might want to find yourself another place. It gets much deeper, you'll have it coming in the door."

"Yeah, I figured I'd probably have to get out of here. I had a radio, but the batteries died. Sounds like a levee gave way up by City Park." He sat down. "Not that anybody's given me any orders. I guess I'm on my own up here."

"I saw a couple guys from your outfit at the Hampton Inn down by the Convention Center. And the department's got an emergency command post at Harrah's. You could head down there."

"Guess I'll have to. Water keeps rising, won't be a whole lot of other places to go." More gunshots, closer this time. The cop raised his shotgun onto his lap. "So what's got you up here, anyway? Last place in the world I'd be walking around tonight."

"I'm looking for some guys who used to work Sixth District Vice."

"*Used* to work it? How long since they been up here?"

"Ten years back, maybe a little longer."

"And you come up here looking for them?" The cop laughed. "Man, sounds like you a little late."

"I'm looking for people who knew them. One guy was named Vince, and he had a partner named Lenny. They work for Jimmy Mancuso now."

The cop was silent. Then he gave a soft cough. "Just my fuckin' luck. Feels like I'm comin' down with something."

"You know the guys I'm talking about?"

"I heard of 'em."

"They buddies of yours?"

The cop laughed. "I don't think you see those two guys hangin' out with the brothers. You know what I mean?"

"Yeah, I guess I do." Danny hesitated. "You ever hear about a place they used to take suspects to interrogate them off the books? Some kind of warehouse?"

"Heard about it, sure. You hear all kind of stories, workin' up here."

"So you've never seen it?"

The cop looked at him in the darkness. "Funny time to be asking these questions. You think it matters now, what the guys who worked up here used to do?"

"Might matter a lot to a guy I know. He was getting ready to testify to a grand jury, but they grabbed him off the street. The best I could find out is that they're holding him someplace they used to take people when they worked as cops."

There was a long pause. Danny heard some kids run past on the street outside, water splashing under their feet.

"You think maybe this is something for *us* to handle?"

"Sure. When you figure that'll happen? You got some officers with free time on their hands?"

"You talk to the FBI?"

"They're in the same boat as you guys. Everybody they got is on emergency duty. Might be weeks before they can free up some agents to look for him. This guy doesn't have that long."

The cop reached down, picked up the water bottle next to his chair, took a long drink. Then he wiped his mouth with the back of his wrist, closed the bottle, and set it back on the floor. "Okay, I see your problem."

"Any way you can help me?"

"There's a bunch of cops who'd know those guys. White guys, mostly. They had a group of 'em used to do things their own way, if you know what I mean. We're talking like ten years ago, back before all the federal investigations. Black cops used to call 'em the Guidos, although half of 'em were Irish, Polish. They all come out of those old cop families, you know? Grew up in the Irish Channel or Mid-City. These guys, they hung together. When I came on the force, first thing everybody told me was, don't cross the Guidos. Just do your job and stay out of their way, they won't bother you none. Lot of that in the old days. Brothers used to say NOPD stood for 'Not *Our* Police Department.' " He shook his head. "Everybody heard the stories, but you figured half of it was just talk. This is the late eighties, early nineties. You really think cops could still get away with hauling guys away to some secret warehouse, takin' care of things off the books? But things don't change as much as you think they do. Or things change, but people, they stay the same. You walk in a squad room, you see more black skin." He waved a hand toward the door. "But look out there, and tell me how much things have changed. How many white folks you see stuck in this city?"

"I'm here," Danny said. "And I'm not the only one."

"What? You mean like those folks down on St. Charles, sittin' in their big old houses?" He shook his head. "We had a couple guys come up here right after the storm passed. It's still raining out there, trees are down everywhere, these guys want to file a crime report. Someone broke into their car, stole the radio. I'm looking at these two guys, and I'm thinking, what the *fuck*? Look around you! There's people dead. You think I give a *shit* about your car radio?"

"What did you tell them?"

He smiled. "Got to be polite. I told 'em, 'I'm sorry, but we're not taking crime reports today. You'll have to come back after the weather emergency is lifted.' You know what one of them says? 'The storm's over. What's the emergency?' I'm thinking, man, I *hope* that's the worst thing you got to worry about today. That would be nice for you."

Danny looked at him. "I'm trying to save a guy's life. You get that, right?"

"Looks like there's a lot of lives need saving out there."

"So how come you're sitting here?"

For a moment neither of them spoke.

"Somebody's got to secure this building," the cop said quietly. "Those are my orders."

"And what happens if the water rises?"

"Then it don't really matter what I do, does it?" Off in the distance they heard a crashing sound, like metal shearing away, and then people cheering. "Look," he said, "I get what you're trying to do. The guy you need to talk to is named Langer. He worked Vice with those guys, back when all that shit was going down."

"Will he talk to me?"

The cop shrugged. "Hard to say. He used to be a drinker, but his wife made him start going to meetings a couple years back. Makes a man think about his past. He might feel like he's got some stuff to get off his chest."

"Any idea where I can find him?"

"I saw him a couple days ago, but that won't help you now. With the rest of the unit, probably."

Danny eased off the wall. "I appreciate your help." He went back around the table. "Okay if I pick up my gun?"

"Go ahead. Just don't forget I'm holding a shotgun."

Danny bent down, felt around by the wall for the pistol. "You mind giving me some light here?"

The cop's flashlight came on. Danny picked up the gun, saw the light follow as he slid it into his pants, pulled his shirt down over it. Then the light went out.

"Good luck," he told the cop.

"Uh-huh. You be careful. Some crazy people out there tonight."

The water on the street was deeper now. Danny waded back down Felicity Street, saw that it had reached the burning funeral home. It was strange to see a building in flames, surrounded on all sides by water. The crowd that had been watching the fire had vanished, and now the street was empty, except for a couple boys on bicycles who were riding through the water, laughing, like they'd been waiting for this day all their lives. A woman came out on the porch of a house, yelled at the boys to quit their foolishness and get on inside, *right now*.

Like that'll help, Danny thought. How long would it be before the water came up over the porch, spilled into the house? They should leave now, before it got too deep. But leave for where? All over the city, there were people wading out of the flood zone carrying a few things in a plastic bag. But where could they go? The water was rising, and soon there would be no place to go except to the high ground along the river. The city would empty as it had filled, a human tide flowing back up the avenues toward the French Quarter, like history unreeling before your eyes. And then what? Would they all climb aboard boats that would carry them away, leaving the city to the alligators and water moccasins? Or slowly rebuild, draining the city to dare history again, until the next time that the winds came and the water rose?

When he reached St. Charles, the Walgreens was silent and dark. Its shattered doors looked like an empty eye socket staring out at the world.

He walked over to the Avenue Pub, found the door unlocked, a small crowd of people inside drinking beer by the light of an oil lamp. But they had a grill going somewhere, and the smell of hamburgers cooking made Danny suddenly feel that he'd fallen down a well. He went over to the bar, leaned against it, feeling the exhaustion catch up with him. The bartender came over, said, "You look like you could use a drink."

"Any chance I could get one of those burgers I smell cooking?"

"You got money?"

"Yeah."

"Then I guess we're in business."

Danny ate slowly, and when he'd finished his beer, he raised the empty bottle to the bartender, who brought over another one.

"Take the edge off?" The bartender tossed the empty into a trash can behind the bar.

"It's a start, anyway. Is it true you stayed open through the storm?"

"We had beer. We had customers. Take a lot more than a storm to close us down."

"The streets are starting to flood up near Claiborne."

"Yeah? That why your shoes are all wet?"

Danny looked down. A small puddle had formed on the floor around him. "Sorry."

"Don't worry about it. We've cleaned up a lot worse than that in here before." The bartender took a rag from under the bar, gave it a swipe while Danny raised his bottle.

"So how deep?"

"Couple inches so far. But it's rising."

"And you think it'll come down this far?"

Danny shrugged. "That guy up at LSU who did the flood predictions said we could lose everything except a couple blocks along the river."

"No shit."

"That's how it looks."

The bartender shook his head wearily. "You live around here?"

"Over on Calhoun Street."

"You come through it okay?"

"I haven't been back to the house since the storm. I was over in the Ninth Ward."

"Seriously?"

Danny nodded. "They're sitting on roofs over there, waiting for a boat to come rescue them. There's twenty feet of water in some places." He looked down at the beer bottle in his hand. Suddenly it tasted flat in his mouth. He set it on the bar, took out his wallet. "I should get going. What do I owe you?"

The bartender went over to the cash register, wrote up a check by hand, brought it back to Danny. "Cash only. We're doing everything by hand, like the old days."

Danny tossed a twenty on the bar, waited while the bartender went back to the register, dug his change out of the open drawer, and counted it out on the bar.

"Stay dry, now."

"Yeah. You guys hang in there."

"We'll be here." The bartender gave a thin smile. "Come hell or high water."

|||| Danny walked up St. Charles toward Audubon Park. There were trees down everywhere, and he saw a couple houses with some serious roof damage, but mostly the Garden District looked like it always did, except that the pale light that usually spilled from the windows of the great houses was absent. The whole city was

dark and silent, as if a shadow had fallen over it. The only light came from a trash can somebody had set on fire near the corner of Napoleon Avenue. A few kids stood around it, their faces lit by the flames. Every few blocks Danny heard what sounded like gunshots off to the north. Other shadows moved through the darkness. He passed a man carrying a baseball bat on his shoulder, like he was just getting ready to step into the batting cage. Danny saw him tighten his grip as the distance between them closed, so he left the street, headed up onto the median ground to walk along the streetcar tracks. Something in the air had changed now that night had fallen. Over the last few hours, as he'd walked across the city, he'd felt a sense of stunned relief, as people emerged from their houses to find that the storm had spared them the worst. Broken windows, splintered trees, roofs torn away. But they'd seen all this before, and you could almost begin to believe that it would take a couple days to get the power back on, and then the city would return to normal. People looked shocked when they heard about the terrible flooding in the Ninth Ward, but not surprised. They'd seen that before too. Somehow, it seemed inevitable. Where else would the disaster fall? In New Orleans, it was always the poor who caught the knife by the blade.

But as the day wore on, something had started to change. Maybe it was the looting, or the sound of gunshots, or the rumors of water rising steadily all across the city, but by the time night fell, the people you saw on the street had begun to take on a frightened look, as if they'd started to realize that the worst hadn't passed them by. Worse was coming; they could feel it now. Darkness fell, and suddenly fear gripped their hearts. Men reached for their guns. You could smell the rage. Across town, people were drowning. But here in the Garden District, where the wealthy lived in pleasure and luxury, he saw men standing on porches with loaded shotguns, ready to kill to protect their property. Which, he wondered, was the greater tragedy? You could lose your life in a storm, but you could also surrender your soul.

He walked on, feeling like something was drawing him. At Calhoun Street, he turned north, walked up toward his house until he felt water splashing under his feet. Then he stopped, stood there looking up the street, still many blocks away from home, and he suddenly knew he couldn't face what he would see if he kept going. He turned around, walked back toward St. Charles. His mother's old house on Octavia Street, now owned by a heart surgeon, looked like it had come through the storm with almost no damage. The ancient oak tree in the front garden had lost a few branches, which lay scattered across the sidewalk, but the house itself looked fine. The streets near St. Charles were dry, so there was still hope that this area might escape the flooding. And then, as if drawn to it, he found himself walking over to Audubon Place, standing outside Jimmy Boudrieux's old house, which had stood empty for almost two years after Jimmy's death, while the IRS dug through his estate, trying to determine how much should be seized and sold at auction as proceeds of a criminal conspiracy. In the end, the house had been sold quietly to an old hunting buddy of a powerful Mississippi senator, who ran an oil exploration supply company with contracts throughout the Gulf states. Danny usually avoided this block. Looking at the house gave him a hollow feeling that he recognized as a combination of anger and guilt. But the house was part of his history, and somehow he'd felt drawn to check on it, make sure it had survived.

There was more tree damage in the yard, and it looked like part of the roof at the southeast corner of the house, over what had once been Jimmy's study, had sustained some damage. Danny could picture every inch of that room; he'd spent hours there, sitting on Jimmy's leather couch, waiting while Jimmy concluded the night's political business and got ready to move on to the more delicate issues that required the services of a man like Danny. Later, when Marty Seagraves played the surveillance tapes for him, he could hear the couch sigh as he shifted his weight, the ice bumping gently against the sides of his glass of single-malt whiskey, and Jimmy's voice, talking, always talking.

"Danny?"

He wasn't sure he'd heard it at first. A whisper behind him in the darkness. He turned, saw a figure emerge from under the trees across the street. He started to reach for his gun, then realized that it was a woman's voice, and that she'd spoken his name. "Who's that?"

"It's Maura."

But he'd recognized her, even before she answered him. In the darkness, you might have mistaken her for a teenage boy: she wore baggy painter's pants, a sweatshirt, and a baseball cap pulled down low over her short hair. But her eyes still had that hungry look he remembered, which made every man she looked at feel strangely ashamed, like a dealer with a pocketful of what she needed to survive.

"What are you doing here? It's not safe to be out alone."

"I could ask you the same thing."

"I wanted to check on my house," Danny told her. "It's a few blocks north of here, over on Calhoun. But the streets are flooded."

"I'm sorry." She looked up at the house where she'd grown up. "I just wanted to see if this place survived."

"How come you didn't leave town?"

"I just got back into town." Then she laughed. "Anyway, I was out partying, and I slept through most of Saturday. By the time I found out the storm was coming, I couldn't get a ride."

"You don't have a car?"

She shook her head. "They took away my license a few years ago. I had some DUIs out in California. Then I hit a school bus."

"You hit a *school bus*?"

"Three, actually. But they were all parked for the night." She took his arm suddenly, drew him back into the shadows at the other side of the street. "Look up there on the porch. There's a guy with a gun."

Danny followed her gaze. The porch was dark, but he could barely make out a man moving around, holding something that looked like a compact assault rifle. "Probably the guy who owns the place. There's people all over the neighborhood sitting in front of their houses with guns."

"I don't think so. I walked past here a couple hours ago, when it was still light out, and they had security guards checking all the doors and windows. You know that company does all the private security work for the oil companies over in Iraq?"

"Blackwater?"

She nodded. "The guy who owns the place now must do business with them. They drove up in a Humvee, all these big guys in Oakley shades and flak jackets, carrying Uzis. They checked out the house, and then two of them stayed when the Humvee took off. There's another guy inside. They take turns out on the porch. You get too close, I think they'd shoot you."

Danny looked at her. "Do you have someplace to stay?"

"I've got an apartment over on Laurel. How about you? You said your house is flooded?"

"I don't know. I haven't been back. There's water in the street."

"So you need a place to sleep."

Danny hesitated. "Maura, I'm married now."

"Hey, fuck you! I just asked if you had a place to sleep, not if you wanted to go to bed with me. I'm not feeling *that* nostalgic!"

He raised both hands. "Okay, sorry. I'm just trying to be a good guy here."

"And your wife plays with guns."

"Yeah, well, that too."

"Your problem, not mine." She looked at him. "Seriously, you got a place? If not, there's a futon in my living room that still has some of you on it."

He winced. "That's more than I needed to know, Maura."

"Don't worry. I bought a cover. You think I'd make my guests sit on that?" She gave a laugh. "Okay, I did. But only for a couple years. And I was broke."

"I'm sure they pretended not to notice."

"You haven't met my friends."

She touched his arm, pointed up onto the porch, where they saw the guard moving around. Danny saw the black bulk of his Kevlar vest, a serious-looking gun that he carried as if he expected to come under fire any moment. He looked like the kind of guy you see in movies guarding the nuclear train, just before the terrorists seize it.

"I thought I was coming home," Maura said. "I barely recognize the place."

"I've been feeling that way about the whole country lately." Danny nodded toward the guard. "Lots of guys like that around these days."

"People are scared."

"People are always scared. This is something else. It's like the guy who's so scared of thieves, he burns his house down." He shook his head sadly. "We're throwing away all the things that we wanted to protect."

"You can't change the world, Danny."

"Why not? They have. Only for the worse."

The security guard came to the edge of the porch, looked toward the sound of gunshots up the street to the north.

"Come on," she said, taking his arm. "There's nothing here but bad memories."

9

Gerald Vickers hated driving east in the morning. Sun coming up, it's in your eyes the whole way, so even with sunglasses you get a headache from squinting. When he was a kid, his father had always made them get up early on Easter for dawn mass, talking to them while he drove over to St. Vincent's about how being up for the sunrise is like accepting God's promise of grace, because you got to see an image of the resurrection. But what did they care about all that? They were just kids, sprawled out in the backseat in their best clothes, whining, trying to grab a couple more minutes of sleep before they got dragged into church and had to sit up straight in the pew, looking like they cared. Grow up Catholic, Vickers had decided, and what you've learned is how to fake it. How to sleep with your eyes open, how to go to confession and tell the priest with a straight face that you've had *impure thoughts*. Like he doesn't? Sitting there in the confessional, taking, like, twenty minutes with the girls, while he sends the boys out to do their act of contrition so fast it felt like brushing your teeth. A whole row of boys kneeling in the first pew, muttering, *O God, I am heartily sorry for having offended Thee, and I detest all my sins because of Thy just punishments, but most of all because they offend Thee, my God. . . .* All of them sneaking looks over at the confessional whenever a girl came out, wondering what she'd told the priest. Do girls have impure thoughts? And if so, about who? The boys had discussed this question at some length on the benches next to the playground behind St. Vincent's.

One kid's big sister had a poster of Mick Jagger on her bedroom wall, and they all agreed that qualified as impure thoughts all by itself.

But now he was headed back to New Orleans, a bright sun blinding him the whole way, and he couldn't shake the feeling that all his acts of contrition had failed, that God was now rising in wrath, not the promise of grace. He knew it was irrational, that the pain in his eyes wasn't the failure of penitence but the natural result of looking into the sun while he drove. As soon as it got high enough in the sky, he'd flip down the visor and the pain would ease. By ten, he'd forget all about the promise of grace and get back to thinking about business. Redemption, he'd learned as he rose from his penance, was the feeling that God's eye had moved on, was not, for the moment, blazing down upon you in judgment. You got to your feet, hurried out of the church, and two boys were fighting in the playground, urged on by a crowd of kids who'd already finished their acts of contrition and were now ready to feel the world and its pleasures settle back around them in a ritual of blood. Confess too much or pray too slowly, and you might miss the show. Get to your feet too quickly, and you might find yourself one of the boys getting beaten to the ground for some mistake you couldn't quite comprehend.

Two days he'd sat in the hotel, watching the whole mess play out on CNN. Aerial cameras flying over the flooded city, zooming in on the crumbled seawalls along the canals, the concrete folded over like pieces of tinfoil.

"It's the soil," he cried out, pointing at the screen. "Can't they see, it's giving way in the foundations?"

"I'm sure they'll see that," his wife said quietly. "You can show them the video."

But she looked at him with empty eyes as she said it, and he could see her starting to get scared. The TV kept cutting away to shots of people waiting in the hot sun for relief at the Superdome, or looters wading through the flooded streets. What did it matter if it was concrete or dirt that gave way? Everybody who'd worked on those seawalls was guilty now. There'd be hearings, lawsuits, prison terms. No one associated with any of it would walk away clean.

"I'm fucked," Vickers said, shaking his head. "You should just walk away right now, because I'm completely fucked."

She didn't say anything, but he could tell that she was thinking about it. *I couldn't believe it,* she'd tell her friends, shaking her head in anger and disgust. *I never had a clue what kind of business he did. All I knew was that he built things from concrete.* A quick divorce, then remarriage to a Houston oilman, and she'd be back in business, going to all the best parties, serving on all the most important fund-raising committees. She wasn't the type to stand by her man, spend her Saturdays driving up to Angola to visit him in prison. Why pay for lawyers when you can marry one, with a partnership in a major firm and a big house on a golf course beneath spreading oaks?

And with that thought, he got angry. Did they think he'd go down without a fight? He stood up suddenly, right there in the hotel room, his wife looking up at him in surprise.

"I'm going back," he told her.

"What are you talking about?" She gestured toward the TV. "The whole city's flooded! They're shooting people in the street."

"It doesn't matter. I have to go back."

He went into the bedroom, started throwing his toiletries back into his suitcase. She followed him. "Where will you stay? There's no power, no water . . ."

"I'll find someplace. I'll pitch a tent out at the plant if I have to."

"How do you know the plant's not flooded?"

"Then I'll find someplace else."

She threw up her hands in frustration. "Well, Jesus. At least wait until morning! You're going to drive back into that city in the middle of the night?"

That stopped him. No power, no light, no place to sleep. "All right," he said. "I'll leave in the morning."

Not that he'd slept any. He lay there staring up at the ceiling, try-ing to see the way ahead, until the clock said 4:22 and he couldn't take it anymore, got up, dressed quietly, and slipped out without waking his wife. He was on the road by the time the first light started to come up in the eastern sky, flying back along I-10, squinting into the rising sun, thinking, *O God, I am heartily sorry for having offended Thee, and I detest all my sins because of Thy just punishments . . .*

But in his heart, he knew there was no contrition. Salvation was the hope of the weak. He'd learned that out behind the church, as the tough boys pounded on their latest victim. A man gets in there and saves his own ass.

|||| Danny woke up sweating. The room was strewn with sunlight, and he could smell the heat already starting to build. He lay there for a moment looking up at the ceiling. There were other smells too. Cigarettes, candles, red wine, perfume. He felt a brief surge of panic, turned his head, but to his relief the other side of the bed was empty. *Well, thank God for that,* he thought. *At least that's one disaster avoided.*

He looked around. Slowly, the wreckage of the night came into focus. An empty wine bottle on the coffee table they'd dragged out of the way when it was time to unfold the futon couch. Two glasses, an ashtray full of Maura's cigarettes. But no pile of clothing, no tangle of sheets on the floor. Nothing, so far, that he'd have to explain or regret.

It wasn't like he hadn't thought about it, just for a moment there as the wine and his lack of sleep started to make the room whirl around him. All her life, Maura Boudrieux had been a slow-motion train wreck, but he'd always found it impossible to look away. Her bed was the battlefield where she fought the world to a bloody draw, and the fury of that battle had never failed to astonish him.

Most men quickly fled, slinking away to nurse their wounds, but Danny had found it exciting, like being swept away by a . . .

His mouth suddenly felt dry. *By a storm.* That's what he'd been thinking. The words came so easily to his mind, with no reality in them. But how could that ever be true again?

Danny got out of bed, went over to the window. The street below was dry, but a large oak tree lay fallen across it, a great sprawl of branches and leaves covering half the block. They'd had to climb over it the night before, and Danny had felt a strange impulse to plunge into the tangle of branches, like a kid clambering around in that green web of sky.

"You remember when we were kids," he'd asked Maura, "and we used to climb that tree in your yard? Your dad had that tree house built for you up there."

"I remember when you fell out of it and broke your arm."

"I didn't fall," he insisted. "You pushed me."

"I never pushed you!" But then Maura hesitated, staring at him. "Wait, did I push you?"

"You did."

"Oh, crap." She raised a hand to her forehead. "I completely forgot that." Then her eyes widened. "Wait, do you remember *why* I pushed you?"

"You were mad at me for something."

"Yeah, but you remember what?"

He shook his head. "Do you?"

"You're damn right I do! We were up there in the tree house playing I'll show you mine if you show me yours. You made me go first, then when it was your turn, you wouldn't do it." She grinned at him. "That's just like you, Danny. All talk and no action."

"I remember lots of action."

"Uh-huh. Twenty years later. You make a girl wait that long, she's got a good reason to push you out of a tree."

"I just wanted to build up some mystery."

She laughed. "Oh, you're good at building up mystery. I'll give you that."

Danny turned away from the window. In the daylight, Maura's apartment was dispiriting. It was a tiny one-bedroom a few blocks from the river, with exposed brick walls that must have looked really cool in 1972. She'd done her best, hanging up framed posters of Miles Davis and Charlie Parker, but it looked like the kind of place a twenty-year-old secretary moves into when she gets tired of sneaking guys into her bedroom in her parents' house. She'd unlocked the door and lit a candle stuck in a wine bottle, watching Danny's face as he looked around.

"It's a rebuilding year for me," she said. "I was planning to get a better place in the fall, but now . . ." She shrugged. "Who knows? Maybe real estate will be cheap after all this is over."

Danny found his pants on the floor beside the futon. He'd tucked the pistol into one of his shoes. They were still damp. He folded up the futon, carried the empty wine bottle and the ashtray into the kitchen, and dumped them in the garbage can under the sink. Then he went down the hall, found the bathroom.

Maura had left the door to her bedroom open. He glanced in. She lay sprawled across the bed in her underwear, one arm flung wide like she was reaching out to catch something that had slipped from her grasp. She'd always been a restless sleeper, flailing angrily and kicking out with her feet. When he'd spent the night with her, Danny had frequently woken up with bruises on his arms and legs. Once, he woke up to find her crouched above him in the bed, murmuring, "I'm sorry. I'm really sorry." He looked down to find himself bleeding onto the sheet from a long scratch on his shin. The strange thing was, he hadn't felt a thing. It was her words that had woken him, that whispered apology.

He left her a brief note on the kitchen counter:

Maura,
Thanks for giving me shelter from the storm.

Danny

He should have written more, but what? *Stay safe? Don't drink the water?* Nothing he could have said seemed like enough.

Out on the street, the air was thick with smoke and a stench of rot like you get out on the bayou. Columns of black smoke rose across the city's skyline. St. Charles was still dry, but as he looked up Jefferson Avenue, he saw water glinting under the morning sun only a few blocks to the north. It didn't look deep yet, but there it was: the city was slowly filling with water.

He walked back toward downtown. It was early still, but the streets were already full of people walking out of the flood zone, carrying a few belongings in plastic trash bags. Some had found shopping carts, which they pushed down the middle of the street. Most were full of food and clothing, but one guy had a mattress balanced across his, a child sitting in the cart and holding it in place as he steered carefully around the storm debris. At the corner of Napoleon Avenue, a man was selling boxes of stale supermarket donuts and bottles of water out of the trunk of his car. Danny paid the guy five dollars for a box of donuts, ate a couple, then gave the rest to a kid standing a few feet away watching. Something about the way that kid stood there, silent, watching people eat their stale donuts struck him as obscene. Was he homeless? Where were his parents? He wanted to ask him, but when he handed the kid the donuts, he ran off, sat on a bench on the median ground, and quickly worked his way through the whole box.

Danny followed the crowds making their way downtown. At one point he stopped to help a man pushing an elderly woman in a wheelchair lift her up over a curb.

"Where's everybody going?" he asked the man.

"Convention Center. They sendin' everybody down there since yesterday."

"Wouldn't the Dome be closer?"

"Nah. They's water all 'round the Dome now. And I heard they got people shootin' at each other in there."

Danny looked at him, surprised. "Wait, you're saying there's people having gunfights in the Superdome?"

"That's what I heard. All them gangs got the place divided up. They up in there robbin' and rapin.'"

"Don't they have police in the Dome?"

The man shrugged. "Have to be a lot of police, all them people they got crowded up in there. And you think all those folks left they guns home?"

"They were putting everybody through security when they went in on Sunday," Danny said. "It was on TV. That's why the lines to get in were so long."

"Well, shit, I don't know. I ain't over there, am I?"

The man walked away. Danny watched him vanish into the crowd of people streaming toward downtown. Was it just fear that had them whispering about violence spreading through every corner of the city? What the man had said made no sense to Danny. Rumors of violence, passed among people who couldn't know what was really happening in the Superdome. But looking around, who could blame them? All the worst predictions about what would happen when the storm hit seemed to be coming true. Massive flooding, fires, gunshots echoing across the city. And where were the police? Where was the National Guard? Danny hadn't *seen* any violence as he walked across the city, but he could feel it all around him, like a fever on the skin. He'd seen looting. But that had looked more like survival, people grabbing what they could. And he'd seen bodies floating in the water. That was the real violence. Maybe that was what lay behind the feeling of rage and fear coming off all these people as they led their children away from their flooded homes.

And he could feel the cold metal of the pistol that he carried shoved into his waistband against his stomach. There were times when the *fear* of violence can be a form of violence. Everybody in this city was a victim; they'd all suffered a terrible loss, and as the water rose, it became clear that even more would be stolen from them with each passing hour. But the fear, the looting, and the sound of gunshots in the night made that almost impossible to see. Everybody reached for their guns, instead of reaching out to grasp each other's hands. Everyone seemed blinded by fear, as if the quiet tide of anger that had flowed through this city for decades had suddenly risen to a flood, carrying all hope away, leaving nothing in its wake.

And so Danny let the tide carry him, following the stream of refugees heading downtown. On Tchoupitoulas Street, the parking lot of the Wal-Mart was empty except for four police cruisers pulled up near the door. Cops in combat gear stood around the trunk of one of the squad cars, where they'd laid out some packaged breakfast food, bottled coffee, and energy drinks that they'd scavenged off the store's shelves.

Danny recognized one of the cops. He was a black officer named Willie Rushton, whose sister had retained Danny to represent her in an insurance claim against an elderly Catholic priest who'd backed into her in a downtown parking garage. Except for the fact that they were suing the archbishop of New Orleans in his capacity as the priest's employer, it was a routine matter, which ended when the diocese's insurance company settled for damages, medical expenses, and lost wages when she couldn't get to her weekend job as a dealer at one of the casino boats in Gulfport. When the case settled, she'd invited Danny to a party at a bar on North Galvez Street, where Willie Rushton had come up to him, put his arm drunkenly over Danny's shoulders, and said, "You took care of my sister. Anything I can do, you just let me know."

Danny walked over. "Hey, Willie."

Rushton looked over. "Yeah? I know you?"

"Danny Chaisson. I represented your sister when she had her accident."

Danny could see that the cop still didn't recognize him, but Rushton said, "Yeah, right. What you still doin' in town?"

"I had some important business to finish up. Then somebody stole my car."

"No shit?" Rushton shook his head. "Man, that's a bitch. Wish we could help you out, man, but . . ." He waved a hand toward the cops in their combat gear. "It's not like we're in a position to take down a crime report right at this moment."

Danny waved a hand. "No problem. The car's probably in Texas anyway."

"Then the guy who stole it is a whole lot smarter than we are." Rushton looked over at the people heading past toward the Convention Center. "My sister got out. She took my parents to Dallas. Wouldn't mind being there with 'em. But I guess this is what I signed up to do. Serve and protect. Spent the whole night out on a boat, pullin' people off roofs. Then they sent us over here to get something to eat." He reached over, took a can of espresso from the trunk of the squad car, offered it to Danny. "You want one of these?"

"Thanks." Danny took it gratefully. The can was warm, but he drained it in a few swallows, then crumpled up the can, tossed it into a cardboard box they were using as a trash can. "You're not Sixth District, right?"

Rushton shook his head. "I'm Third District. But we're all flooded out, so they sent us down here to dry out."

"I'm looking for a guy named Langer, works Sixth District Vice."

"There's a bunch of Sixth District guys inside the store. Most of 'em are over on the West Bank, but they're talking about moving back over here, using this place as a command post. Maybe he's in there."

Danny looked over at the store. The doors had been smashed,

and the interior was as dark as a cave. "They won't shoot me, I go walking around in there?"

Rushton shrugged. "Hell, they might. Or arrest you for looting. C'mon, I'll take you in there."

They walked across the parking lot and into the store. Rushton switched on his flashlight, used it to pick his way through the dark store. The place had been trashed. Shelves were tipped on their sides, merchandise lay in all the aisles. Rushton led him back to the furniture section, where a group of cops sat around on office chair samples or lay stretched out on futons.

"Any of you guys know a cop named Langer?"

The cops looked up at Rushton, and in the glow of his flashlight, Danny could see the exhaustion in their eyes.

"I know him," one of the cops said. "Why?"

"This guy's looking for him." Rushton pointed the flashlight at Danny, and all the cops followed it with their eyes, like dogs lined up on a sidewalk, watching a cat in a house cross in front of the window.

"I need to talk to him," Danny said. "You know where I could find him?"

"He was over in Algiers this morning. They're all in the parking lot of the Breaux Mart on General Meyer, sleeping in their cars."

"Any way I could get hold of him over there?"

The cop shrugged. "You got a ride?"

"No. I'm on foot."

"Then I guess you better start walkin'."

Rushton walked back out to the parking lot with him. "Sorry, man. I had a car, I'd run you over there, but everything's all fucked up."

Danny looked at the squad cars lined up in the parking lot. "Any way we could use a radio in one of those cars, find out if he's over there?"

Rushton hesitated. "It's emergency only, man. They'd have my badge."

Danny walked on up Tchoupitoulas. When he got to the express-way, he found a crowd of people sitting on the base of the ramp.

"Yo, man," a kid called out. "You still got my piece?"

Danny looked over, surprised, saw one of the boys from Jabril's boat get up, walk over to him. They shook hands, and Danny asked him, "These all people from the warehouse?"

"Most of 'em. We picked up a couple others walkin' over here. Jabril over at the Convention Center, lookin' for a way out of the city. Somebody told him there's all these city buses just sittin' in a lot a couple blocks from here, but they all locked up, and the water's risin' all around there. Police say we go take 'em, they'll lock us up." He shook his head. "It's crazy, man. Nobody knows what's goin' on. Those people over at the Convention Center, they just sit-tin' there. No food, no water. People *dyin'* over there. Some old guy died on the sidewalk, they just threw a blanket over him, left him lyin' there. So Jabril, he say, 'Fuck this shit. We just gonna *walk* out.' Cross the bridge, get on out of here. Like the exodus out of Egypt, man. We gonna cross the waters, go find us someplace where some-body gives a shit whether folks in this city live or die."

"Might be a long walk."

"Tell me 'bout it. Look like we be walkin' to *Canada*, way things goin'."

Danny looked up at the bridge rising high above them. "You said Jabril's over at the Convention Center?"

"Uh-huh. You know how he is, he gets to talkin'. He's tryin' to get some a them to walk out with us. But those people scared, man." He shook his head sadly. "They hear shootin' at night, see cops runnin' around with guns in their hands, they figure it's open season on black folks. They just gonna sit there, wait for somebody to show up and help them."

"I'm headed across the bridge too."

"Yeah? Well, you don't mind waiting a little while, you can walk out with us. You got enough people, nobody mess with you."

Danny nodded. "Maybe I'll head over there, have a talk with him, see what he's got in mind."

"Suit yourself, man. But I got a feeling we gonna be doin' a lot of walkin' soon enough."

Danny started to walk off toward the Convention Center, but then a thought struck him, and he turned back. "Hey," he called out to the kid. "You want your piece back?"

The boy grinned. "Nah, man. I was just messin' with you. I got a better one now." He lifted his shirt, and Danny saw he had a Glock 9mm pistol shoved into his waistband. "Jabril gave it to me. Told me I got to use front sights and foresight. Man never misses an opportunity to mess with your mind."

Danny walked over to the Convention Center. There were many more people standing around outside now, and he could feel the anger coming off the growing crowd. They were tired and hot and hungry; he could see the feeling of betrayal in their eyes. Where was the help they'd been promised? Wasn't it somebody's job to *plan* for this? An old woman sat on the neutral ground, staring off into the distance. Beside her lay a body on a lawn chair, covered with a yellow comforter. A TV crew had set up across the street, filming the misery. A small group of people had gone over, and the reporter was interviewing them. One woman burst into tears, and he put his arm around her, while the cameraman moved in close for the money shot.

Up the street, in front of the Hampton Inn, a different cop sat in the same lawn chair, a rifle across his lap. But he'd pulled the chair back into the shade of the building's entrance, so you could barely see him, and he kept glancing over at the crowd nervously. He looked like a kid, barely out of high school, and the combination of the assault rifle lying across his lap and fear in his eyes made Danny's heart sink.

Inside the Convention Center, Danny could barely see in the unlit corridors. But the smell alone was enough to tell him what life in that building had been like for the last three days. It was the stench of sweat and fear and death. *Prison camps must smell like this,* Danny thought, covering his mouth and nose. *Hospitals in third world plague zones, where people come to die.* All he could see were shadows slumped along the walls, and eyes gazing up at him. When his eyes finally began to adjust, he saw that people were sitting along every wall, and anywhere there was an open piece of floor someone had stretched out there, marking off the territory with pieces of clothing or a dirty sheet, as if trying to cling to some private space among the crowd of refugees.

A woman called out to him, "What you lookin' at?"

Danny raised both hands. "Sorry. I'm just looking for somebody." He moved on down the hall. The smell got more powerful as he made his way deeper into the building. It felt like falling into a well, seeing the bright sky recede as the darkness takes you. The faces that looked up at him as he passed were drained and hopeless. They were simply waiting, but without any expectation that their suffering would be relieved. All they had now was a few inches of filthy carpet and foul air, and the look in their eyes seemed to say that they knew that worse was still to come.

Ahead, Danny heard two young men arguing loudly in one of the ballrooms. People were glancing over anxiously, and a few got up, gathered up their things, and moved away. They didn't say a word, but it was enough to tell Danny that they'd spent three days listening for the sound of voices raised in anger. New Orleans was a violent city at the best of times: heat and poverty combined to bring out the killing rage in men's hearts, and the streets were full of illegal guns. Every night the police hauled away the dead who lay sprawled on sidewalks and empty lots across the city. And now thousands of people from the city's poorest neighborhoods had been driven from their homes by the rising water, crowding into this building and the broiling streets outside; they were angry and afraid. Every man in the crowd knew that there were enough guns scattered through the crowd to turn what remained of the city into Mogadishu, and if he'd found his way here, there was a good chance that his enemies from the next street, the next block, or even the next building had made the same journey. Men who'd shot at each other only a few days before might now meet in a crowded hallway, or stake out opposite sides of a ballroom, glaring at each other as the temperature in the building rose with every passing hour.

But then Danny heard a voice he recognized. He followed it, pushing past the people moving away from the dispute, and just inside the entrance to one of the ballrooms he found two groups of young men squaring off, with Jabril standing between them, arms folded, looking down at the floor with an expression on his face like he was disgusted by the whole thing.

Finally, he raised his eyes, looked at one of the leaders, and said, "That your mama over there?"

His words made the anger on the boy's face vanish like wind blowing paper off a table. He glanced over, and something like embarrassment came into his eyes. "Why you want to know?"

"You over here arguin'," Jabril said, "and your mama's sittin' over there in this stink like she ain't nothin' to the people who run this town but an animal. So what I want to know is, where the fuck is your *head*? How'd you let this happen to your *mama*? You got more important things to do, like fight with this guy, while your people are dyin'?" He turned to look at the other boy. "How 'bout you? You got all that anger in your eyes because somebody *disrespected* you?" He waved a hand around the room. "Look around you, man. This how you earn respect, by fightin' over a couple feet of the pigsty they keepin' you in?"

The boy looked at him resentfully. "Man, you don't know nothin' 'bout me."

"So show me somethin' 'bout you I don't know!" Jabril shook his head sadly. "You see all those TV cameras outside? They here to tell your story, man. And you can bet the whole world's watchin'. This what you want 'em to see? This the best you got? Those people, they take one look at you, and they think they know, man. You ain't even worth savin'. You just a nigger with a gun. Some white guy sittin' up in Ohio, he's got no reason to feel ashamed of what he sees on his TV, 'cause you makin' it *easy* for him. How much respect you think you're gonna get from him?"

The boy scowled. "What you expect me to do? We stuck here like everybody else."

"You love your mama?"

"Damn right."

" 'Cause she does stuff for you, or 'cause she's your mama?"

" 'Cause she's my mama."

Jabril nodded. "So how come you askin' that question? This city's your mama too. Some people treat your mama bad, you got to find a way to make it better. Not go makin' it worse by fightin' with each other over who gets her stuff when she's dead."

The boys were silent, eyeing each other with suspicion. Then one of the two leaders shrugged, said, "Ain't nothin' to me." He turned, walked back to a corner of the room, sat down against the wall, pulled his baseball cap down low over his eyes. The rest of his gang followed. For a moment the other boys stood there, as if they were waiting for Jabril to say something else. But he just folded his arms, looked down at the ground. So they drifted away, settling along the opposite wall. The two groups of boys did their best to ignore each other.

Danny walked over to Jabril. "Doin' the Lord's work?"

Jabril shook his head in disgust. "It's like preaching to the dead. Most of their daddies are in jail or dead. Now they're doin' their best to go join them. Best you can do is to stop them killin' each other for a couple days. Forget tryin' to get them to help anybody else." Jabril looked at Danny. "So what you doin' in here, anyway? I thought you were out lookin' for the cops. Won't find any of them in here."

"They're over on the West Bank," Danny told him. "At least the ones I need to talk to are. I was on my way over there, and I ran into some of your people waiting by the bridge. They said you were going to walk out."

Jabril nodded. "Thought I could talk some of these people into coming with us. But they keep hearin' somebody's coming with buses to take 'em to Baton Rouge in a couple hours. Sounds like they've been hearing that for the last two days."

"Would make sense to get some buses in here."

"You want to sit around here until they make up their minds how to get it done?"

"You're asking the wrong guy," Danny told him. "I used to work for a politician. I know how it works. I've helped more people cover their asses than Calvin Klein."

Jabril looked at him. "You just make that up?"

"It's been a long couple days."

"Yeah, and we just gettin' started." He turned back toward the building's entrance. "Come on. Let's get out of here."

IIII "Boat."

Lenny raised his head, looked at Vince wearily. "Where?"

"Couple blocks up."

Lenny let his head sink back down onto his arms. He was sitting against the wall a few feet from Sams, knees drawn up, arms folded across them, like he'd played out his hand, couldn't even work up the energy to reach for the next round.

"He's comin' this way," Vince said. And he leaned out the window, started waving his shirt around, like he did every time a boat went past.

It was like watching somebody play with a dog, Sams thought. Doesn't matter how many times you fake him out, pretending to toss the stick, the dog gets excited, starts jumping around like he's gonna go racing off and catch it every time.

285

Lenny raised his head. "How many people you figure are hanging out their windows, waving their shirts at this guy? You think you're the only one?"

"In this neighborhood? Yeah, I think I might be the only one. There's nothing around here but warehouses and factories."

"That's why they're all goin' someplace else."

"So what are you saying? I should stop?"

Lenny sighed, shook his head. "Nah, man. You go right on doin' it. Knock yourself out."

He shot Sams a glance, like, *You believe this guy?* Then he closed his eyes, laid his head back down on his arms.

Sams waited a moment to make sure he wasn't looking, then went back to working at the rope tied around his wrists. In the movies, you see guys slip out of ropes all the time. They start moving their hands around, and the next thing you know, the rope comes loose, and they're ready to punch out one of the guards, grab his gun, and make a break for freedom. What they don't show you is how knots can tighten when you start twisting them, and how quickly ropes can strip the skin from your wrists, so you feel blood running down the back of your hand, dripping off the tips of your fingers.

He could hear the sound of an outboard engine approaching, and then Vince called out, "Hey, we could use some help over here!"

The last few boats had just kept on going, never getting close enough for Vince to draw his gun and wave them in. But now Sams heard the engine slow, and a man's voice call up, "What you doin' in *there*? That building's been empty for thirty years!"

"My partner and me, we got caught in the storm," Vince called out, leaning against the side of the window and reaching back casually, his hand coming to rest on the pistol holstered on his belt. "We busted in here, then the water started rising, and we got stuck."

There was a pause, and the man gunned the engine slightly to hold the boat in place while he considered this. "You cops?"

"Used to be. We work private security now."

"I heard there's cops come 'round in this building sometimes."

"Used to be, back in the old days. That's how we knew about the place."

There was another pause. Lenny raised his head, said, "Will you just shoot the guy already?"

Vince ignored him, called out, "You got room for us in that boat, we could sure use a lift."

"I got some people on a roof a couple blocks from here. You wait a couple hours, I'll come back and get you."

Vince sighed, drew the gun from its holster, and pointed it out the window. "I got a better idea."

⫼ They walked up the bridge's long ramp, over two hundred of them in a group, taking it slow in the hot sun. At the top of the bridge, they paused, looked back at the city. It shimmered in the midday heat, the light glinting off the water that filled the streets. From a distance it almost looked beautiful. You couldn't see the wreckage and death out in those flooded neighborhoods, or smell the stench of chemicals, sewage, and rot; there was just a smooth expanse of water flowing between the buildings, strangely green in the sunlight. Only when you looked over at the Central Business District could you get a sense of the violence that had been visited upon the city. The buildings looked shattered, like they'd been beaten with a stick. The Superdome looked like a piece of fruit that had been left out in the sun, its roof peeled back as if it simply exploded from the heat building up inside. And then there were the fires: Danny counted six columns of smoke rising from different points across the skyline. Helicopters hovered over one of the worst of the fires, over in Bywater, near the docks. Watching, Danny realized that they weren't there to fight the fire, but to film it. TV news choppers, sending images of the ruined city out to people around the world, who'd sit on the sofa watching it, shaking their heads at the misery they saw. How many times, he wondered, had he done that? Beirut, Somalia, Rwanda, Aceh . . . it was strange to think of that now, as if he'd never understood the reality of those scenes until it struck home. Was that why America was so pitiless in its judgments? The world on his television was always suffering, always dying. Famine, flood, and war. Blinding disease, which makes you look away when the child in the African hospital with oozing sores appears on the screen. All so hopeless, and so far away. But how can you feel pity, if you've never suffered? He'd sent money for famine aid and tsunami relief. But men can grow smug in their charity, the way a healthy man looks down on the sick. It's not real until it's you. And then you suddenly realize how the rest of the world must be seeing you.

A police car passed, heading back toward New Orleans, slowing way down as it passed the crowd of people. Danny saw the white cop behind the wheel get on his radio, his eyes wide. But he didn't stop, just punched the gas and got out of there.

"You see that guy?" Jabril shook his head. "Looks like we put the grease on his skids."

"He looked scared," Danny said. "Why would he be afraid of people who just want to get out of the city?"

Jabril looked at him, amused. "Look around you, man. Lot of black skin in this crowd. They probably figure we've looted all the stores in New Orleans, and now we're headed out lookin' for more."

"You serious? The whole city's flooded. They have to know people are going to be looking for a way out."

Jabril smiled. "Way that guy sees it, all the *people* already left, before the storm. All that's left is dangerous niggers."

Danny's face got serious. "If that's true, then we're all in trouble."

"You don't think we're in trouble already? Look back behind you, man. Whole city's gone. We got nothin' left *but* trouble."

They walked on across the central span of the bridge. As they started down toward the West Bank, Danny saw several more police cars heading up onto the bridge. One of them came to an abrupt stop, turned sideways, blocking the road, and the other two pulled up behind it, forming a barricade across the entire span. Officers piled out of each car and lined up behind them, holding rifles and shotguns, which they pointed toward the approaching refugees.

"Well, I guess there's your answer," Jabril said. "Still think they don't see us as a threat?"

"Okay, I see what you mean," Danny said. He turned to the crowd, called out, "Everybody stay calm but keep walking. They won't open fire on unarmed people."

Jabril studied the cops standing behind their barricade. "You sure about that, man? They look serious."

"So we show them we're serious too."

They kept walking, and Danny saw the cops start to glance at each other. One of them leaned into his squad car and grabbed a microphone. Then he straightened up, raised the microphone to his mouth, and said through the car's public address system, "This bridge is closed to all traffic. You need to turn around and go back to the city."

His voice made Danny think of rocks rattling around in a tin cup. It was the voice you hear when things go very wrong, when men cease to be men you might sit down and have a beer with, becoming only the voice that echoes through the machine, telling you to stay calm, not to panic, and to await further instructions, while the life slowly seeps from your body.

"What's he mean, the bridge is closed?" a woman asked. "Cars been driving over it all day. I seen 'em do it when we were sitting on the ramp."

Danny kept walking. He could feel the rest of the crowd hang back slightly, like they were starting to get nervous, but they stayed with him, slowly closing the distance that separated them from the line of police cars.

"We're evacuating," Danny called out to the officer with the microphone. "The city's flooded."

"This bridge is closed," the officer repeated into the microphone, although they were close enough now to hear him without it. "You need to return to the city."

"It's flooded," a man behind Danny called out. "Look over there! You can see it!"

"Let us past," a woman shouted.

The officer said something to the cop standing next to him, who raised his M16, fired three quick shots into the sky above them. In the crowd, several people ducked. Others cried out, dropped back a few steps. For a moment nobody moved.

Danny was shocked. He'd seen movies about the Russian revolution, where soldiers fire on a peaceful crowd, seen it again in TV documentaries about the dirty wars fought by right-wing governments in Central America against their own people, but he'd never imagined he'd see it happening in the city where he grew up.

"Looks like you a little optimistic," Jabril said quietly. He reached out, laid his hand on the arm of the boy standing next to him, whose hand was drifting toward his waistband.

"Have everybody stay here," Danny said. "I'll go talk to them."

"You think you do your lawyer thing, they'll just let us past?"

"You got a better idea?" Danny walked toward the police cars, saw a couple of the cops swing their rifles over to follow him. He suddenly became very conscious of the gun shoved into his pants, raised both hands out in front of him, letting the cops see they were empty. "What's the problem here?"

"No problem," the officer holding the microphone said, "except you don't seem to be understanding me. This bridge is closed, and it won't be reopening until further notice."

He spoke to Danny quietly, but he kept the microphone in his hand, like he wasn't afraid to use it.

"Why is it closed? We've seen traffic crossing on it all day."

"I can't tell you what happened all day. My orders are to close this bridge now, and I'm carrying them out."

Danny glanced around at the bridge surface. "Is it damaged?"

"I don't know anything about that, sir. All I can tell you is that this bridge is closed, and your people need to turn around and go back where they came from."

Danny looked up at him. "Go back where they *came* from? Did I hear you right?"

"Public shelters have been set up at several locations, sir. Your group can receive food and water at those locations, and transport out of the city will be provided for them at an appropriate time."

Danny looked down the row of cops, all watching him over their guns. Every face was white. "You realize," he said, "how this looks? You've got a group of white officers turning back a group of black citizens who are only trying to escape from the flooding."

The cop glanced over at the news choppers circling the fire down along the docks. None of them had caught sight of the confrontation yet, but it was only a matter of time.

"All I know is I've got orders to stop all pedestrian traffic across this bridge. Emergency vehicles only. That means you and your group will have to turn around and return to one of the designated emergency shelters."

"And if we refuse?"

The cop gave Danny a hard look. "Then we'll be forced to arrest anyone who doesn't comply."

"Can I talk to your commanding officer?"

"He's got other things to worry about at this moment. This is a public safety situation, and I've got full authority to do anything necessary to maintain order."

"All right," Danny said. "Nobody's questioning your authority, and there's no need for any arrests. I'll tell these people that they have to go back to the expressway and look for another way out of the city. But that's not why I'm here. I'm looking for some Sixth District cops who evacuated to the West Bank."

The cop shook his head. "I don't know nothing about that. My job is to clear this bridge, and that includes you. So I'm going to have to ask you to leave with everybody else."

Where did they all learn it? Danny wondered as he walked back to Jabril. Every cop he'd ever known took the same tone when challenged, like they were explaining something to a very young child, and it required infinite patience. They were mostly blue-collar guys, but put them in a uniform and they stiffened up, like they'd suddenly found themselves speaking a foreign language, in which you punctuate every sentence with "sir," making it sound like a stiff-fingered jab.

"They're not going to let us past," Danny told Jabril. "They say the bridge is closed to everything but emergency vehicles."

Jabril looked up at the row of cops with their rifles pointed at the crowd. "I don't know why I'm surprised. You go over to the West Bank, they'll pull you over for driving while black. Makes sense they wouldn't want a bunch of niggers walking around in their neighborhoods."

"Maybe you can walk out on the expressway, try to pick up I-10 toward Baton Rouge. Might be better to head that way anyway. It would take you out of the storm's path."

Jabril nodded. "Unless the Jefferson Parish sheriffs stop us at the parish line. This shit makes it look like they're trying to turn the city into a concentration camp. Keep us all in here so we don't go 'round lootin' and killin' while they decide what to do with us."

Danny glanced over at the cops. They were watching over their assault rifles to see what the crowd did next. "We should get these people moving before something bad happens."

Jabril looked at him. "What exactly is your definition of *bad*?"

▓ Hope dies, like men, suddenly. It can hang on longer than anyone thought possible, growing slowly weaker. But when the end comes, it comes abruptly, just something that was once there and is now gone.

For Louis Sams, the end of all hope came when they shot the old man in the boat and shoved his body over the side. Until that moment, he'd thought there was a small chance that they might leave him alive. They were cops, once. Maybe there was still a line they couldn't easily cross. But the flood seemed to have swept all the old borders away, so that men redrew them at their own convenience: there was, it struck him, nothing natural about this disaster. Men had built here, where the waters rose; they had ignored the warnings and their own history; and now it was men who let the compassion fade from their hearts, rage and hatred flooding in to take its place.

Not that there was any rage or hatred in the way they killed this man for his boat. They shot him as casually as you would slap a mosquito, then Vince dumped his body over the side while Lenny took his place behind the boat's wheel. Neither said a word after that as they turned the boat around, headed up past the rows of warehouses and rail yards, deeper into the flood zone. Sams slumped in the bottom of the boat, closed his eyes. They were going to kill him. First they'd take him out to the plant and beat the truth out of him. Then, when they had what they wanted, they'd put a bullet in his head, or simply shove him down in the filthy water and hold him there until he drowned. There was something calming about this knowledge. No panic, just a feeling of tiredness and relief that it would all soon be over.

The sun on his face was like a blessing. *After so much*, he thought. The pain, the flood, the death of all hope. He could hear nothing but the roar of the boat's engine. There were ropes cutting into his wrists, and he knew he would die soon. But still, there was this feeling of sun against his skin, and the warm, thick air flowing over him as the boat carved its way through the dark water.

|||| "I got somebody here you should talk to."

Danny looked up, shielding his eyes against the late afternoon sun. The two men were just shadows against the sky. But one stood with the bent-at-the-hip posture of an old man for whom every step was painful, as if hard work and the passing of time had slowly twisted him like a corkscrew.

"This here's Erwin Shapard," Jabril said. "He knows where you can find that warehouse you been lookin' for."

Danny got up, shook the old man's hand. His grip was strong, and his eyes looked into Danny's with a piercing gaze, but his face sagged slightly on one side, as if he'd suffered a palsy. "Were you on the force?"

The old man made a rasping sound in his throat, which Danny realized after a moment was laughter. "Nah, sir," Shapard said, shaking his head. "Wouldn't nobody who knew me mistake me for no police. But I seen my share of police stations. Prisons too. Did seven hard years up at Angola, back when them guards still loaded their shotguns up with rock salt, shot it at your ass if you movin' too slow."

"Were you in the warehouse?"

The old man shook his head again. "Wouldn't be here if I was. They took you in there, that was the last time anybody seen you. They found out what they wanted to know, they'd take you out in the bayou, feed you to the gators. Wouldn't be *nothin'* left." He looked at Danny intently for a moment, like he was making up his mind about him. "Jabril say you lookin' for somebody they got up in there. That right?"

Danny nodded. "It's not police who are holding him. These guys got kicked off the force a while back."

The old man shrugged. "Don't make no difference. They still act like your ass *belong* to them, they got you shoved up against a wall, put that gun up to your head. That's a habit. Does something to their brains, just like them kids out on the corner, smokin' that rock. Can't just stop."

"But you can tell me where the warehouse is?"

"Sure. Ain't hard to find. You just head up Franklin till you hit the tracks. There's a bunch of old warehouses up in there. It's next to a place got a big old coffee sign on the wall. They took you up there, people used to say you been *roasted*."

Danny waited for the old man to say more, but he just turned, looked out across the flooded streets, said, "Ain't gonna be easy to get over there. That's some deep water up that way. Whole place probably flooded." He looked back at Danny. "They used to keep people in a room on the first floor, had egg cartons on the walls, so you couldn't hear 'em screamin'. They had your boy in there, he probably drowned when the water came up."

Danny said nothing. They were sitting in a forlorn group on the expressway overpass, the heat slowly draining them of all hope. They could see the Superdome, crowds sitting on the elevated walkways, surrounded by piles of garbage. All around them, the streets were flooded. More fires were burning across the city, columns of smoke rising into the summer sky.

"Doesn't matter," Danny said. "I have to try."

Jabril nodded. "Thought you'd say that. Some of my boys are still usin' that rubber boat. They're bringin' people out St. Claude to the bridge. We could head on back there, meet up with them the next time they come out."

Danny looked at his watch. "We'd better get moving, then. It'll be getting dark soon."

IIII Gerald Vickers had two central business philosophies. The first was, *It helps to be lucky, but don't go counting on it.* The other was simply an extension of the first: *It helps to have friends.* Spread enough money around, and you make both luck and friends.

He'd spent six hours talking his way past roadblocks manned by exhausted cops in combat gear, with three-day beards and dark circles under their eyes, waving traffic across the median ground on I-10, back onto the westbound lanes. "Sorry, road's closed, sir. I need you to turn your car around and head back the way you came." Saying it just like that, every one of them, "I *need* you to turn your car around . . ." Like it was something personal, a compulsion to stand there in the middle of the road and send everybody right back the way they came.

"I run a concrete plant," he explained, trying his best to look like a doctor rushing to the scene of an accident. "We worked on the seawalls. I need to get the plant running so we can help with the repairs."

The cops looked doubtful, but they waved him on around the barriers, told him to watch out for the trees and power lines that were down in the roads, then turned to the next car, whose driver was forced to make the slow U-turn across the highway, watching in frustration as Vickers vanished up the road. But the closer he got to New Orleans, the harder the look in the cops' eyes, like fragments of mirrors reflecting the shattered world around them. Trees, wires, and traffic lights down, buildings with walls or roofs torn away, everything spilling out. Anything still standing looked like it had been sandblasted, its skin peeled away. It was a world scraped to raw muscle and nerve, and the cops looked like they felt the same way. Some stood with guns cradled in their arms, and he could feel the anger pouring off their bodies with the stench of their sweat. Everything they'd ever known was gone, and they were left standing on a sun-scorched road, guarding the ruins. They glared at him as they waved his car to a stop, came up to his window with a look on their faces like they'd just caught him rooting through somebody's garbage.

They really expect people to come driving in on I-10, start hauling away TV sets and washing machines? But maybe that wasn't such an unrealistic fear. He used to hear stories about oil companies evacuating their workers from offshore rigs before a hurricane;

two hours after the storm passed, they'd fly the workers back out there and find the rigs had already been stripped. There were Cajun guys down along the bayous who'd take off in their boats while the storm was still blowing, tie up alongside an oil platform or a fishing boat that had run up on a reef, and strip it down to the bare decks in a couple hours. Some of those Cajuns were direct descendants of the Barataria pirates, and when a storm blew through, you found out how little had changed in those bayou towns.

But somehow Vickers didn't think it was good old Cajun boys come up off the bayou that these cops were watching out for. White skin, expensive car, they still weren't cutting him much slack, but he could see them ease up a notch when they bent down beside his window, got a look at him. Still, it took him twenty minutes of explaining and two hundred dollars in cash to get past a roadblock out by the Belle Terre Country Club. Even longer by the airport, where he saw a whole row of National Guard trucks lined up along the highway, waiting for an armed escort into the city. *Jesus*, he thought, looking over at them as a soldier armed with an M16 came over to his window. *If the National Guard's scared to go in there, things must be pretty bad.*

When he told the soldier where he was going, the man just looked up the highway, shook his head. "I wouldn't try goin' in there alone. We got all kinds of reports of shooting. Sounds like gangs have taken over parts of the city. And anyway, the road's underwater in a couple places. You won't be able to get through."

"But I need to get to my plant."

The soldier looked over at the row of trucks. "I might be able to get you a place on one of those trucks. They're all we got right now that can get through the high water. There's a couple Black Hawks over at the airport. You could try to get on one of those, you're in a hurry."

"When are the trucks leaving?"

"Couple hours. They're waiting for more security."

Vickers turned his car around, headed for the airport. There, he found an emergency triage set up on one of the runways, where they were bringing in people lifted off rooftops across the city, bandaging up the minor injuries and sending the most seriously injured into an emergency room they'd set up in a baggage claim center. It looked like something from an old war movie, except that most of the people laid out on stretchers or plastic sheets on the ground were elderly, suffering from heart attacks, heat exhaustion, or dehydration. Vickers couldn't believe the smell. It was like they'd all decided to take a swim in a sewage plant before heading over there for some medical care. Couldn't someone hose them off?

Then he saw a face he recognized among the Air National Guard officers supervising the helicopter refueling: it was Jim Kahler, an official from the state Department of Transportation and Development who'd helped him out on some highway contracts in the past. They'd gone fishing a couple times out at a camp Vickers rented out on the salt near Cocodrie, and Vickers had sent him season tickets on the forty-yard line at LSU stadium every August, along with a note that said, *Yell louder. They got to win sometime.* Now he was wearing a flight suit, standing there watching the guys from the re-fueling truck like he considered the Black Hawk his baby and he didn't want them scratching the paint. Vickers walked over.

"They really let you fly one of these things?"

They shook hands, and he saw Kahler look down at his clothes, which were still reasonably clean, even after hours of driving. "You just get back in town?"

"Drove in from Houston," Vickers told him. "I saw the flood walls go, and I figured the Corps of Engineers would be needing concrete."

"Your plant come through the storm okay?"

"That's what I'm trying to find out. But I can't get over there. Any chance I could catch a ride with you?"

Kahler hesitated. "We're doing search-and-rescue. It's not like we got room for passengers."

"All I need's a flyover. If the plant's dry, you can set me down right there."

"It's over on Industry Street, right?"

"That's right. Back by the tracks."

Kahler shook his head. "There's ten feet of water all up through there. We set you down there, we're just going to end up coming back to pull you off a roof."

"So drop me where I can get a boat. There must be someplace you can set me down."

"I can drop you down by the Riverwalk, but there's no way you're going to find a boat. Every boat that wasn't wrecked by the storm is out on the water already. NOPD's running three shifts, and there's old men in pirogues pulling people off roofs down in the Ninth Ward."

"You get me down there," Vickers told him, "I'll find a boat."

And so forty minutes later he was strapped into a rear seat on Kahler's Black Hawk, looking down at the flooded city. The sun was getting low in the sky behind them as they flew east along I-10. Looking out the open door, Vickers could see flooding all along Airline Highway, east of Causeway. The Metairie Country Club was underwater; and along his street, only roofs were visible. He looked away. His house was gone, under a good eight feet of water.

They flew out across City Park, which was now a lake, only the tops of the trees sticking up out of the water. When they got to Industry Street, made a low pass over the concrete plant, Vickers saw that the water was up over the office doors and covered the lower level of the production plant.

Kahler's voice came over Vickers's headset. "Looks like it's going to be a while before you get this place back up and running. You still want me to drop you downtown?"

But Vickers wasn't listening. He'd spotted something down amid the ruins of the plant. It was a small boat, tied up next to the building that housed the offices. Somebody was down there, searching through the wreckage.

"Set me down," Vickers shouted into his headset. "Right here!"

"You crazy? Water must be almost ten feet down there."

"So put me on the roof," Vickers yelled. "You pull people up, you can put me down." He saw Kahler glance back at him from the cockpit, jerked his finger down, hard.

"Okay," Kahler said wearily to one of the crewmen in the back of the chopper. "Hook him up."

|||| Jabril and Danny carried the rubber boat between them, wading up Franklin Street until the water was deep enough to launch it. Then Danny climbed into the front, and Jabril took up his place at the stern, and without a word they dug in with their paddles.

It was the silence that seemed strangest to Danny. They paddled past rows of empty buildings—gas stations, storefront tabernacles, dry cleaners, corner markets—all empty and silent in the moonlight, water lapping gently against the tops of the doorways, like it had always been there, if only as an idea. Danny used his oar to fend off the edge of a Laundromat's flat roof. What a fragile thing a city is! You drive around on a normal day, it looks so solid, rooted deep and sprawling like a patch of weeds that can't be torn up. But then a wind comes, and in a day it's all gone; not the city, but its life. What's left behind is only an empty husk.

He felt a current pushing against them at every intersection. It surprised him. The water looked so lifeless, like a muddy lake, but beneath its oily surface it was flowing, spreading out through every part of the city. Somewhere under it, there were cars, mailboxes, street signs, but all he could see on the surface was the black water and the dark mass of buildings up ahead.

And then he saw it: something floating in the water. In the darkness, it looked like a log. But as they got closer, he saw that it was a man's body. It lay facedown in the water, arms flung out, a large T-shirt billowing out as the water gently rocked him.

Danny felt his chest tighten. He brought them up beside the body, reached out and caught hold of it, then, gripping one arm tightly, turned it over.

It was a white man, in his late fifties. His eyes were open, gazing blankly up at the night sky. And there was a bullet hole in the middle of his forehead, smaller than Danny would have imagined, a perfect round hole, too neat, somehow, to have caused so violent a death. A watery veil of blood had leaked from that hole, and it lay across the man's face like a piece of lace that someone had draped carefully over him. But it wasn't Louis Sams, and Danny couldn't help feeling relieved.

"That the place you're lookin' for?"

Danny looked up, saw Jabril pointing with his paddle at a row of buildings in the next block. One of them had a faded image of a coffee cup painted on one wall, along with the words SMELL THE FRESHNESS!

Danny let go of the dead man, and he drifted slowly away. They paddled over to the coffee warehouse. As they got closer, Danny saw that there was a sloping roof that extended out a few feet over what must have once been the loading dock. Now it lay just below the water, and he could have climbed out onto it, walked right up to one of the second-floor windows.

Next to the coffee warehouse, the old man had told him. Danny looked up the block. There was another empty warehouse about a hundred yards away. The windows along the second floor looked broken, and something hung out of one of them, trailing in the water like an old sheet.

"Up there," Danny said, pointing. "I'm guessing that's it."

They paddled across the narrow alley separating the warehouses, came up alongside the sheet trailing out the window. It turned out to be a strip of old canvas, which someone had wound tightly at the top so he could use it as a rope. The bottom had come unwound and lay spread out on the water. Danny reached up, got a good grip on the canvas, and stood up in the boat, using it to balance himself. He gave the canvas a tug, trying to judge how solid it was.

"You think it'll hold?"

Jabril shrugged. "Only one way to find out."

"Wait here, okay?"

"You sure?"

"Not really, but somebody has to stay with the boat." Danny braced one foot against the brick wall and heaved himself up out of the boat. The base of the window was about six feet above the waterline, and he had to pause to get a better grip, then reached up, got a hand on the window ledge, and pulled himself up. The window frame was studded with ancient shards of glass. The edges glittered in the moonlight, and Danny could see that somebody had carefully broken them off along the base of the window where the canvas hung out. The canvas was dry down to a few inches above the water, so he figured it probably hadn't been hanging out there during the storm. Somebody had escaped out that window, tying off the canvas to something inside and tossing it out so they could climb down. But where? Had a boat come by to rescue them?

And suddenly it occurred to Danny that the canvas might just as easily have been for somebody to climb *in*. The warehouse was dark, so he'd assumed it was empty. But now he realized that the whole city was dark, and it was far from empty. The moonlight made men into shadows, moving through the deeper shadows of the silent city.

He slid the gun out of the waistband of his jeans, moving quickly out of the rectangle of moonlight that spilled through the window onto the floor. He stood there motionless, his back pressed against the wall, waiting for his eyes to adjust to the darkness. He listened, feeling the space opening out around him, and the smell of the place—a combination of dust and mold and concrete and stale air, like you get in an empty attic. But the only sound he heard was the soft lapping of water. At first he thought it was coming from outside the window. Then he realized that it had a faint echo, like the sound of an indoor swimming pool after hours. The floor below him was flooded, he realized, the water slapping gently against the walls.

His eyes adjusted slowly, until he could see a few yards beyond the square of moonlight near the windows. Where had he read that some Native American tribes had herbs that allowed them to see in the dark? Some weed that dilated the pupils, so their eyes absorbed even the faintest light, like cats' eyes. Warriors ate it before going into battle, then crept up on their enemies at night, their hands trembling with the high, so powerful that some men didn't even realize they'd been wounded until hours after the battle, when the herb wore off.

Weird thought to come to him now. But it was always like this. There had been other moments when he'd stood in dark rooms, a gun in his hand, and he'd found that his mind sped up, skipping like a rock across the surface of a pond, while his eyes and hands became very still. And then, when he was ready to move, his mind went completely silent. Like stepping up to the plate in a baseball game, no thought in your mind beyond the smell of the infield dirt, the feeling of the breeze against your face, and the hollow slap of the catcher's glove as he goes into his crouch.

But now he'd reached that moment, and there was nothing for him to do. The building was silent and empty. Somebody had been here recently; he could smell smoke in the air—not the thick smoke that rose from the burning buildings and drifted across the city, but the sharper smell you get from a fire lit with paper or wood. He could just make out a dark spot on the concrete floor, not far from what looked like an opening to the floor below. He took a step toward it, then froze as something skittered across the floor and vanished into that hole.

Rats. They'd been frozen, just like him, watching him cautiously in the darkness. But now that he'd moved, they suddenly came to life, and he saw almost a dozen take off at a run, scattering into the far corners of the vast room, or vanishing with a quiet splash into the flooded stairway below. That was where he had to go, he realized. If he wanted to look for Sams, he'd have to dive into that water, swim down into the darkness while the rats patrolled the surface, find the cell the old man had described, and somehow get the door open.

He suddenly felt stupid, standing there. It was impossible. Sams could be only a few feet away, but he'd never know. He'd never be able to find anything in that dark water, and if he didn't drown trying, he'd probably have to be hospitalized just from swimming around underwater with his eyes open. He'd wasted his time coming out here.

He went over to the stairs, took a few careful steps down, and sure enough, there was the water, just a few inches below the concrete floor. He went back to the window, then felt his way carefully around the outer wall of the warehouse until he found the stairs going up to the floors above. Moving as quietly as possible, he checked the rest of the building, but it was empty. There was nothing to do but head to high ground. He went back to the window, started to climb out onto the ledge. But as he reached for the canvas to lower himself down into the boat, he saw light flickering in one of the buildings across the street. He paused, watching it. The building looked like another abandoned warehouse. The windows were all broken, and most of the steel security grates hung askew, like somebody had used a crowbar to pry them away out of the wall. How was that possible, he wondered, on the second floor? Then he saw that, like the building up the street, it had a sloping roof over the loading dock, which ran along the whole front of the building. All anybody had to do was climb up on that roof with a crowbar, and you could go to work on those windows. Most of the roof was underwater now, but a few feet still rose above the waterline.

And now Danny saw the light again. It was faint, like the flicker of a small fire burning somewhere on the second floor. If he hadn't been standing on the ledge, he'd never have seen it. But as he watched, he saw a man's shadow pass against one of the walls. The building wasn't burning. Somebody was in there, with a fire going for light.

Danny climbed down the canvas sheet and slid carefully into the boat. "There's somebody in the building across the street."

Jabril nodded, and they paddled silently across until the boat ran up on the loading dock's sloping roof. Danny climbed out, stood there for a moment listening. He could hear singing. *Ain't I goin' down to New Orleans*, an old man's voice growled. *Ain't I gonna see my baby?* It sounded like something you'd hear on a scratchy old record, some guy they found in a bus station slapping his guitar when he couldn't find the chords. The guy's name would be Tupelo Slim or Blind Lemon Pledge, and white men from the Upper West Side of Manhattan with law degrees and cardiology practices would argue at dinner parties about whether he did his time at Angola or Parchman, while their expensive wives stood gazing down into their wineglasses.

But all Danny could think, listening to him, was, *What are the chances a guy like that is going to have a gun?* Any man who holes up in an abandoned building way out in the flood zone, you've got to figure he's not looking for company. But he's not hiding either. He's in there singing, got a fire going. Last thing he expects is somebody to come walking up to his window. Danny looked down at the water dripping off his clothes. His gun was clearly outlined where the shirt clung to his belly. He thought about sliding it around back, where it wouldn't be the first thing the man saw. But then he changed his mind. *Let him see it. At least that way he'll know the score.*

When he was a kid, Danny had spent one summer with some cousins who lived on a farm in Ohio. One night their parents took them out to a drive-in movie, pulled the pickup in backward so the kids could lie on air mattresses in the bed of the truck and watch the movie. Danny couldn't remember what the main feature was, some stupid comedy where cars jumped over bridges and girls in tight shirts somehow didn't mind that they'd been sprayed down with hoses, but as night fell, they'd opened with a remake of *Swamp Thing.* When the first shot of the swamp came up on the screen, one of his cousins, a girl two years older than Danny, on whom he'd developed a fierce crush, turned to him and said, "Is that where *you* live?" And after that, whenever they went to the local pool for the rest of the summer, Danny would climb out of the water, and all his cousins would run away, shrieking, "Look out! It's Swamp Thing!"

Now, as he climbed through the window, Danny saw the old man look up at him with an expression that suggested the same thought had just flashed through his mind. He was sitting on a wooden packing crate, with a gallon jug of cheap red wine on the floor between his feet. His eyes widened when he saw Danny, his mouth opened, and when he caught his breath, it made a whistling sound through the gap in his front teeth.

"I heard you singing," Danny said quickly, holding out his hands to show he meant him no harm. "And I saw your fire."

Danny saw the man's eyes move down to the gun in his waistband, then come back to his face. "Where you come from? There ain't nothin' out there but water."

"I've got a boat. I came up here looking for some people in the building across the street."

The old man studied his face. "Friends of yours?"

"One of them might be. Black guy in his early forties. But I don't think he was there by his own choice. I think he was brought here by two men. White guys, look like cops. They brought my friend here a couple days before the storm hit."

The old man gave this some thought, then he looked down at the fire, gave it a poke with a stick. "They gone. Took off a couple hours ago."

"So you saw them?"

"Uh-huh. Two white cops and a black man, looked like his hands weren't workin' too good."

"You mean like they had him handcuffed?"

The old man shrugged. "Cuffed, tied. Don't much matter. He wasn't in no shape to go anywhere."

"You see where they went?"

He shook his head slowly. "Nah, sir. Just headed on up the street in a boat. They shot that poor man for his boat, then just took on off."

Danny stared at him. "What man?"

The old man gestured toward the window. "He layin' out there in the water. Just some man come by in a boat, tryin' to help. And they shot him."

"You saw it happen?"

"I was sittin' right there by the window. Couldn't hardly miss it. I was lucky they didn't see me, or I'd be lyin' out there in the water right now too."

"So which way did they go?"

The old man raised an arm, pointed north. "Up that way. Under the highway. Looked like they was in a hurry too."

They weren't headed back to high ground, then, but up Franklin, which took them even deeper into the flood zone. Danny looked down at the fire, thinking about the concrete plant over on Industry Street. It was just a few blocks away, but only God and FEMA knew how deep the water might be over there, and neither one was talking. If Louis Sams had managed to hold out on them, to keep from telling them about his testimony and the evidence against Vickers, then they might take him out there to go through his files, hoping to gauge the extent of the danger he'd put them in by his cooperation with federal prosecutors.

Danny looked up at the old man. "Sorry I can't offer you a ride out. You want us to send someone back to get you?"

"Hell, no." The old man grinned, and Danny saw his tongue dart forward to fill the gap between his front teeth. "I got food, I got some wine, and ain't nobody gonna bother me out here. I usually sleep over by the stadium in City Park, and I only come up here when it gets cold. But there's always kids messin' 'round up in these buildings, doin' their drugs. You ain't watchin', they'll piss all over your stuff, just for somethin' to do. A couple of 'em almost beat me to death once, just come up on me while I was sleepin' and started whalin' away on me." He shook his head. "Nah, this the first time I been able to sleep without worryin'. Feel like I'm on a desert island or somethin'. Get me a parrot to talk to, I be all set."

He stood at the window, watching as Danny climbed into the boat, headed on up Franklin into the darkness. "Stay dry," the old man called out. "Look like some nasty shit swimmin' 'round in that water."

And then Danny heard him laughing as he vanished from the window.

||| "I've had it with this shit." Vince pointed his flashlight down into the flooded hallway below them, the surface of the water only eight inches from the ceiling. "He comes flying in on a chopper, ropes down here like he's Commando Joe, and for what? So he can sit there and tell us how bad we fucked things up."

Lenny didn't answer. They'd found a couple more flashlights and a cordless circular saw in the plant with some charge still in its batteries, used the saw to cut a hole in the ceiling of the office building. Now they were sitting in the crawl space above the row of glass cubicles, shining their flashlights down into the darkness below them. Louis Sams was up to his shoulders in the black water, standing on a desk or something, feeling around with his feet to see where it dropped away.

"You know what I think?" Vince's flashlight went out, and he shook it. The light flickered, then came back on. "I think this whole thing's a fucking joke. There's no *way* we're gonna find a disk in here. Even if we knew right where it was, we'd still be fucked. All this water? That thing's gone."

Lenny didn't answer. He watched as Sams took a deep breath and vanished beneath the surface of the water. They followed him with their flashlights, his white shirt clearly visible, even through the filthy water, as he felt around in the open drawers of the desk. They both had their guns out, in case the guy tried to make a break for the door while he was swimming around down there. But Vince felt sure that if he took off, one of them would have to go after him. He shook his head. No *way* would he put his face under that water. Vickers wanted that disk so bad, let him get his fat ass over here and dive for it himself. But no, he was over there on the upper level of the plant, trying to figure out how much of his equipment would have to be replaced. Told them that he'd pay them each ten thousand, in *cash*, if they came up with the disk. Which raised an interesting question . . .

Sams surfaced, gasping for air, reaching up to grab the metal frame that held the building's drop ceiling, hanging there for a moment to catch his breath. Then he let go, dove under the water again.

"Lenny, listen." Vince leaned over, spoke quietly. "Let's say he finds the disk. Where you think this guy is gonna come up with all that money from? You really think he's got it *on* him?"

Lenny shrugged. "Probably keeps some cash here in the building."

"Uh-huh. So what good is that to us? We find the disk, then

we're gonna have to go dive for the money?" Vince spread his hands. "Why bother with the disk? Why not just find the cash and get the fuck out of here?"

"Jimmy said—"

"Fuck Jimmy! Jimmy's dead. Or even if he ain't dead, you think he cares anymore? Look around you! There's nothing left here for a guy like Jimmy. He's probably in Miami by now. Got himself some new guys to do his shit work."

Lenny raised his eyebrows. "You think?"

"Makes sense. What's a guy like Jimmy Mancuso gonna do here? There's no restaurants."

"He could make some serious money on the rebuilding."

"What rebuilding? You really think anyone's going to want to come back here? For what? So they can wait for the next storm to blow in?"

Lenny shook his head. "No way they'll just abandon this city. They'll fix the levees, drain the water out, and start building again. Same way they always have."

"Okay, so let's say that's true. There's going to be some *serious* money coming into this city. Federal money, insurance payments. Think about it."

"That's what I'm saying. Jimmy's not going anywhere."

"*Fuck* Jimmy. I say we grab some of that for *us*."

Lenny looked at him. "You got something in mind?"

Sams came back up, gasping. He looked up at them, exhausted. "I can't find it."

Vince raised his gun, pointed it down at him. "Then you ain't looking hard enough."

Sams wiped his face against his forearm, looked down into the water. "Everything's all scattered around. There's papers floating everywhere, and all the stuff from the desk floated away."

"You hid it, you find it. That's how it works."

Sams shook his head wearily. Then he took a deep breath, slipped back under the water.

"Think about it," Vince went on. "What's this disk matter? We go down in Vickers's office, you don't think we'll find all kinds of papers and contracts with the same exact stuff on it?"

"Yeah, so?"

"So *that's* where we should be looking. Find the money, get the papers, we could go into business for ourselves. Put in bids on the reconstruction projects, then call up all the people he's been paying off, put the squeeze on 'em to make sure we get the job."

"How's that make us any money?" Lenny asked. "We don't know shit about construction."

"So we sell the contract to one of the guys who didn't get it. Sub-contract. They do the work, we get a cut. You think any of these guys with contracts in Iraq actually do the work? They hire some Iraqi guys to do it, while they sit back and collect."

"And that's legal?"

"Most of it. You put the squeeze on somebody to get the contract, I guess that's technically extortion. But look around. How you think this guy got rich? He's paying people off, watering the concrete. Why you think we're sitting here?"

Lenny gazed down at Sams swimming around down there in the pale light from their flashlights. "The cash is probably in a safe."

"So we find it, then we make Vickers tell us the combination." Vince smiled. "You can be pretty convincing, you put your mind to it."

Lenny thought about this for a moment, then shrugged. "Okay, let's do it."

Sams came back to the surface, and Vince said, "All right, that's enough. Forget the disk. We got another little job for you."

▯▯▯▯ "There it is."

Danny sat forward, gazing intently at the concrete plant rising up before them in the moonlight. The sand and gravel silos stuck up out of the water, a pair of conveyor belts sloping down through the roof of the main production building. The casting yard, where the huge concrete forms were laid out awaiting shipment to construction sites, was underwater. Danny saw that the water rippled slightly where it flowed over something large lying just below the surface. Off to the right, a set of metal stairs led down into the water from the upper level of the production plant. A few yards away he saw the small office building, mostly submerged, and beside it a small boat tied up to an air-conditioning duct that rose up out of the water, entering the building just below the sloping roof.

"What's the story?" Jabril asked quietly.

"Looks like they're here." Danny pointed to the boat tied up beside the office building. "It's not really clear how they got into that building. The water's up over the door. They could break a window, I guess, if they don't mind swimming."

"I'd use that air duct to get up on the roof," Jabril said. "Then you could cut a hole in the roof and climb down, use all the wiring and pipes up in the ceiling to stay out of the water."

"Cut a hole with what?"

Jabril looked over at the plant. "That's the factory, right? Must be plenty of stuff over there you could use to bust a hole in a roof."

Danny followed his gaze. "You really think these two guys are gonna get their feet wet looking for something in a flooded building?"

Jabril shrugged. "Your boy Sams hid it, they'll make him go get it. Why go splashing around in that water if you don't have to?"

Danny nodded. "So the question is, where would he hide it?"

A light moved across a window on the second floor of the main production building, and then it vanished, like somebody was swinging a flashlight around.

"I guess there's your answer," Jabril said.

"I guess so."

They dug in with their paddles, and the boat silently moved toward the metal stairs that rose out of the water toward a door high up along the outer wall of the building.

IIII You build a business with your own two hands. You're still a young man then, so you've got energy and hope. Over time, you nurture it, spread some fertilizer around, and watch it grow. Nobody has a clue how it feels unless they've done it. Maybe if you've raised a child. But Gerald Vickers had one hundred and forty-one employees, and he thought of them all the way a father thinks of his children. And as with a parent, it breaks your heart when your children disappoint you—lying, stealing from you, taking for granted all the things you do for them.

When he thought about Louis Sams, Vickers couldn't help feeling angry. Was loyalty too much to expect?

And now, wandering through the production plant, shining his flashlight across the half-submerged machinery, he felt the loss even more acutely. All the time they'd put in together, all the effort it would require now to rebuild. As if the challenges they faced weren't enough, without this kind of trouble and the solution it required. He sighed, shook his head. What a mess. Everything would have to be replaced.

He heard the door open on the upper catwalk while he was bent over the railing looking down at a dust collector, trying to figure out how much of the electrical system would have to go. The compressors were all underwater, but the central electrical panel looked like it had stayed dry. At least the filters were okay, so they might be able to get away with reconditioning that unit.

He heard footsteps coming up behind him, straightened up, saying, "You guys find what you were looking for?"

A flashlight shone directly into his eyes, blinding him. "Not yet. But it looks like we came to the right place."

|||| "What the fuck is this?" Vince stared down at a wad of sodden papers that Sams had passed up to him.

"Contracts. You told me to find them for you."

"I can't read this shit! The pages are all stuck together, and the ink's all smeared."

"What'd you expect? They've been underwater for two days."

Vince glared at him. "This ain't helping you any. You realize that, right?"

"Yeah? So what's that mean? You're going to kill me twice?" Sams closed his eyes wearily. "Let's just get it over with, then. I've had enough of this bullshit." Lenny reached down, grabbed a handful of his hair, and jerked his head up so Sams was looking right up into his eyes, his eyes startled and tearing with pain. "I'll only kill you once, but you mess with me, I'll make sure it's real slow. You hear what I'm saying?"

"I hear you," Sams gasped.

Lenny let go of his hair, wiped his hand carefully on his pants. "What about the money?"

"The safe's down there, but it's locked." Sams reached up, rubbed at the top of his head slowly. "The only one who has the combination is Vickers."

"Could be all kinds of stuff in that safe," Vince said. "Cash. Bonds. Might be where he keeps all the really valuable information. But even if we get the combination, we open it down there, everything's gonna get soaked, just like these papers." He tossed the wad of contracts into the water. "Another big fucking waste of time."

Lenny looked up at the metal beam running the length of the building just above their heads. "We could try raising the safe out of the water."

"You serious? You know what one of those things weighs?"

Lenny shrugged. "Three of us, we could do it." He nodded to Sams. "He's an engineer. Ask him."

Vince looked down at Sams. "So? He's full of shit, right?"

Sams looked up at the beam, and Vince could see him calculating. "You find a block and tackle, we could probably do it. It's a small safe, and we'd be pulling down, not up, so we could use our body weight as a counterbalance." He reached up, pulled down some more of the acoustic ceiling tiles hanging from their metal tabs. "Have to clear these out."

"No problem." Vince kicked at the remaining ceiling tiles below him, and they tumbled into the water. "How's that?"

Sams didn't answer. He was studying the problem now. He looked at the beam, then reached up, pointed Vince's flashlight toward a corner of the office below him. "Keep the light right there," he said, then he took a deep breath and vanished under the water.

"You believe this guy?" Vince looked over at Lenny. "He's all into it now."

"He's an engineer. You give him a problem, he'll solve it."

Sams came back to the surface, wiped the water from his face. "Be easier if the beam were directly over it, but it's possible." He floated there, looking up at them. "You sure there's money in that safe? This isn't a cash business."

"He's got a safe in his office. What do you think he keeps in there, his lunch?"

"Okay. I've just never seen any cash lying around. Everything's done by contract."

"You kidding? This guy's been paying people off all over town. You think he wants a favor, he writes the guy a *check*?"

"I don't know anything about that."

"You don't, huh?" Vince grinned. "You'd said that to the U.S. attorney, you wouldn't be in this mess."

Sams looked away.

"All right," Lenny said. "This ain't getting us anywhere." He looked down at Sams. "You got any idea where we could find what we need to raise this thing?"

"There's an equipment locker over in the plant."

"Show me."

|||| "Let me ask you something. You think all this is my fault?" Vickers waved a hand at the rows of flooded machines behind him. "I've lost more than anyone. My house, my business. It's all gone."

"My heart bleeds for you." Danny had his gun out, holding it loosely against his leg. He kept his flashlight pointed at Vickers's face. "I've been over in the Ninth Ward. People are dying over there."

"I'm sorry to hear that. But how's it my fault?"

"Go look at the seawalls. They washed out, just like Louis Sams said they would."

"Come on! You know why those seawalls gave out? I've seen the pictures on TV. It wasn't bad concrete. You can see where the soil washed out from around the foundations." Vickers shook his head. "That's not *my* fault. Go ask the Corps of Engineers why they didn't require a firmer foundation, or build up the earth levees so they could take the water pressure. Go ask the Congress why they didn't appropriate the money so we could build it *right*. You want to make me the bad guy here, 'cause I cut some corners. But you ever try to bid on one of those jobs? We're building on the cheap because that's the way people want it. It's tax money paying for those jobs. You think people want to pay more taxes so we can do the job the way Louis Sams thinks it should be done? You think some guy in Indiana wants to pay more so New Orleans can have flood protection? Sorry, but that ain't how this country works. Our whole society runs on two basic principles: *Fuck you, and gimme what's mine.* You get what you pay for, and nobody wanted to spend the money. That's why those levees washed out. But nobody's going to want to admit that. You watch: they'll go looking for somebody like me to blame, so the politicians can say it wasn't their fault. But they're the ones who wouldn't write the check."

Jabril looked over at Danny. "Man's got a point there."

"They'll all say that," Danny said bitterly. "You watch. They'll have televised hearings, a congressional investigation, and in the end they'll agree that they're all national heroes and they did everything they could."

Jabril watched Danny rub the gun against his thigh gently. "Ain't nothing new, man. That's how it's always been."

"That doesn't make it right."

Vickers was eying the gun now too, and Jabril could see he was trying to gauge the seriousness of the situation. "Look," he said. "There's a time to worry about who's at fault. Right now we all need to focus on repairing the damage. Why do you think I came back now? My wife's in Houston, but when I saw the flooding on the news, I knew they were going to need people like me to get this city back on its feet."

Danny smiled. "People like you."

"You know how to make concrete?" Vickers waved a hand at the machines. "You can do it better, then be my guest. If not, then how about you get off my case and get out of my way?"

Danny rubbed the gun against his leg. "Lots of money to be made, they start rebuilding those levees. And I'll bet you won't lose a dime on all this flooding. You're probably insured up the ass and out the eyeballs."

"You're right. I got insurance. And there's no question that somebody's going to make a shitload of money pouring concrete when the rebuilding starts." Vickers looked at them and raised his eyebrows. "You boys want a piece of that action? A chance like this doesn't come around but once a century. A man plays it right, he could end up owning half the city. There's gonna be a lot of cheap real estate out there in the next six months. You make some quick money, put it into property, you'll be set for life."

Jabril looked at Danny. "He's kidding, right? He's trying to talk us into investing in *real estate*?"

Vickers grinned. "What goes down must come up. People need a place to live."

"Or maybe," Danny said, "they just learn from their mistakes."

Vickers shook his head. "Never happen. People don't live where they do because it's smart. They live there because it's what they know. Maybe all those people who left town won't come back, but a lot of them will. They'll get sick of Houston or Baton Rouge. They'll think about what this town used to be like, how they felt living here, and they'll say, *Fuck it. This ain't living*. And then they'll pack up their stuff and move back." He spread his hands. "I don't know about you, but I'd like to make that possible for them."

"Damn." Jabril grinned. "You got the peddler's gift, don't you?"

"I'm serious about this. We've got to think about the future."

"Uh-huh. And like you said, there's a shitload of money to be made."

"I'm not worried about what happens to your business," Danny said. "That's up to the U.S. attorney. Where's Sams?"

Vickers gave a sigh. "He's over in the office, okay? As far as I'm concerned, you can have him."

"He's alive?"

"He was when I last saw him."

Jabril looked at Danny. "I'll go take a look," he said, and then he disappeared into the darkness.

"He should be careful," Vickers said. "I don't think Lenny and Vince are going to be in any hurry to hand him over to you. They're looking at some serious charges if he walks out of here, and I gather Jimmy isn't going to be around to protect them."

"You're not worried?"

"Me?" Vickers shook his head. "I'll say that I hired them to secure the plant, and they caught him breaking in during the flood. Black guy climbing in the window? They thought he was a looter. Anybody else would have shot him."

"So you just tortured him."

"He doesn't look too bad. And they were just holding him until the police arrived. Took a couple days, and then I showed up, recognized the poor guy."

"I've got a better idea," Danny said. "The U.S. attorney doesn't care who he prosecutes on this corruption charge. So cut a deal. Give 'em the people up in Baton Rouge who took the payoffs. They're the ones who've really corrupted the system." He waved a hand at the water around him. "You think any of this would have happened if they'd done their job?"

Vickers looked interested. "What about Sams? He was all set to testify against me."

"You let him keep his job, he's got no reason to go after you. All that evidence he's collected shows is that you paid off some people to get jobs. That's what you'd be saying to the grand jury, so it just corroborates your story. You get immunity for your testimony, you're in the clear."

"And the kidnapping charge?"

Danny shrugged. "They try to come after you for any of this, just say those two guys exceeded their authority. Those guys are nothing without Jimmy. He's not around, they're disposable. And there's nobody to collect on what you owed him. I'm guessing nothing's on paper, so you collect the insurance on this place, you're out of debt. You can rebuild without having to worry about paying his percentage."

Vickers thought about this for a moment, then he laughed. "You know, I never thought about that."

Danny heard footsteps on the catwalk above him, turned just as a flashlight came on, blinding him. He raised a hand to shield his eyes, felt it brushed aside as something hard came crashing down against the side of his head. He cried out in pain, fell to his knees.

"Jesus," he heard Vince say. "What the fuck did you do that for?"

"If there's anything I hate," Lenny said quietly, "it's a fucking lawyer."

IIII "This isn't going to work."

"Shut up." Vince pointed his flashlight at Sams, shining it in his eyes so he winced and looked away. "You had your say. Now just shut the fuck up and pull!"

"I'm just saying—"

"What part of shut the fuck up don't you understand?"

Sams looked at Danny, shrugged. The safe was an old-fashioned floor unit that looked like it belonged in an old movie, Butch and Sundance squatting beside it, deciding how much dynamite to use. Danny and Sams were standing in the water in Vickers's office, a series of ropes slung over the beam in the ceiling.

They'd searched the equipment locker, finding coils of rope but no block and tackle. "It was there last week," Vickers had told them, all helpful now. His eyes kept flicking over to check out the blood streaming down Danny's forehead. "One of my guys was doing some repair work on a batcher. He might have needed it." He'd stood there in silence as they told him they wanted their money up front, and *dry*, none of this wadded-up cash they'd have to hang out on a clothesline, they ever wanted to spend it. He kept glancing at the gun in Lenny's hand as Vince spoke, then he just nodded. "Won't be easy to get that safe up without the right equipment."

"You think?" Vince pointed to the coils of rope in the equipment shed. "We toss those over the beam, these guys get down in the water, they can heave the safe up."

"It's not the same," Sams tried to tell him. "A block and tackle spreads the weight out, so you're lifting with two or three different ropes at the same time. You don't have to use as much force, and the ropes don't have to take as much weight."

"You're telling me two guys can't lift one fucking safe?"

"He's right," Vickers said. "It isn't about the number of men you've got doing the lifting. It's the carrying weight of the rope and the efficiency of the force you can apply."

Vince looked at Lenny. "You know what we need in here? An engineer. That would solve all our fucking problems."

They'd cut a second hole in the metal roof, this one at the back of the building, directly above Vickers's office, and now Lenny, Vince, and Vickers sat up there on a beam supervising, while Danny and Sams worked in the water below. Danny's head had finally stopped bleeding, but it hurt like hell, and he didn't like the look on Lenny's face, or the way he rubbed the tip of his thumb gently against the grip of his pistol as it lay against his leg. And then, just as they got the ropes rigged up, Lenny's flashlight died. He shook it, and it flickered briefly, then went out. Without a word, he dropped it into the water. "Hurry it up," he said quietly.

All the polish had rubbed off his surface, so now all you could see was the violence hidden just beneath. A guy like that could walk around New Orleans with a cop's badge for almost fifteen years, earn himself a detective's shield by keeping the violence just barely under control, unless you counted dragging the occasional suspect into a dark alley and teaching him the meaning of *excessive force*. In the old days, a guy like that would have put in his twenty, then retired with a pension to go work security at Jefferson Downs or one of the casinos on the Gulf Coast. But the city had outgrown such men, or at least it pretended it had. But all it took was a few bad hours, when the wind blew hard and the waters rose, to see what lay just beneath that polished surface. Lenny had come in hard and fast, surprising Danny with the sudden violence of his attack, and then calmly crouched down beside him, drew back the hammer on his pistol, and pressed it against the side of his head. He looked up at Vickers, said, "How much you keep in that safe in your office?"

Eighty thousand. Not as much as they'd hoped, but enough to make it worth hauling it up out of the water so they could clean it out. And more than enough to kill their prisoners once they'd got the safe opened. Danny figured that was the plan. Just a couple more victims of the storm, their bodies floating among the wreckage.

Jabril was out there somewhere in the darkness. Had he seen them forced to climb up onto the roof of the office building at gunpoint? It was enough to give Danny a flicker of hope, just knowing these men had no idea that someone was waiting for them in the dark.

Danny saw Sams catch his eye and then glance up at Vince's flashlight. The batteries had grown weaker over the last hour, and now it gave no more light than a candle. How much longer until it went out also? Danny and Sams had taken their time down in the water rigging the ropes around the safe, watching the flashlights slowly get weaker above them. Now, with one of the flashlights gone, when you slid beneath the surface and swam down to the safe you were lost in darkness. If Danny and Sams could drag out their struggle with the safe until the other flashlight went out, then they could dive under the water in the darkness and slip away.

Vickers looked down at his office, framed pictures of him landing a marlin off Cozumel barely visible in the faint gleam of the flashlight on the nearest wall. The water rippled with every movement they made, so the fish in the photograph almost looked like it was leaping free, seeing its chance to make a break for it. Papers and framed family photographs from his desk floated on the surface of the water around him. He was playing along with this effort to raise the safe, but Danny could see that he was thinking about what they'd talked about earlier, trying to figure the best way to slip away from these two guys and leave them holding the bag when the law returned, as he knew it would, and started coming down on people for the things they'd done out here in the darkness. Let them take the eighty thousand, he was thinking. He'd grab the papers he needed, then clear out, claim it was an armed robbery.

"You heard the man," Vince said. "We ain't got all night."

They gripped the ropes and heaved. The ropes drew taught across the beam, and their faces contorted. The safe rose an inch off the floor, swung slowly in under the beam. Sams jumped back out of its way, and it settled there. Danny let go of the rope, straightened up.

"It's too heavy," he said. "We'll never get it out of the water."

"C'mon," Vince said. "You moved it. I saw you."

Lenny just snapped the hammer back on his pistol, pointed it down at Danny. "I'm getting tired of this," he said.

They tried again. This time they got it halfway out of the water before it slipped back.

"Much better." Vince grinned. "You see what you can accomplish when you put your mind to it?"

"We get it up there," Sams said to Danny, "we're going to need some way to tie these ropes down, so we won't have to hold it up there while they get it open."

Danny looked around. "What about the desk?"

Sams looked at it, shook his head. "What would we tie off to?"

"You could run the ropes under it," Vickers suggested. "It's a heavy desk, solid oak. You're standing on it, so it won't go anywhere. Then the desk takes some of the weight."

Sams thought about this. "We'd be pulling up against the desk, instead of down from the beam. We'd lose some power."

"Yeah, but you wouldn't need to pull as hard," Vickers told him. "It'll work just like a block and tackle. Every point of contact cuts down on the force you need."

Sams looked at Danny, who shrugged. "You guys are the engineers. I'm just a lawyer."

They tried it. Sams slid under the water, ran the ropes under the legs of the desk, then came back up, handing the ends up to Danny. He climbed back onto the desk, shook the water off his hands, and wrapped his rope around one of his hands to get a better grip. "You ready?"

Danny nodded. Once again they heaved, raising the safe a few feet. But this time they could hold it there, shift their grip, and heave again, setting their own weight against it. Before long the safe came up into the light, water streaming off it. It seemed lighter once it was out of the water, and they heaved it right up to the beam, steadied it there.

"Now we're talking," Vince said triumphantly. He shoved his gun into his belt, leaned over, rested a hand on top of the safe, and held the flashlight down close to the dial. "So what's the combination?"

"Thirty-two," Vickers told him. "Twenty-four. Forty-eight."

"Ah, that's real sweet." Vince started to spin the dial. "You used your wife's measurements."

Sams glanced at Danny. Danny nodded slightly, and they both watched as Vince spun the dial more slowly now, peering at it closely. He gave the dial one last turn, bringing it home. Danny heard the lock click into place, and Vince grinned. "I always wanted to be a safecracker." He grabbed the lever, turned it, and the safe's door swung open.

Vince peered inside, shining the flashlight across the shelves. "Now, that," he said, "is a lovely sight."

Danny saw Vince reach inside. Lenny leaned over to look. Sams must have been watching just as closely, because they let go of their ropes at exactly the same moment.

"Shit!" Vince lost his balance, dropping the flashlight as he tried to catch hold of the beam. The safe hit the water first, sending out a huge wave that caught Danny by surprise, sweeping him off the desk at the same moment that the flashlight hit the water and the office was plunged into darkness. Danny heard a shout and another large splash. Then, suddenly, it was as if a thunderstorm had broken right over their heads—bright flashes of light, as Lenny fired down into the darkness wildly.

Danny heard a scream. He took a deep breath and dove under the water, kicking out for the door into the hallway. He missed it by inches, cracking the fingers of one hand painfully on the doorframe. But he managed to get a grip on the door with his uninjured hand, pulled himself out of the room into the darkness beyond.

|||| "We've got gunshots."

ATF Special Agent in Charge Jim Fisher was at the wheel of one of the boats they'd liberated from a dealership up on Airline, cruising slowly up North Broad Street, shining their spotlight on the buildings on either side of the road, when the call came in over his radio. Mickie Vega, her voice calm, just calling it in, the way she'd been trained. He grabbed the radio off his belt, keyed the microphone, said, "What's your location?"

"Industry Street, a couple blocks from I-10."

"What's your cross street?"

"East of Marigny . . ." There was a pause. "And just north of the railroad tracks, looks like."

"I'm just down the road from you. Sit tight, and we'll be there in a minute to back you up." Fisher slipped the radio back onto his belt, then spun the wheel, put the boat into a tight turn, and punched it, feeling the boat dig in and throw water as he headed east along Florida Avenue. He'd really started to like this boat. A little Cobia bay skiff with a four-stroke Yamaha outboard that could fly across the water when he needed it to. Mostly they'd prowled the neighborhoods at a slow cruise, looking for survivors, but twice now he'd had to punch it to answer an emergency call, and the three agents grabbed hold of the sides, the wind whipping up around them. It might almost have been fun if he hadn't had to worry about slamming it into a submerged car or ripping out the bottom on a street sign. But the water here was deep enough to open it up and let her run, skimming past the submerged buildings, fast enough to earn himself a ticket on this stretch of road, if there'd been a cop dedicated enough to still be out there to write him up.

He cut over onto the railroad tracks at Elysian Fields, then turned north on Marigny, cutting his speed. Soon the cement plant's silos appeared, sticking up out of the water on his right, and suddenly there was Vega's boat coming out of nowhere in the darkness to swing up alongside him. She leaned over, shouted something he couldn't make out over the sound of their engines, then gestured with one hand toward a low building that looked like the plant's offices. He nodded, motioned for her to swing around behind the building, saw her spin the wheel, and her boat raced away. He cut his own wheel to the left, eased off on the throttle, and coasted in toward the building's front entrance, while his men crouched in the front of the boat, watching for any movement over the barrels of their squat Heckler & Koch assault rifles.

Beautiful, he thought. *Like a dance in the moonlight.*

|||| "You're a mutt. That's what you are."

"Fuck you! How was I supposed to know they'd let go?" Vince climbed out onto the building's tin roof, water dripping off him. "Anyway, we still got this guy."

Sams lay on his back beside Vickers, trembling. There was a bullet hole in his left arm, and he was bleeding heavily.

"We should do something about that arm," Vickers said.

"Fuck him," Lenny said. "He didn't want to get shot, he shouldn't have fucked with me."

"He won't be much good to us if he bleeds to death."

"He wasn't much good to us before." Lenny got up, went over to the edge of the roof. "Son of a bitch!"

"What?"

"Somebody put a hole in our fucking boat!" Lenny crouched down, drew his gun, peering out into the darkness. He glanced over at Vince, who was crouched over Sams, examining the wound. "Will you leave him? We got bigger problems here. We don't find a boat, we're stuck here."

Vince peeled off his shirt, rolled it up, and began tying it around Sams's upper arm as a tourniquet.

"Hey," Lenny said. "Where's your gun?"

"I dropped it."

"You *what*?"

"I dropped it. When I fell in the water."

"Jesus Christ." Lenny shook his head in disgust. "Take this one. It's got a couple rounds left in the clip."

Vince looked at him. "You're giving me your gun?"

"It's not my gun. I took it off the lawyer back in the plant." Lenny reached around behind, pulled a semiautomatic pistol out of his belt. "This is *my* gun." Then he froze, looked off into the distance. "You hear that?"

"What?"

"It sounded like a boat."

|||| Danny did his best to move quietly through the darkness, but he knew that if anyone was listening, they could track him along the hall by the quiet sighing of the water. He was working his way along the hallway toward the faint light at the entrance, taking it

slowly, trying not to give away his position. Had Sams gotten out? Twice Danny almost whispered his name. But then he hesitated. He couldn't hear anyone behind him. And he wanted to be damn sure just what was out there in the darkness before he gave away his position.

He was moving from office to office, trying to stay out of the hallway. If you got caught out there when someone started shooting, there'd be no place to hide. Danny thought about going over the low glass walls that separated the cubicles, but when he tested one, the glass groaned under his weight and he quickly let go, slid back into the water.

"Damn," Jabril said from the end of the hall. "You *think* you could make any more noise?"

IIII   Mickie Vega eased the boat in toward the back of the office building, then reached over, touched the shoulder of the agent crouched on her right. He switched on the spotlight, and they saw three men on the roof, shielding their eyes from the sudden blaze of light. Two of them were holding guns, and Mickie saw the agents in the front of the boat tense up, their fingers moving to the triggers of their assault rifles.

"NOPD," one of them called out, and he laid his pistol on the roof beside him, stood up slowly, and held his hands out wide so they could see he was unarmed. "We've got an injured man here!"

Mickie saw that a fourth man, this one black, lay stretched out on his back, a shirt wrapped around his upper arm as a tourniquet. "ATF," she called out. "We heard gunfire."

The man nodded, pointed down into the building below him. "Looters," he yelled. "We got this one. There's another one still in there."

And now Mickie saw that a section of the building's metal roof had been cut away. A boat was tied up to an air-conditioning vent just below them, but it wasn't going to be much use to anyone. It was half full of water and sinking fast.

"You have any ID?"

The man hesitated. "We lost everything in the flood," he called out. "We were working security." He gestured toward one of the men beside him. "This guy is the owner. We came out here to check on his place, and found some guys trying to open the safe."

Two of them sure looked like cops. White guys with bad haircuts and athletic builds gone soft from too much beer and fried food. And their clothes looked like they'd bought out the sale rack in the men's department at JCPenney's. But something about the whole thing felt wrong to Mickie. Maybe it was the slightly pleading tone in the guy's voice. Not pissed off the way a local cop would sound if a bunch of Feds showed up and held him at gunpoint. More like a kid trying to lie his way out of trouble, anxious that you believe him, his voice getting more plaintive the wilder the story gets.

"Tell your friend to put his gun down," she called out.

For a moment nobody moved. Then the second man reached out very slowly and laid his gun on the roof a few inches away. His hand came slowly back to rest on his knee.

The agents in the front of the boat kept their guns trained on the men, but their fingers drew back off the triggers of their assault rifles, moved to the front of the trigger guard.

"How many looters?"

"Two. We got this one, but the other guy's still inside." The man glanced down through the hole in the ceiling. "And he's armed."

Mickie slid the radio off her belt, keyed the microphone, and said, "Jim?"

Fisher's voice came back. "Go ahead."

"We've got four men on the roof. Two identify themselves as New Orleans police, and one claims to be the owner. The fourth guy is injured, and they say they caught him looting the place. They also say they exchanged fire with one more looter. They believe he's still inside the building."

"Roger that. We've got the entrance covered, but the water's pretty deep here. You see any entrance points back there?"

"Looks like they went in through a hole in the roof."

"Can you get in that way?"

"No problem. What do you want us to do with these four?"

"Get 'em in the boat, so they'll be out of your line of fire. You say one of them's injured?"

"That's right." Mickie looked at the man lying on the roof. "Looks pretty serious."

"You got somebody there who can look after him?"

"We'll manage. Can you give us some light through the windows when we go in?"

"You got it. Let me know when you're ready."

Mickie slid the radio back onto her belt, then fed the boat's engine a little gas so that it slid in next to the roof. She killed the engine as two of the agents jumped out, tossed a rope to one of the cops. They got the wounded man on board, and then the two cops and the plant's owner climbed down into the boat. Mickie told one of the ATF agents to stay with the boat, then she climbed out onto the roof, checked her weapon. She slid the radio off her belt, said, "We're ready."

"Roger that," Fisher said. "We'll give you three minutes to get inside, then we'll hit the lights."

Mickie put the radio away, took out her flashlight, and shone it down into the hole in the roof. It was some kind of office. She saw ropes wrapped around one of the support beams just below the roofline, trailing in the black water. *Weird,* she thought. *Most looters just kick in a window.*

But this wasn't the time to speculate on such things. Her mind was like a wire drawn taut, focused on disarming the man still hiding in the darkness below.

"Let's do it," she said, and then she dropped through the hole in the roof into the water below.

On the boat, Vince watched her vanish into the hole. He grinned, shook his head. "Damn," he said. "She's something else. Seriously, I'm filled with admiration." He turned to the remaining ATF agent, who was bending over Sams, wrapping his wound with a bandage he'd taken from a first-aid kit. "What's a guy got to do to get some of that?"

The agent ignored him. He drew a combat knife out of a leather sheath on his belt, used it to cut the bandage, then reached for some medical tape to secure the loose end.

Vince sighed, looked over at Lenny. "Man, that's the Feds for you. No cooperation."

Lenny shrugged. He bent, picked up a metal ammo case off the deck of the boat, hefted it once, then raised it and brought it crashing down on the agent's head. The man slumped to the deck. Lenny tossed the ammo case aside, crouched down, and checked his pulse.

"He'll live," he said. Then he picked up the agent's assault rifle, wound his arm through the strap. "Climb back up there on the roof," he said to Vince, "and grab our guns. We're out of here."

⫼ "I'm going back in there," Danny said.

"You want to get shot?"

"I came here for Louis, I'm not leaving without him."

Jabril looked back along the dark hall. "You think they still got him?"

"I kept listening for him, but I didn't hear anything."

"Well, if they got him," Jabril said, "they ain't taking him nowhere. I put enough holes in their boat, you could strain spaghetti."

They were floating in the reception area, the water up over the tops of the doors, but Jabril had swum down and broken one of the glass doors, then made his way inside just in time to see the lights go out and all the shooting begin.

"Lend me your gun," Danny said now. "I'll go after him."

"You're gonna swim back in there, start shooting?"

"They won't expect me to come back, or to have a gun."

"Won't stop them killing your ass."

Behind them they heard a loud splash. They froze. And suddenly white light filled the reception area, throwing their shadows against the rear wall.

"ATF!" a voice called out from the hallway behind them. "Put your weapons down and come out where we can see you."

Jabril looked at Danny. "That who I think it is?"

"Sure sounds like it."

Jabril tossed his gun aside, put his hands up high. "Damn," he said. "We ain't *never* gonna hear the end of this one."

IIII Lenny eased the boat away from the building, keeping the engine just above an idle. When the searchlights came on in front of the building, Vince shot him a look, but Lenny didn't seem concerned, just steered the boat slowly back among the cluster of gravel silos, keeping to the shadows, one hand resting on the throttle, ready to punch it if somebody spotted them. Vince glared at his back. *Okay*, he wanted to say to Lenny, *but tell me that wasn't some slick shit back there, getting all those ATF to go in there and do our work for us.* The guy always acting like he had to do everything and you're just along for the ride. But could he have talked his way out of the situation like that? That searchlight came on, they're standing there with guns in their hands, a guy who's been shot right there at their feet. Man, that's *caught*. But you got to stay loose, work with what you got, even if that means making shit into shoe shine. Work it hard enough, it'll catch the light.

Vickers was sitting in the front of the boat, looking around like he kept expecting somebody to jump out of the darkness any second and grab him, just like in one of those slasher movies. As long as they had him, they could claim they were just securing the property, and as long as they had Sams, Vickers wouldn't be able to cut out on them. But now one of the ATF agents appeared on the roof, looking around for the boat. Vince had to laugh, imagining the guy's face getting that surprised look, like, *What the fuck?* But then he must have caught movement out of the corner of his eye, because he looked over toward the gravel silos, shouted, "Hey!" He raised his assault rifle, then thought better of it, grabbed for the radio on his belt instead.

"Time to go," Vince shouted to Lenny. They were just coming out around the last of the silos, about fifty yards to clear the back of the production plant and they'd be in open water, the railroad tracks straight ahead. Lenny pushed the throttle forward, and Vince felt the bow of the boat leap out of the water, the stern slewing from all that sudden power. He grinned, raised a hand to wave good-bye to the ATF agent back on the roof as the boat vanished behind the production plant, when without warning the boat slammed into something hidden just below the surface of the water. Vince was thrown onto his back next to Sams, and he saw Lenny stumble, grabbing for the wheel mount, only to land on his knees in the bow.

"Son of a *bitch*!" Vince grabbed the side of the boat, pulled himself up to his knees. The bottom of the boat was filling with water. "What the fuck did you do?"

Lenny didn't answer, and Vince saw that he was on his side, doubled over in pain, gripping his right knee. He'd landed, Vince saw, on the metal ammo box. The thought of it made him wince. *Jesus, sharp metal edge? That's one way to fuck up your knee good.*

He heard an engine rev up, and a boat appeared around the far end of the office building, its spotlight lancing out into the darkness among the silos, searching. Vince glanced back at Lenny, then thought, *Fuck it*, and slipped over the side of the boat.

He landed on a huge mound of gravel. The boat had run up on it, so the water was only ankle-deep, but he slid down the gravel into deeper water, then plunged in, swimming toward the open doors of the production plant.

‖‖ "There they are." Danny stood on the roof of the office building, pointing toward an area of open water just beyond the gravel silos, where the spotlight on Fisher's boat had swept past a dark shape on the water, then quickly tracked back to fix on it. The stolen boat lay dead in the water, listing slightly to one side. Danny saw no movement.

"Get down," Mickie told them. She had her assault rifle raised, keeping it fixed on the stolen boat while Fisher swung wide around the silos to come up on it from behind. Then the engine on Fisher's boat abruptly died, and Danny saw the agents on board raise their assault rifles in one motion. Lenny was on his feet, holding the stunned ATF agent in front of him, his assault rifle pointed at the men in the boat.

"Put your guns down," Lenny yelled. "Now!"

For a moment everything seemed to freeze. Danny could feel the tension coming off Mickie as the ATF agents watched their worst nightmare—an agent held hostage—take shape before them. She had the angle to take a shot, but Lenny's boat was moving now, shifting sideways under their weight, and she hesitated, not wanting to hit the agent. Vickers sat frozen in the front of the boat, staring at Lenny like he couldn't believe what he was seeing. Lenny had his arm around the ATF agent's throat, holding him up. Danny saw that he was trying to keep his weight off one leg, his face contorted and shining with sweat.

Then Danny saw Sams get to his feet. He stood in the bow of the boat behind Lenny, looking disoriented. His shirt was drenched with blood, and somebody had tied a tourniquet around one arm just below the shoulder. Mickie swung her gun to the left to cover him.

"Don't shoot," Danny yelled, pushing Mickie's gun down. Then he saw Sams take in the situation. His eyes moved from the ATF agents to Lenny, and then he took two steps forward, shoved Lenny from behind. Lenny stumbled, let go of the agent. He cried out in rage and pain, grabbed for Sams. The sudden movement made the boat slide sideways; it tipped up on one side as it hit the water, throwing everyone on board into the water.

Without thinking, Danny dove off the roof into the water. He swam through the legs of the gravel silo and grabbed the bow of the boat that was hung up there. The water beyond the boat was still and empty.

Fisher's boat had come alongside, and two agents had the injured agent under both arms, hauling him on board.

"Where'd they go?" Danny yelled up to Fisher.

Fisher pointed toward the open doors of the production plant. "They swam in there."

Danny pushed off from the boat, swam across the stretch of moonlit water and into the darkness of the plant.

|||| Sams clung to a support bracket that braced a large cement mixer to the building's metal frame, keeping the machine between him and the open water beyond. His left arm hurt like hell, and he had no memory of how he'd made it here, just a vague sensation of struggling against the water, grasping at anything that came within his reach, then struggling on. He'd been thrown into the water when the boat overturned, felt Lenny grabbing for him, and kicked away. The plant's entrance gaped directly ahead of him, and without thinking, he swam toward it. He had to hide; that was all he knew. He wanted to get into a dark corner and stay there, his head barely above the water, just enough to breathe.

He knew these machines, had spent many hours back here solving problems in the production process. The men who worked the production floor called this mixer Janelle, joking that it looked like one of the women who worked in the accounting office, so fat across the ass that when she waddled out to her SUV at the end of every workday, she had to slide the driver's seat back and then grab the roof to hoist herself in behind the wheel. The machine was temperamental, and every now and then it would seize up on them, so they had to back a dump truck up under its release valve and purge the load of wet concrete manually. *Janelle's taking a dump*, somebody would call out, and all the men working the production floor would laugh.

That's where Sams was hiding now, up behind the mixer, among the wires and pipes that ran toward its electric motor. Just above him was a control panel with the manual lever they'd pull to dump the load. Most of the time one of the production workers had to climb a metal ladder to reach it, but the water was so high that he floated only a foot or two below it, hanging on to one of the pipes that ran off toward the master controls.

But now he heard someone moving around out there quietly. Slipping through the water, between the machines, only a few feet away. He kept very still, listening as whoever it was slowly moved away. He was too tired to feel any fear. If they wanted to kill him, there was nothing more he could do. He'd wait there in the dark water for death or morning, not making a sound.

Twenty feet away, Vince was also listening. He clung to the bottom of the metal stairs that rose up along the outer wall of the building to a catwalk, wondering if he could risk easing himself around to climb up onto the steps, get out of this filthy water, and go looking for a way out of there. He was starting to regret ever hiding in the plant. Why hadn't he just kept swimming, out across the flooded parking lot, gotten lost among the warehouses up the street? He'd be long gone by now—or at least far away from those

ATF guys—out there clinging to a streetlight, waiting for somebody to come by in a boat and save his sorry ass.

He still had the gun; it wouldn't fit his holster, so he'd shoved it into his belt under his shirt. But now it felt like a weight that might pull him down into that black water. How long, he wondered, before those ATF guys brought their boat up to the door, shone that spotlight around in here, ready to open up on him if they spotted a gun? Fucking Lenny had to go and put the hurt on one of their people, so now they weren't going to be in any mood to screw around.

He heard something moving in the water nearby. His first thought, no lie, was that it was a fucking alligator come way up out of the bayou for a couple days on the town. Like, seriously, *on* the town, swimming around, looking down at all the buildings like he owned the place now. Hell, maybe he did. But then he realized that was stupid. He'd never even *hear* an alligator. They moved silently through the water, with only their eyes visible above the surface, coming up on you nice and slow. . . .

He swam around to the front of the metal steps, eased up out of the water. No *way* he was going to stay down there in the water, just waiting for something to slide on up there and take a bite out of him. And now that he was out of the water, he thought, *Shit, just keep going. Head right on up the catwalk, wait up there until the ATF guys show up in their boat down below, then ease right on out the door at the top of the stairs. Play it right, you could be out the door and gone before anybody even notices you're not floating around down there with the snakes.*

He almost made it. Shoes off, up the steps, moving quietly through the darkness, feeling his way with one hand on the cold metal railing. He could see the catwalk door just above him, open a crack, the moonlight shining through it, when suddenly he heard the sound of a boat's engine coming up on the entrance to the plant, and then a bright light filled the interior of the building, the boat's spotlight darting between the huge machines. Vince froze, looking up at the door only a short flight of stairs above him. A shadow rose up just beyond it, blocking out the sky. An ATF agent, he realized, coming up the catwalk, closing off that escape.

He glanced down at the searchlight, saw it still moving among the machinery, and slowly backed away from the door. Suddenly he was afraid. There was a smell in this building of dust and mud and rusting metal and stagnant water, and he recognized it as the smell of a place where men die in a sudden flare of light. He'd seen those rooms many times, walked into them as a cop after the killing was finished to find men lying splayed in a pool of blood, the same surprised look on all their faces. Now he could feel his face taking that same shape, the muscles around his eyes tightening, the corners of his mouth drawing up in something like a smile.

The searchlight was moving up along the stairs now, and he felt it looking for him. *Don't move*, he thought. *Not a muscle. So what if they arrest you? Nobody's dead; nothing's stolen. It's just their word against yours. They'll hold you for a couple days, then end up dropping the charges.* So he turned, faced into the searchlight as it moved up to the landing, found him standing there, grinning slightly, like a kid who's been caught in the back of the store trying to shove a dirty magazine down his pants.

"Drop your weapon," somebody shouted. "Put it *down!*"

Huh? Vince looked down at his hand, confused. His gun was under his shirt, stuffed into his belt. He was holding his shoes, a pair of black leather ECCOs he'd paid almost two hundred dollars for just a couple weeks ago, now dripping and ruined in his hand. Couldn't they see that?

He raised them, so the ATF could see it was just a pair of wet shoes. But it was a long way up to that high landing from the boat, and the searchlight threw strange shadows. Vince didn't even realize his mistake until the first bullets exploded in his chest. Later, everyone would agree it was a tragic mistake, but by then it was all water under the bridge, just a drop in the bucket of that filthy water that rises to wash all the world's sins away. Now it was all blood and cracking bone and Vince's face not grinning anymore as he stumbled back, then fell, so slowly, into that dark water below.

|||| Danny watched the body fall from high up on the metal stairs, splash into the water in the shadows at the back of the building. Movement, off to his left. He held very still. He was floating in the shadow of a huge machine, one hand resting on a pipe that ran out to join a cluster of other pipes before they climbed up toward the ceiling. Everything coming together, right here. Or coming apart.

And now the boat was moving, shifting its position so the agents could send the searchlight way up into the dark corners at the back of the building. Danny saw Mickie crouched in the ATF boat's bow, water dripping off her so he knew that she'd dove into the water behind him, swam across to get back in the fight. She leaned forward, tracking the searchlight with her assault rifle.

Danny caught the movement from the corner of his eye, not in the light, but in the shadows behind one of the huge machines. It was Vickers, his hands held high, moving toward the light. He'd seen what happened to Vince, and he was taking no chances. Surrender, let the lawyers get him out of this mess. That's what a man does when his business isn't based on violence, but on cultivating the self-interest of other ambitious men. He had powerful friends; he wasn't meant to die this way.

But then, none of us believe we're meant for what awaits us. We're special, we think; we should be excluded from the accidents, the illness, the acts of God or man that bring disaster down upon us. By the time we realize our mistake, it's too late. The storm is blowing the house away, and around us the water is rising.

Lenny waited until Vickers had moved out into the light, all the ATF agents' guns swinging over to cover him, before he opened fire, taking out the searchlight and plunging the whole building into darkness. Vickers never stood a chance. The building erupted in gunfire, bright flashes in the darkness, which only ceased when the agent at the boat's wheel gunned the engine, spun them out into the open water. Danny plunged under the water when the firing started, got behind the machine's support leg, hearing bullets *whang* off the metal above him. He waited there until the firing stopped, then quietly surfaced into silence and darkness.

That was bad, Danny thought. Mickie would be livid. They'd let that situation get out of their control, and once the firing had begun, they'd forgotten their training, simply fired wildly into the darkness. Clinging to the pipes, he gazed out at the entrance to the building. The boat's propeller had stirred up the water as it sped out of the building, and he watched the small waves lap against the doors in the moonlight. Then something floated into view. It was a body, arms outflung, facedown in the water. Vickers.

Somebody was moving again, behind him now. He could hear the soft movement of water from somewhere back among the machines, where Lenny had been hiding when he opened fire. Danny realized now that he was in a bad spot. If Lenny was behind him, he might catch a glimpse of him outlined against the moonlight outside the building. He took a deep breath, let himself sink beneath the water, then pushed off from the machine's leg, swam deep among the cables and pipes, almost catching his foot in that treacherous tangle. He came to the surface against one wall, under the metal stairs. And now he saw that he'd been right. Just off to his right, between him and the moonlight spilling through the open door, he saw the dark shape of a man's head barely sticking up above the water. It was Louis Sams, Danny saw, his hair cut tight against his skull. He'd frozen at the quiet sound of Danny emerging from the water, and now his head turned slowly to peer back into the darkness, trying to locate the danger.

Danny wanted to say something to reassure him, but at that

same moment he heard someone else moving nearby. He'd made too much noise, he realized, coming to the surface. It wasn't only Sams who'd caught it, and now Lenny was moving quietly toward them, his gun raised above the water. He'd want a hostage, somebody to hide behind when he made a break for those dark buildings out there beyond the open water. The ATF boat had drifted slowly back into view, so Lenny was being careful, staying close to the machines, even passing under them where he could, to avoid emerging into the open water where he might be spotted.

Now Sams heard him too, and Danny saw his neck tense as he realized that there were *two* men in the darkness nearby. He listened for a moment, then reached up slowly with one hand, grasped something above him, like he was getting ready to pull himself up out of the water.

"I know you're there," Lenny said quietly. "I can fucking smell you."

Neither of them spoke. He was only a few yards away, on the other side of the huge cement mixer.

"I'm leaving here," Lenny said. "And as much as I'd like to just put a bullet in your head, I need you to get out of here. You can come out easy, or you can come out the hard way. Personally, I don't care. It's your choice."

Did he think it was only Sams hiding there in the dark water? That's how it sounded. But he was talking to Danny, moving under the machine toward him now.

Above them, a door opened. An ATF agent came out onto the catwalk, pointed a flashlight down into the water below him. Lenny paused as the light swept past them, moved off among the machines, then he raised his gun and pointed up at the agent.

"Don't!" Danny braced his feet against the metal stairs, got ready to lunge toward him, but just as he did, he saw Sams rise up in the water suddenly, then just as quickly sink back down. There was a rumbling sound, and without warning a huge load of cement spilled out of the base of the machine. Lenny screamed, then vanished beneath the dark water. A wave rushed out from under the machine, and Danny felt himself slammed against the stairs behind him, then just as quickly swept out across the floor of the plant. He grabbed at a pipe, but his hand slipped off it. Then the water swelled up around a massive gravel bin, spun him around, and flung him out toward the plant's entrance. A flashlight picked him up as he drifted into the open water, and Danny felt the ATF agents' guns train in on him. Then he heard Mickie shout, "Don't shoot!" as the tide carried him out beyond the silos and into the open water. They found him floating there in the darkness.

Fisher's boat carried them slowly back into the city, its engine straining under the weight of both ATF teams, Danny, Jabril, and Sams shivering in the stern, and two bodies wrapped in wet canvas that lay in the bottom of the boat, everyone taking care not to brush against them with their feet. Mickie had barely spoken a word to Danny since they'd pulled him from the water; she was busy recovering first Sams, whom they found clinging to an outflow pipe near the plant's entrance, and then the bodies, which floated facedown among the machines. The third body would have to wait until the flooded city was drained. It lay beneath a huge pile of cement on the factory floor. Fisher brought his boat right in close to the mixer, and they pointed their flashlights down into the dirty water, but they could see nothing except a gray pile, slowly hardening into stone.

"It won't set right," Sams said quietly. "Too much water's bad for cement."

Danny looked down at the water. "I think it'll do the job."

Fisher eased the boat out of the building, and they headed west through neighborhoods with only roofs visible above the water in the moonlight. They had to take it slow, two agents sitting up in the bow watching for submerged structures and debris floating in the water. As the sun began to rise, they picked up City Park Avenue and followed it down to the cemeteries. Everything, Danny saw, was gone, vanished beneath the waters that spread out in every direction.

The air was still cool, but they'd stopped shivering. Sams looked at the sun rising and said, "What day is this?"

Jabril thought about it, then shook his head. "Damned if I know."

Danny leaned forward, said to an agent, "You know what day it is?"

The agent shrugged. "Day after yesterday. That's all that matters."

Mickie had been talking quietly with Fisher, but now she came back and sat beside Danny. "How you doing?"

"Tired. You?"

She nodded. "One of us needs to get up to Baton Rouge."

"I'll go," he said. "They need you here."

She took his hand in hers. She was wearing her half-finger assault gloves, and she curled one finger in so that its tip rested gently in his palm. "I'm furious at you," she said.

"You understand why I stayed?"

She looked over at Sams, then nodded.

"People need your help, you got to be there."

She didn't say anything, just looked out across the water at the flooded city. "You been to the house?"

He shook his head. "Couldn't get to it. The water's pretty deep up through there."

Mickie got up, went forward and spoke to Fisher. He looked at her for a moment, then shrugged, spun the wheel to head south under the expressway. They followed the highway down past Xavier, the university's buildings strangely beautiful rising above the water that shimmered with early morning light. Then Fisher turned south on Jeff Davis Parkway, and they followed it down to where it joined Octavia Street, then cut over to Calhoun.

The water was up among the branches of the oak tree that stood in front of their house, and Fisher had to slow the boat to a crawl to navigate past it. He brought them right up below the second-floor window, and Danny was surprised to feel the boat bump against the house, a sensation that was too strange to be real. But he stood up and, as two agents grasped the window ledge to hold the boat steady, climbed up, raised the window. He looked down at Mickie, but she shook her head.

"I can't," she said. "It's too painful."

He crawled in through the window. It was Anna's room. Her tiny bed, piled high with stuffed animals, was exactly as they'd left it. Her closet was open, and he saw a row of small dresses Mickie had hung up neatly, a shelf of shoes arranged just below it. He saw there was a tiny doll sitting in one of her shoes, like a man rowing a boat. Danny went down the hall to the stairs, looked at the water lapping at the steps a few feet below. Then he went back into the bedroom he shared with Mickie, stripped a pillowcase off one of the pillows on the bed. He opened the closet, saw an album of family photographs they'd left behind on an upper shelf, tossed it into the pillowcase. He pulled some clothing out of his dresser, piled it on top. Then he stripped the case off Mickie's pillow, went into Anna's room and filled it with stuffed animals from her bed. When he'd finished, he looked around.

Just stuff. Everything important was gone from the house.

He went to the window, tossed the pillowcases down to Mickie in the boat, then climbed out onto the window ledge, and dropped into the boat.

Fisher looked back at him. "Get everything you need?"

"Yeah." Danny looked over at Mickie. "I got everything I need right here."

Fisher nodded, eased forward on the throttle, and the boat slid away from the house.

Mickie reached out, took Danny's hand. He turned, watched the house vanish behind them. Then he sat back, closed his eyes.

Mickie was watching him closely. "You okay?"

"I left the window open."

She turned, looked back at the house. "You want me to have them turn around?"

He shook his head. "I always forget something," he told her. "And the rest I leave behind."

"You'll be back." She reached up, ran a finger gently down the back of Danny's neck. "You belong here."

Like she's offering me a blessing, he thought, looking at the flooded houses, the ancient oak trees rising out of the water.